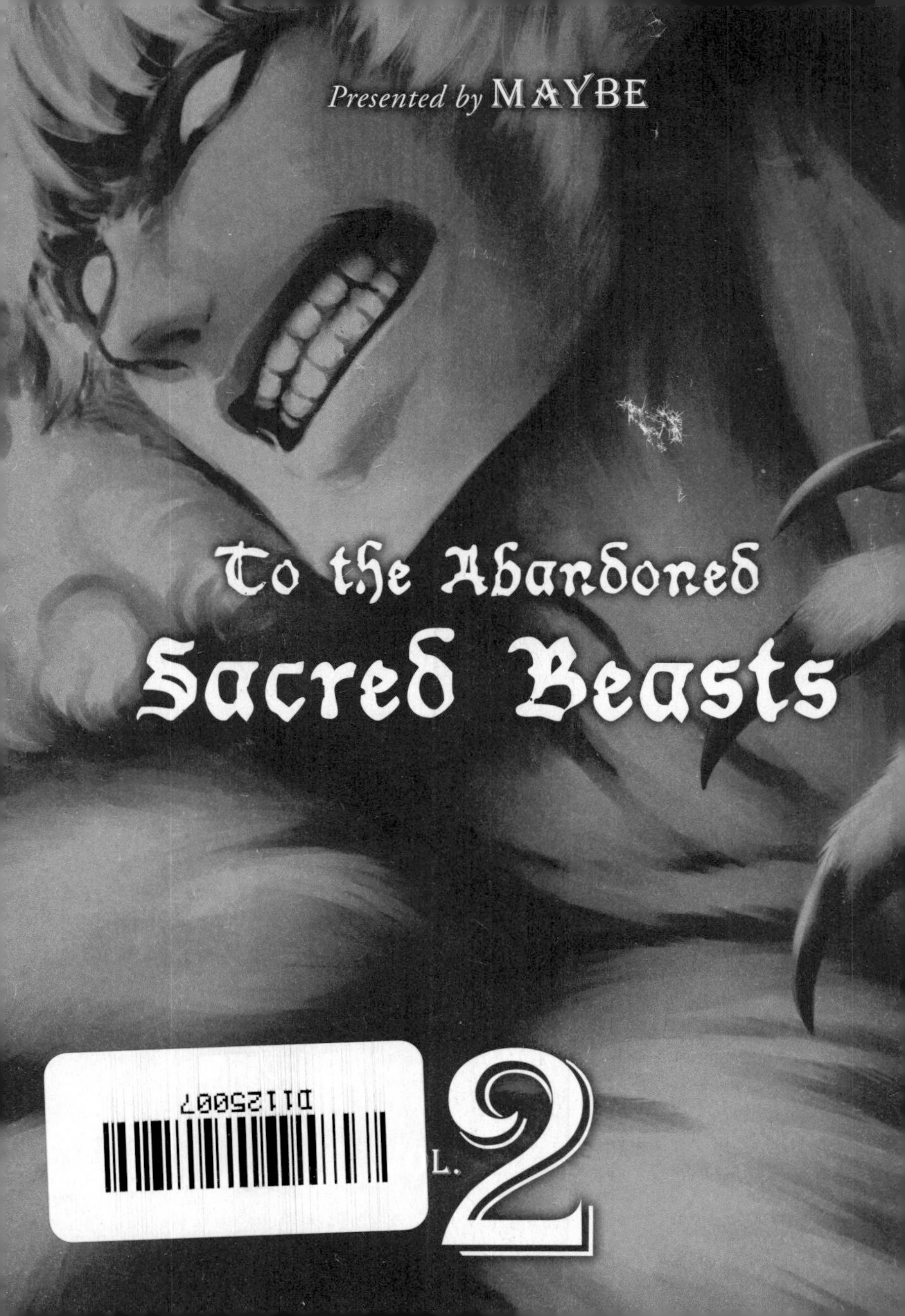
Presented by MAYBE
To the Abandoned
Sacred Beasts
L.
2

CONTENTS

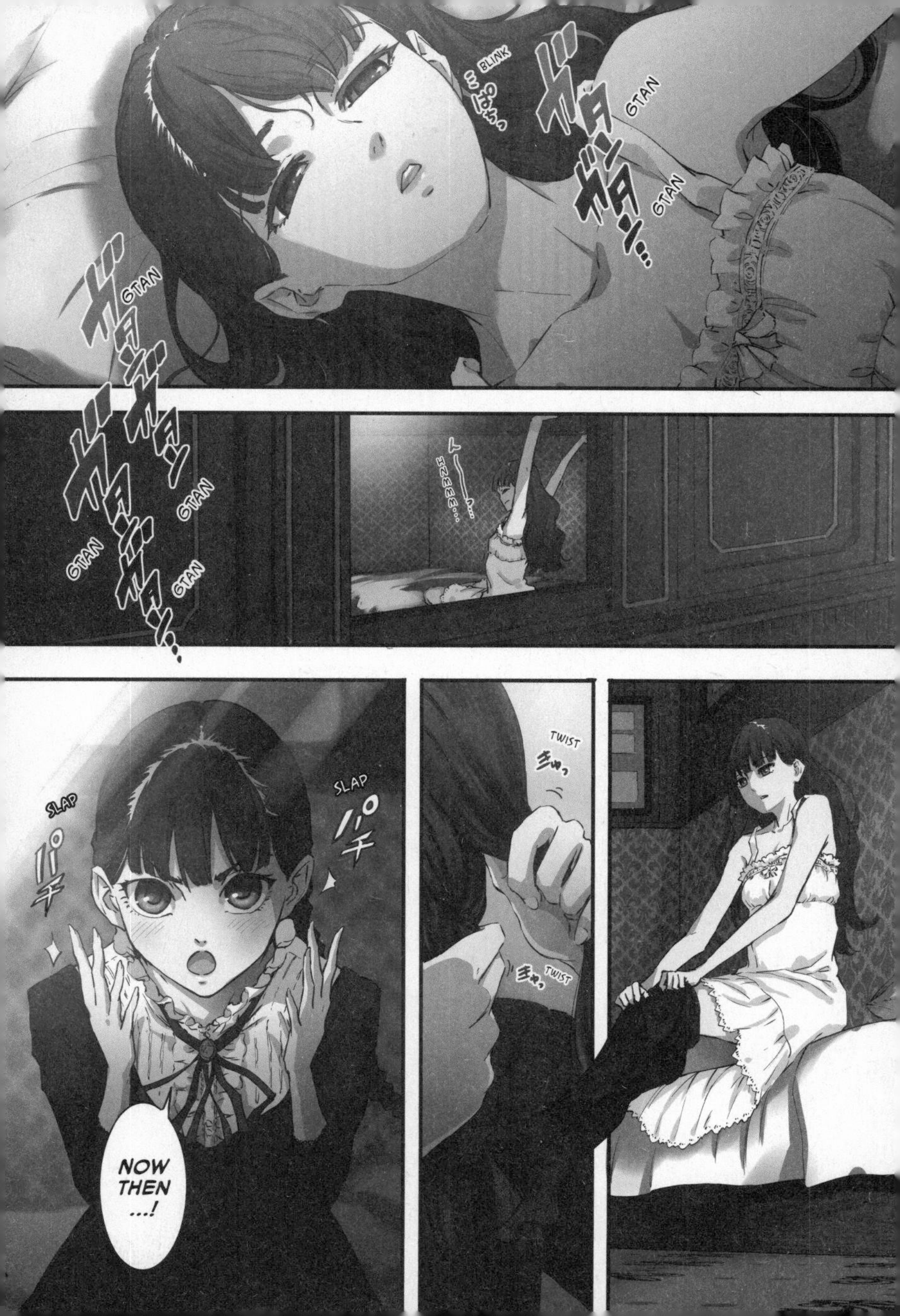
BLINK
ぱちっ
GTAN
GTAN
GTAN
GTAN
GTAN
GTAN
HMMMM...
TWIST
きゅっ
TWIST
きゅっ
SLAP
パチ
SLAP
パチ
NOW THEN ...!

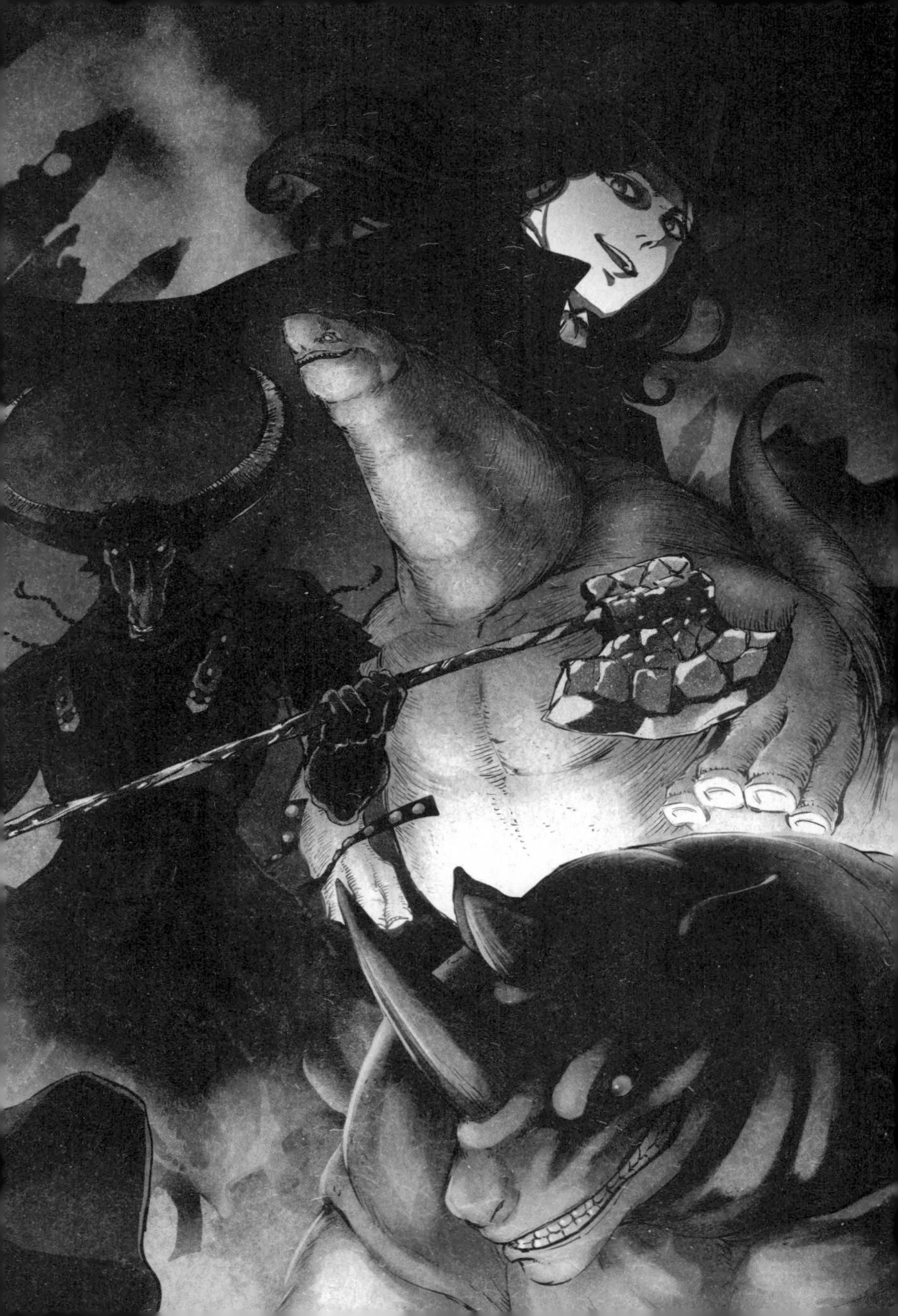

Chapter 6: Beasts Unbound

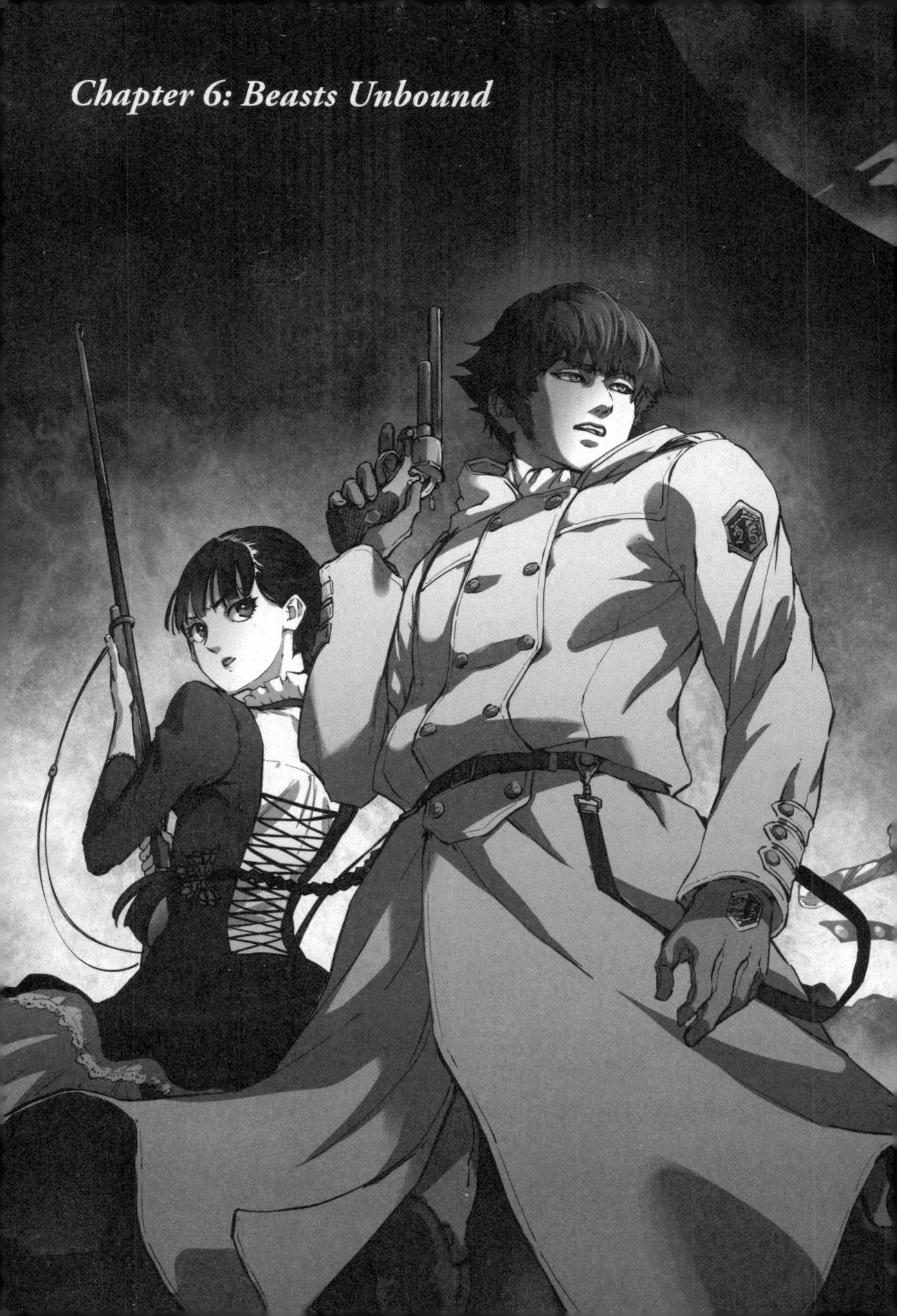

To the Abandoned
Sacred Beasts

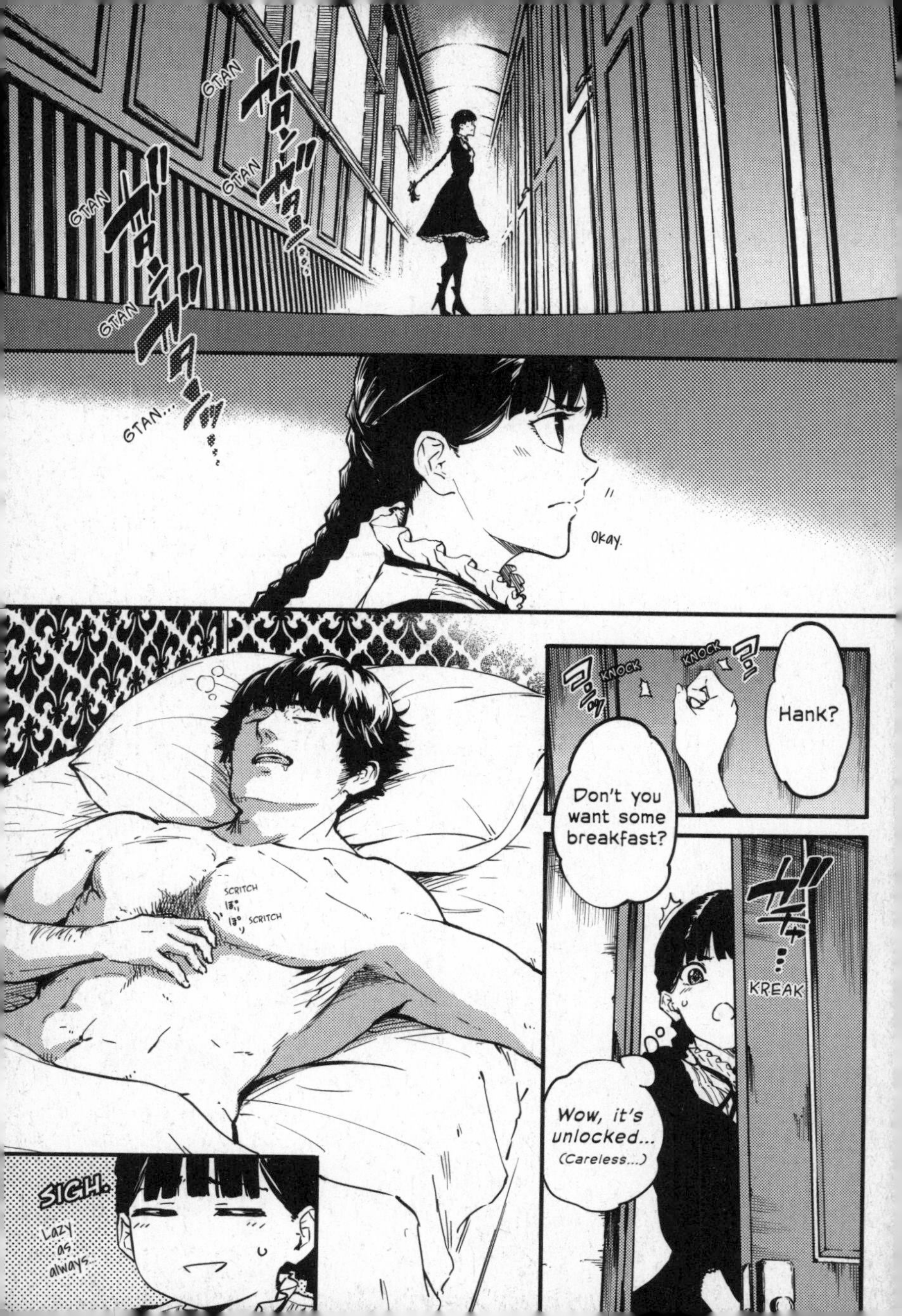
GTAN
GTAN
GTAN
GTAN
GTAN...
Okay.
Hank?
KNOCK
KNOCK
Don't you want some breakfast?
KREAK
Wow, it's unlocked...
(Careless...)
SCRITCH
SCRITCH
SIGH.
Lazy as always...

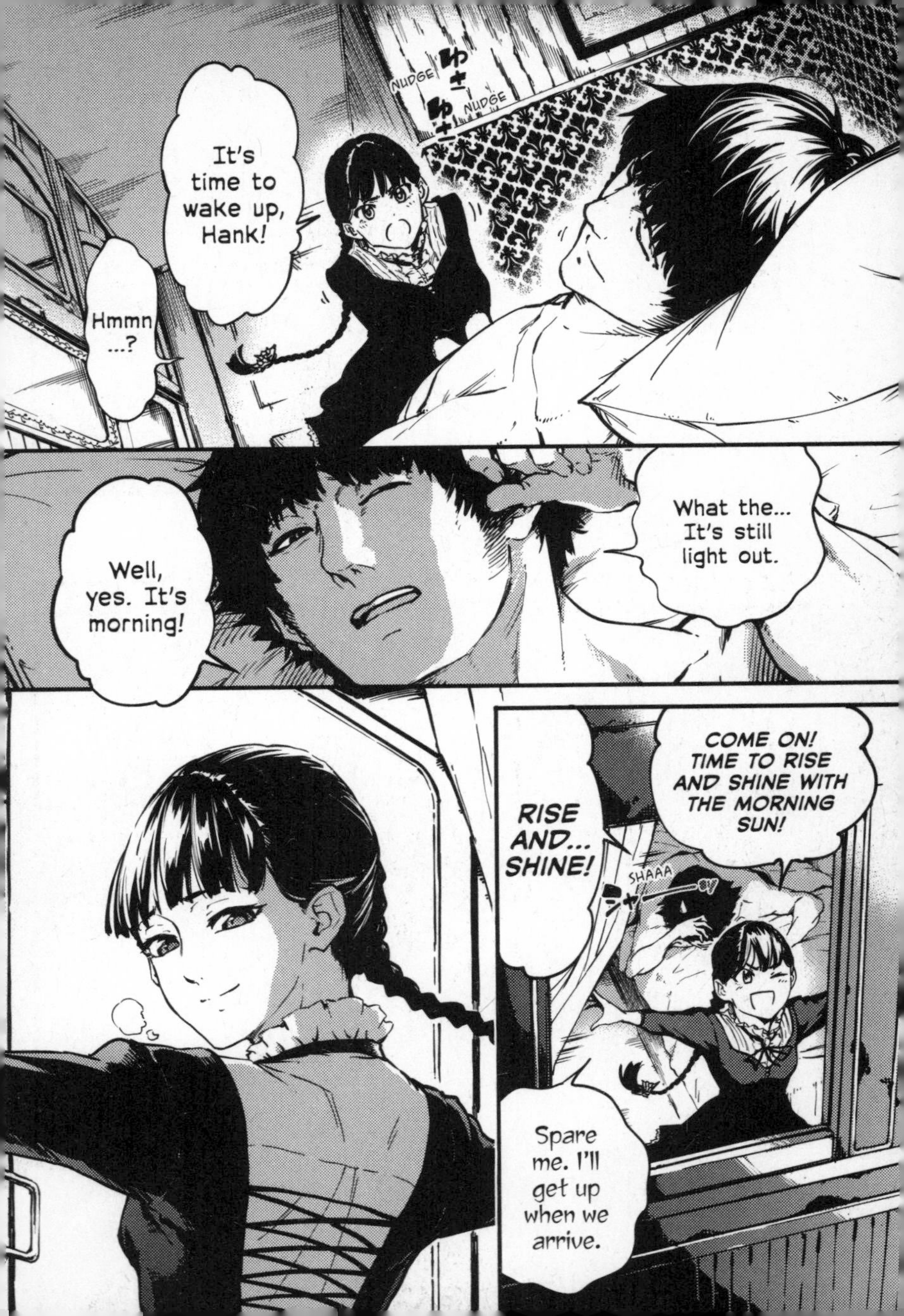
NUDGE
NUDGE
It's time to wake up, Hank!
Hmmn ...?
What the... It's still light out.
Well, yes. It's morning!
COME ON! TIME TO RISE AND SHINE WITH THE MORNING SUN!
RISE AND... SHINE!
SHAAA
Spare me. I'll get up when we arrive.

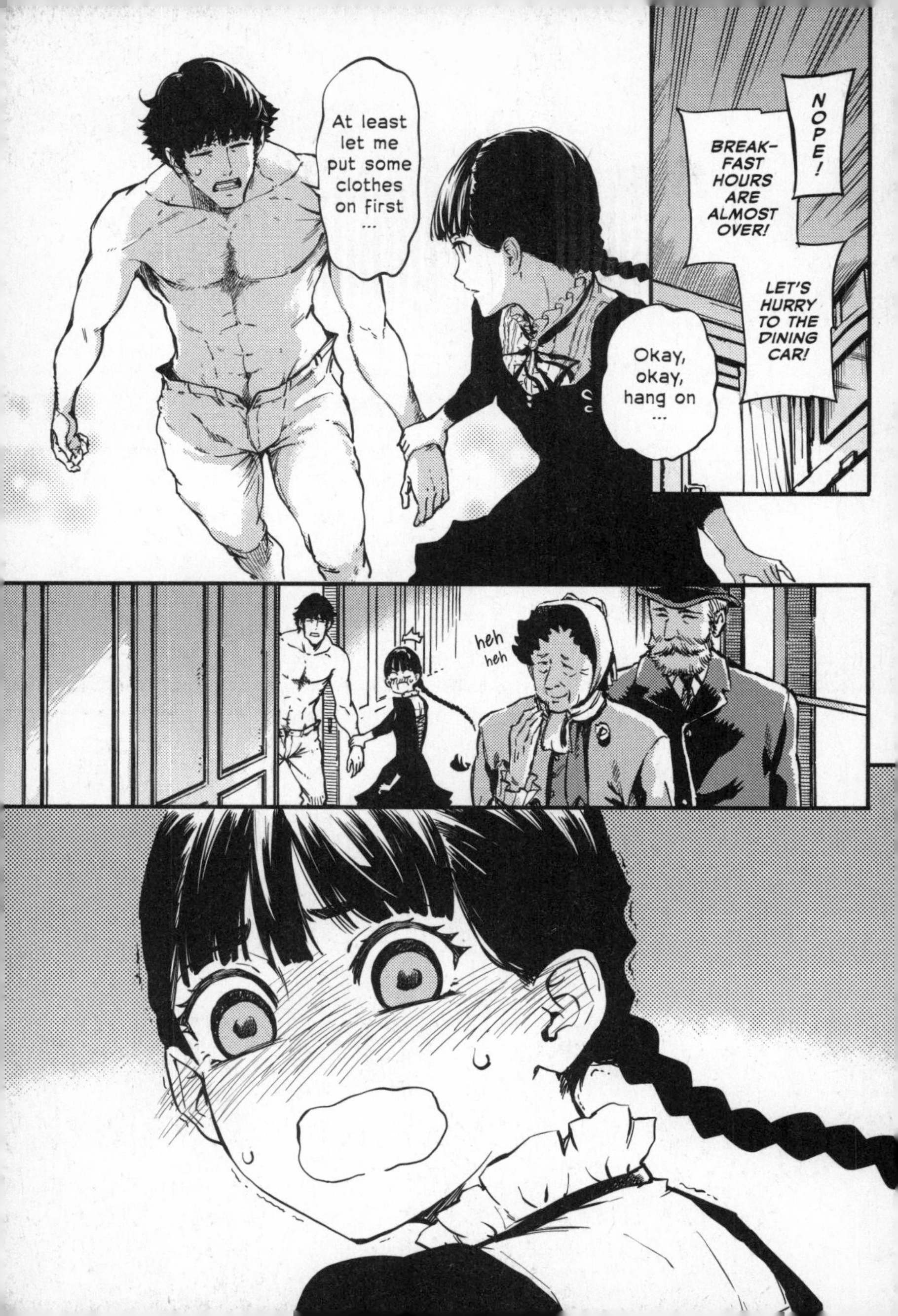
NOPE!
BREAK-FAST HOURS ARE ALMOST OVER!
LET'S HURRY TO THE DINING CAR!
At least let me put some clothes on first ...
Okay, okay, hang on ...
heh heh

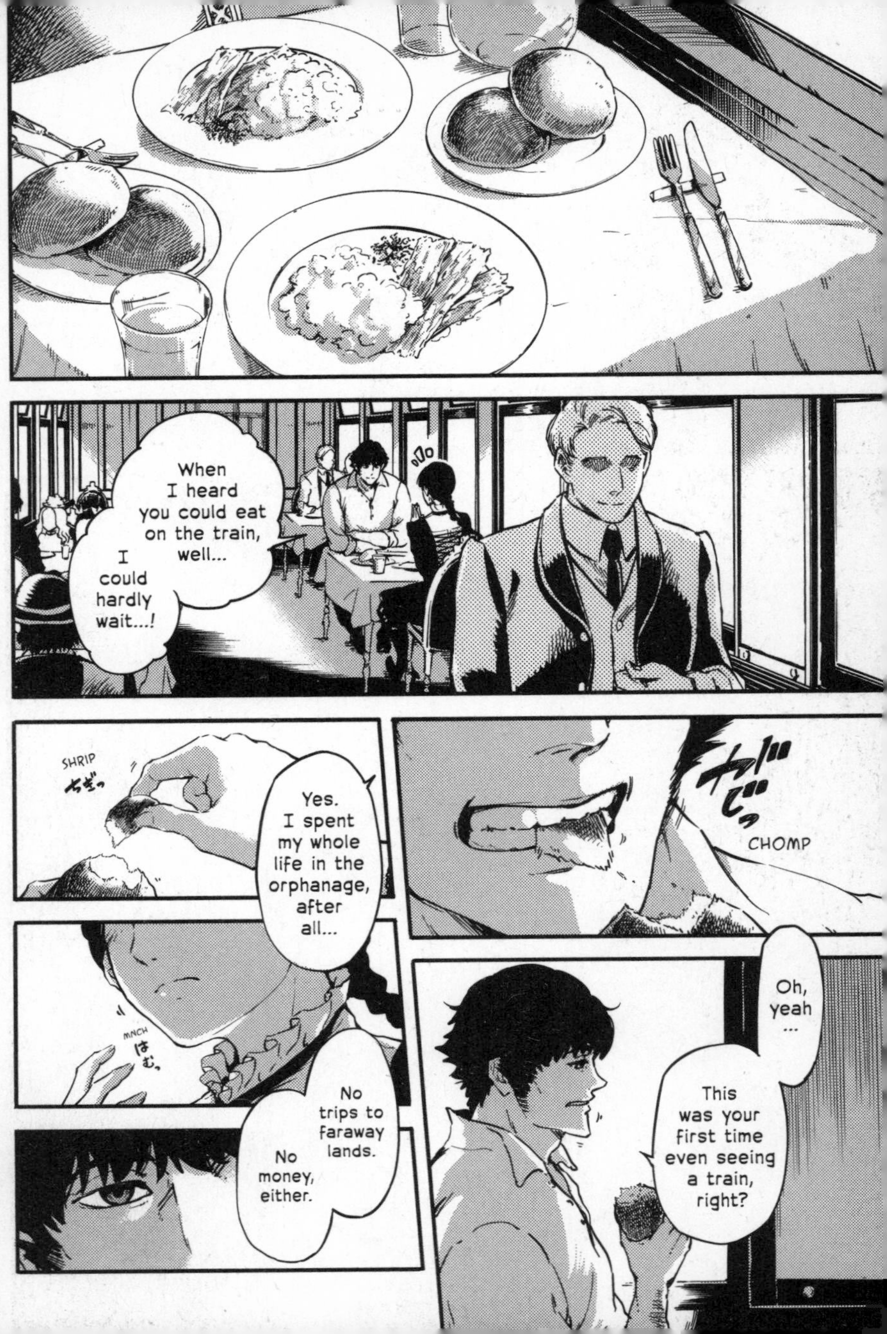
When I heard you could eat on the train, well...
I could hardly wait...!
CHOMP
SHRIP
ちぎっ
Yes. I spent my whole life in the orphanage, after all...
Oh, yeah ...
This was your first time even seeing a train, right?
MNCH
はむっ
No trips to faraway lands.
No money, either.

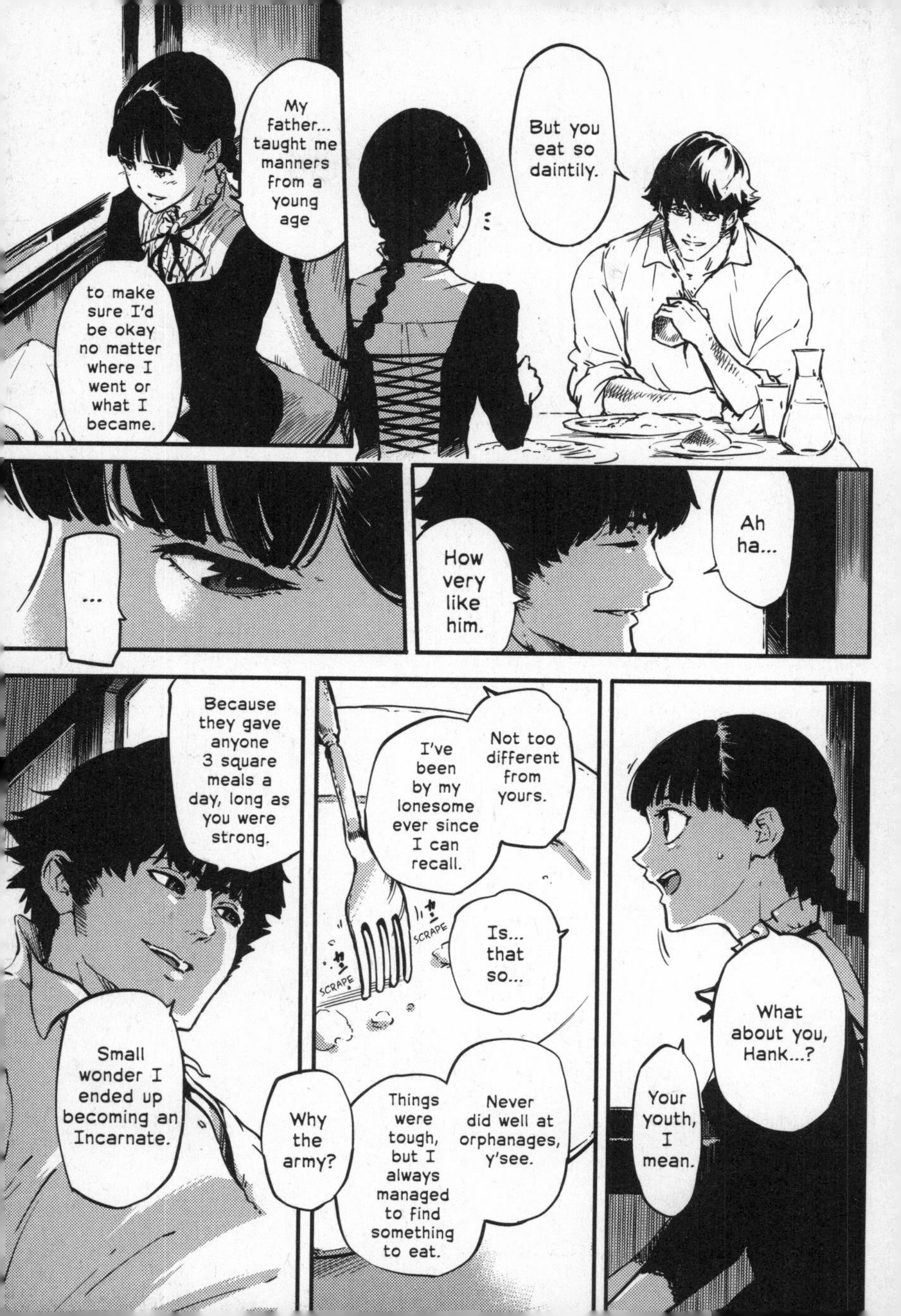
But you eat so daintily.
My father... taught me manners from a young age
to make sure I'd be okay no matter where I went or what I became.
Ah ha...
How very like him.
...
What about you, Hank...?
Your youth, I mean.
Not too different from yours.
I've been by my lonesome ever since I can recall.
SCRAPE
SCRAPE
Is... that so...
Never did well at orphanages, y'see.
Things were tough, but I always managed to find something to eat.
Why the army?
Because they gave anyone 3 square meals a day, long as you were strong.
Small wonder I ended up becoming an Incarnate.

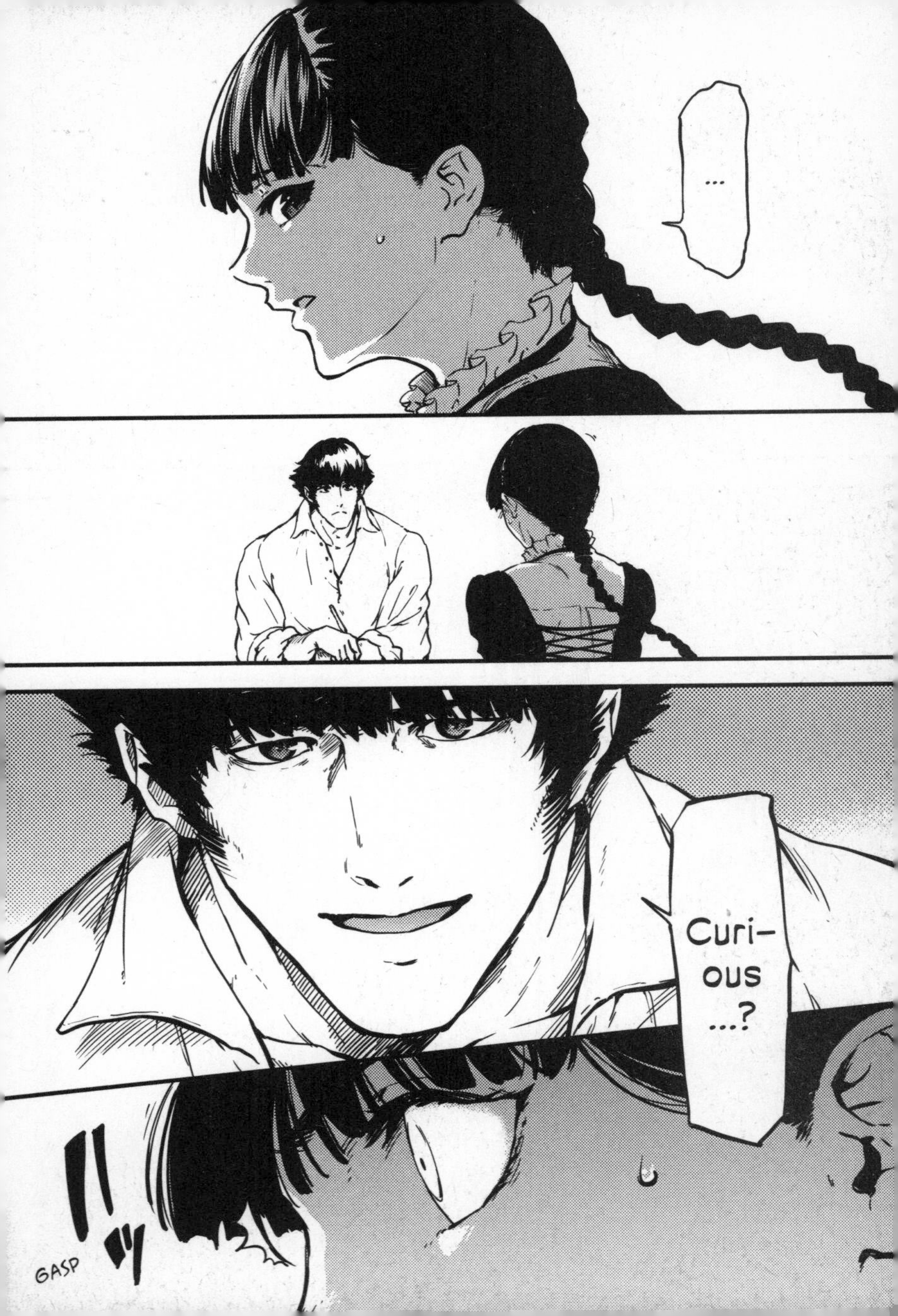
...
Curi-
ous
...?
GASP

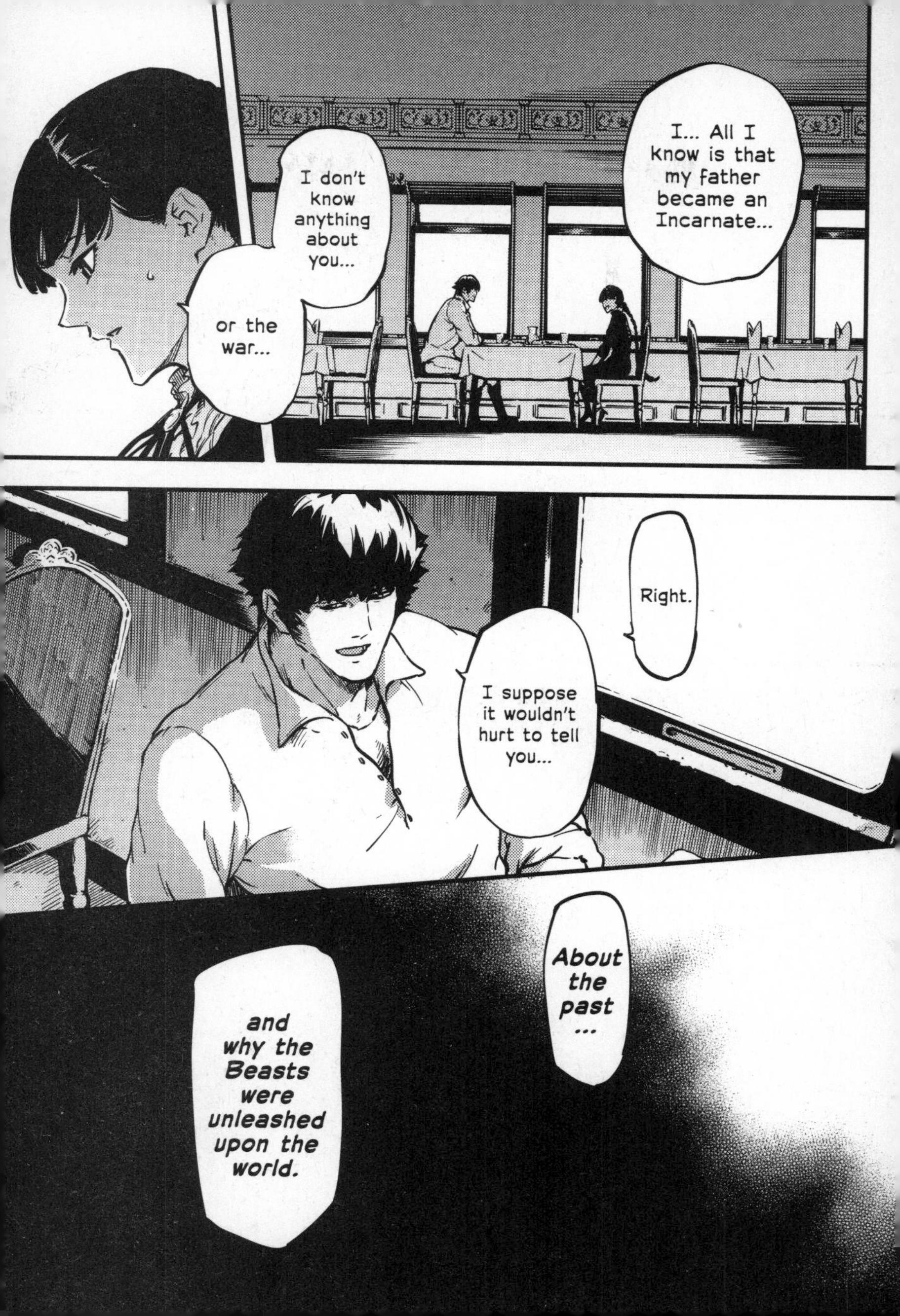
I... All I know is that my father became an Incarnate...
I don't know anything about you...
or the war...
Right.
I suppose it wouldn't hurt to tell you...
About the past...
and why the Beasts were unleashed upon the world.

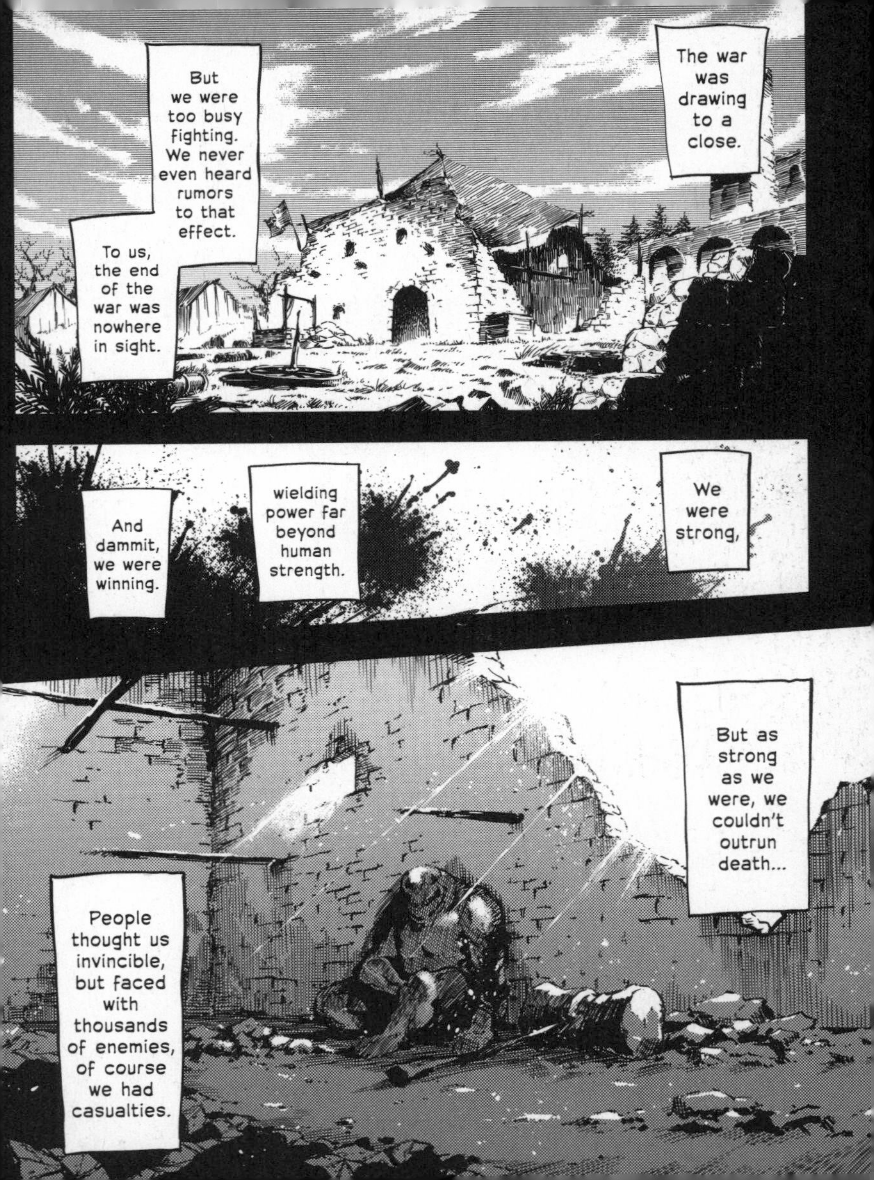
The war was drawing to a close.
But we were too busy fighting. We never even heard rumors to that effect.
To us, the end of the war was nowhere in sight.
We were strong,
wielding power far beyond human strength.
And dammit, we were winning.
But as strong as we were, we couldn't outrun death...
People thought us invincible, but faced with thousands of enemies, of course we had casualties.

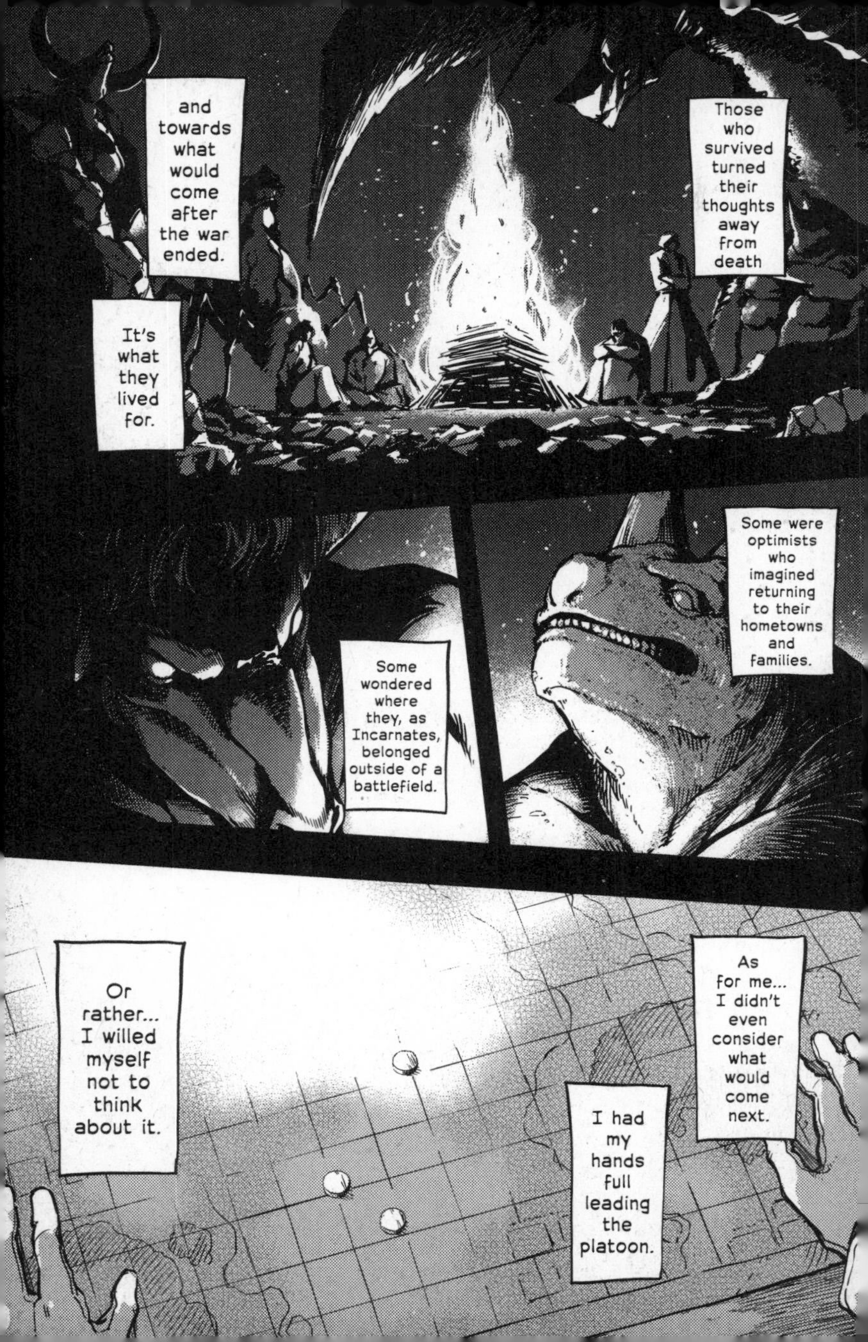
Those who survived turned their thoughts away from death
and towards what would come after the war ended.
It's what they lived for.
Some were optimists who imagined returning to their hometowns and families.
Some wondered where they, as Incarnates, belonged outside of a battlefield.
As for me... I didn't even consider what would come next.
I had my hands full leading the platoon.
Or rather... I willed myself not to think about it.

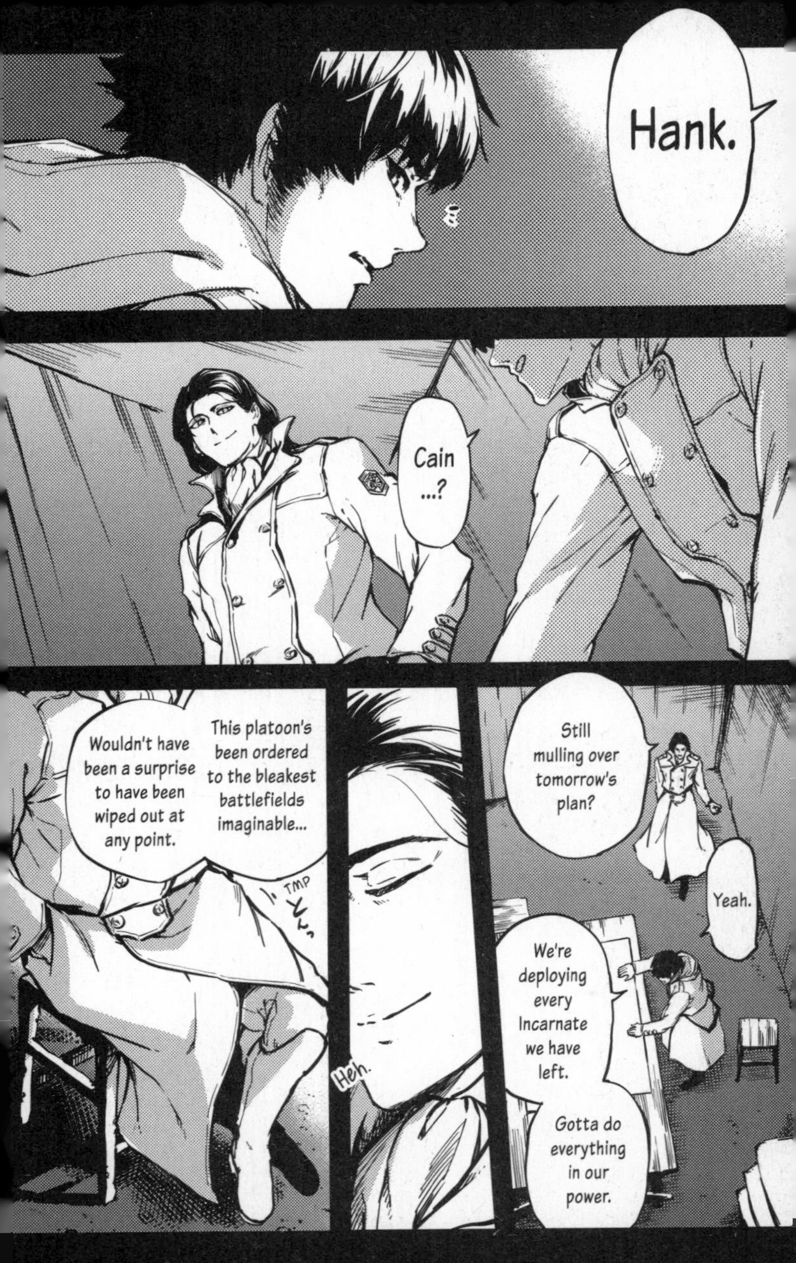
Hank.
Cain ...?
Still mulling over tomorrow's plan?
Yeah.
We're deploying every Incarnate we have left.
Gotta do everything in our power.
Heh.
This platoon's been ordered to the bleakest battlefields imaginable...
Wouldn't have been a surprise to have been wiped out at any point.
TMP

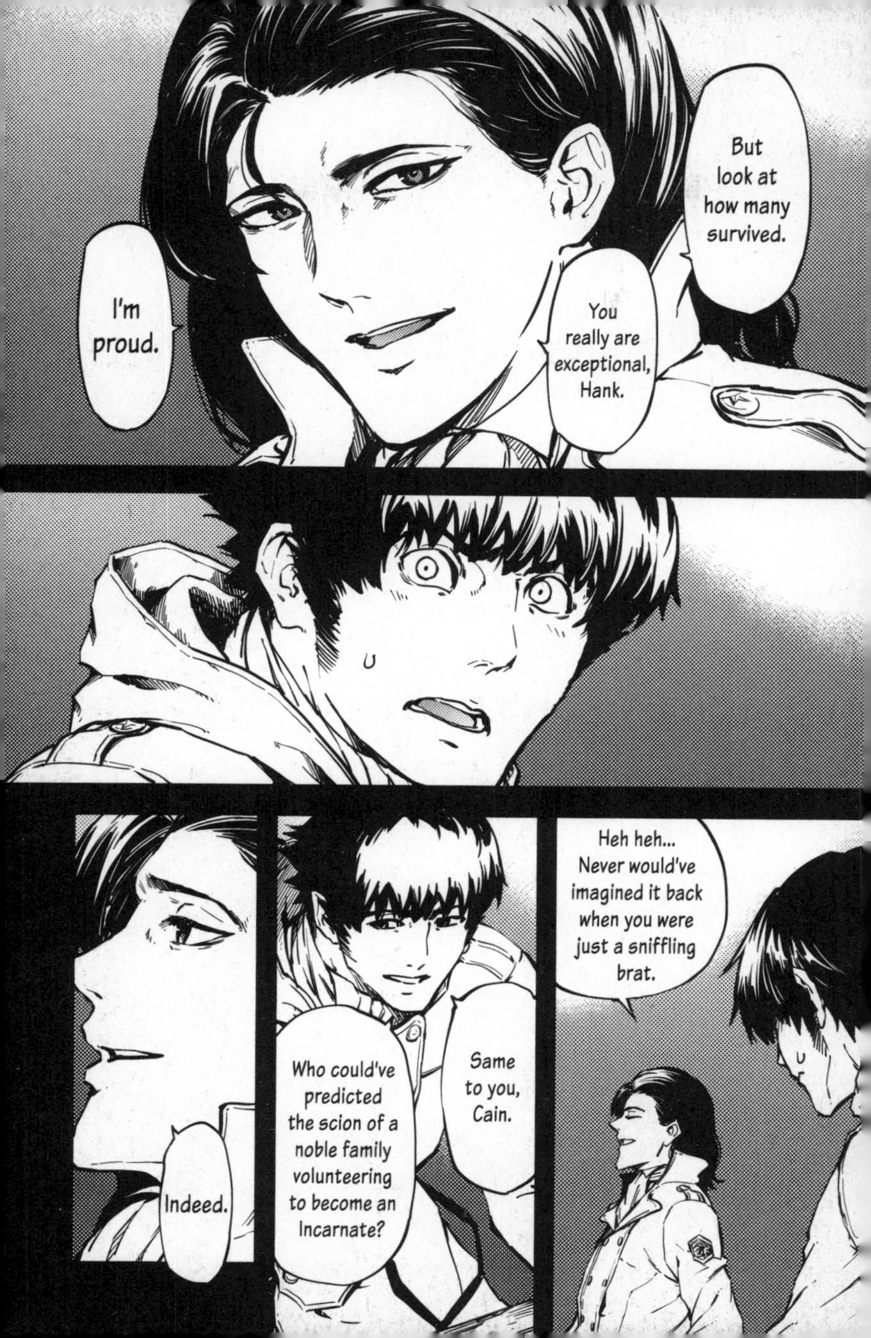
But look at how many survived.
You really are exceptional, Hank.
I'm proud.
Heh heh... Never would've imagined it back when you were just a sniffling brat.
Same to you, Cain.
Who could've predicted the scion of a noble family volunteering to become an Incarnate?
Indeed.

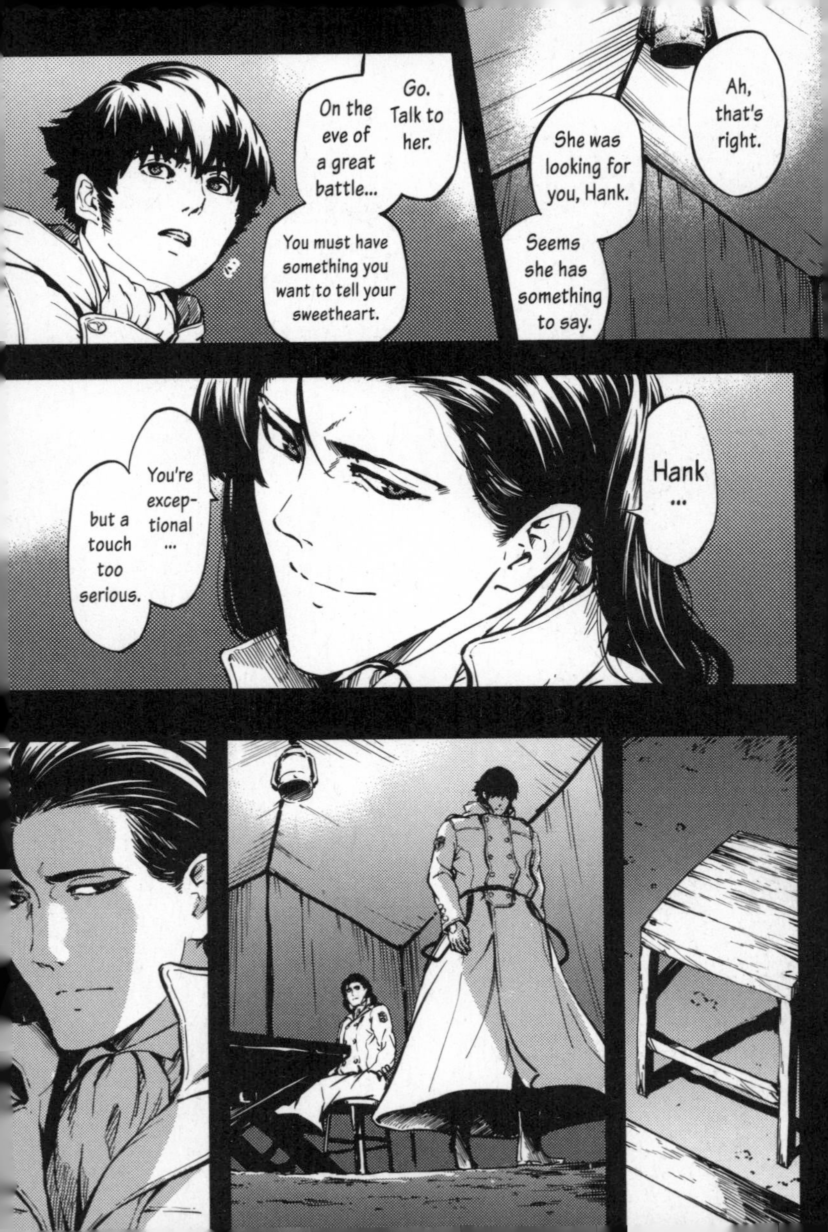

Ah, that's right.
She was looking for you, Hank.
Seems she has something to say.
Go. Talk to her.
On the eve of a great battle...
You must have something you want to tell your sweetheart.
Hank...
You're exceptional...
but a touch too serious.

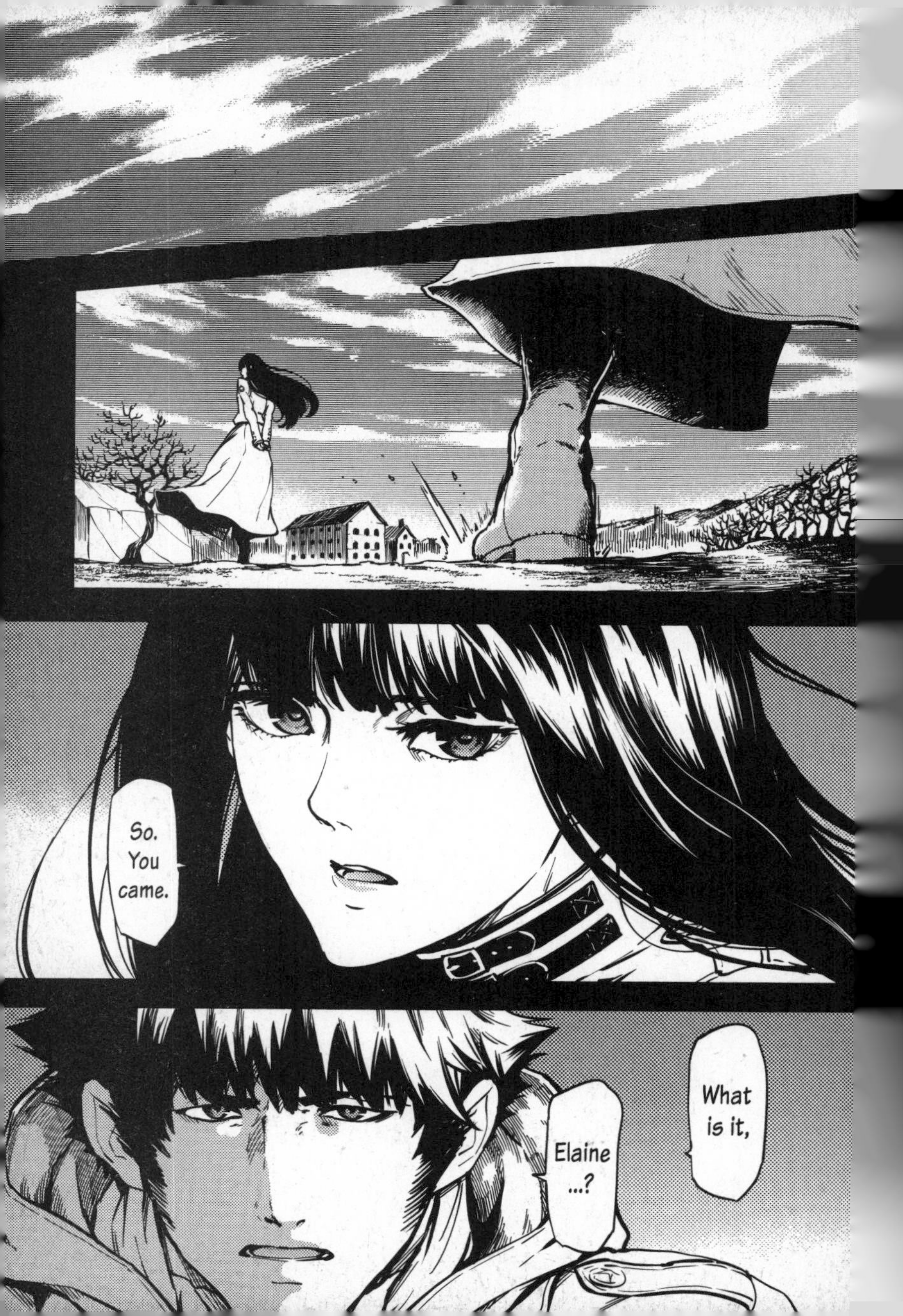
So. You came.
What is it,
Elaine ...?

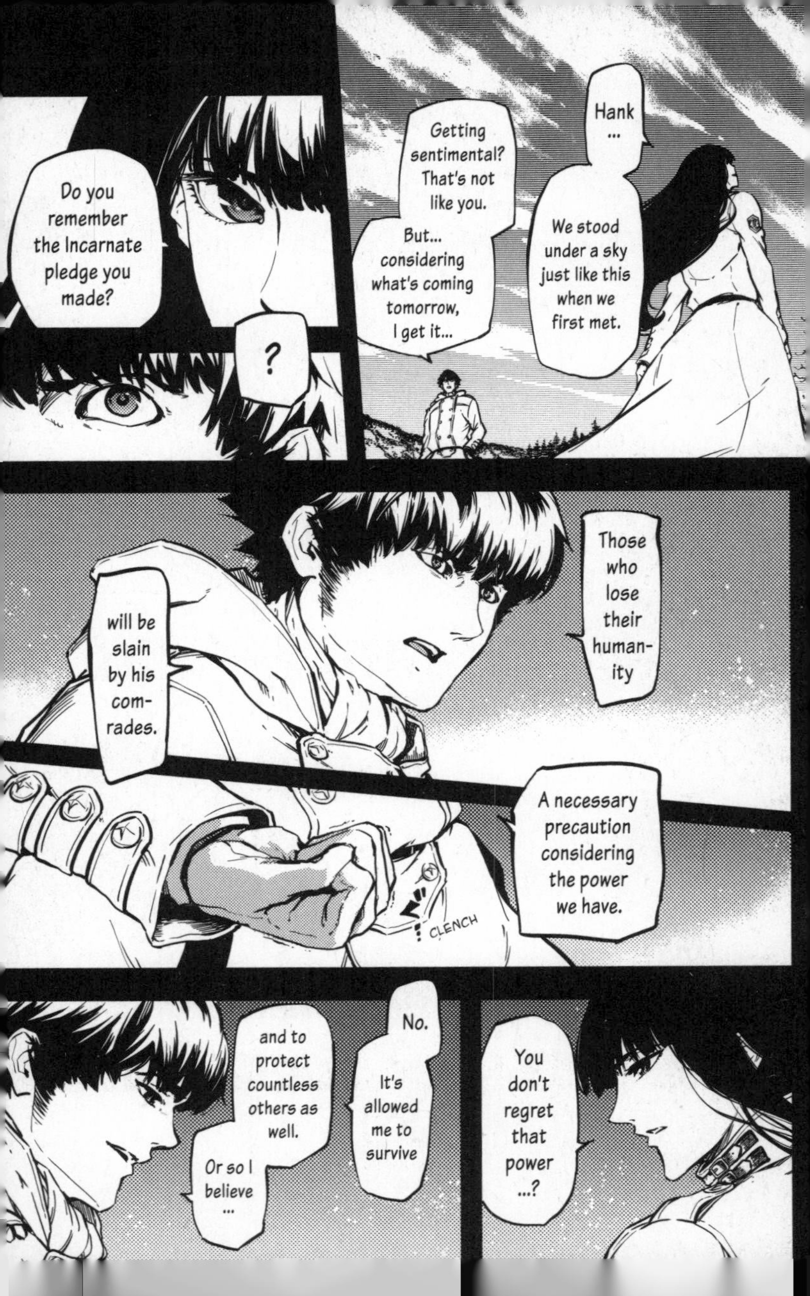
Hank ...
We stood under a sky just like this when we first met.
Getting sentimental? That's not like you.
But... considering what's coming tomorrow, I get it...
Do you remember the Incarnate pledge you made?
?
Those who lose their human-ity
will be slain by his com-rades.
A necessary precaution considering the power we have.
CLENCH
You don't regret that power ...?
No.
It's allowed me to survive
and to protect countless others as well.
Or so I believe ...

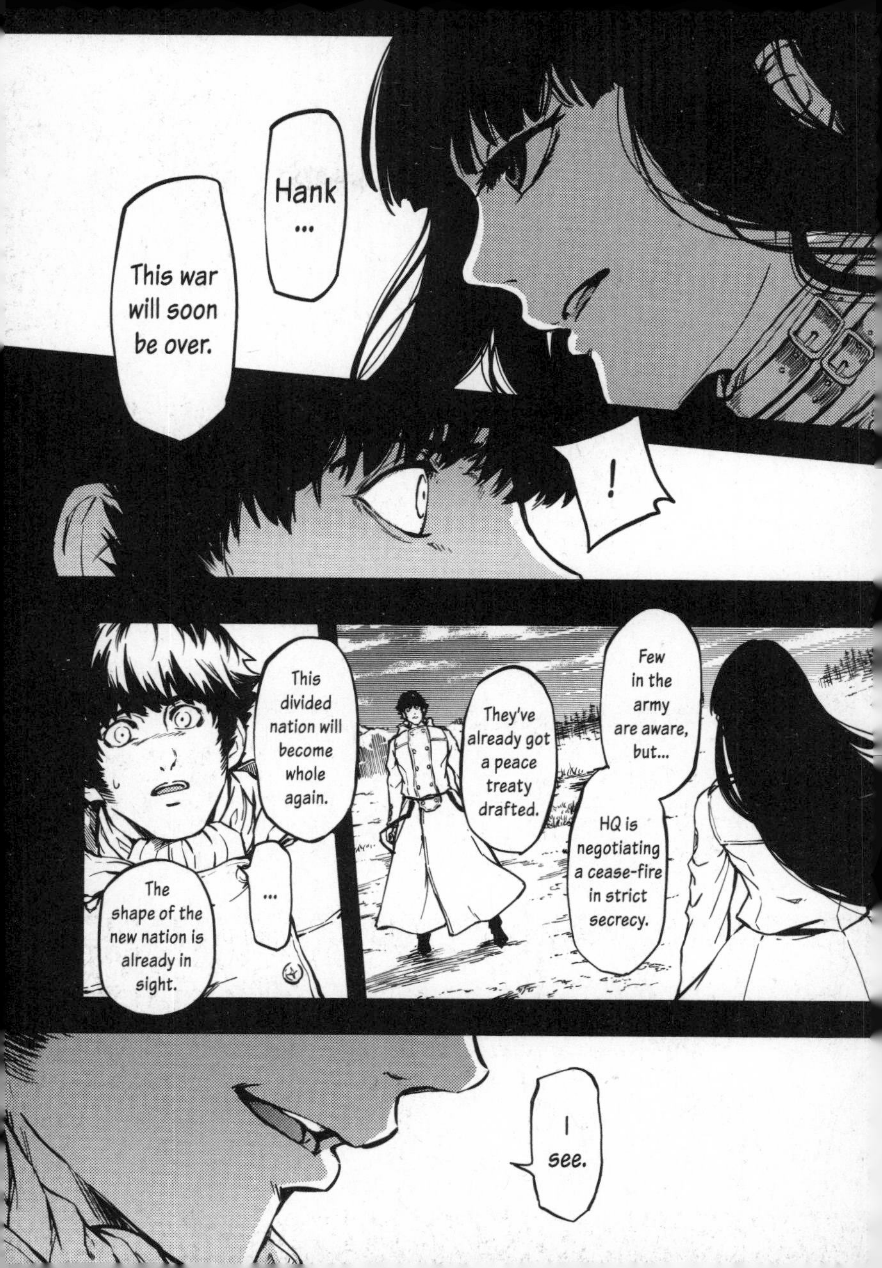
Hank ...
This war will soon be over.
!
Few in the army are aware, but...
HQ is negotiating a cease-fire in strict secrecy.
They've already got a peace treaty drafted.
This divided nation will become whole again.
...
The shape of the new nation is already in sight.
I see.

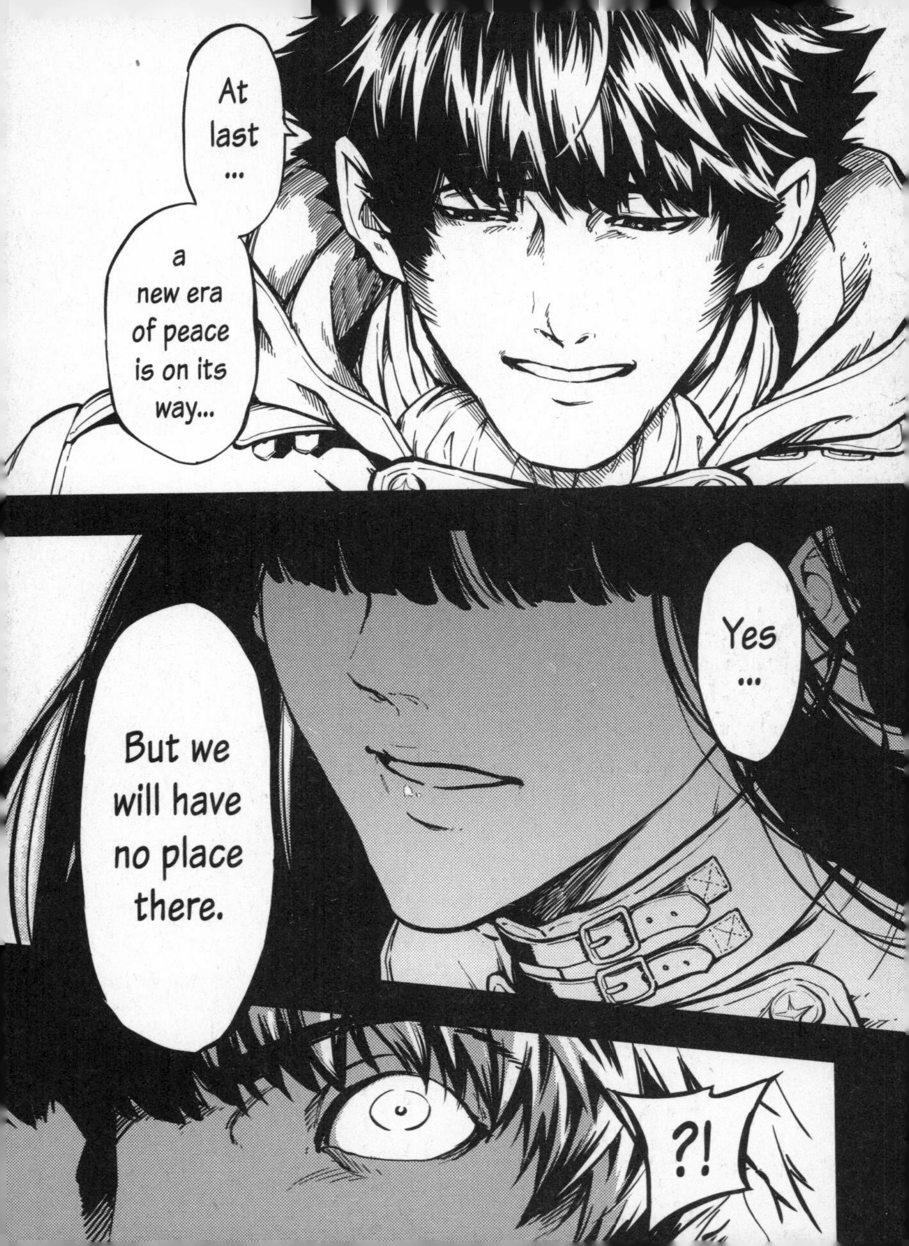
At last ...
a new era of peace is on its way...
Yes ...
But we will have no place there.
?!

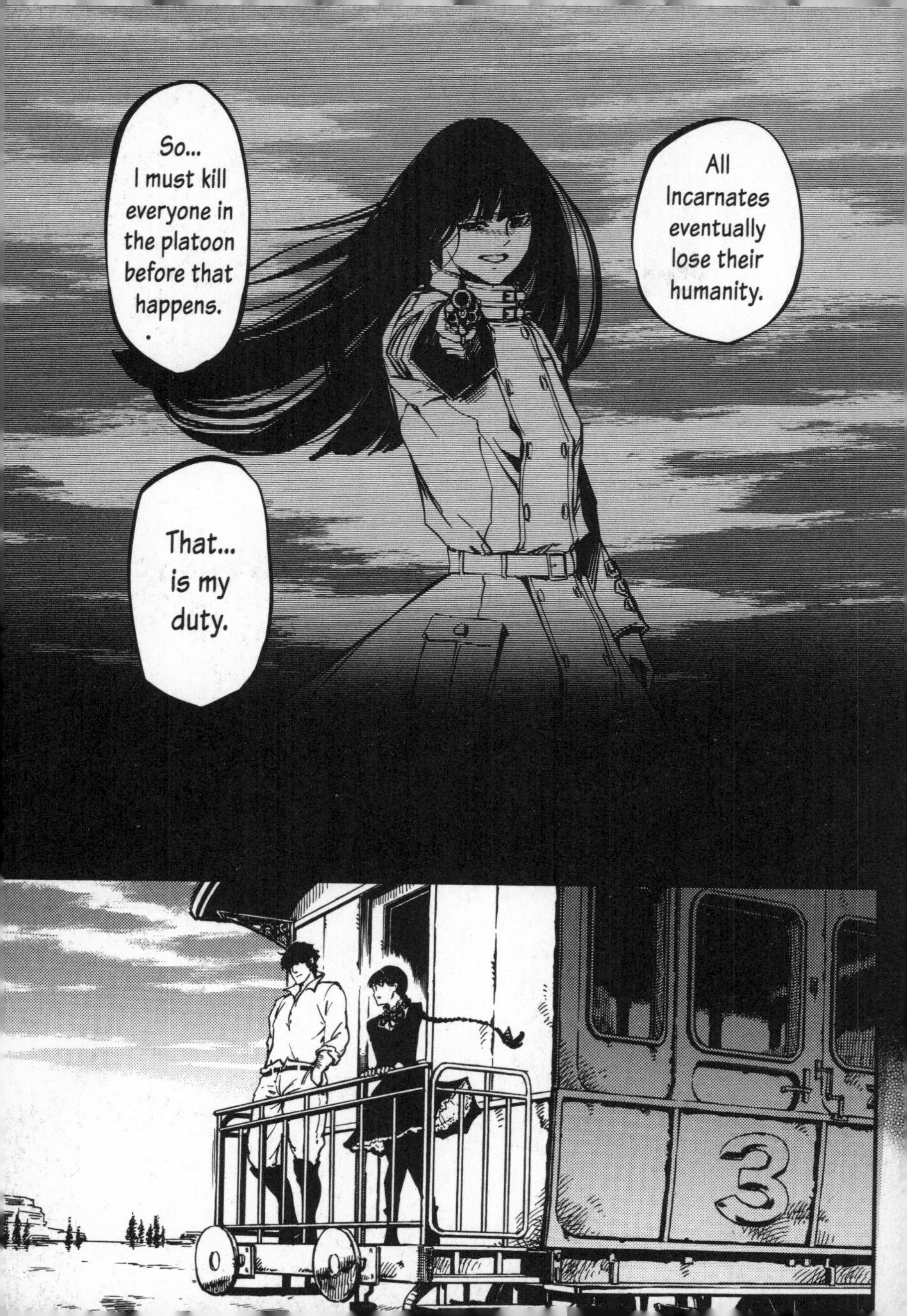
All Incarnates eventually lose their humanity.
So... I must kill everyone in the platoon before that happens.
That... is my duty.

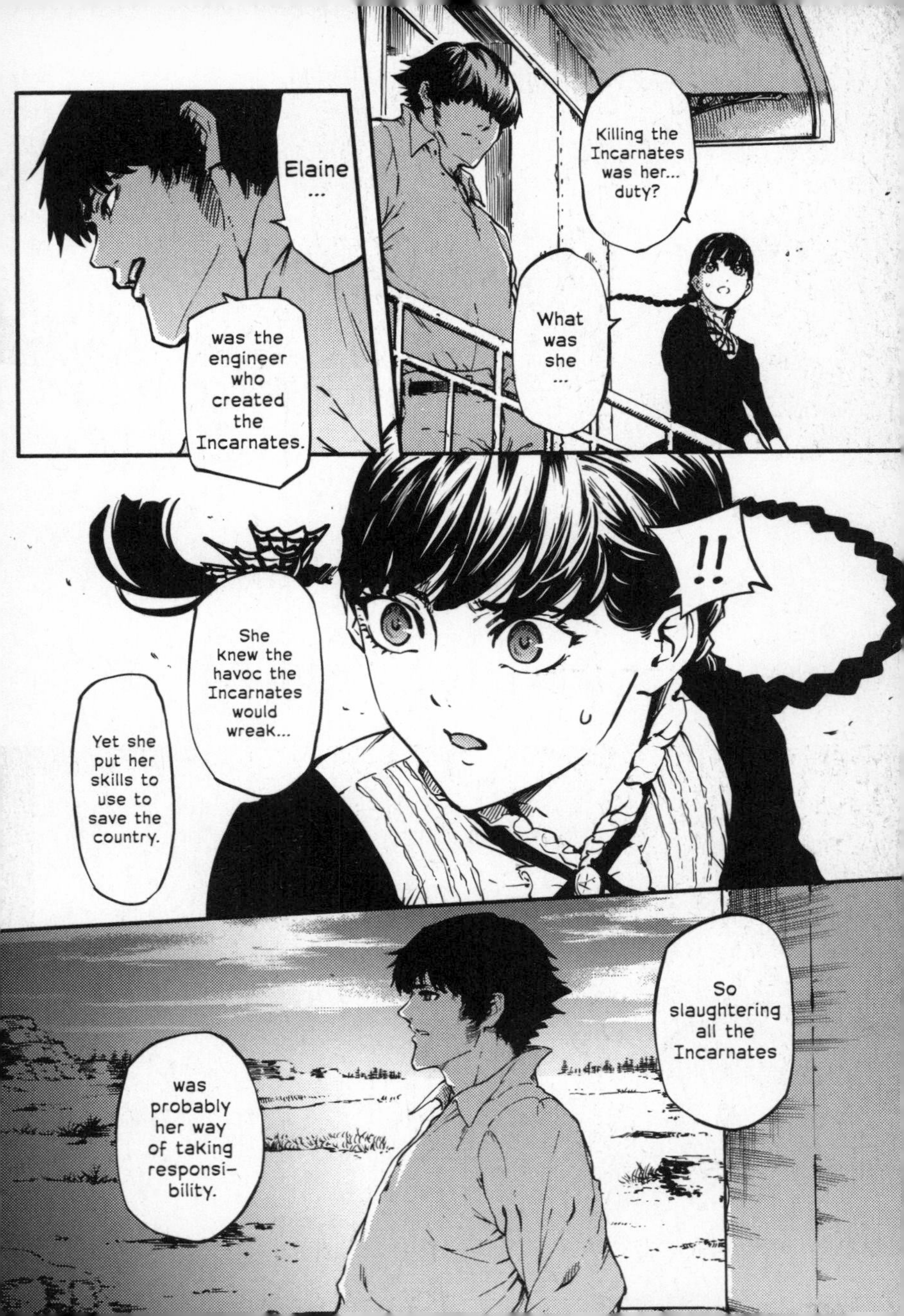
Killing the Incarnates was her... duty?
What was she ...
Elaine ...
was the engineer who created the Incarnates.
!!
She knew the havoc the Incarnates would wreak...
Yet she put her skills to use to save the country.
So slaughtering all the Incarnates
was probably her way of taking responsi-bility.

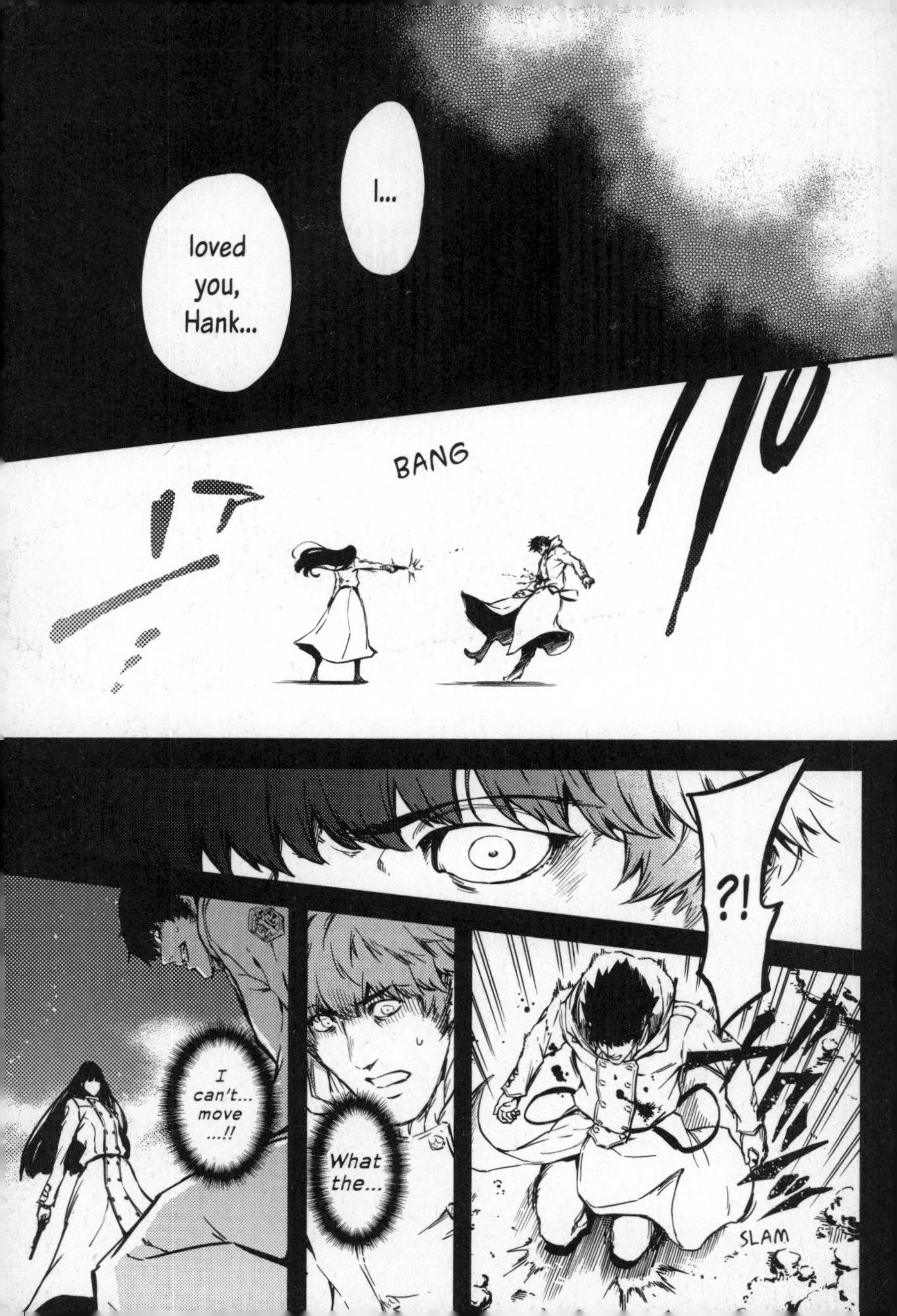
I...
loved you, Hank...
BANG
?!
SLAM
What the...
I can't... move ...!!

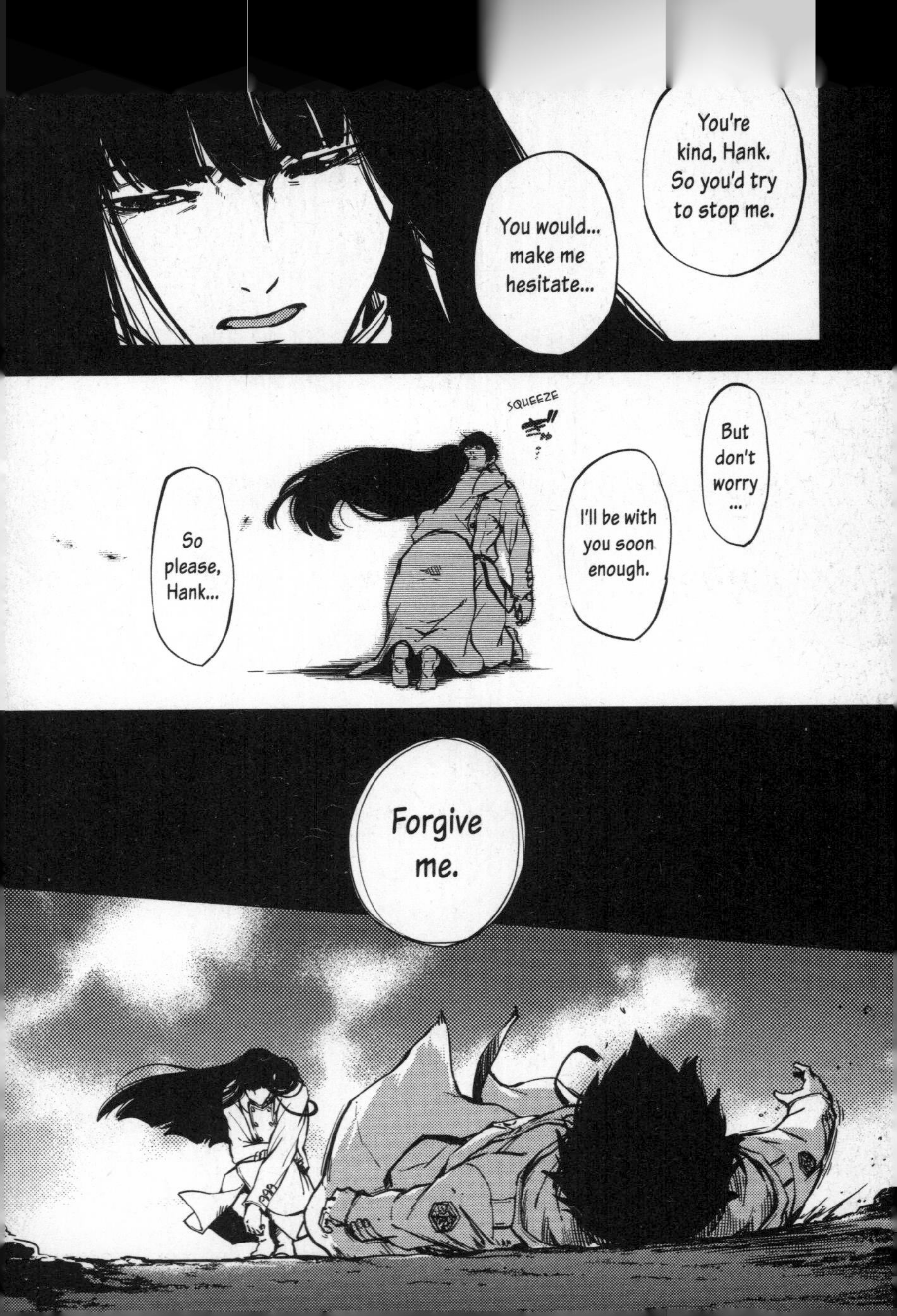
You're kind, Hank. So you'd try to stop me.
You would... make me hesitate...
But don't worry...
I'll be with you soon enough.
SQUEEZE
So please, Hank...
Forgive me.

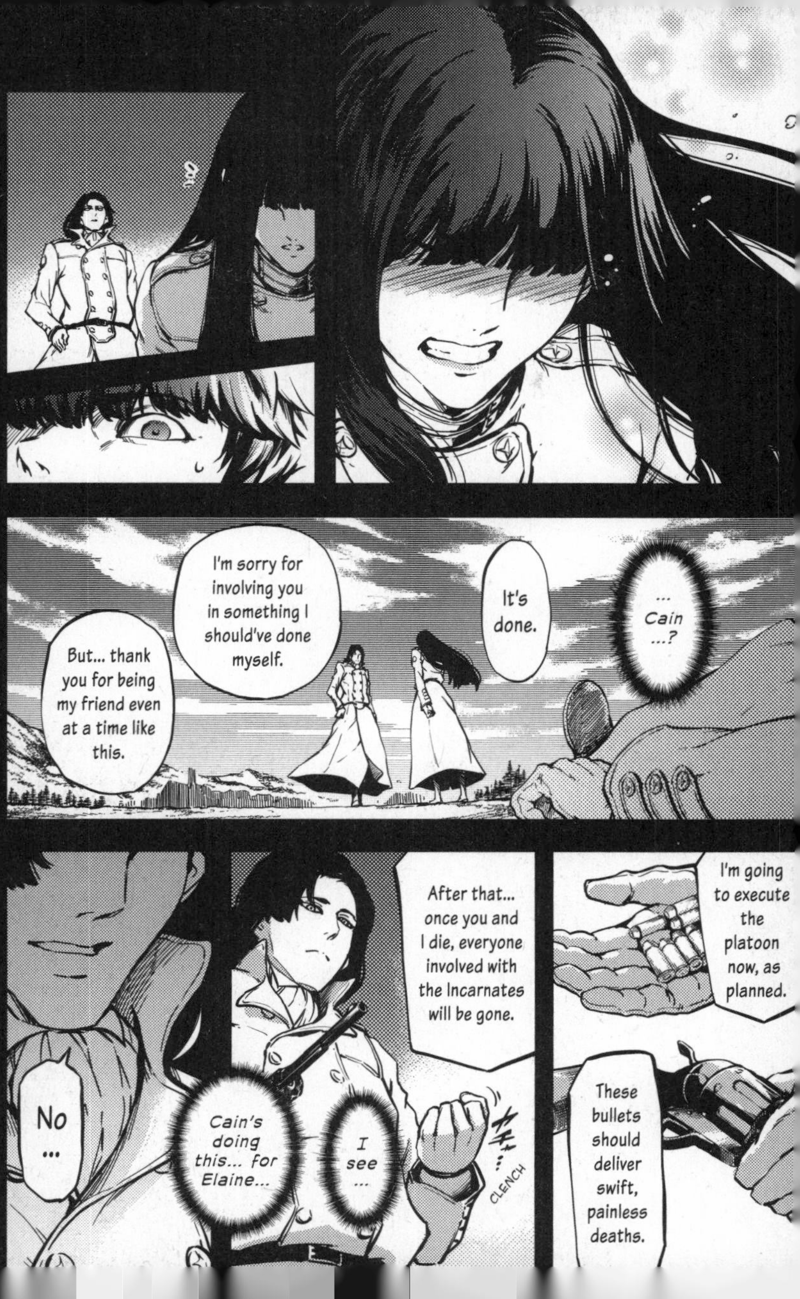
... Cain ...?
It's done.
I'm sorry for involving you in something I should've done myself.
But... thank you for being my friend even at a time like this.
I'm going to execute the platoon now, as planned.
These bullets should deliver swift, painless deaths.
After that... once you and I die, everyone involved with the Incarnates will be gone.
CLENCH
I see ...
Cain's doing this... for Elaine...
No ...

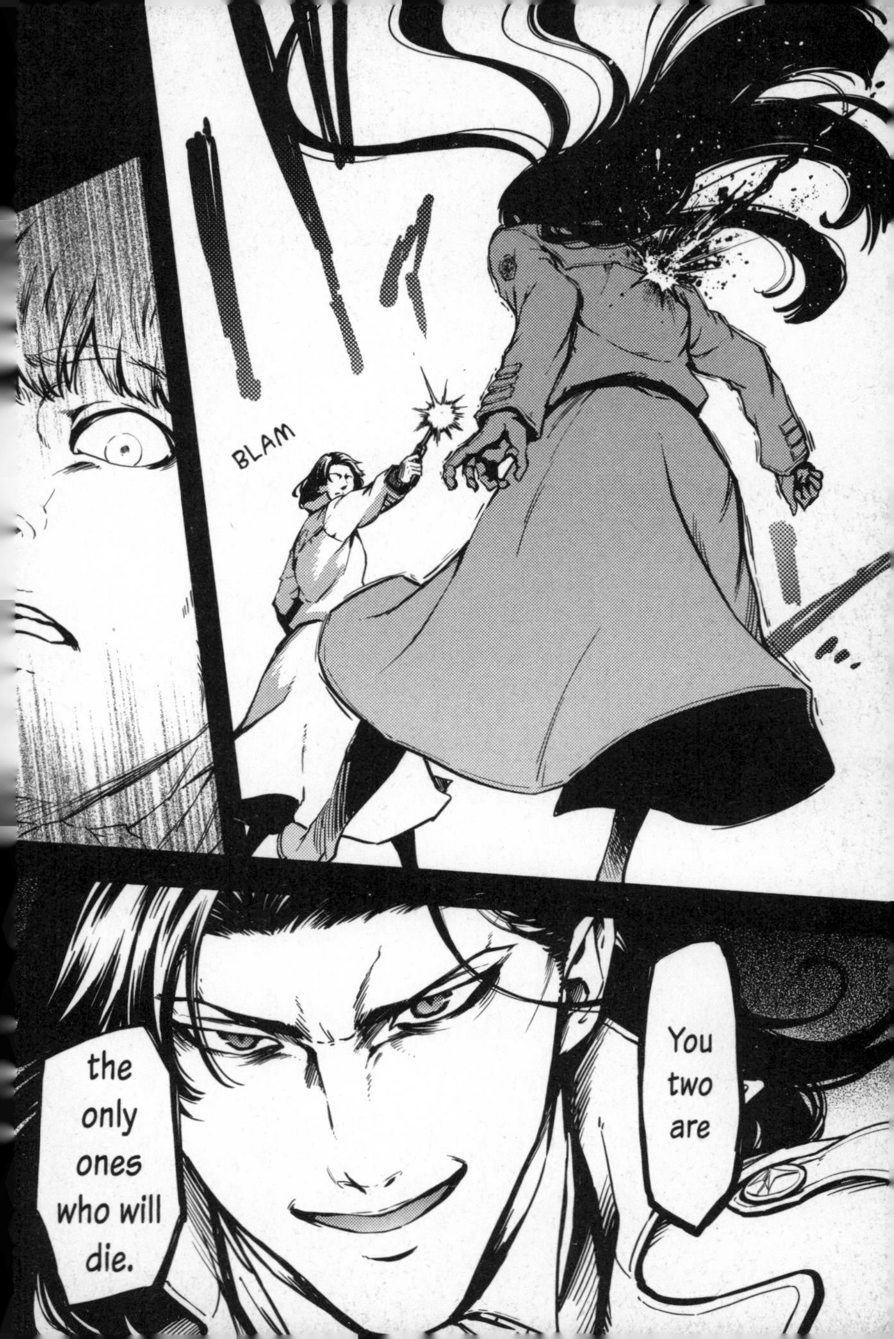
BLAM
You two are
the only ones who will die.

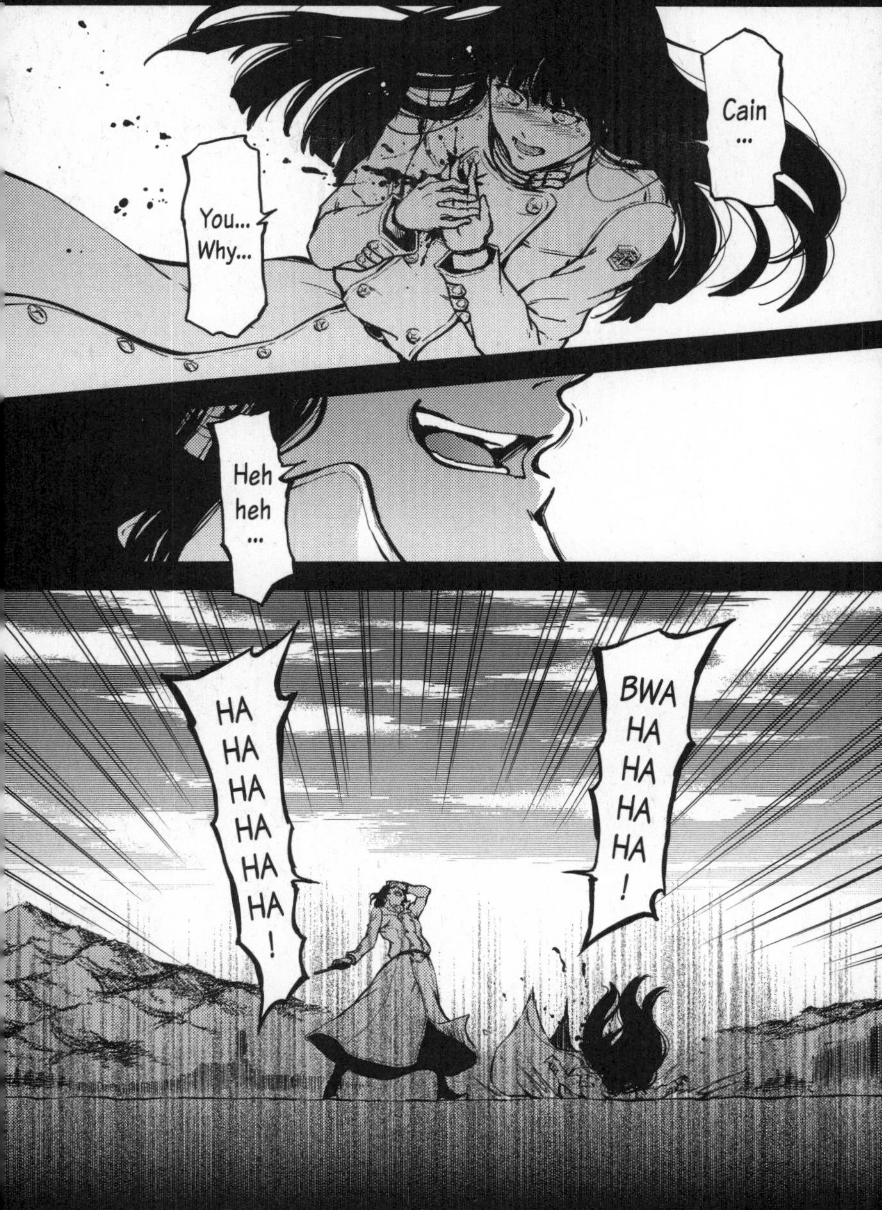
Cain...
You... Why...
Heh heh...
BWA HA HA HA HA HA!
HA HA HA HA HA HA HA!

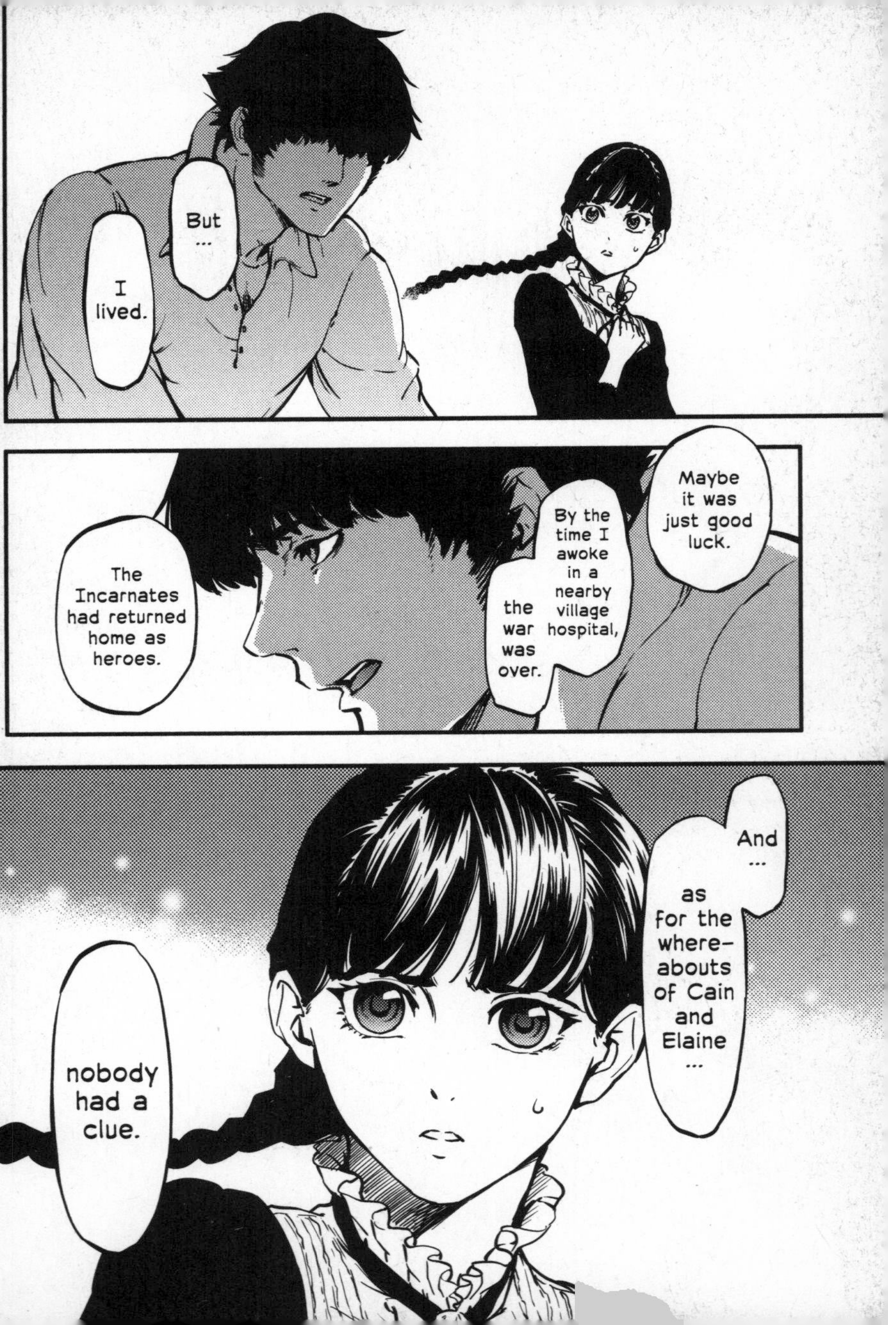
But ...
I lived.
Maybe it was just good luck.
By the time I awoke in a nearby village hospital, the war was over.
The Incarnates had returned home as heroes.
And ... as for the whereabouts of Cain and Elaine ...
nobody had a clue.

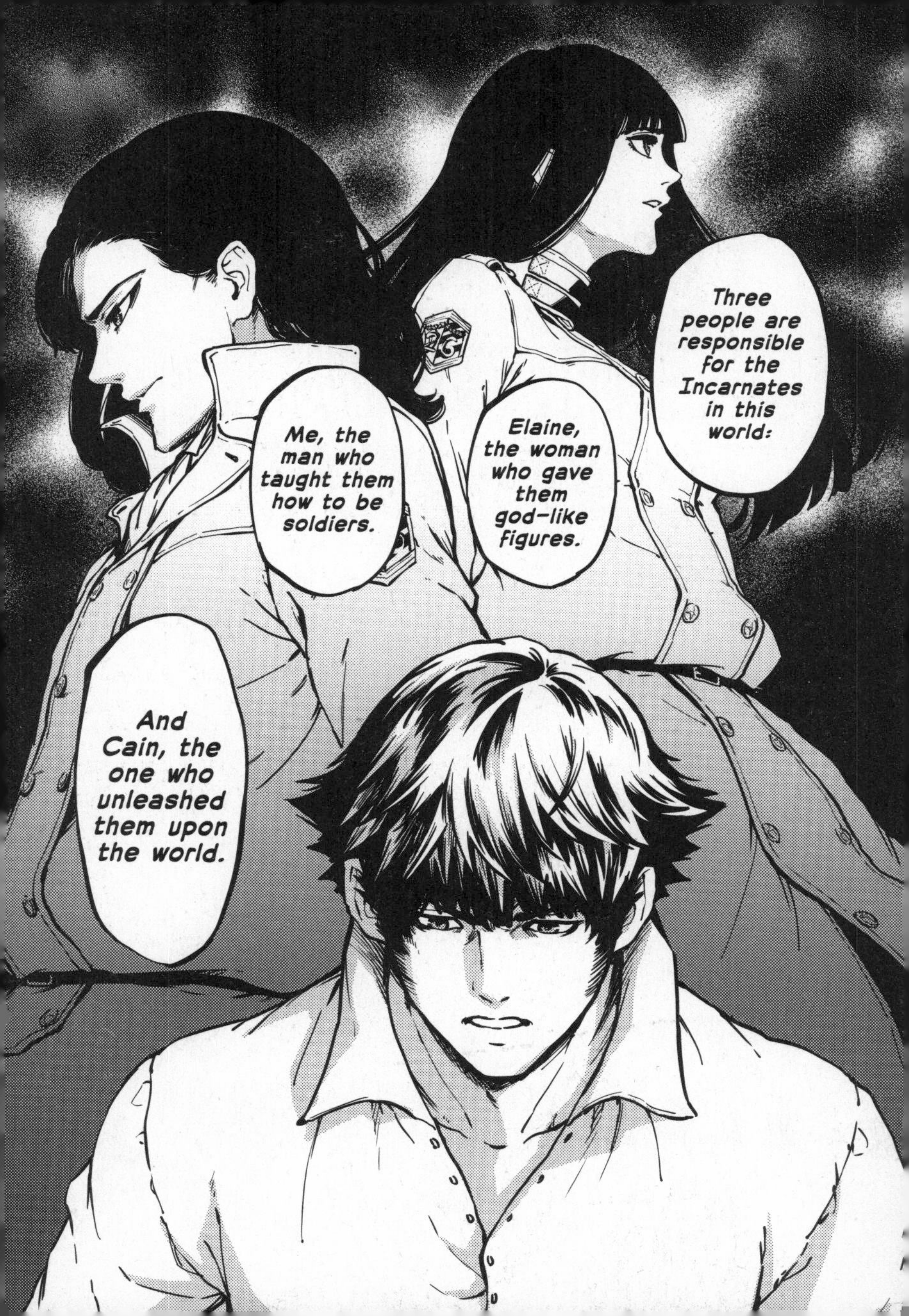
Three people are responsible for the Incarnates in this world:
Elaine, the woman who gave them god-like figures.
Me, the man who taught them how to be soldiers.
And Cain, the one who unleashed them upon the world.

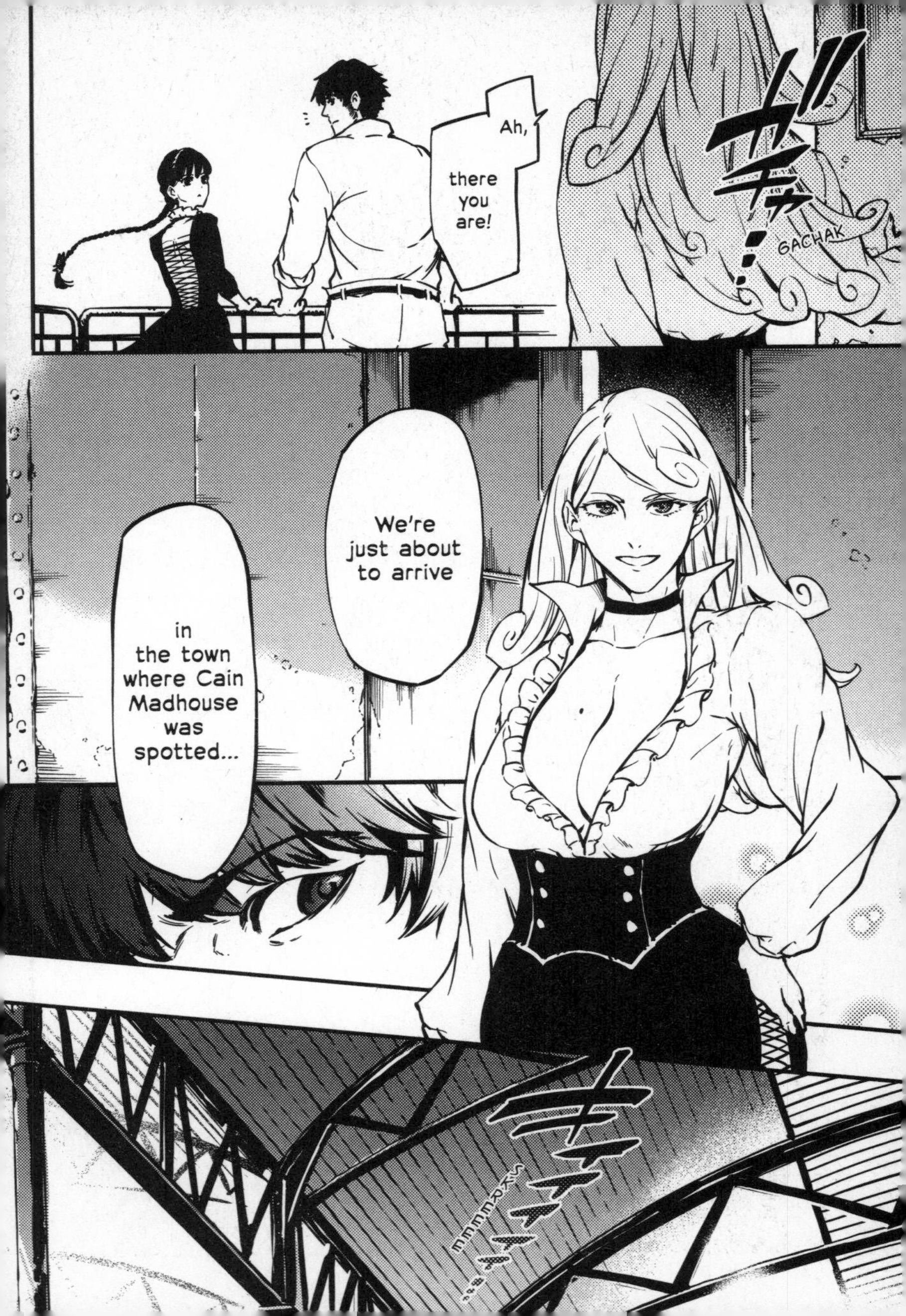
GACHAK
Ah, there you are!
We're just about to arrive
in the town where Cain Madhouse was spotted...
SKREEEEE

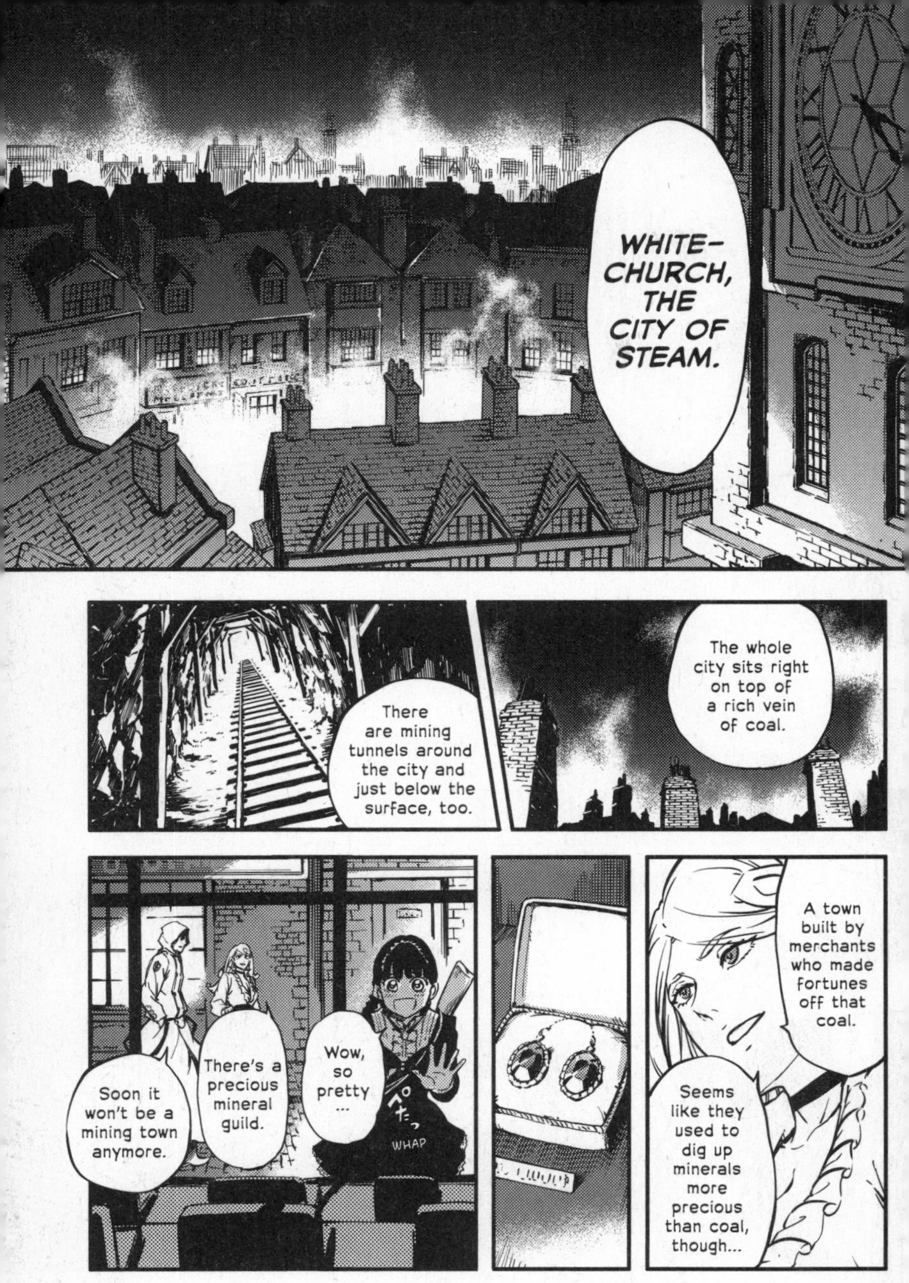
WHITE-CHURCH, THE CITY OF STEAM.
The whole city sits right on top of a rich vein of coal.
There are mining tunnels around the city and just below the surface, too.
A town built by merchants who made fortunes off that coal.
Seems like they used to dig up minerals more precious than coal, though...
Wow, so pretty ...
WHAP
There's a precious mineral guild.
Soon it won't be a mining town anymore.

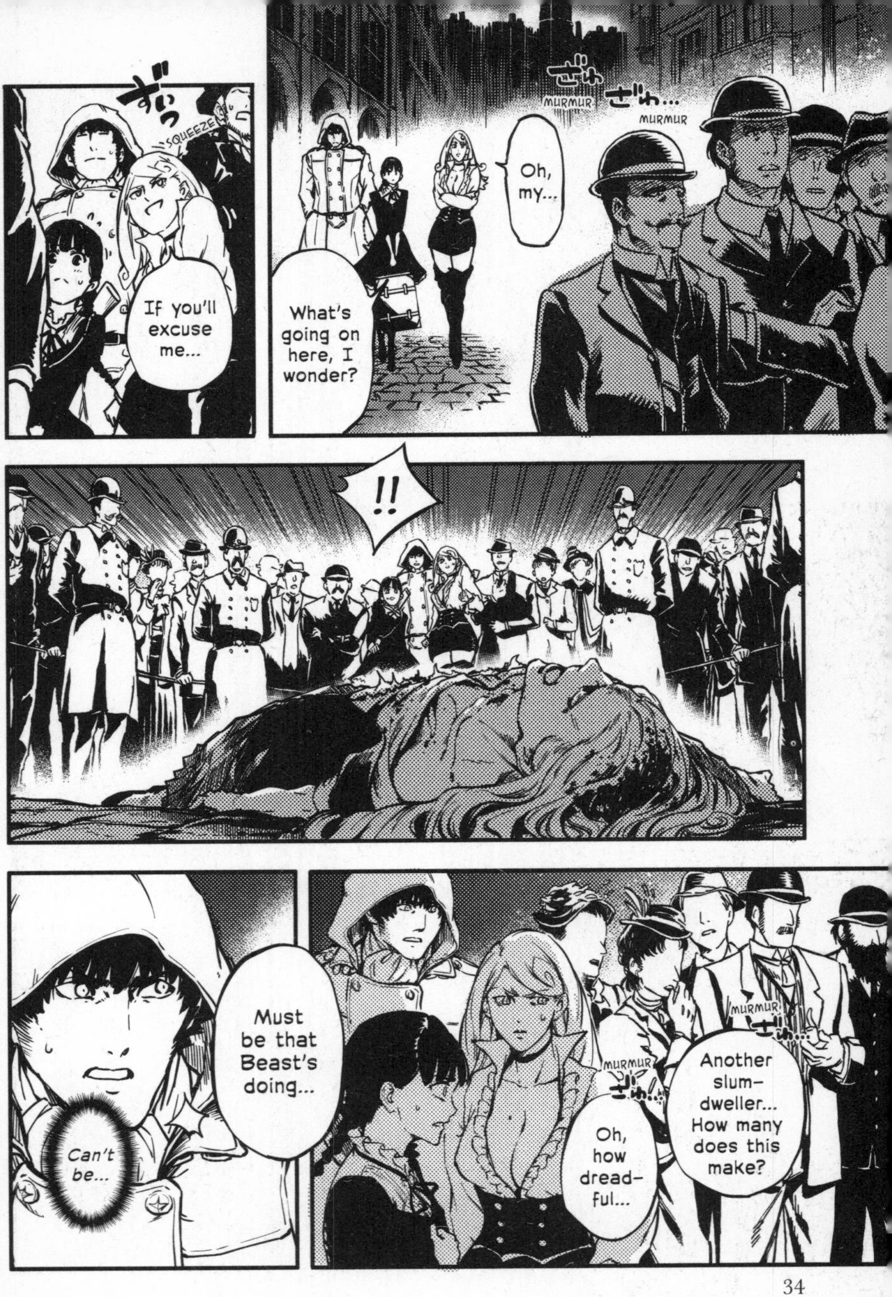
ざわ ざわ...
MURMUR
MURMUR
Oh, my...
What's going on here, I wonder?
SQUEEZE
If you'll excuse me...
!!
MURMUR
Another slum-dweller... How many does this make?
MURMUR
Oh, how dreadful...
Must be that Beast's doing...
Can't be...

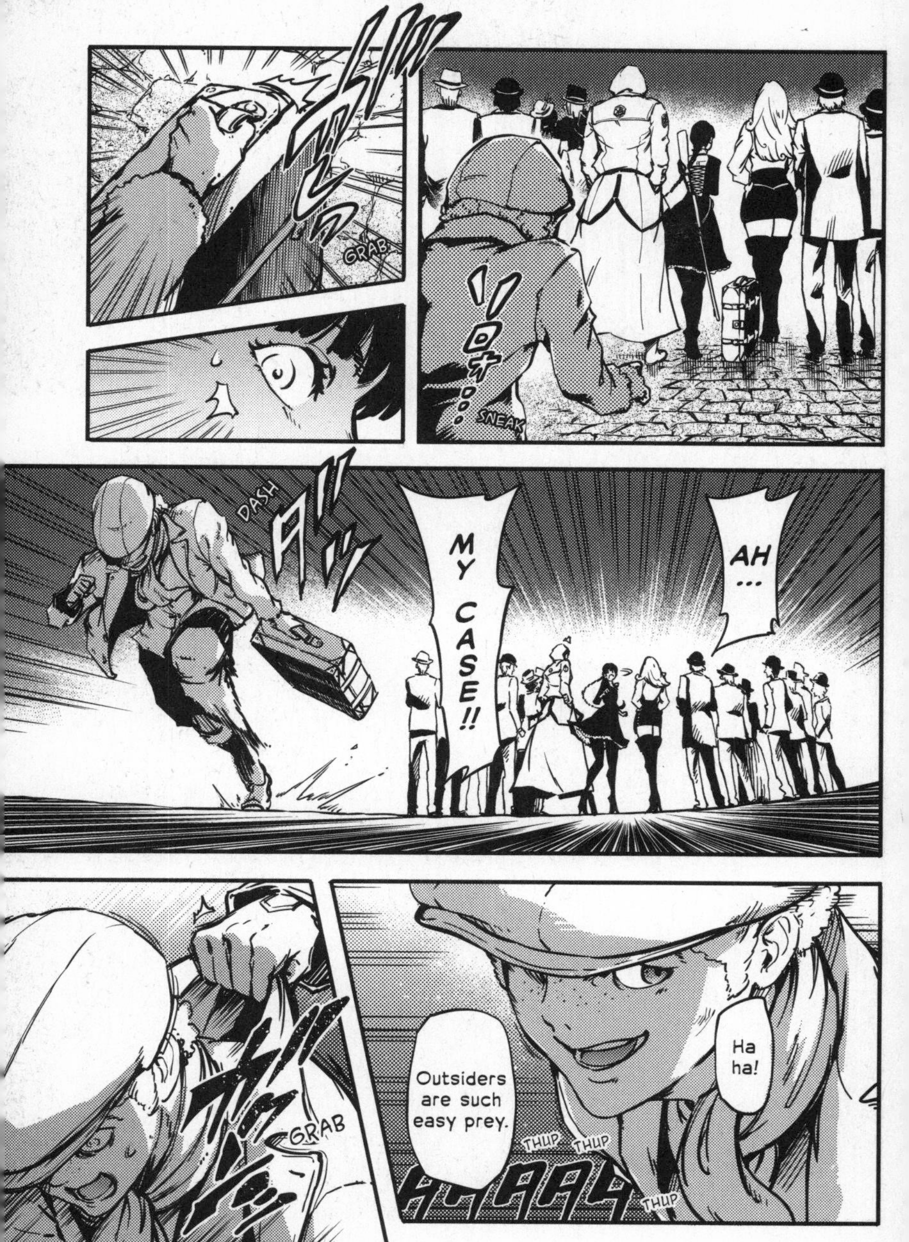
SNEAK
GRAB
AH...
MY CASE!!
DASH
Ha ha!
Outsiders are such easy prey.
THUP
THUP
THUP
GRAB

No ...

?!

He caught up to me in an instant ?!

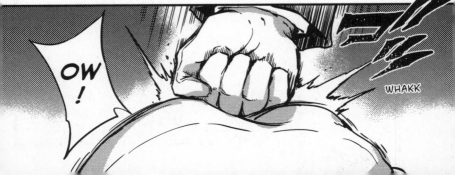

OW !

WHAKK

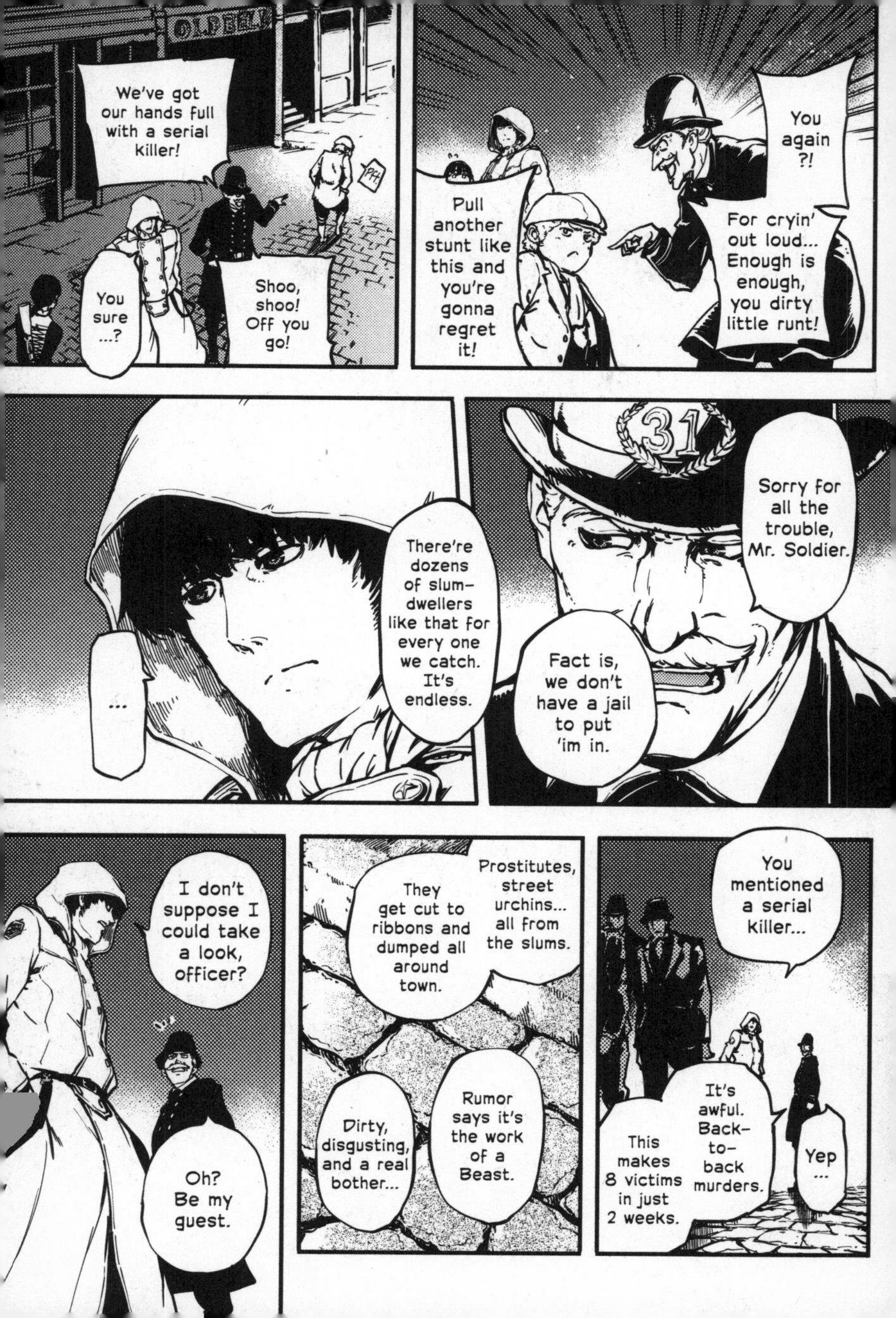
You again ?!
For cryin' out loud... Enough is enough, you dirty little runt!
Pull another stunt like this and you're gonna regret it!
We've got our hands full with a serial killer!
PFF
Shoo, shoo! Off you go!
You sure ...?
Sorry for all the trouble, Mr. Soldier.
Fact is, we don't have a jail to put 'im in.
There're dozens of slum-dwellers like that for every one we catch. It's endless.
...
You mentioned a serial killer...
Yep ...
It's awful. Back-to-back murders.
This makes 8 victims in just 2 weeks.
Prostitutes, street urchins... all from the slums.
They get cut to ribbons and dumped all around town.
Rumor says it's the work of a Beast.
Dirty, disgusting, and a real bother...
I don't suppose I could take a look, officer?
Oh? Be my guest.

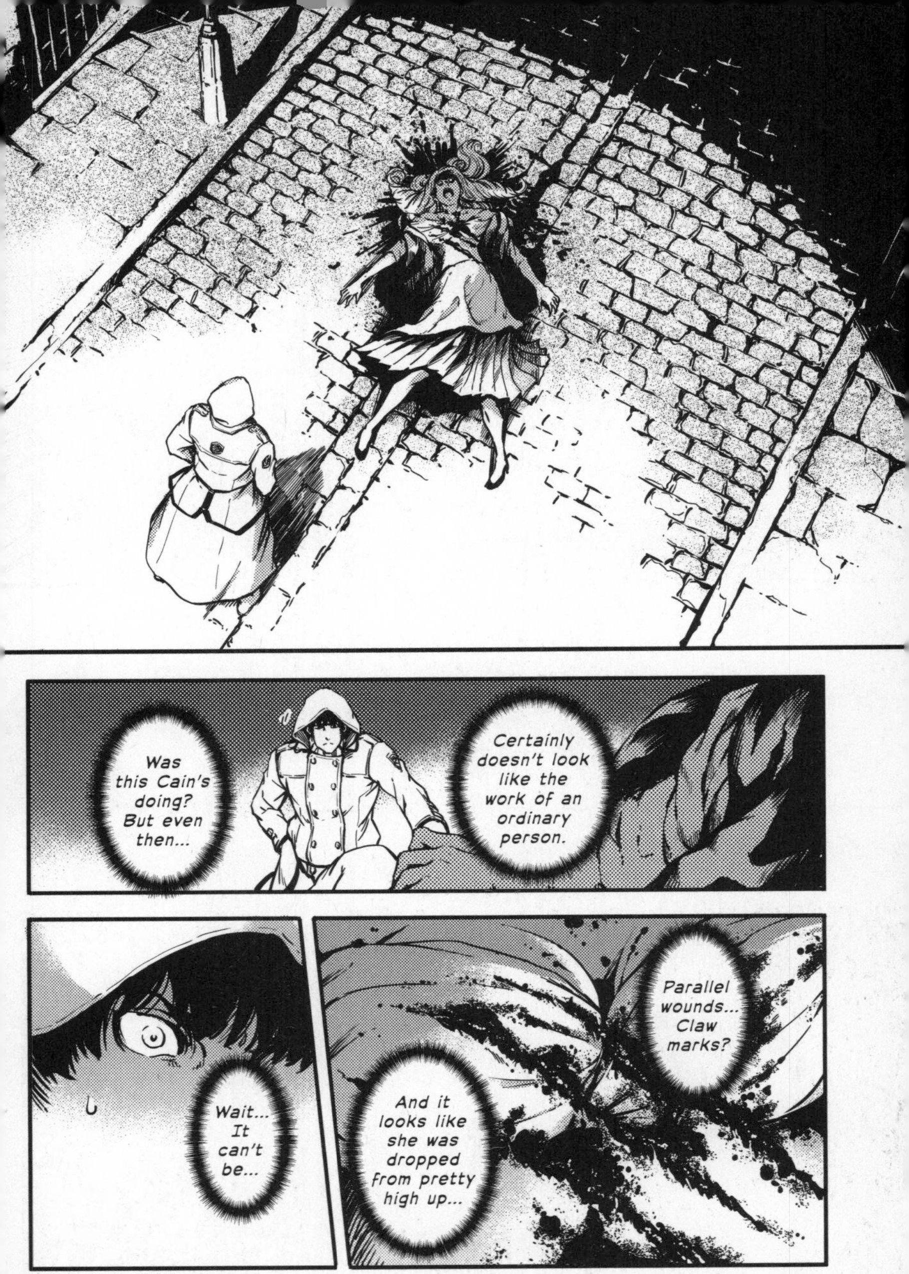
Certainly doesn't look like the work of an ordinary person.
Was this Cain's doing? But even then...
Parallel wounds... Claw marks?
And it looks like she was dropped from pretty high up...
Wait... It can't be...

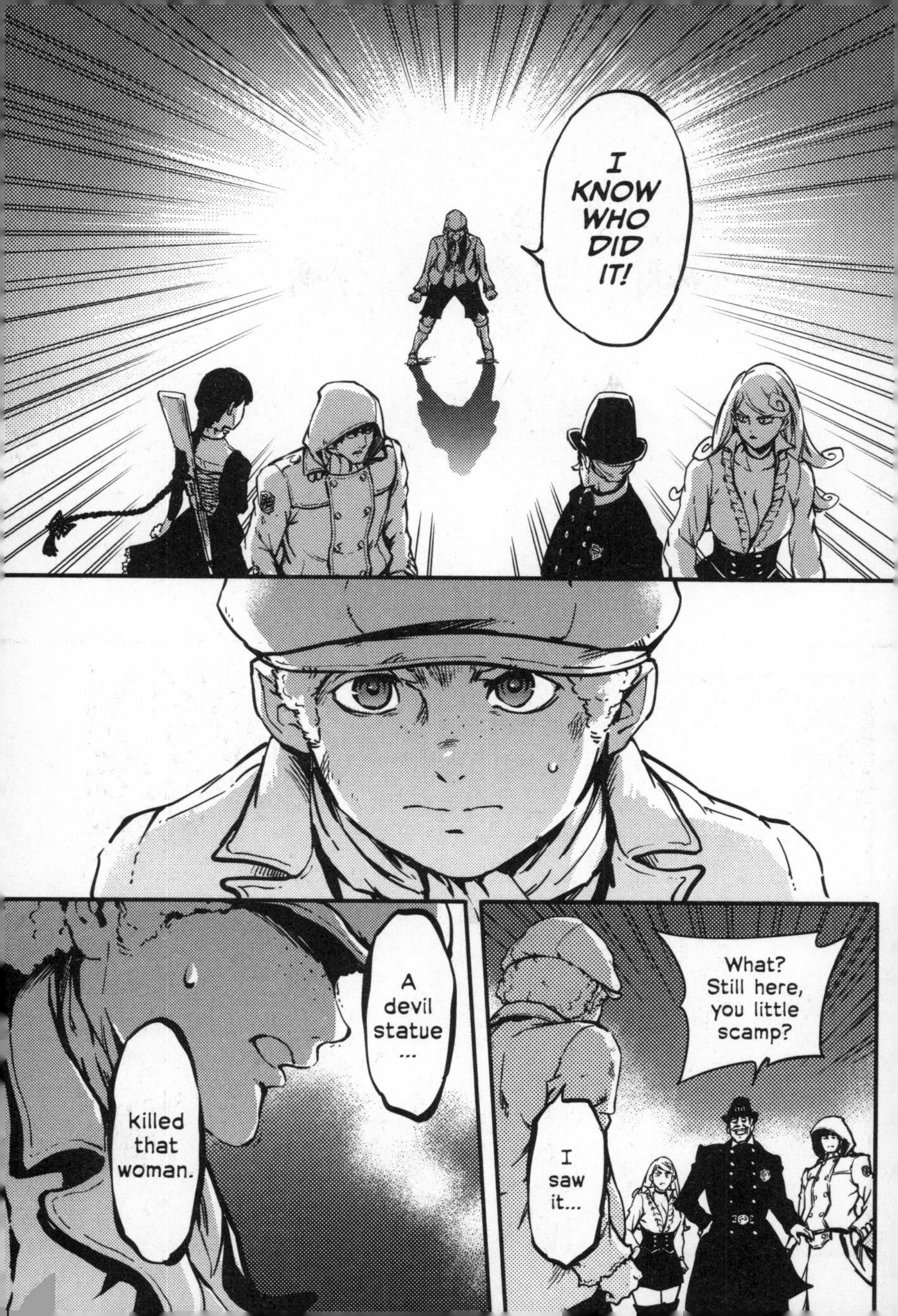
I KNOW WHO DID IT!
What? Still here, you little scamp?
I saw it...
A devil statue...
killed that woman.

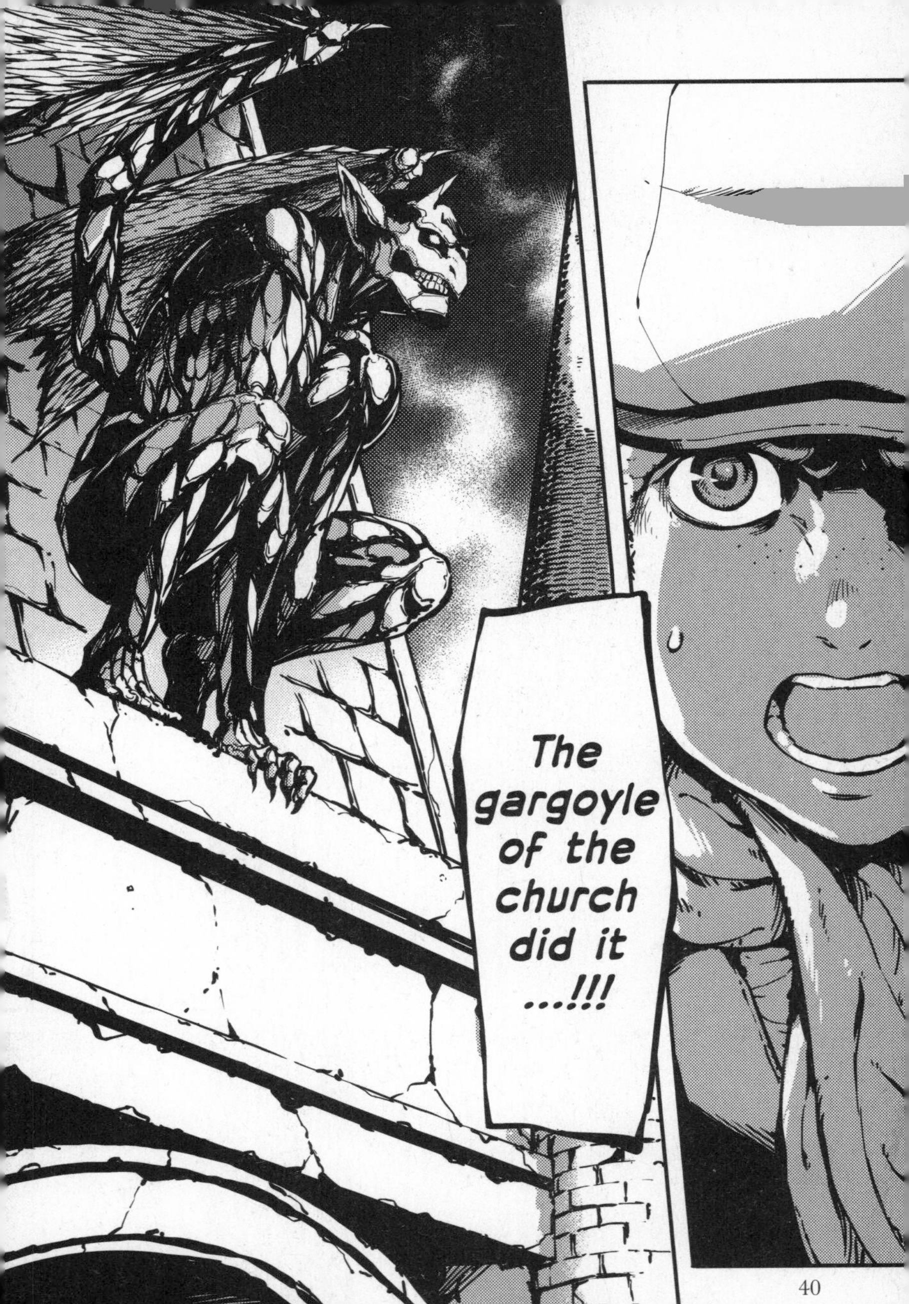
The gargoyle of the church did it ...!!!

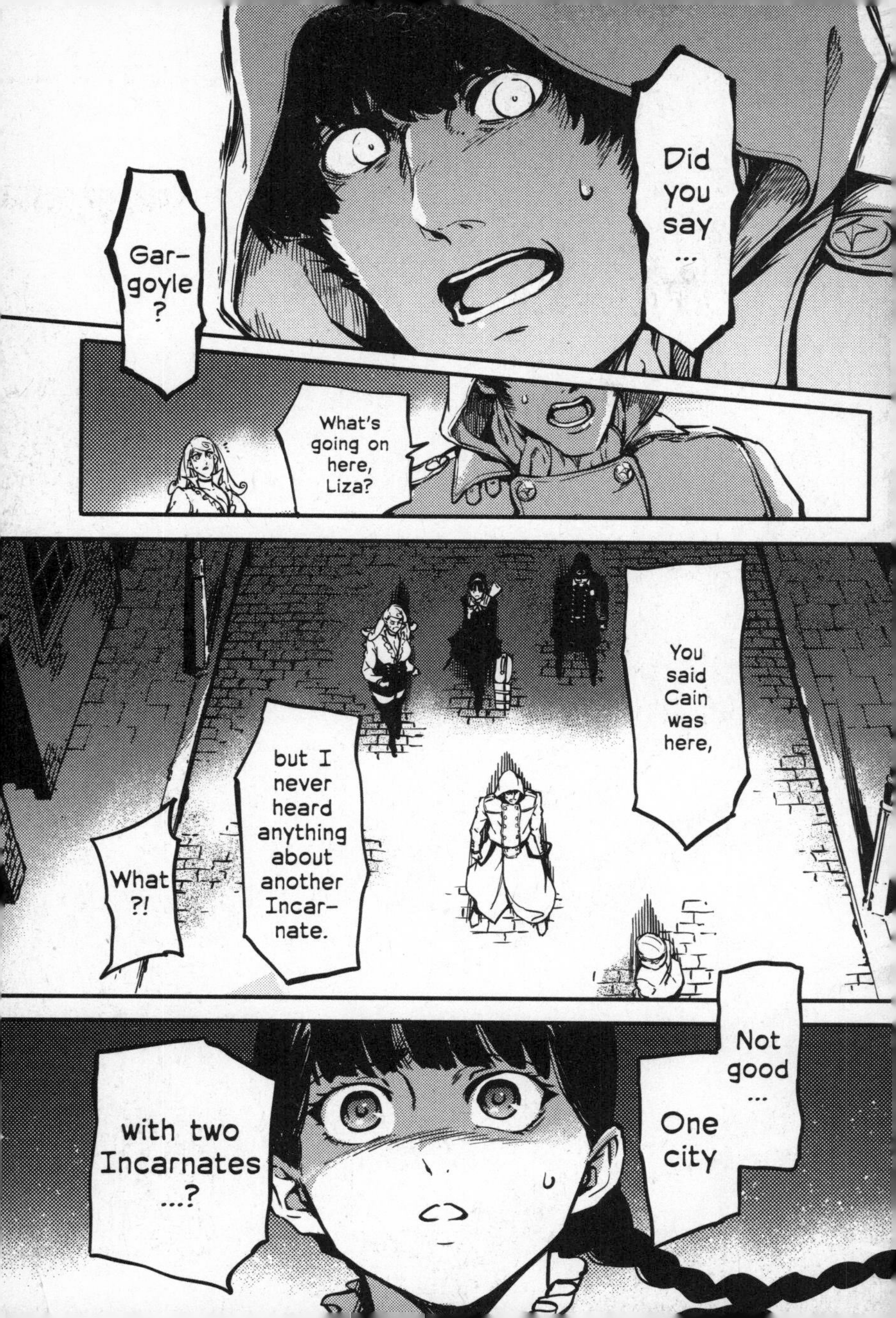
Did you say ...
Gar-goyle?
What's going on here, Liza?
You said Cain was here,
but I never heard anything about another Incar-nate.
What?!
Not good ...
One city
with two Incarnates ...?

To the Abandoned
Sacred Beasts

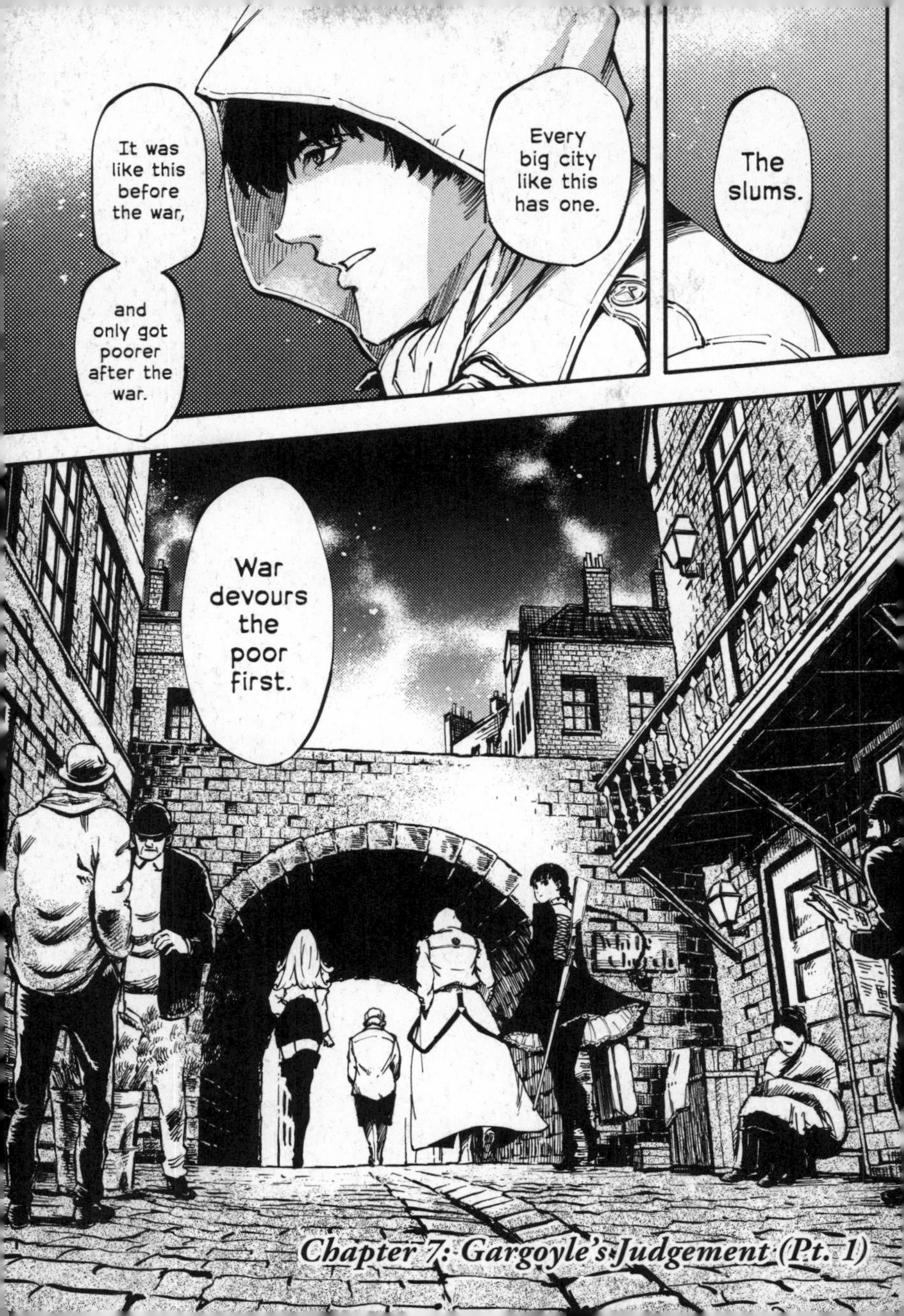
The slums.
Every big city like this has one.
It was like this before the war,
and only got poorer after the war.
War devours the poor first.
Chapter 7: Gargoyle's Judgement (Pt. 1)

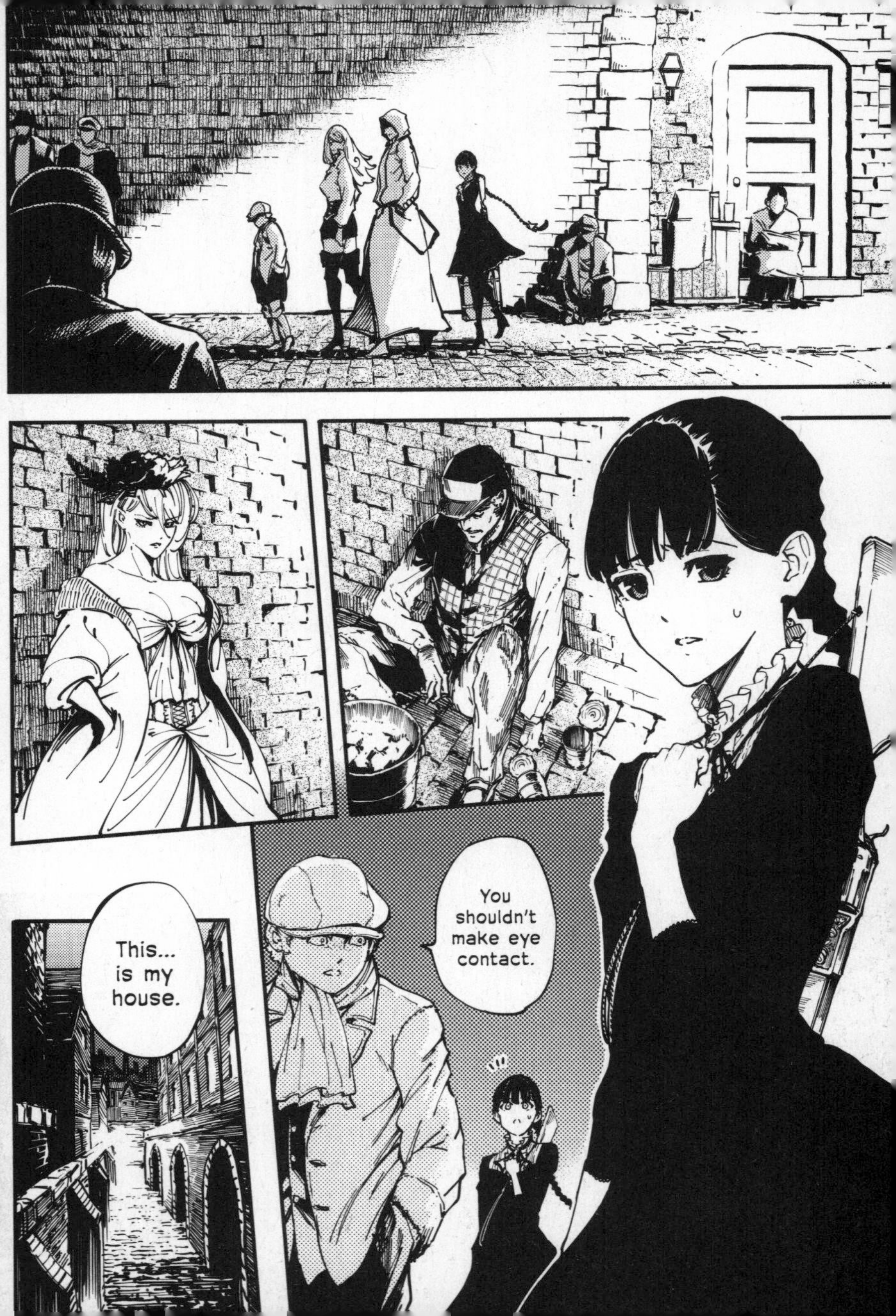
You shouldn't make eye contact.
This... is my house.

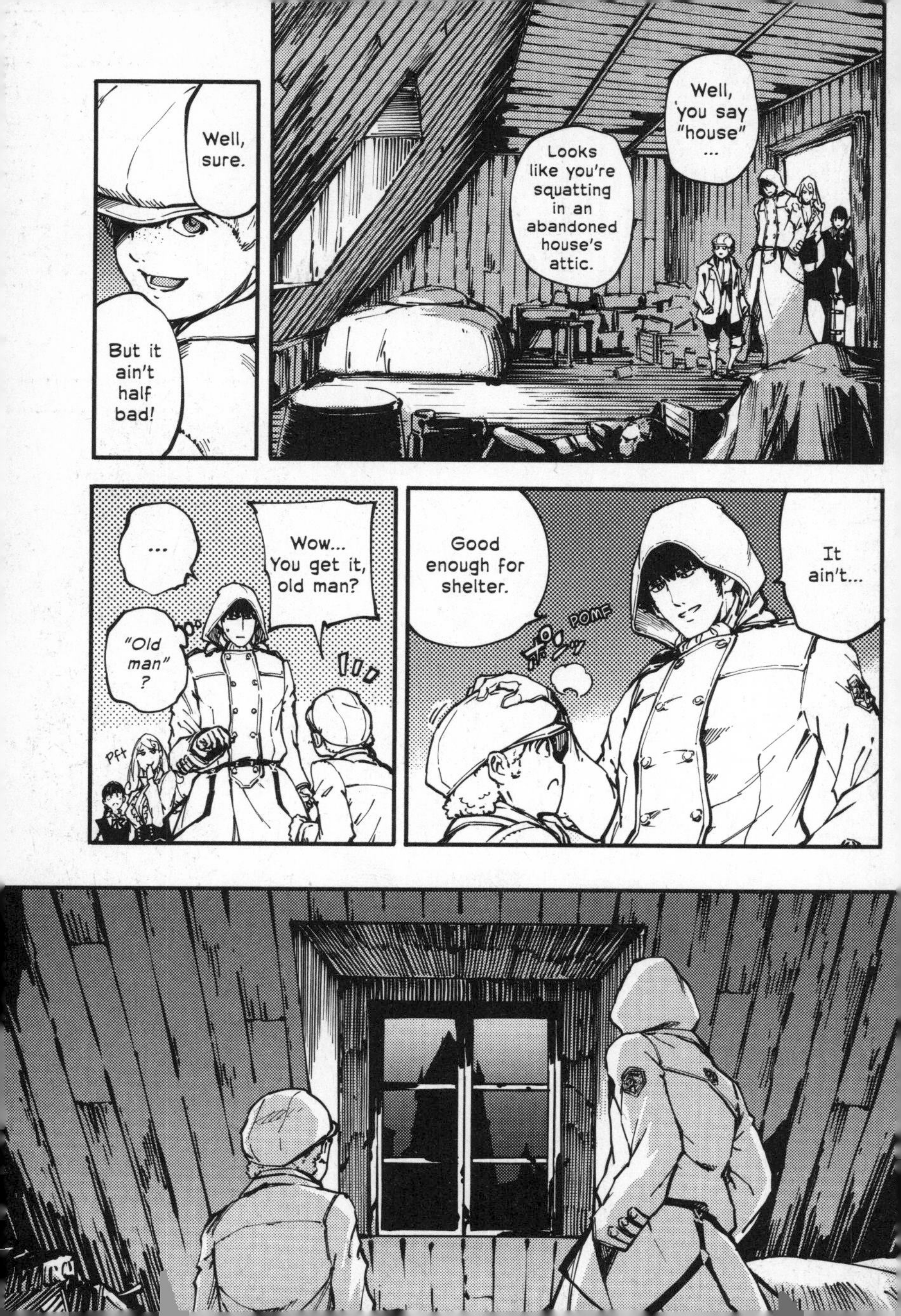
Well, you say "house" ...
Looks like you're squatting in an abandoned house's attic.
Well, sure.
But it ain't half bad!
It ain't...
Good enough for shelter.
POMF
Wow... You get it, old man?
...
"Old man"?
pft

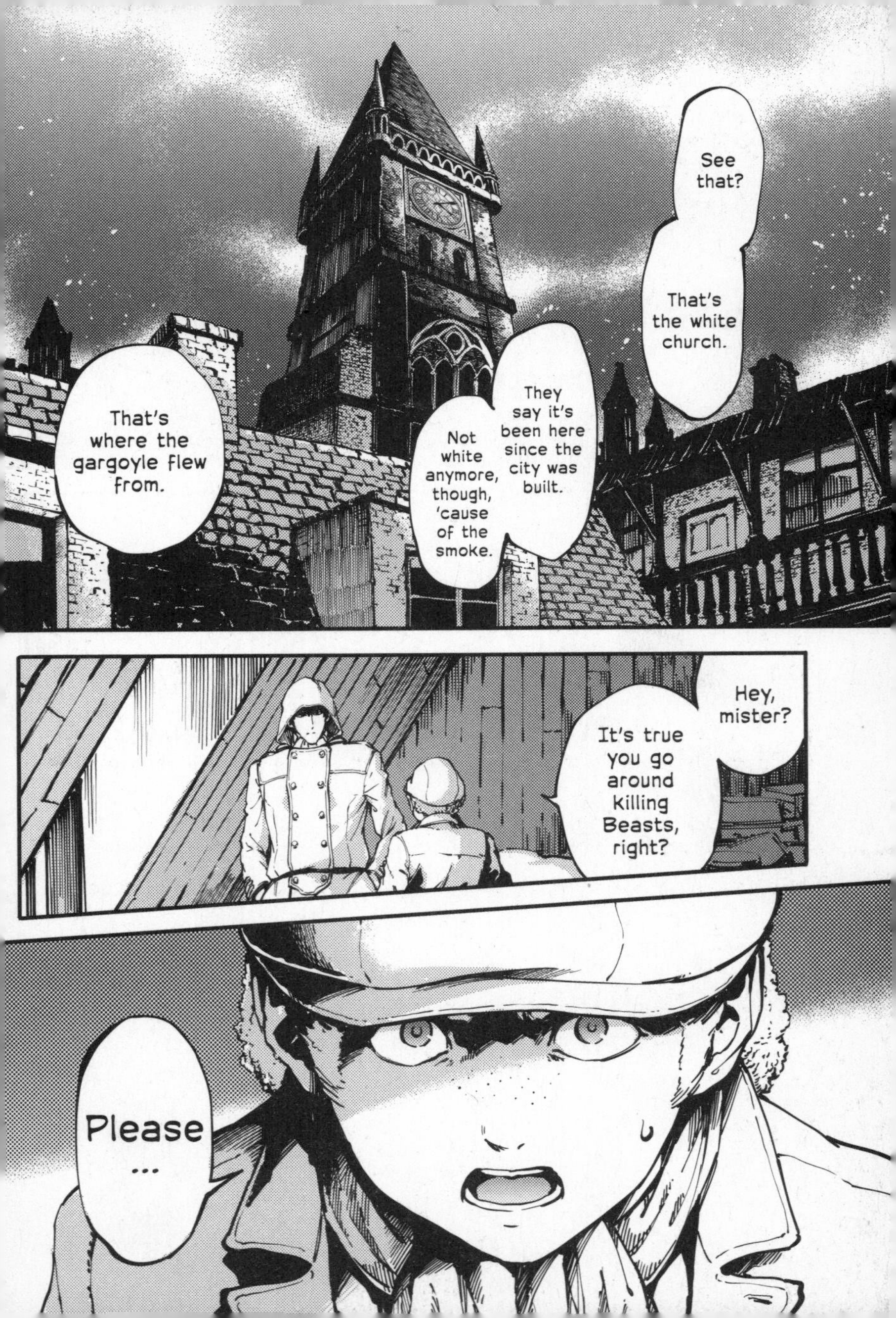
See that?
That's the white church.
They say it's been here since the city was built.
Not white anymore, though, 'cause of the smoke.
That's where the gargoyle flew from.
Hey, mister?
It's true you go around killing Beasts, right?
Please ...

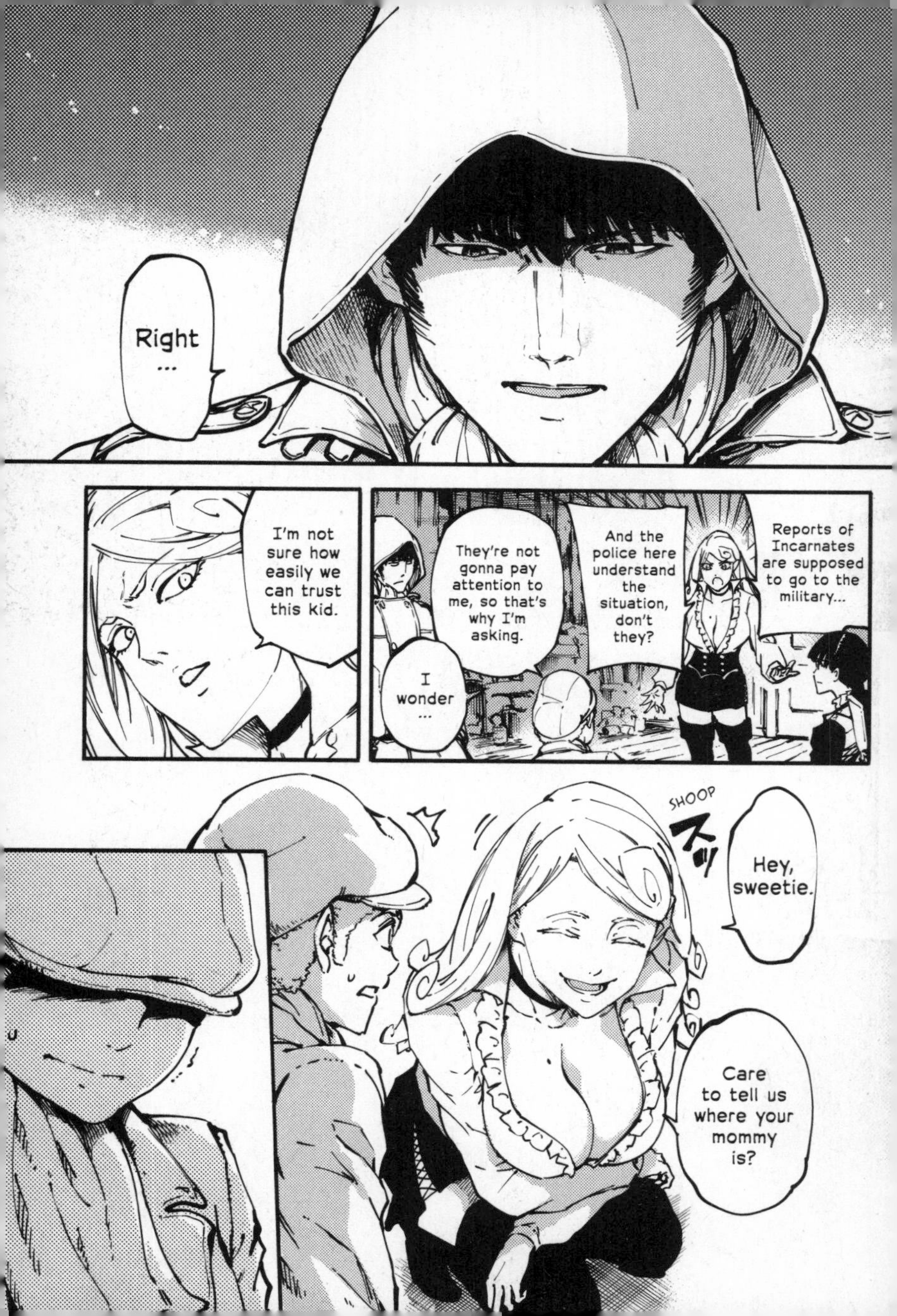
Right ...
Reports of Incarnates are supposed to go to the military...
And the police here understand the situation, don't they?
They're not gonna pay attention to me, so that's why I'm asking.
I wonder ...
I'm not sure how easily we can trust this kid.
SHOOP
Hey, sweetie.
Care to tell us where your mommy is?

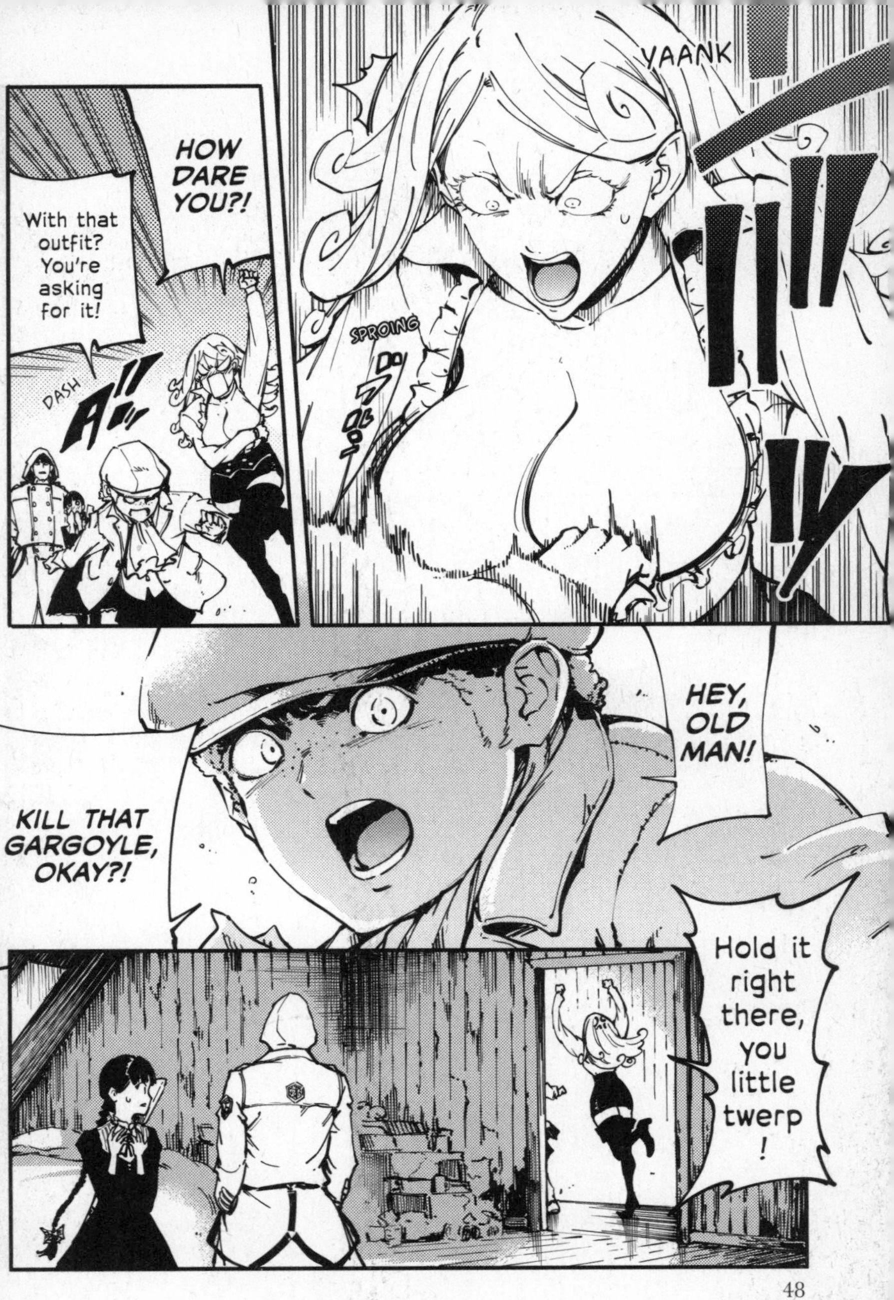
YAANK
SPROING
HOW DARE YOU?!
With that outfit? You're asking for it!
DASH
HEY, OLD MAN!
KILL THAT GARGOYLE, OKAY?!
Hold it right there, you little twerp!

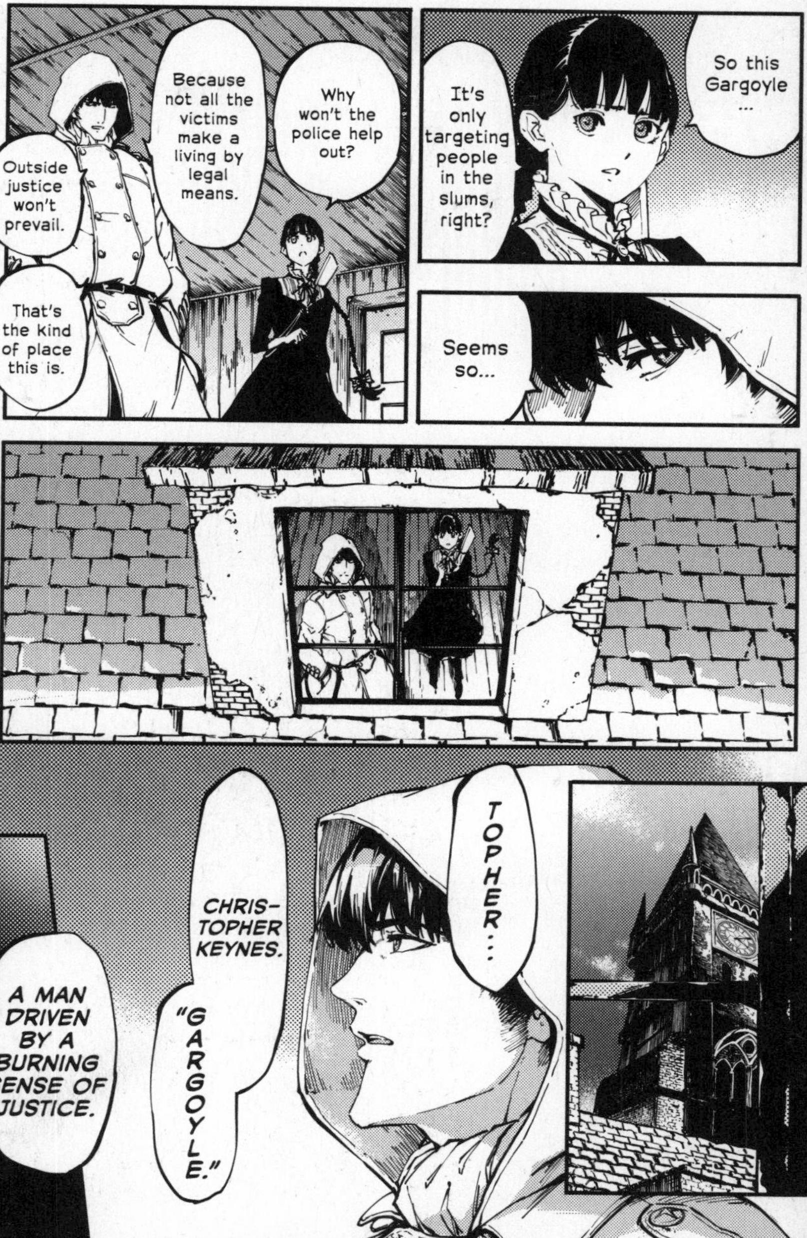
So this Gargoyle ...
It's only targeting people in the slums, right?
Seems so...
Why won't the police help out?
Because not all the victims make a living by legal means.
Outside justice won't prevail.
That's the kind of place this is.
TOPHER...
CHRIS-TOPHER KEYNES.
"GARGOYLE."
A MAN DRIVEN BY A BURNING SENSE OF JUSTICE.

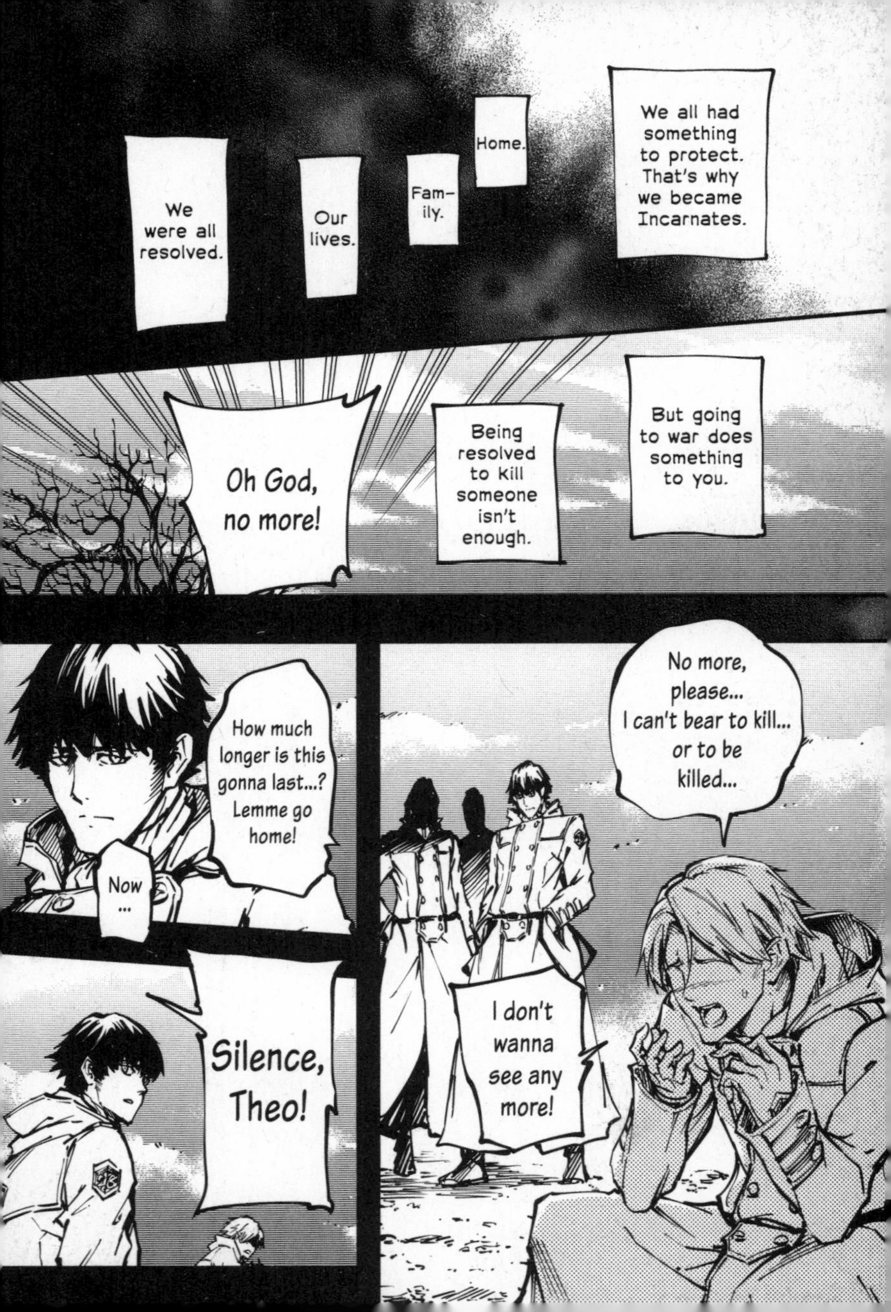
We all had something to protect. That's why we became Incarnates.
Home.
Fam-ily.
Our lives.
We were all resolved.
But going to war does something to you.
Being resolved to kill someone isn't enough.
Oh God, no more!
No more, please... I can't bear to kill... or to be killed...
I don't wanna see any more!
How much longer is this gonna last...? Lemme go home!
Now...
Silence, Theo!

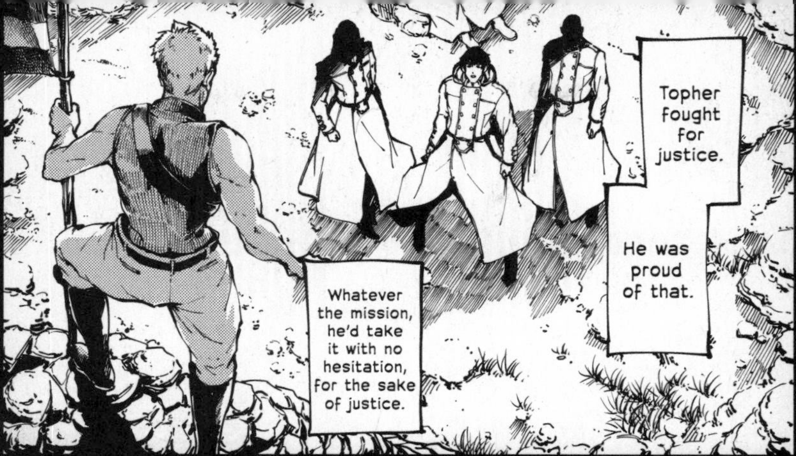
Topher fought for justice.
He was proud of that.
Whatever the mission, he'd take it with no hesitation, for the sake of justice.

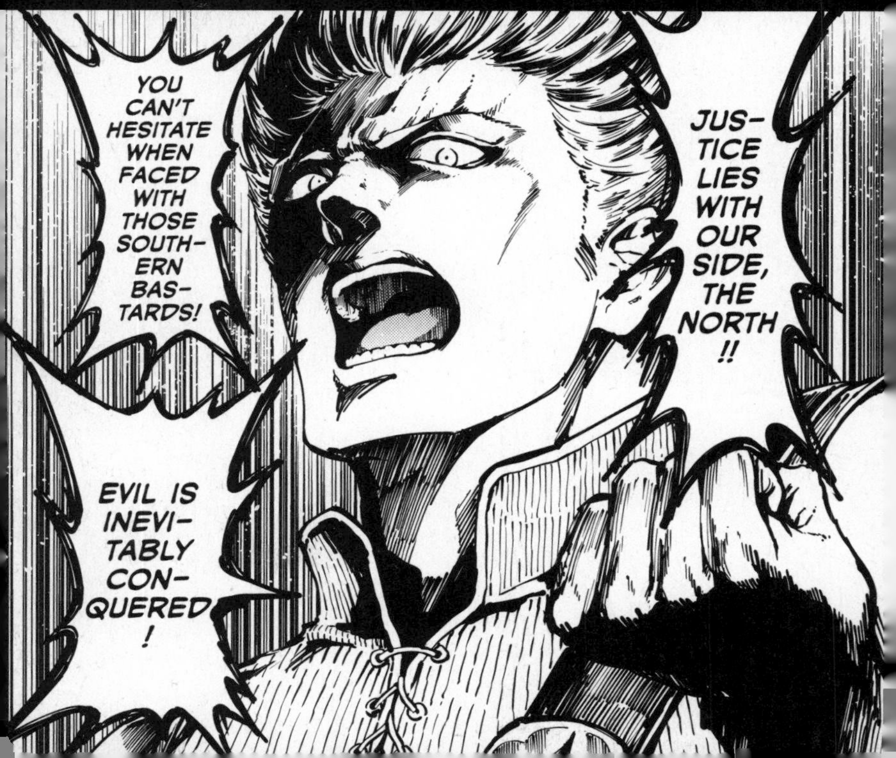
JUSTICE LIES WITH OUR SIDE, THE NORTH!!
YOU CAN'T HESITATE WHEN FACED WITH THOSE SOUTHERN BASTARDS!
EVIL IS INEVITABLY CONQUERED!

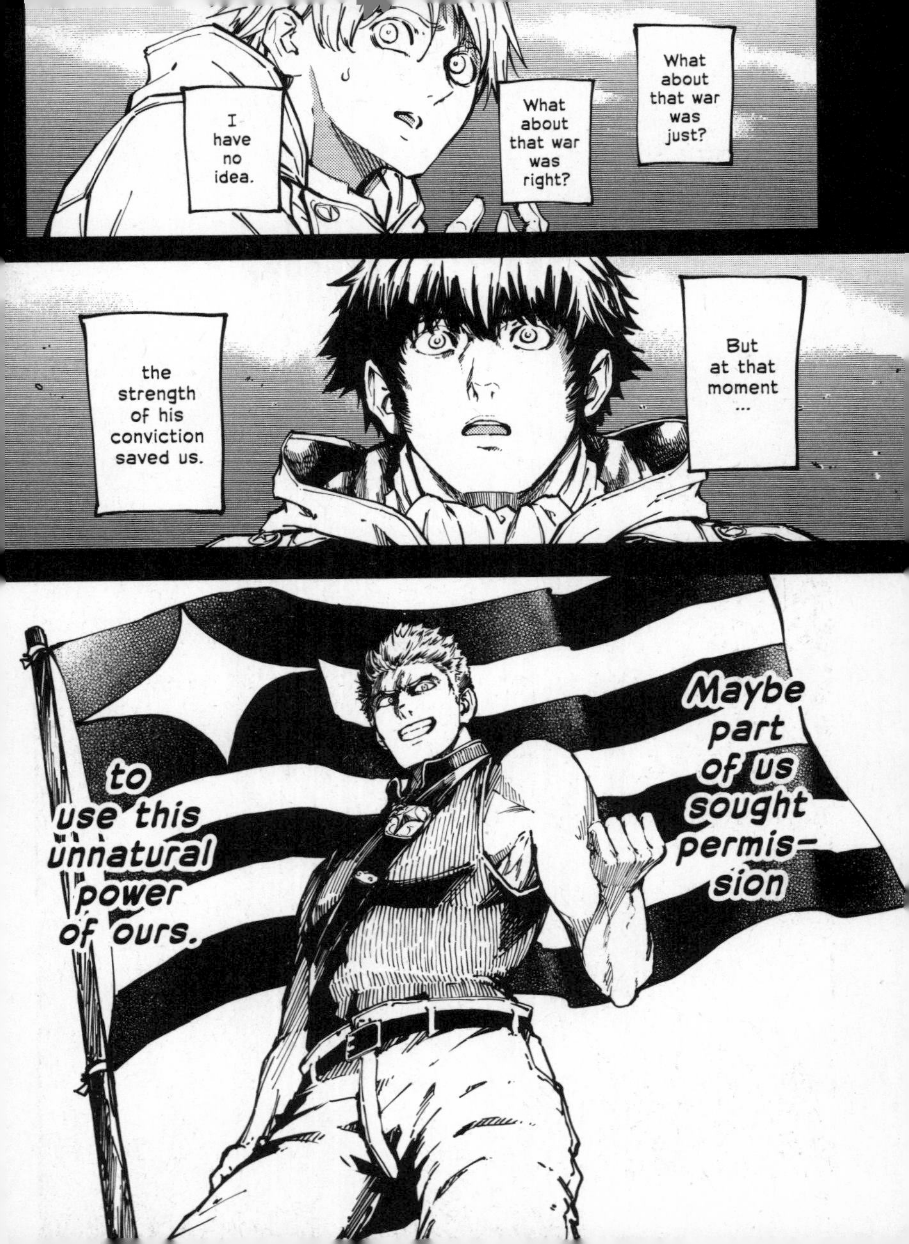
What about that war was just?
What about that war was right?
I have no idea.
But at that moment ...
the strength of his conviction saved us.
Maybe part of us sought permis-sion
to use this unnatural power of ours.

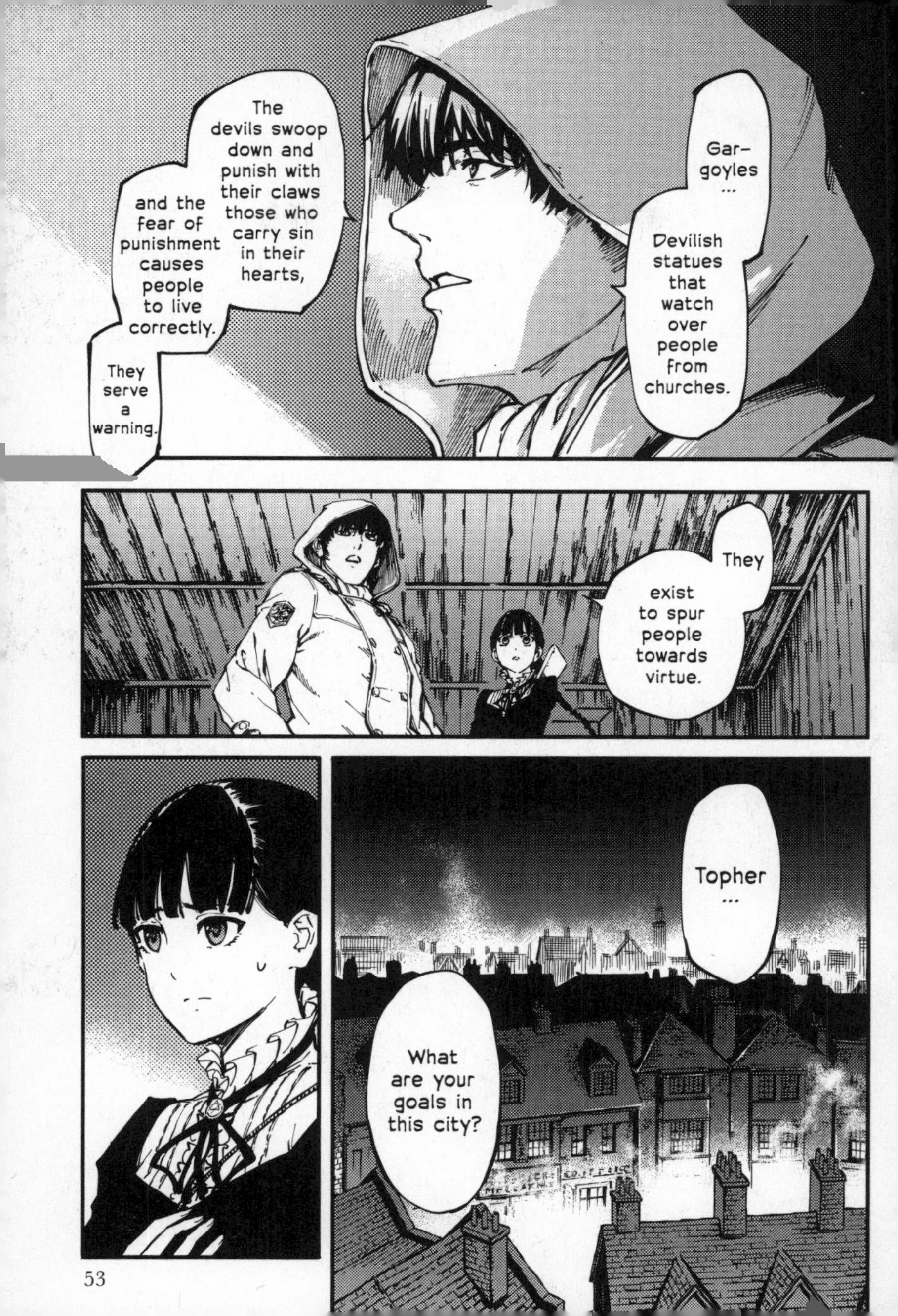
Gar-goyles ...
Devilish statues that watch over people from churches.
The devils swoop down and punish with their claws those who carry sin in their hearts,
and the fear of punishment causes people to live correctly.
They serve a warning.
They exist to spur people towards virtue.
Topher ...
What are your goals in this city?

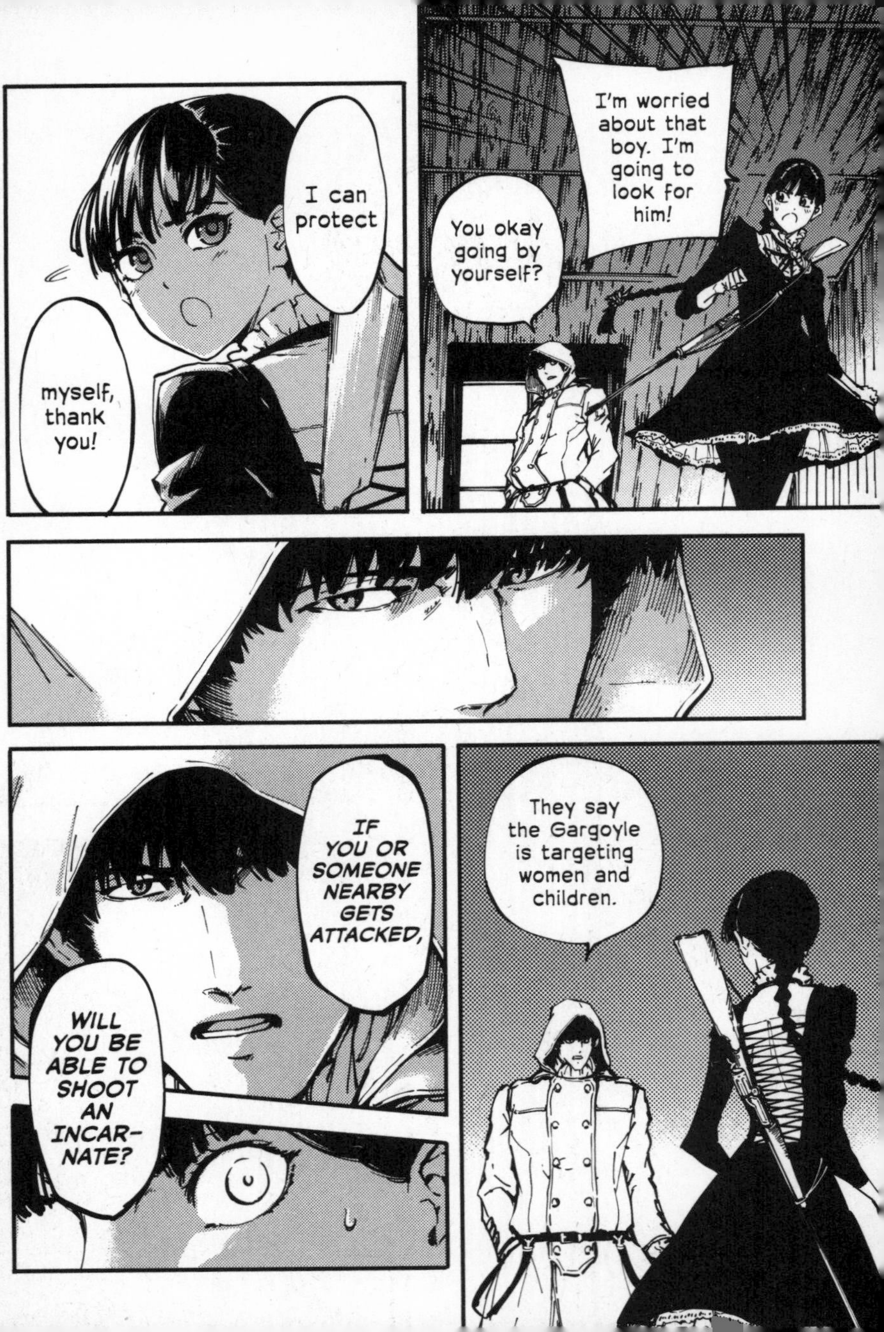
I'm worried about that boy. I'm going to look for him!
You okay going by yourself?
I can protect
myself, thank you!
They say the Gargoyle is targeting women and children.
IF YOU OR SOMEONE NEARBY GETS ATTACKED,
WILL YOU BE ABLE TO SHOOT AN INCAR-NATE?

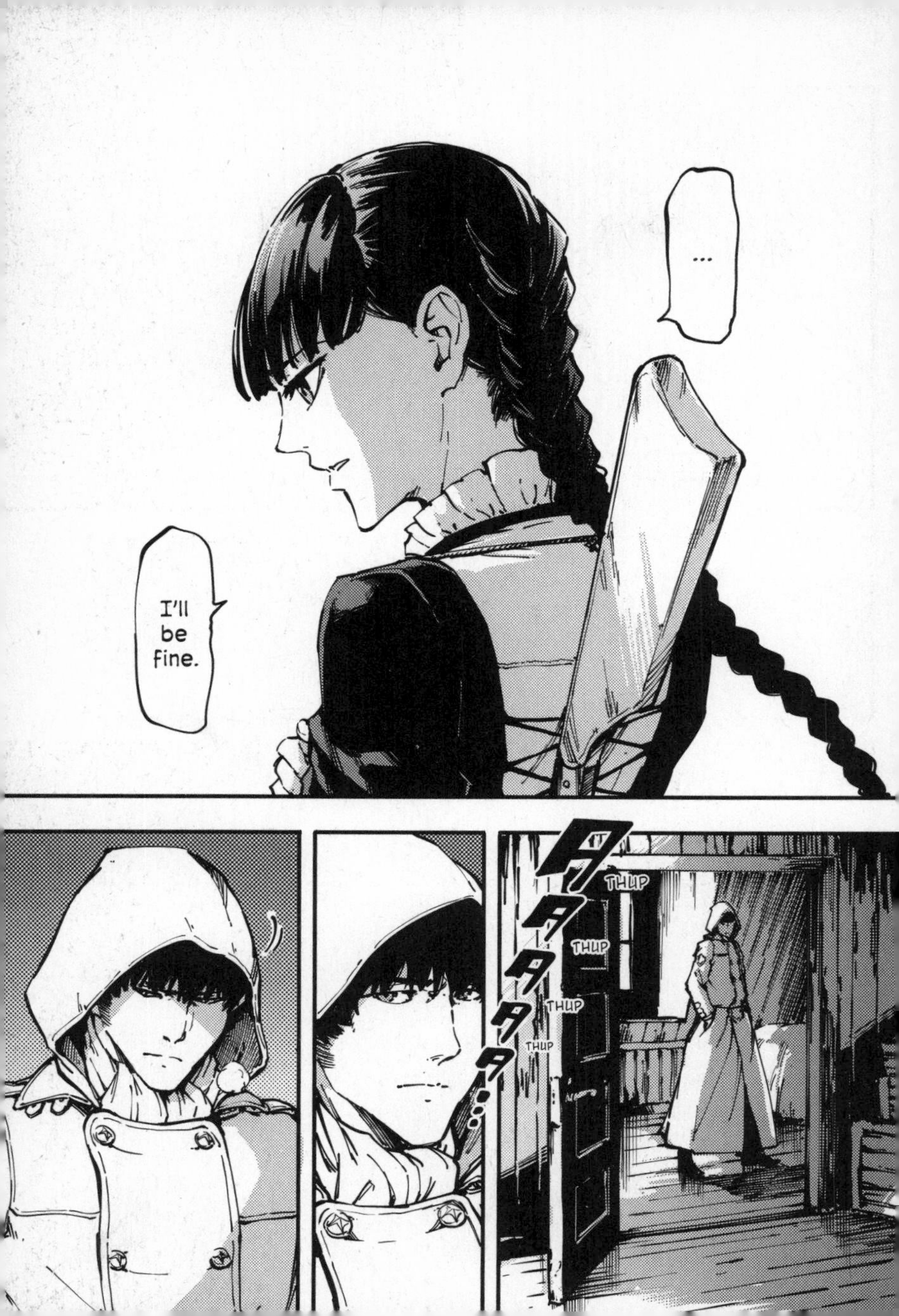
...
I'll be fine.
タタタタタ…
THUP
THUP
THUP
THUP

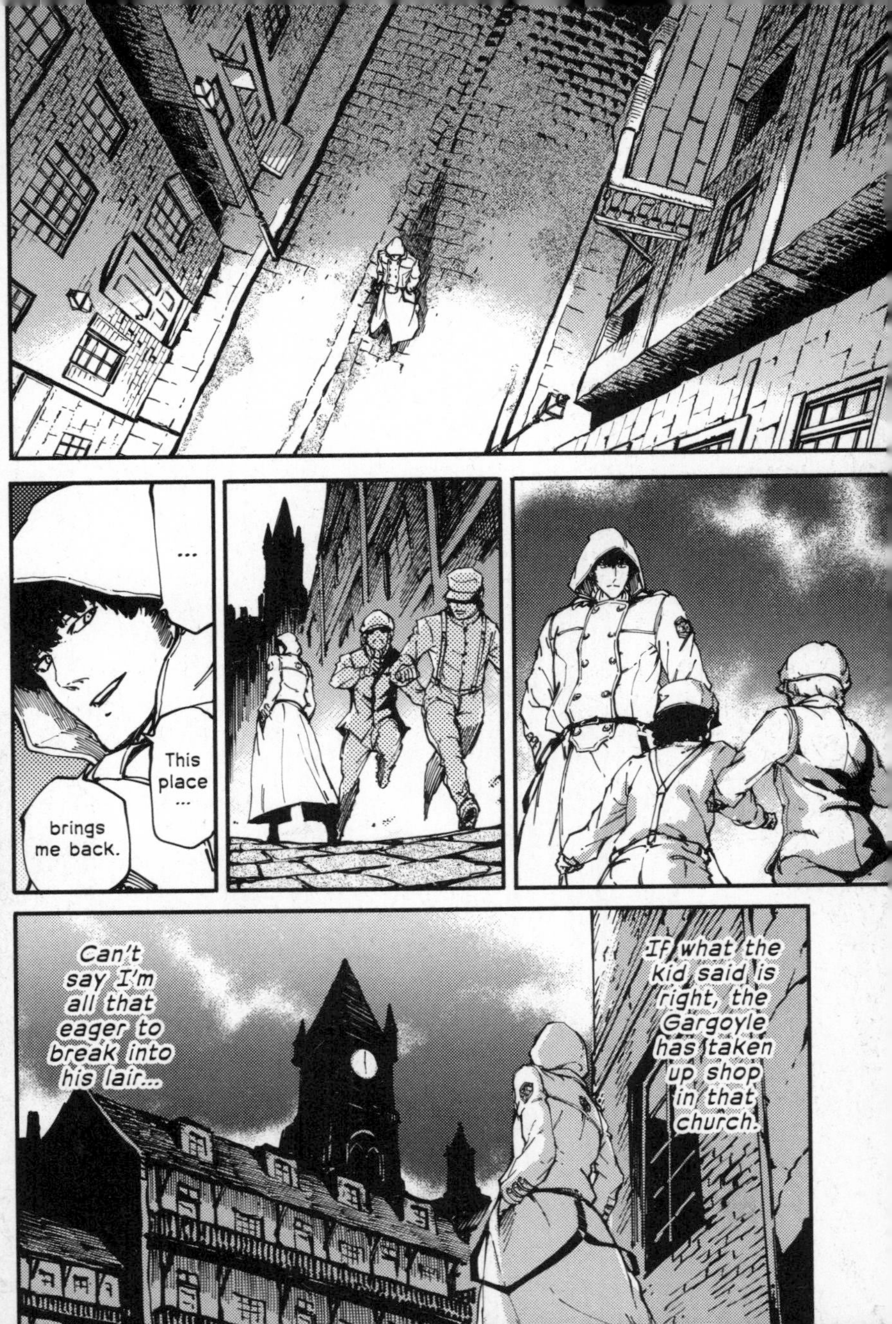
...
This place ...
brings me back.
If what the kid said is right, the Gargoyle has taken up shop in that church.
Can't say I'm all that eager to break into his lair...

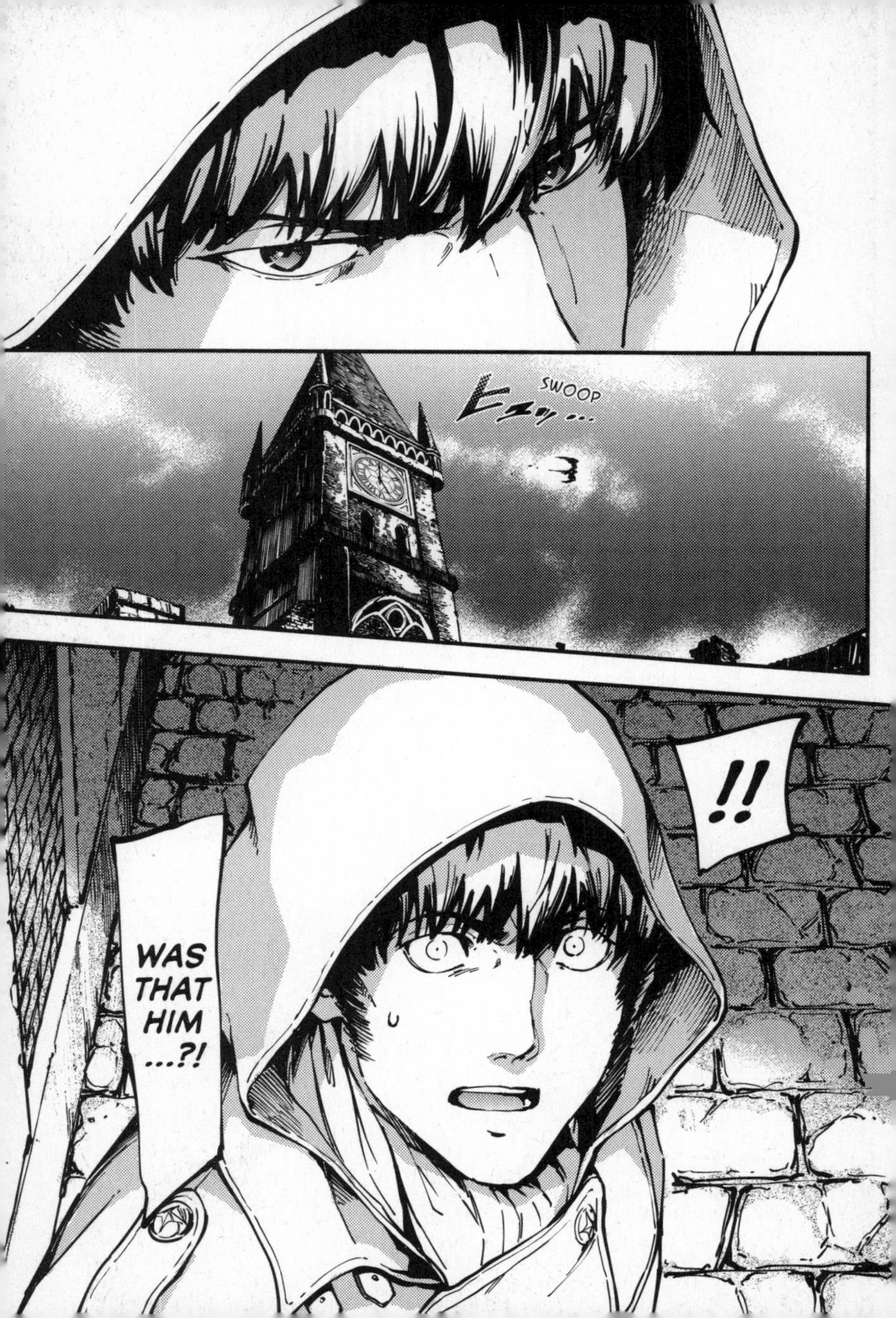
SWOOP
!!
WAS THAT HIM ...?!

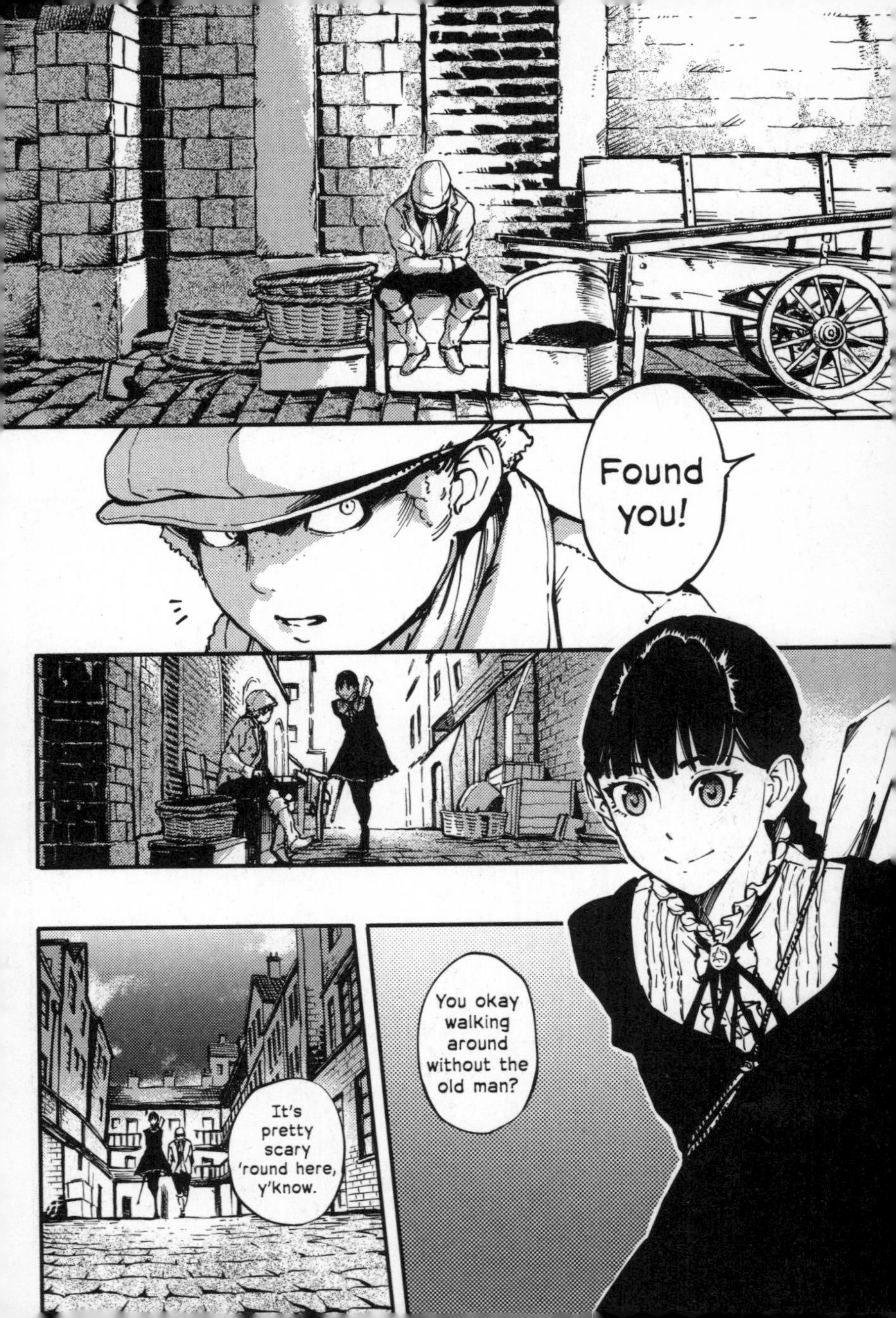
Found you!
You okay walking around without the old man?
It's pretty scary 'round here, y'know.

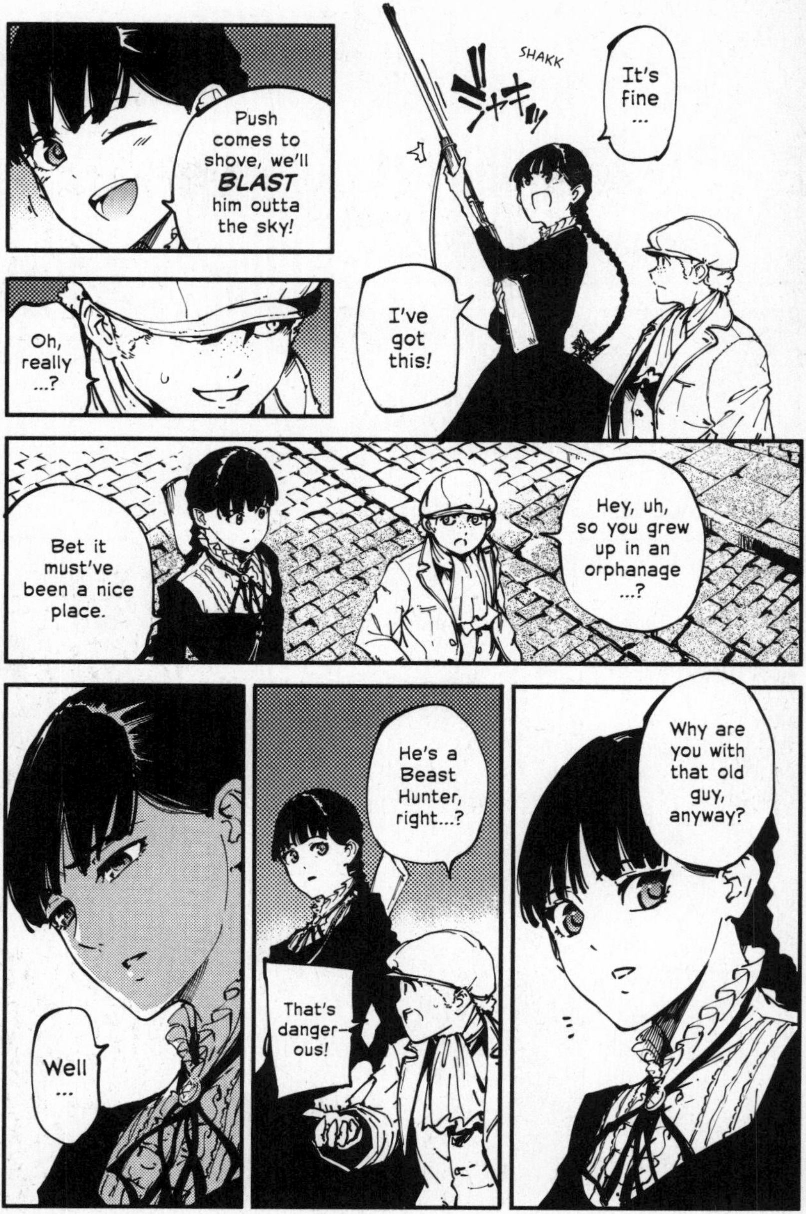
SHAKK
ジャキッ
It's fine ...
I've got this!
Push comes to shove, we'll **BLAST** him outta the sky!
Oh, really ...?
Hey, uh, so you grew up in an orphanage ...?
Bet it must've been a nice place.
Why are you with that old guy, anyway?
He's a Beast Hunter, right...?
That's danger-ous!
Well ...

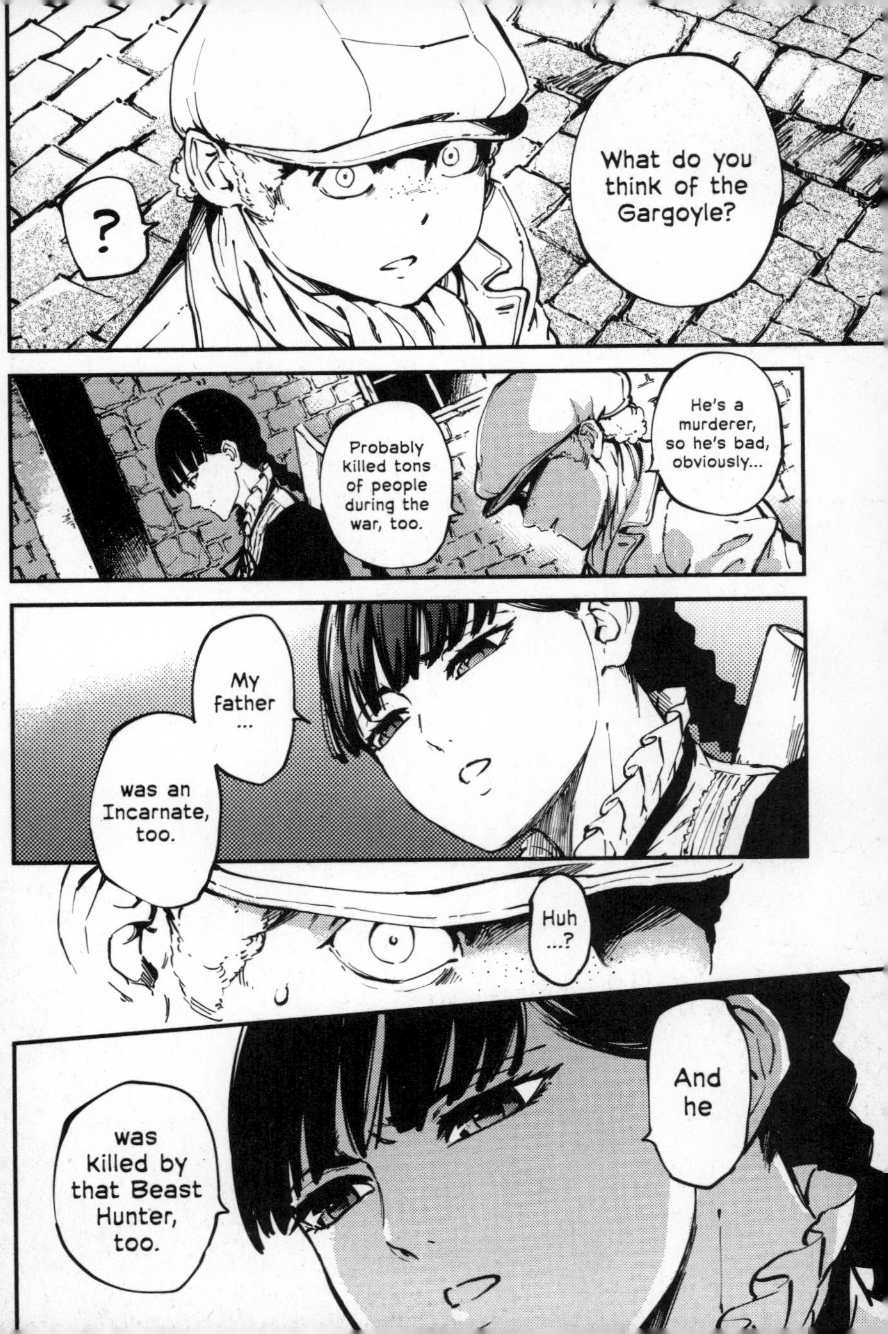
What do you think of the Gargoyle?
?
He's a murderer, so he's bad, obviously...
Probably killed tons of people during the war, too.
My father ...
was an Incarnate, too.
Huh ...?
And he
was killed by that Beast Hunter, too.

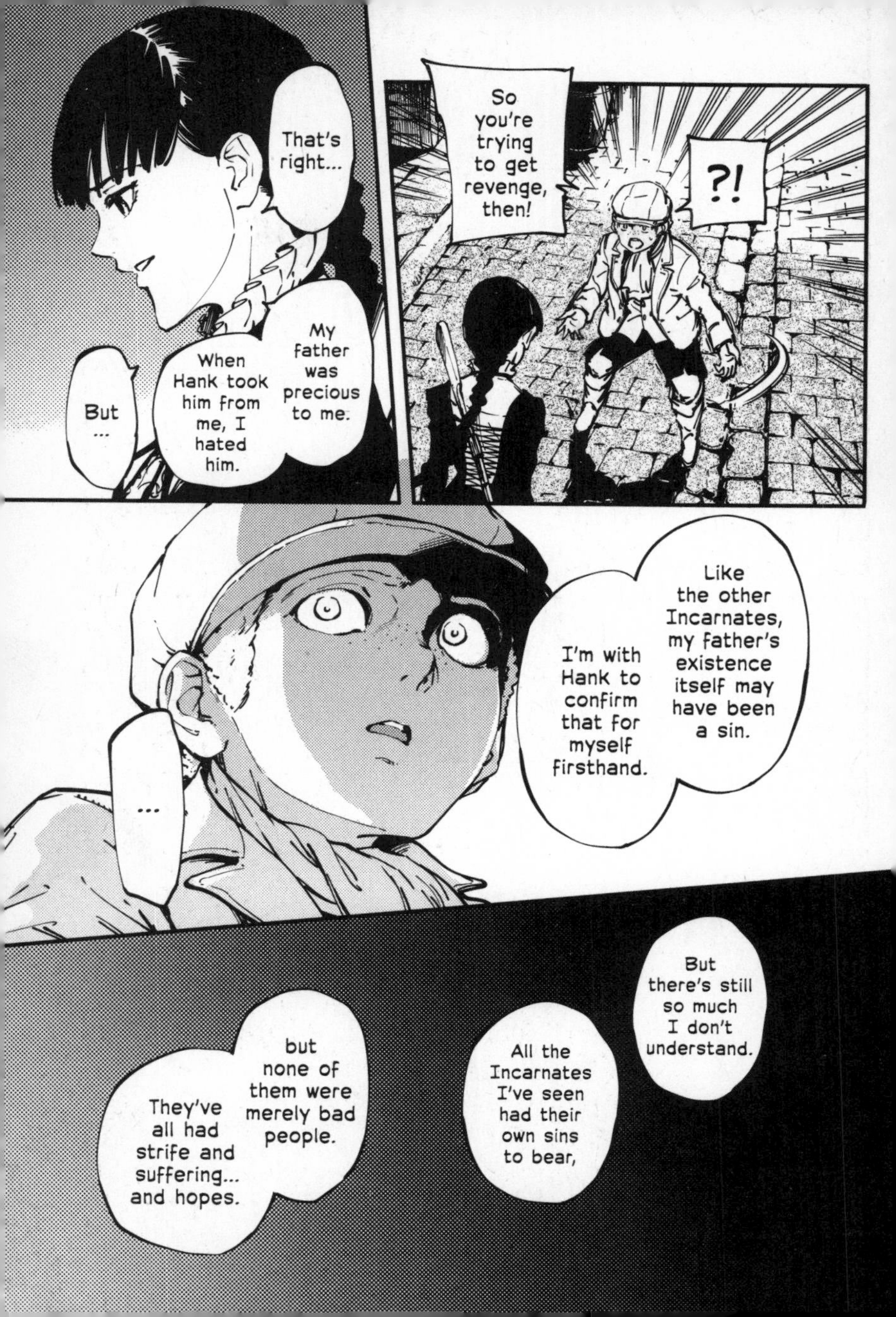
So you're trying to get revenge, then!
?!
That's right...
My father was precious to me.
When Hank took him from me, I hated him.
But ...
Like the other Incarnates, my father's existence itself may have been a sin.
I'm with Hank to confirm that for myself firsthand.
...
But there's still so much I don't understand.
All the Incarnates I've seen had their own sins to bear,
but none of them were merely bad people.
They've all had strife and suffering... and hopes.

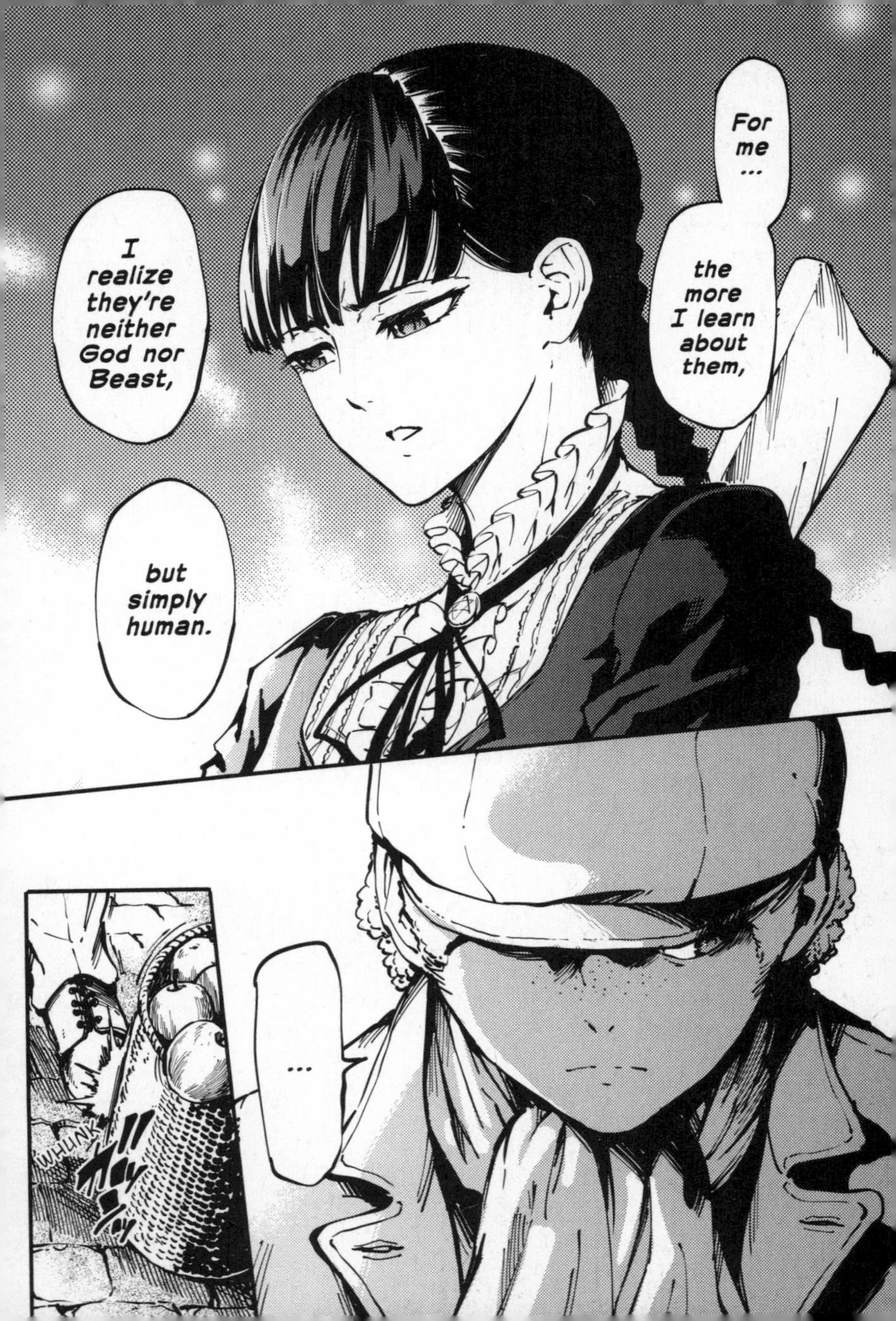
For me ...
the more I learn about them,
I realize they're neither God nor Beast,
but simply human.
...
WHUNK

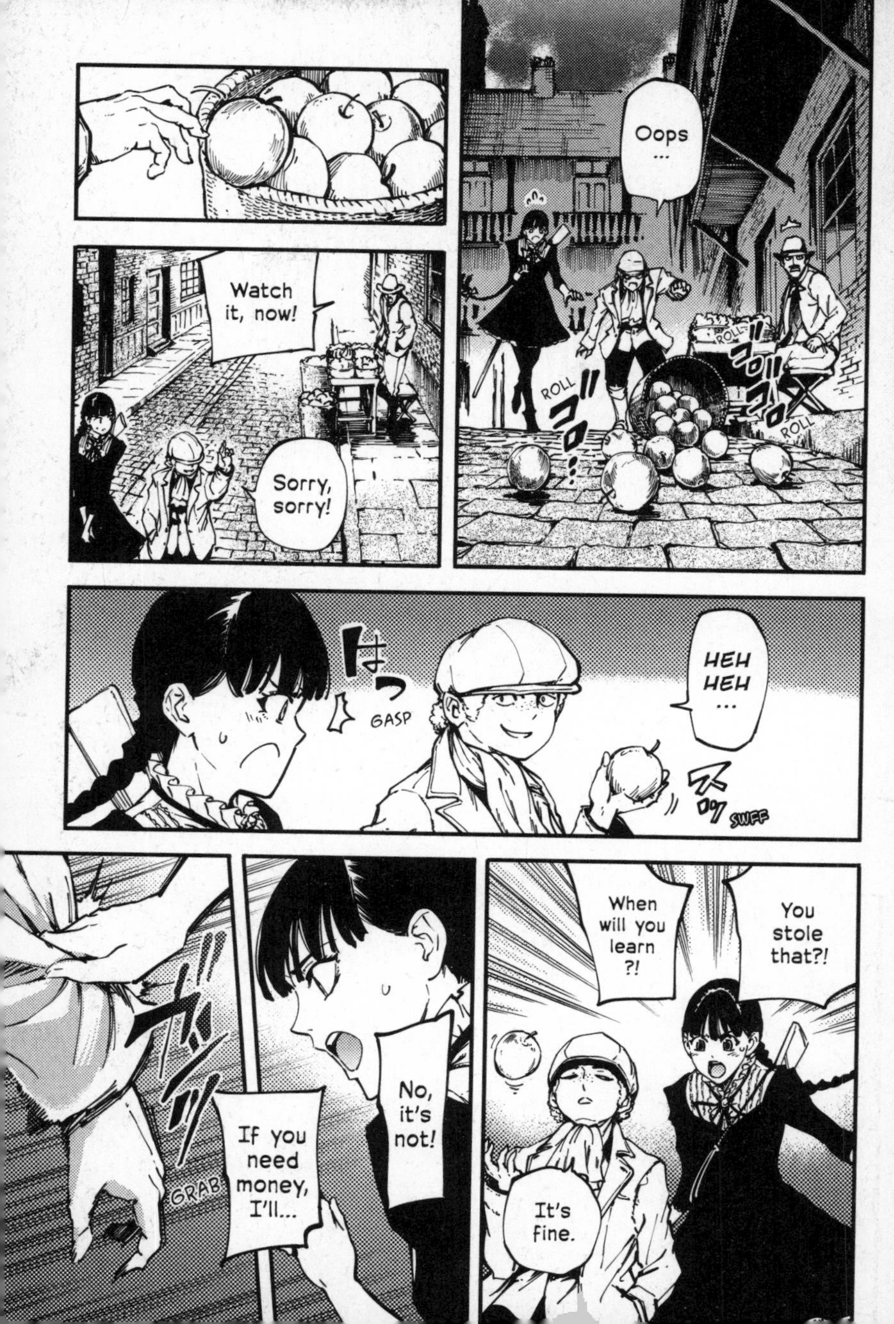
Oops ...
ROLL
ROLL
ROLL
Watch it, now!
Sorry, sorry!
HEH HEH ...
GASP
SWFF
You stole that?!
When will you learn ?!
It's fine.
No, it's not!
If you need money, I'll...
GRAB

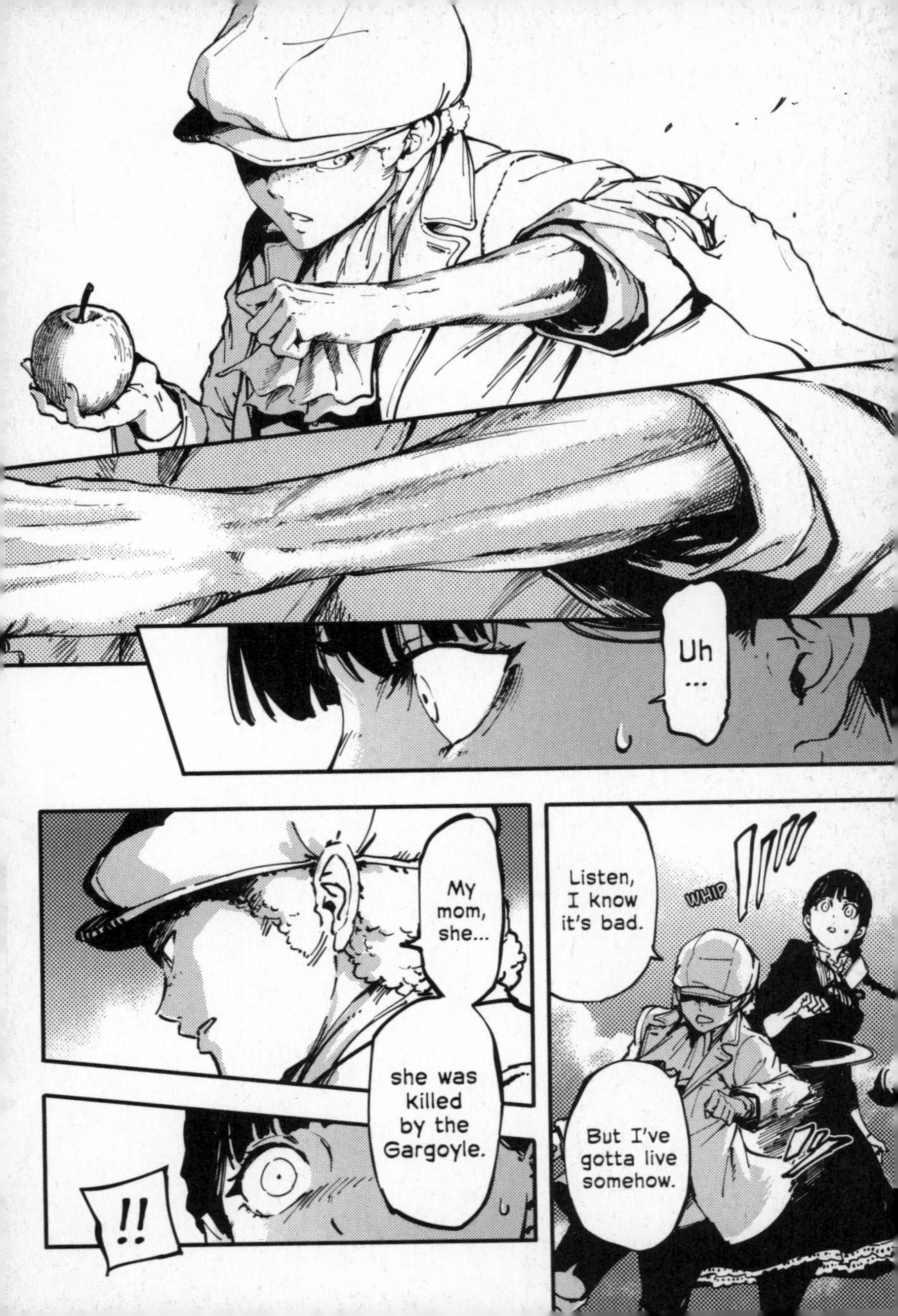
Uh ...
Listen, I know it's bad.
WHIP
But I've gotta live somehow.
My mom, she...
she was killed by the Gargoyle.
!!

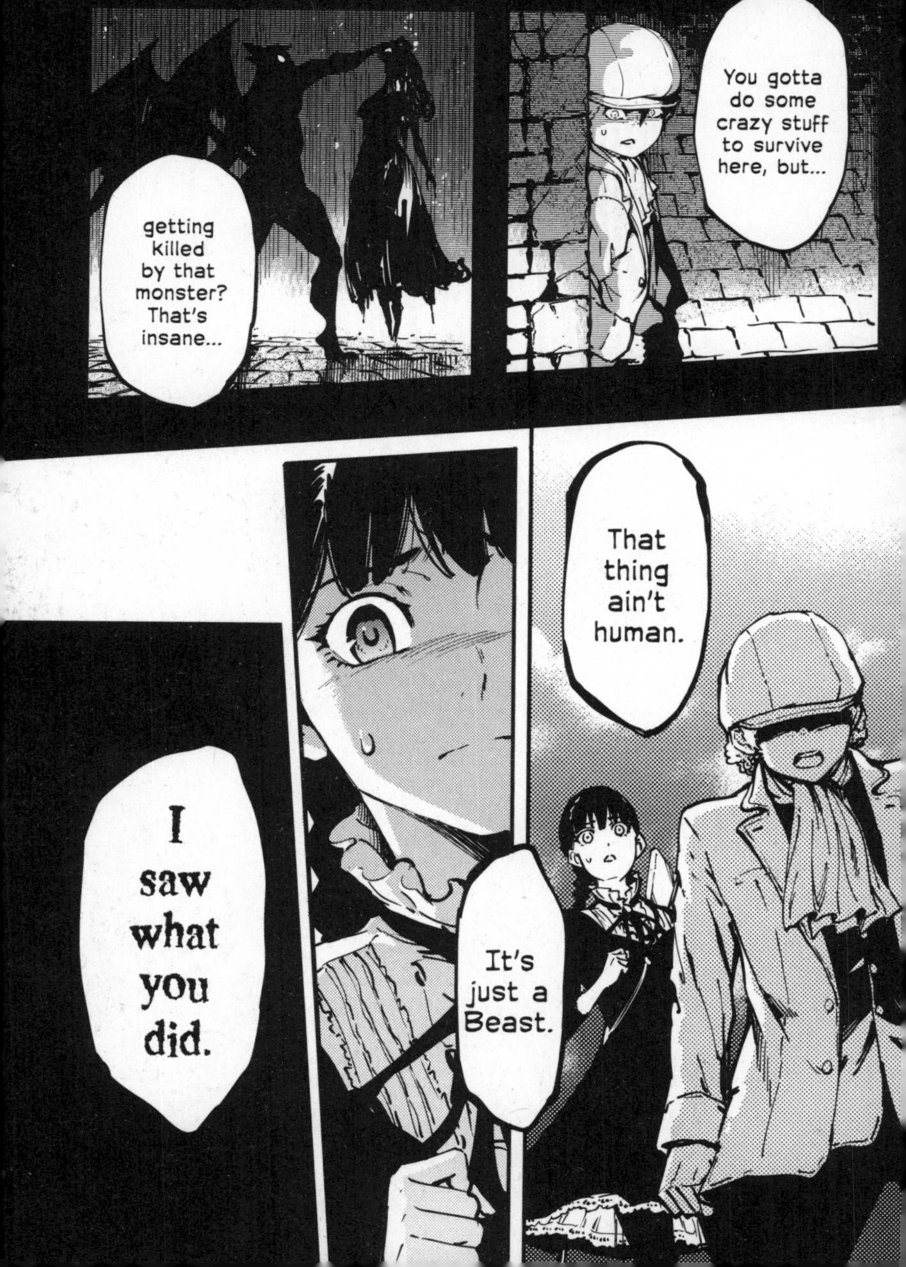
You gotta do some crazy stuff to survive here, but...
getting killed by that monster? That's insane...
That thing ain't human.
It's just a Beast.
I saw what you did.

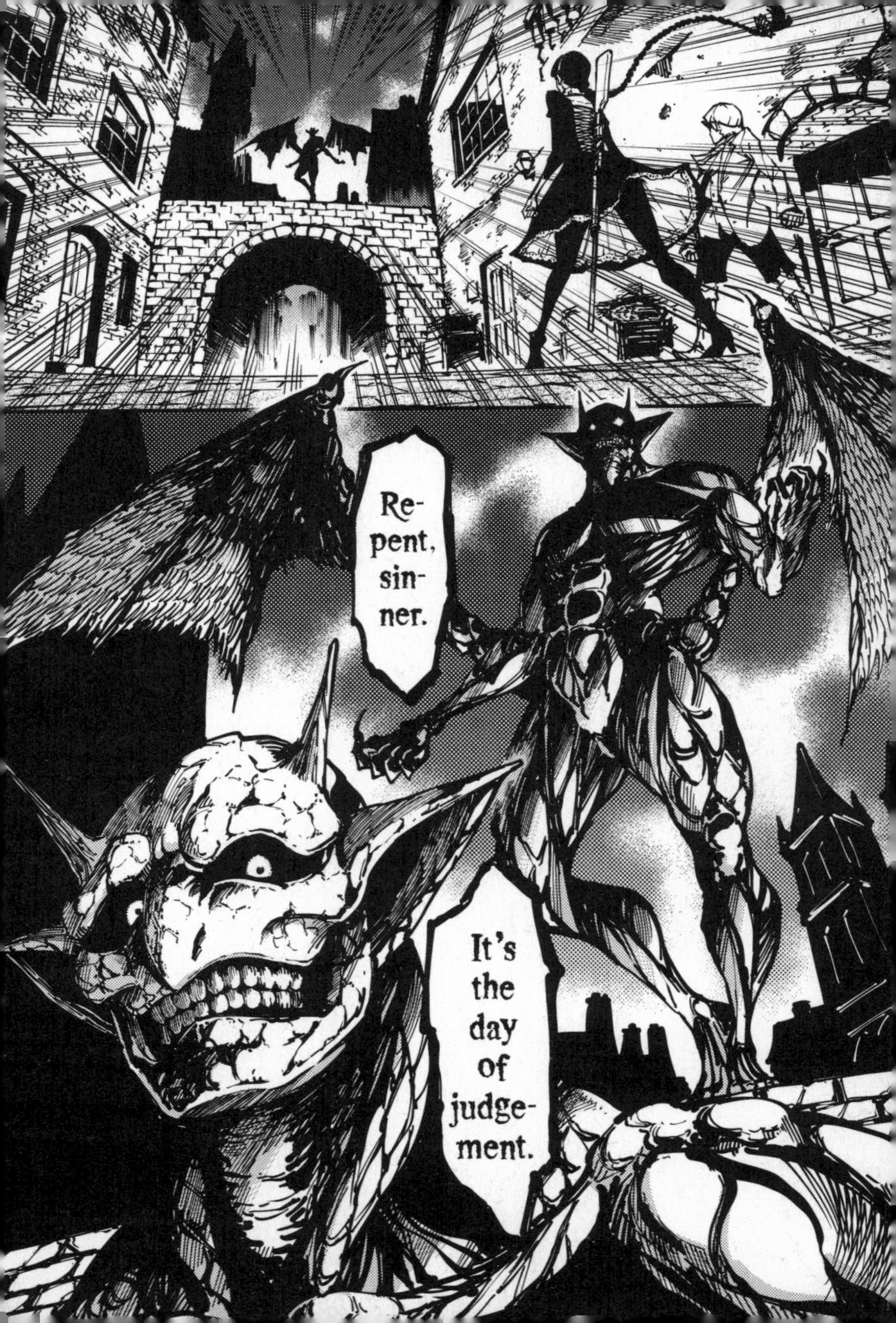
Re-pent, sin-ner.
It's the day of judge-ment.

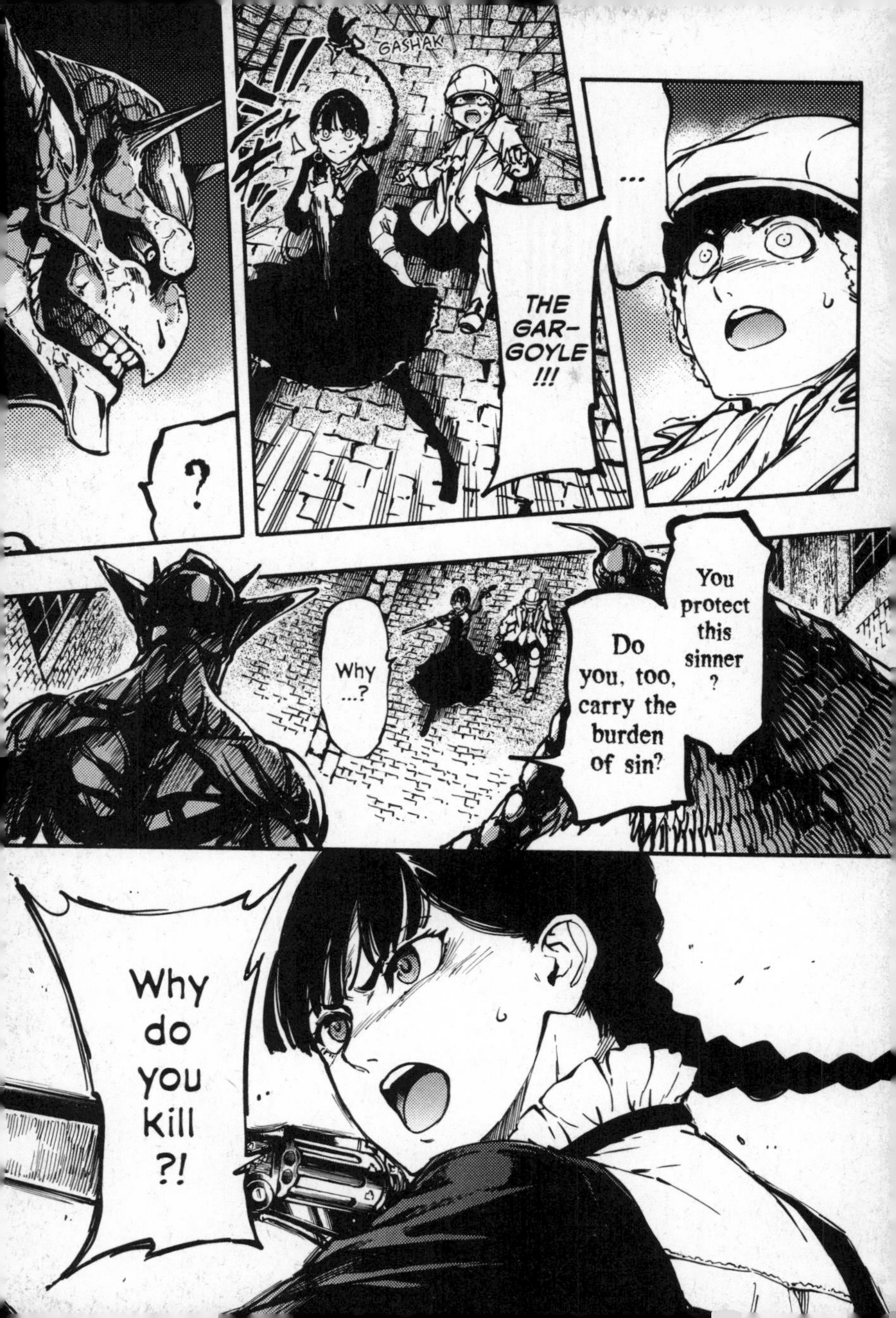
...
GASHAK
THE GAR-GOYLE !!!
?
You protect this sinner ?
Do you, too, carry the burden of sin?
Why ...?
Why do you kill ?!

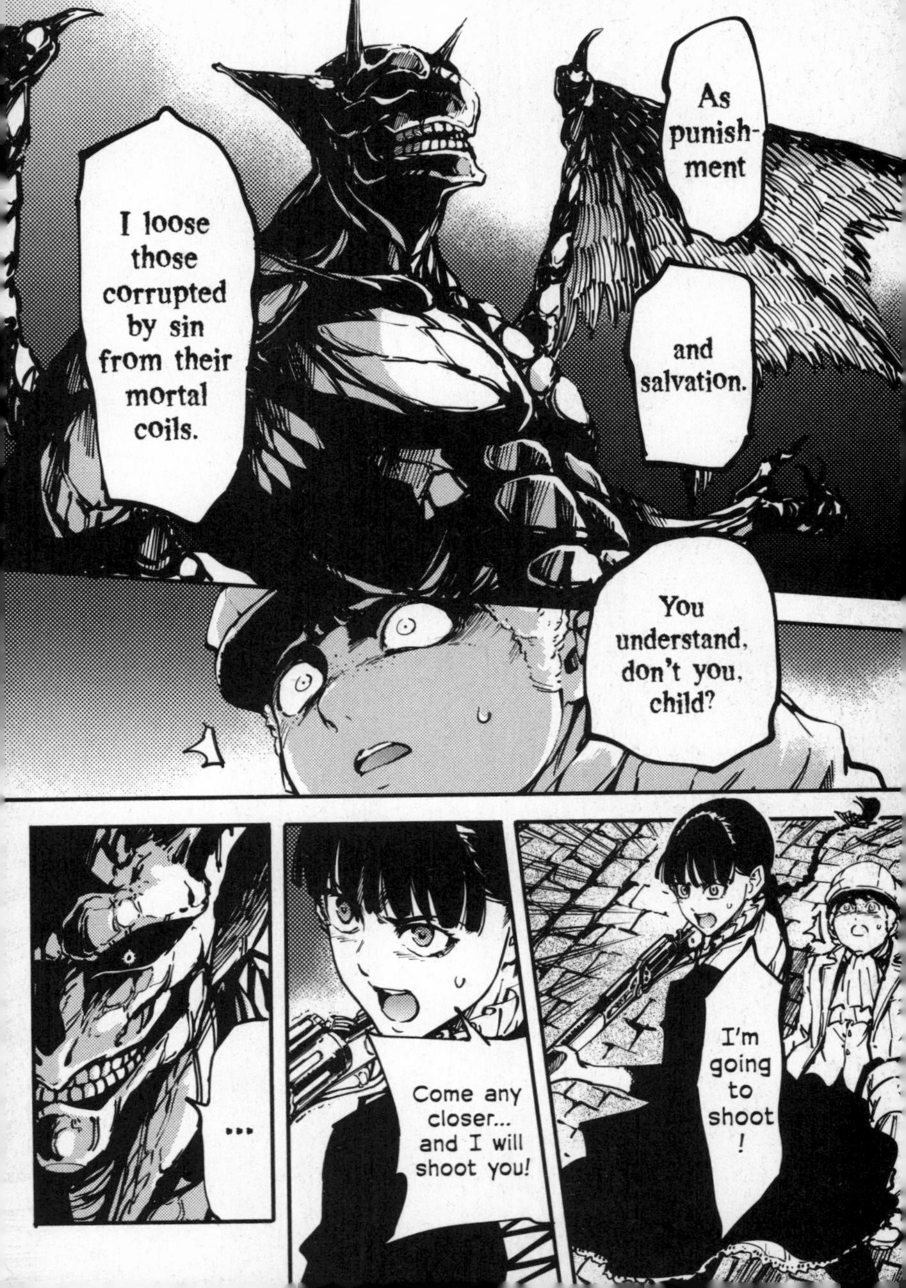
As punish-ment
and salvation.
I loose those corrupted by sin from their mortal coils.
You understand, don't you, child?
I'm going to shoot!
Come any closer... and I will shoot you!
...

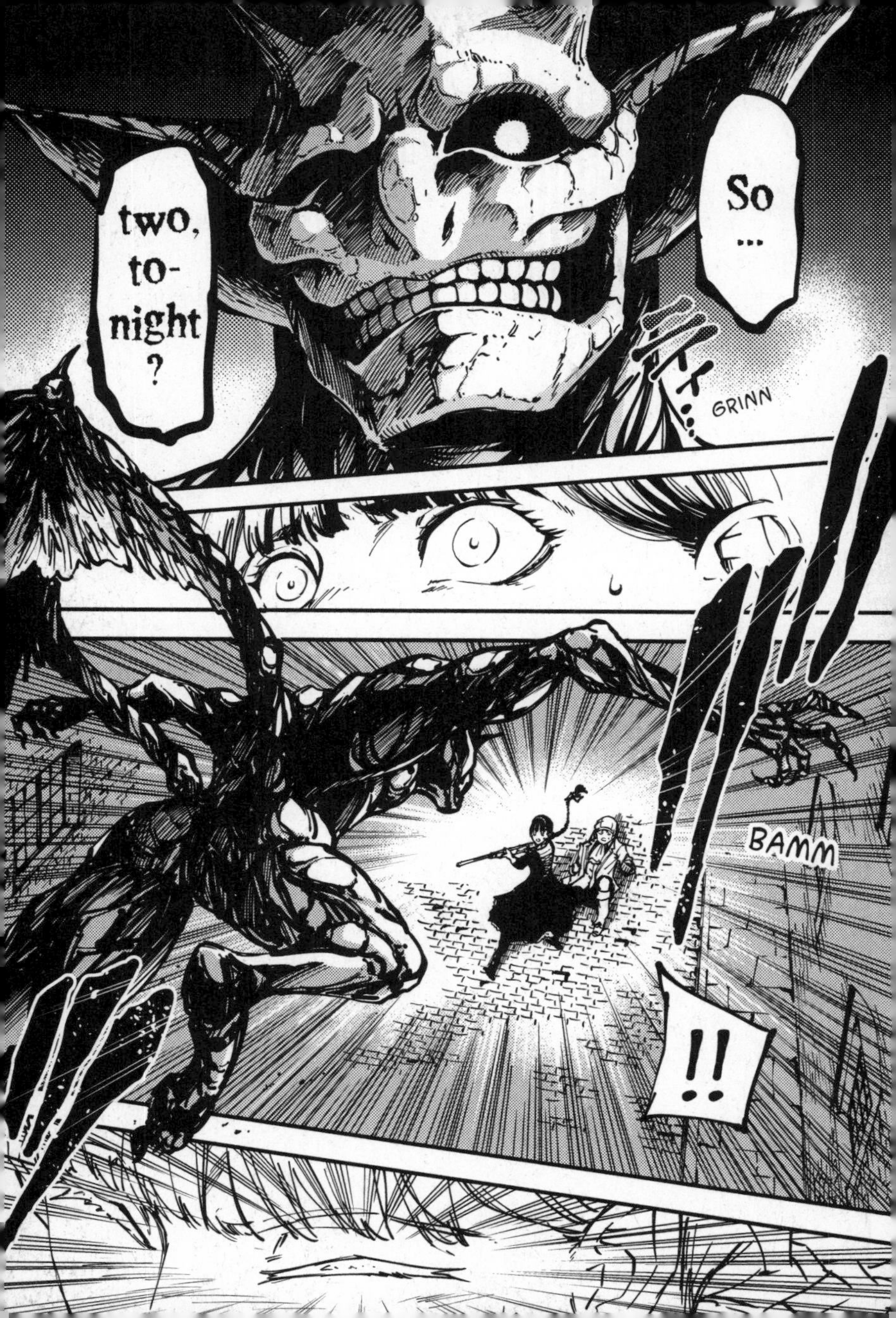
So ...
two, to-night?
GRINN
BAMM
!!

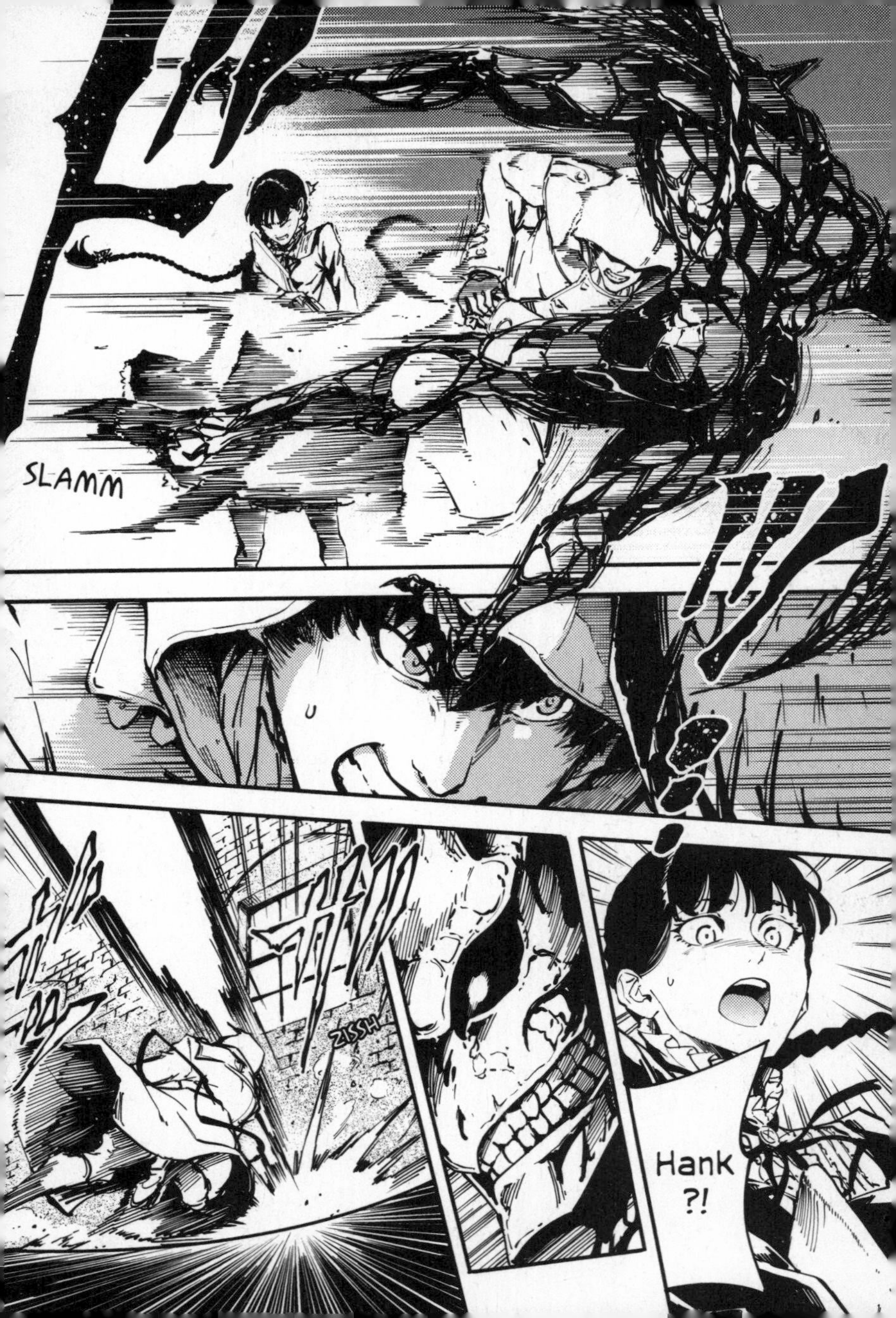
SLAMM
Hank ?!
ZISSH

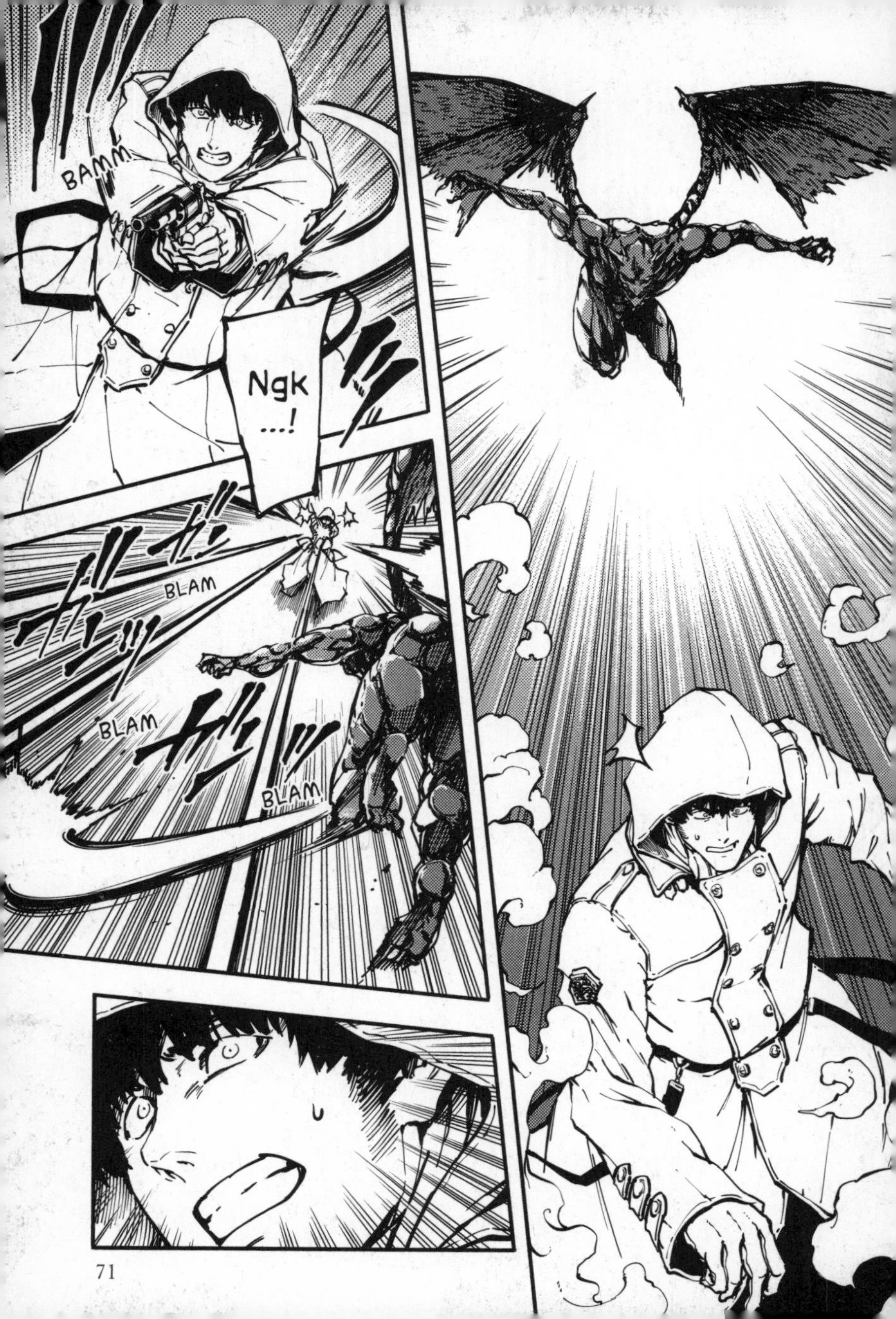
BAMM
Ngk
...!
BLAM
BLAM
BLAM

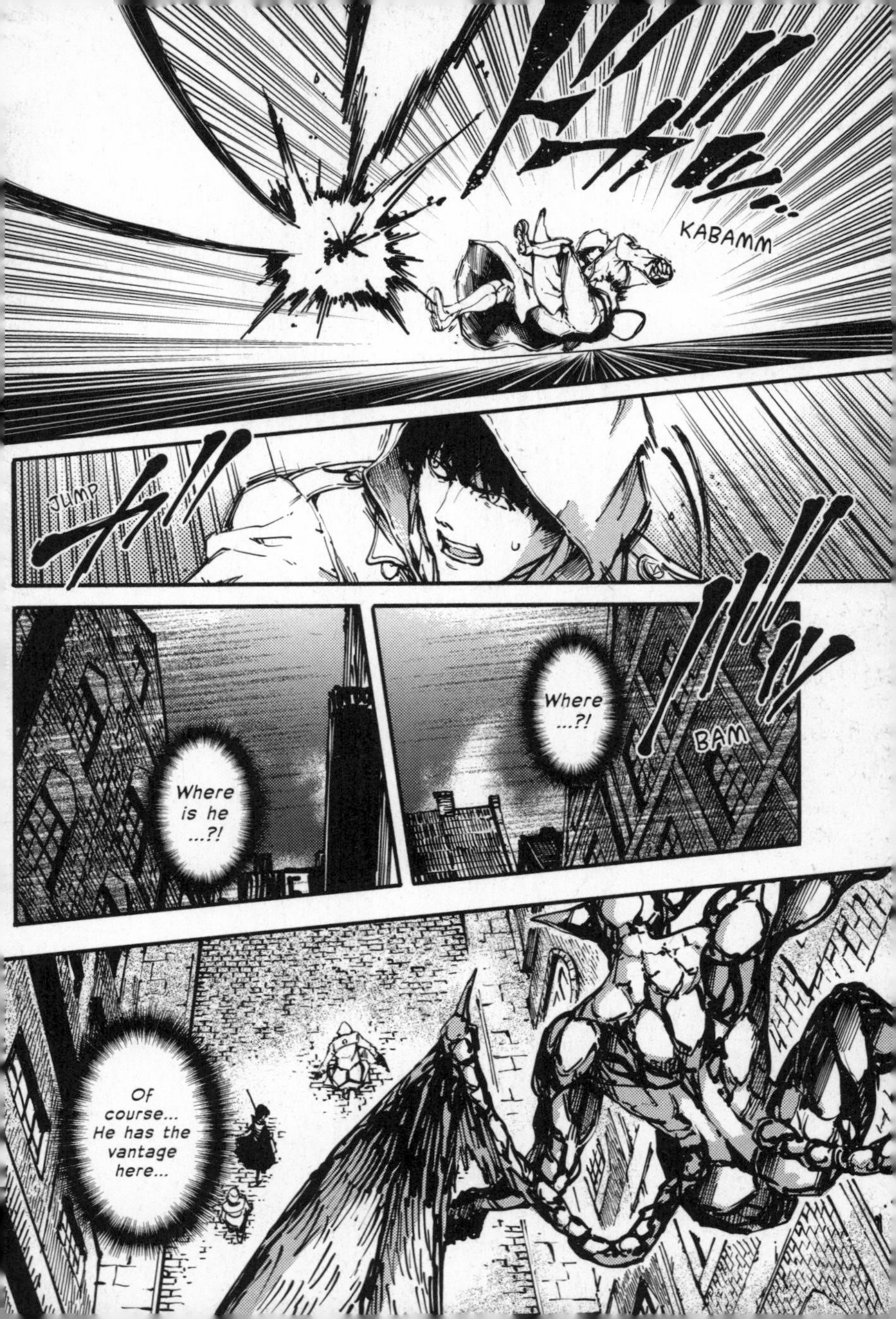
KABAMM
JUMP
Where ...?!
BAM
Where is he ...?!
Of course... He has the vantage here...

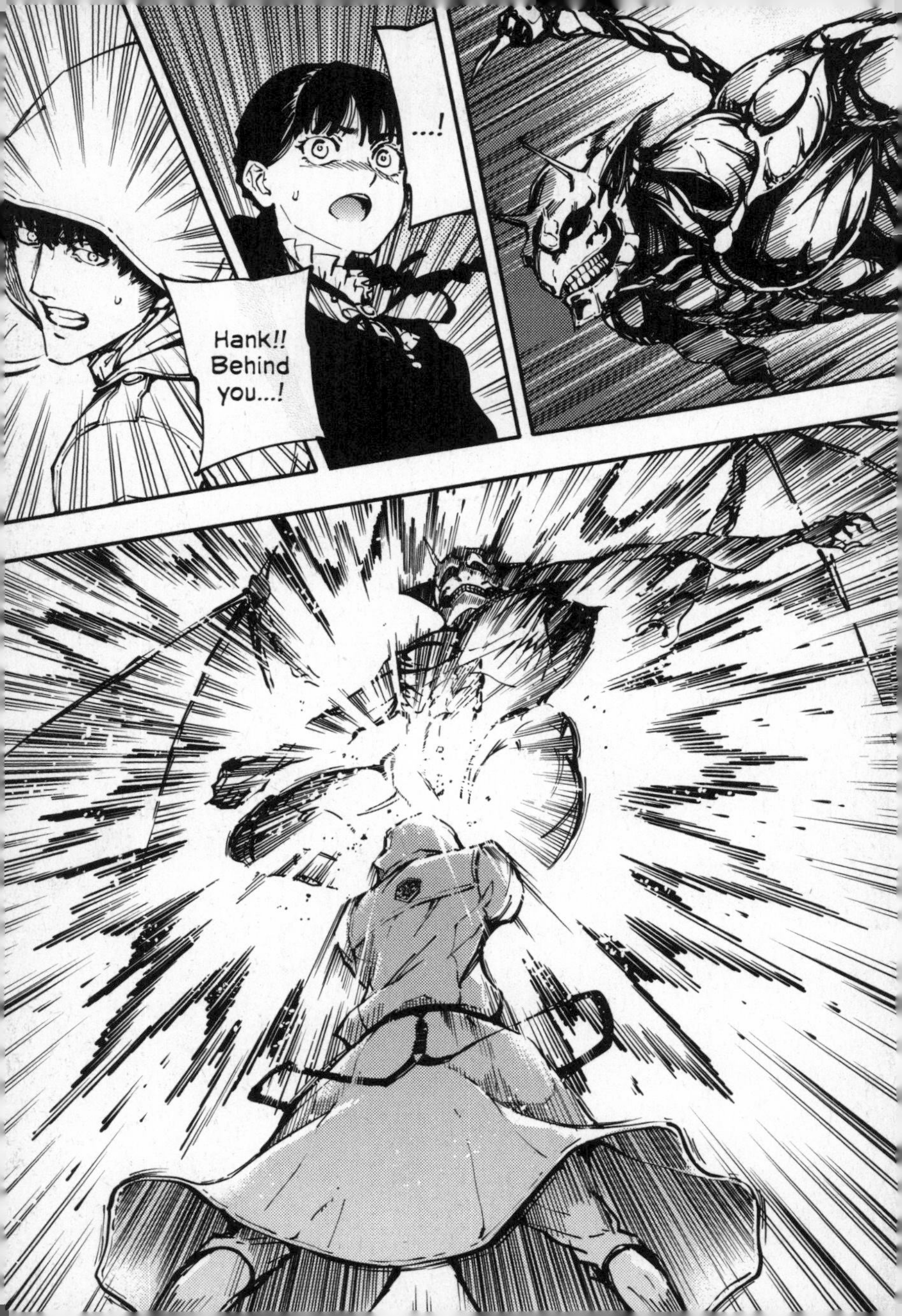
...!
Hank!! Behind you...!

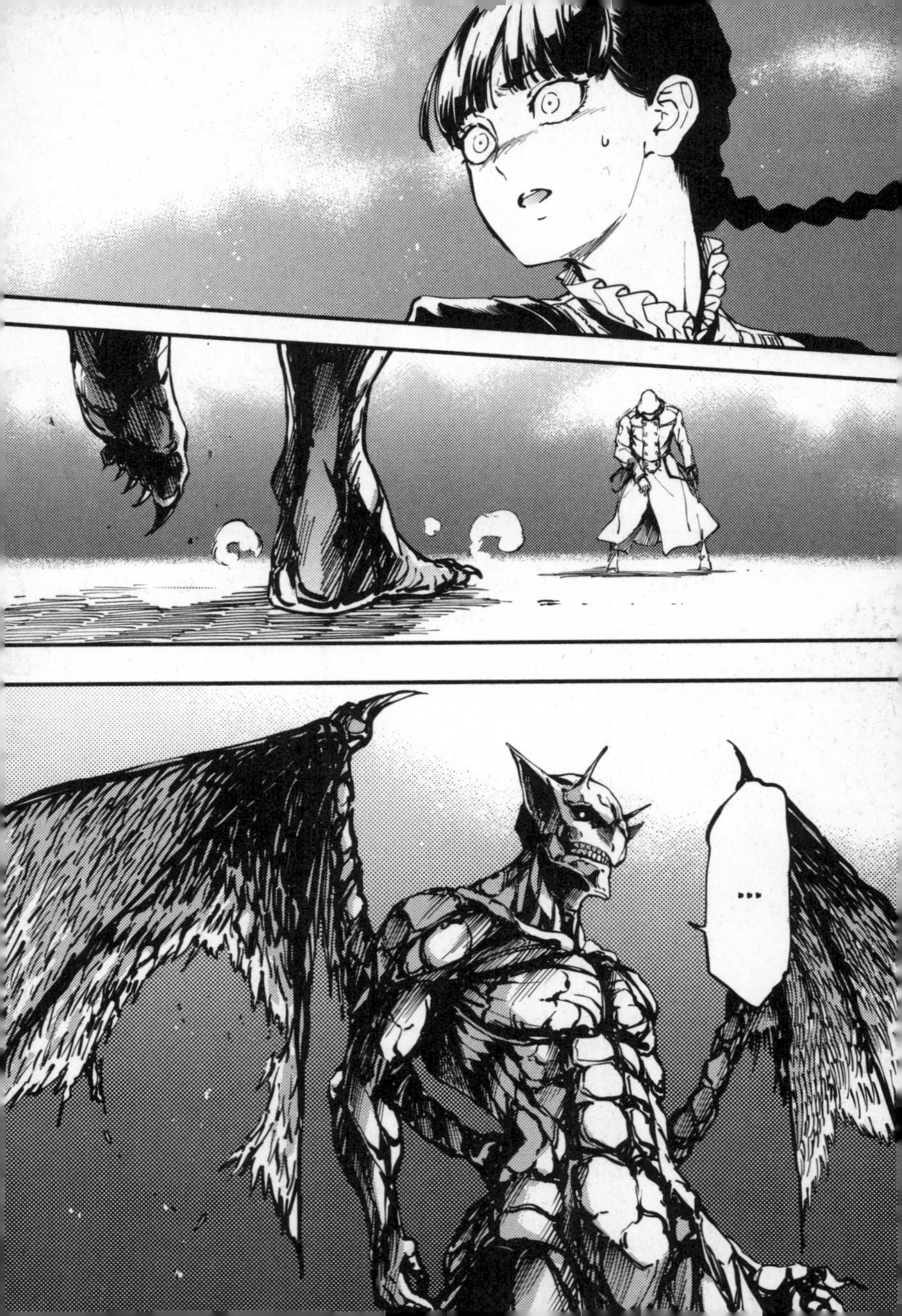
...

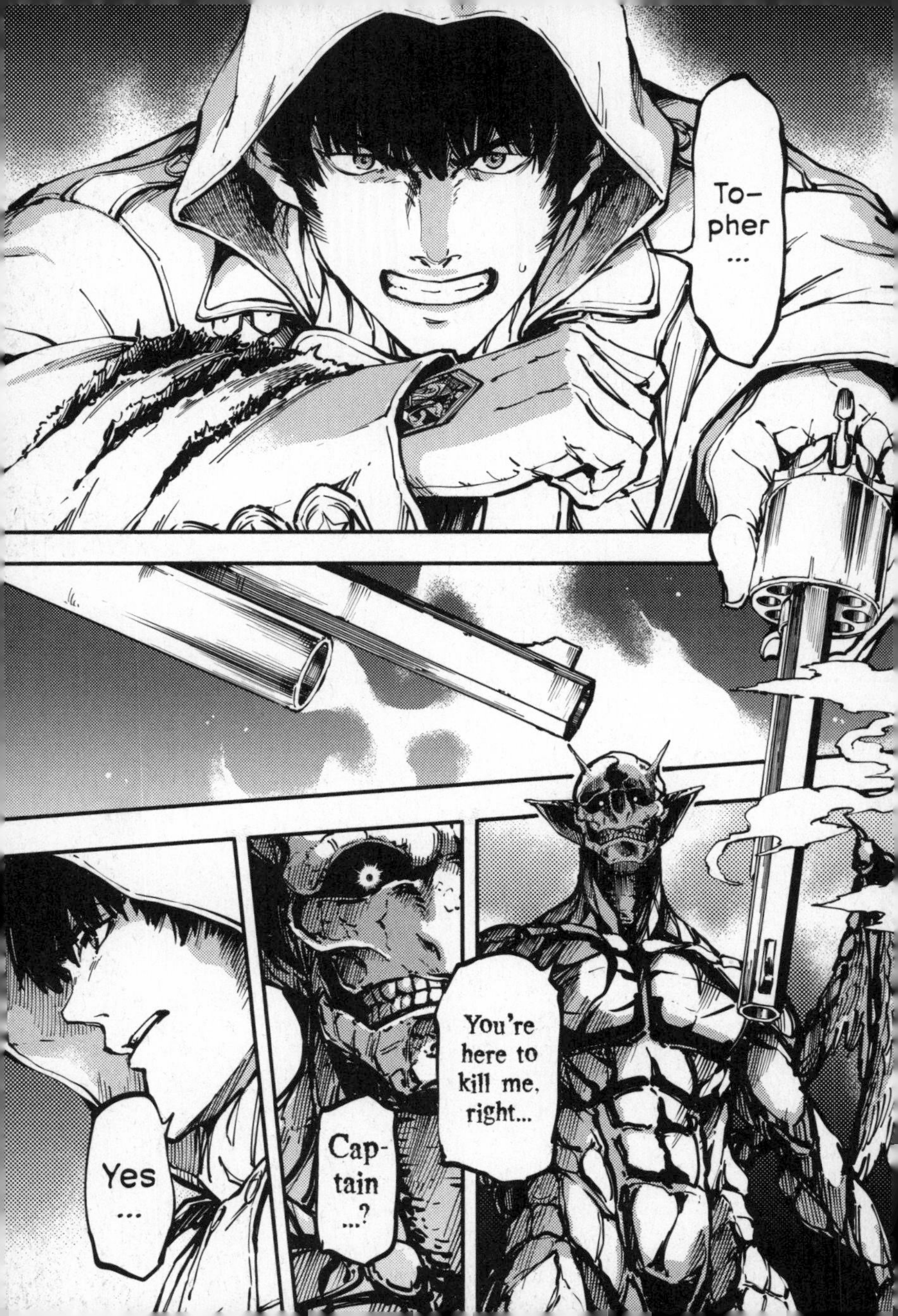
To-pher...
You're here to kill me, right...
Cap-tain...?
Yes...

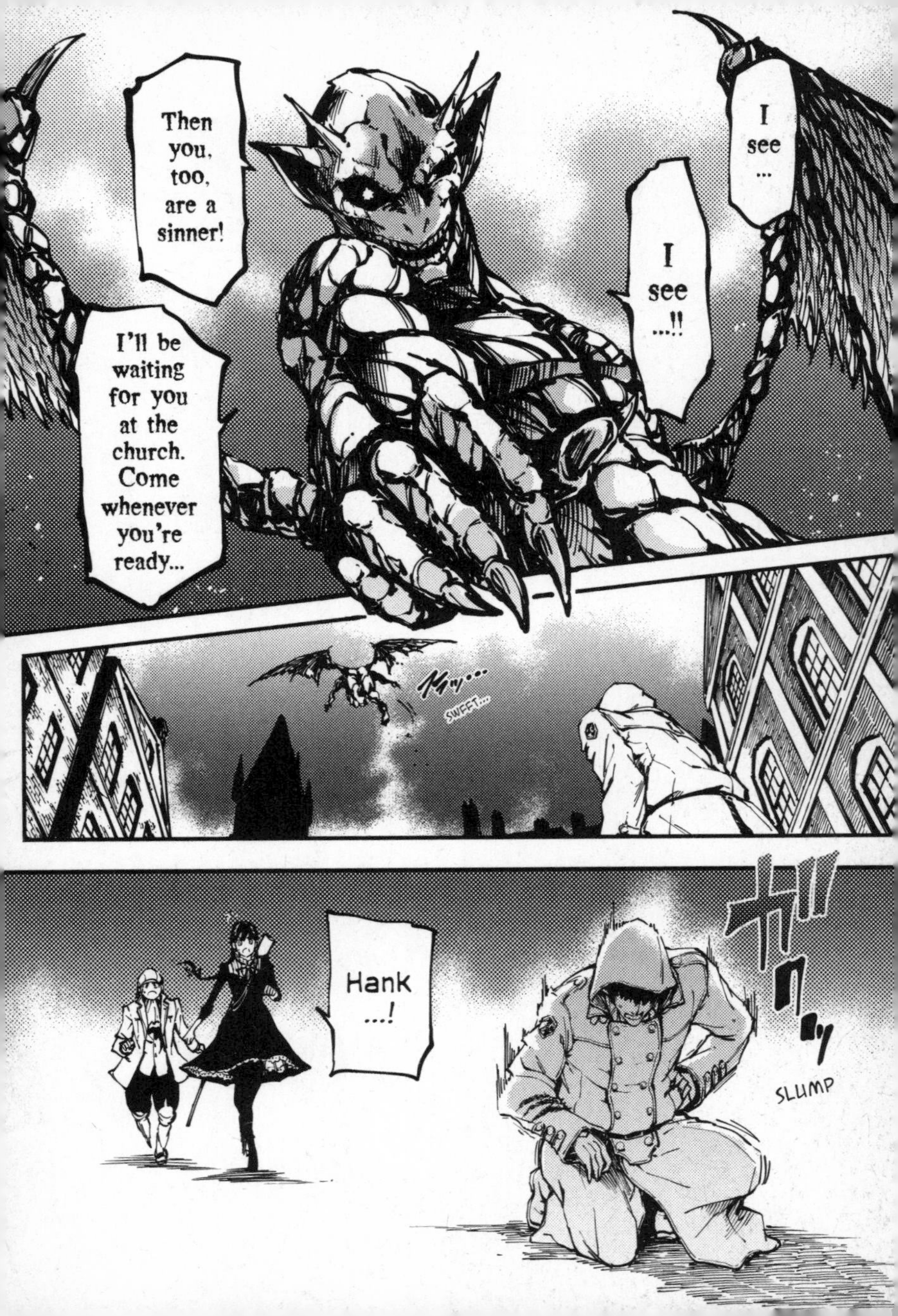
I see ...
I see ...!!
Then you, too, are a sinner!
I'll be waiting for you at the church. Come whenever you're ready...
SWFFT...
SLUMP
Hank ...!

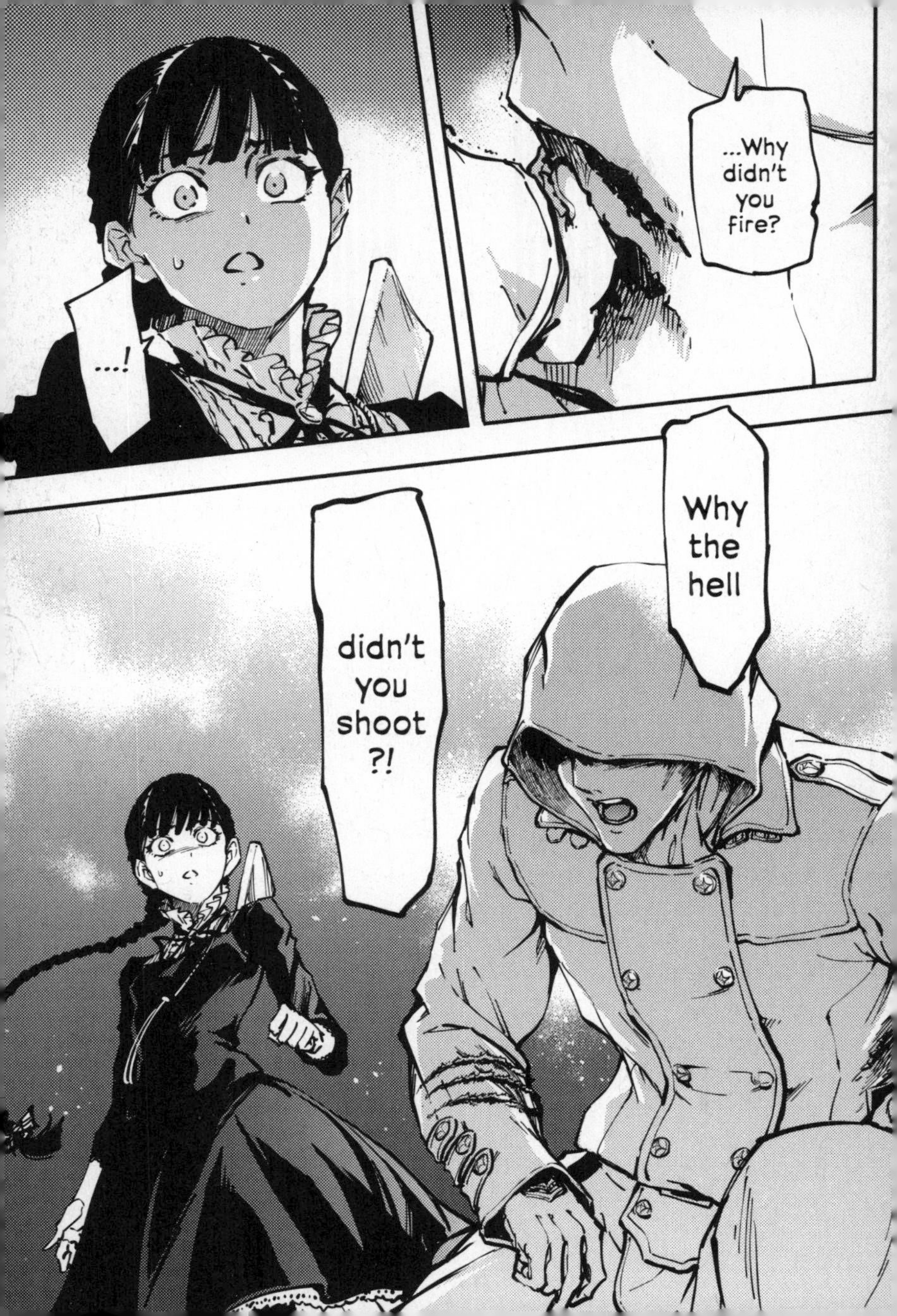
...Why didn't you fire?
...!
Why the hell
didn't you shoot ?!

To the Abandoned
Sacred Beasts

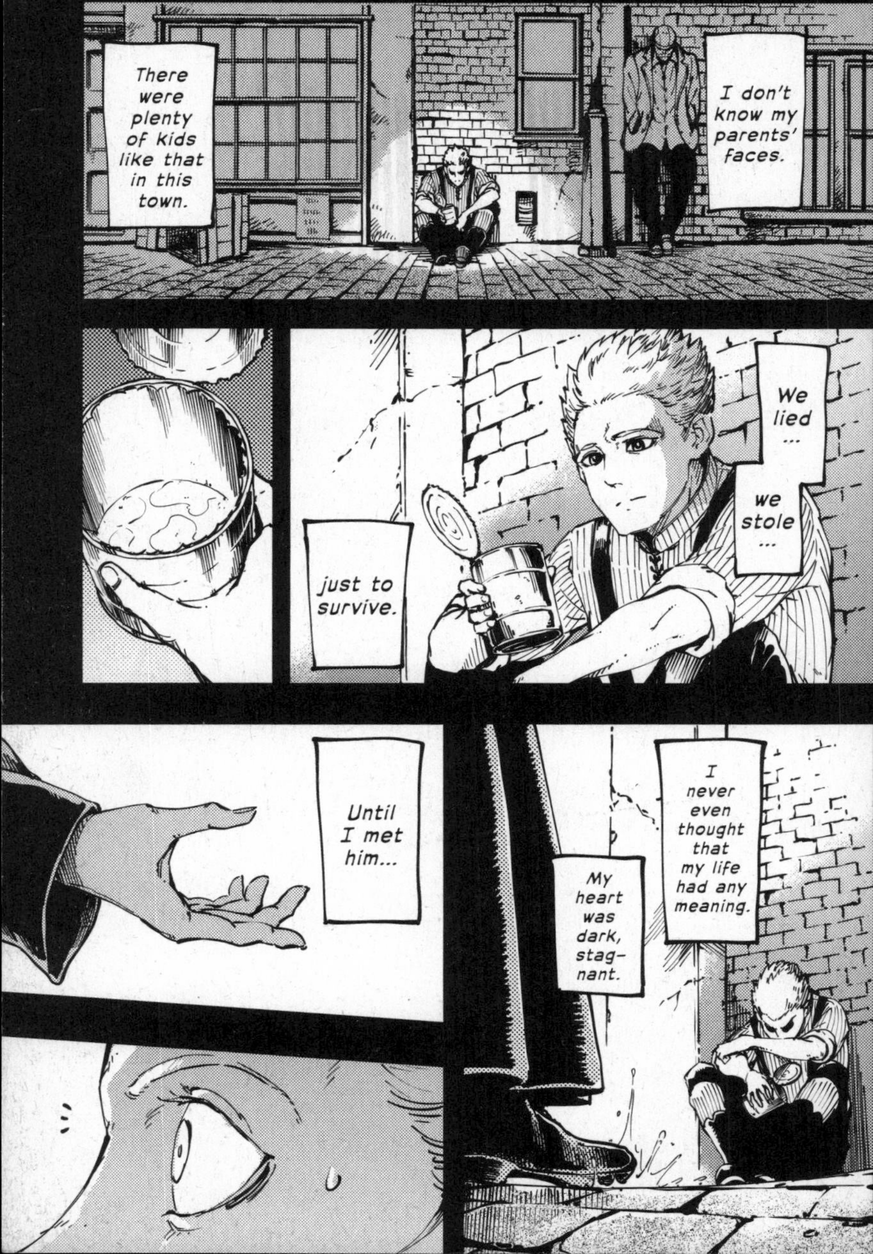

I don't know my parents' faces.
There were plenty of kids like that in this town.
We lied ...
we stole ...
just to survive.
I never even thought that my life had any meaning.
My heart was dark, stagnant.
Until I met him...

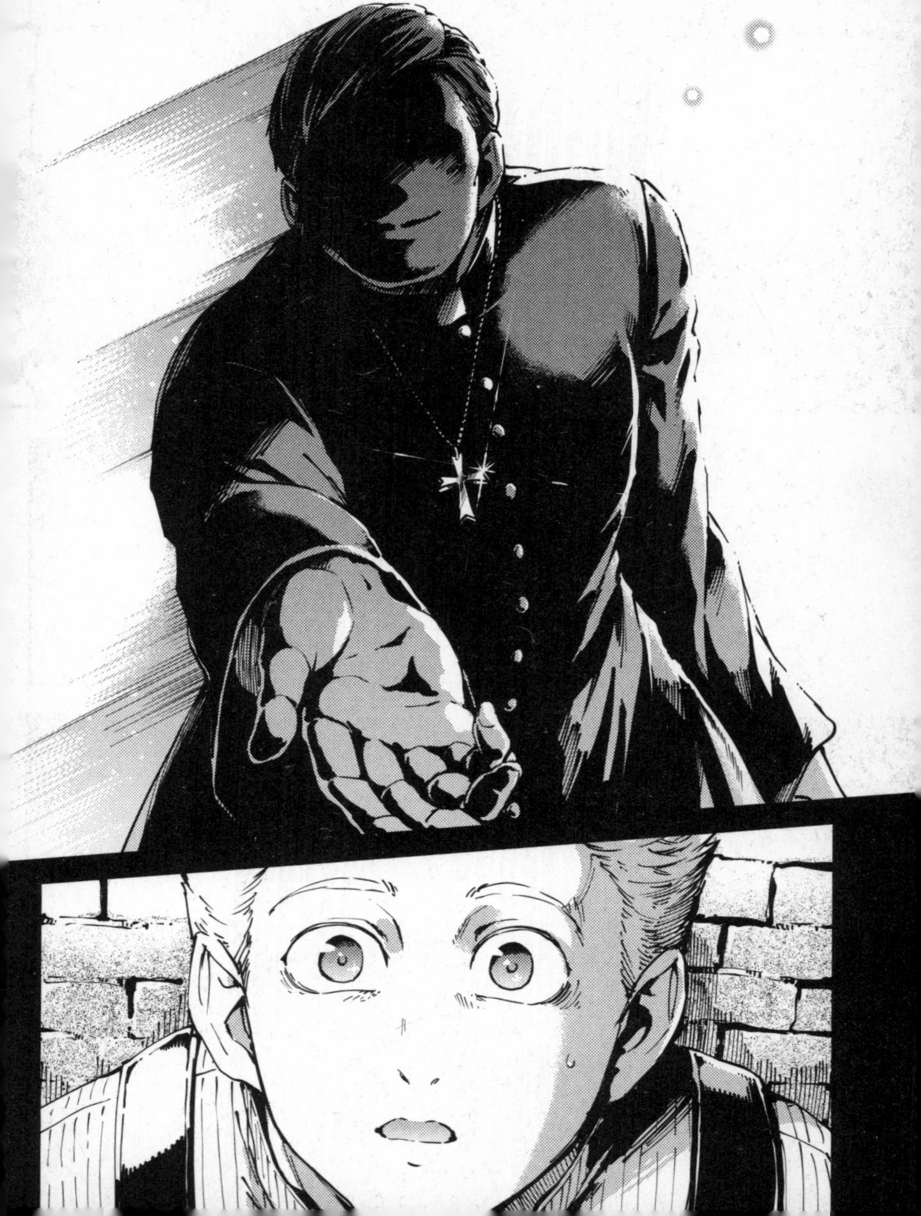

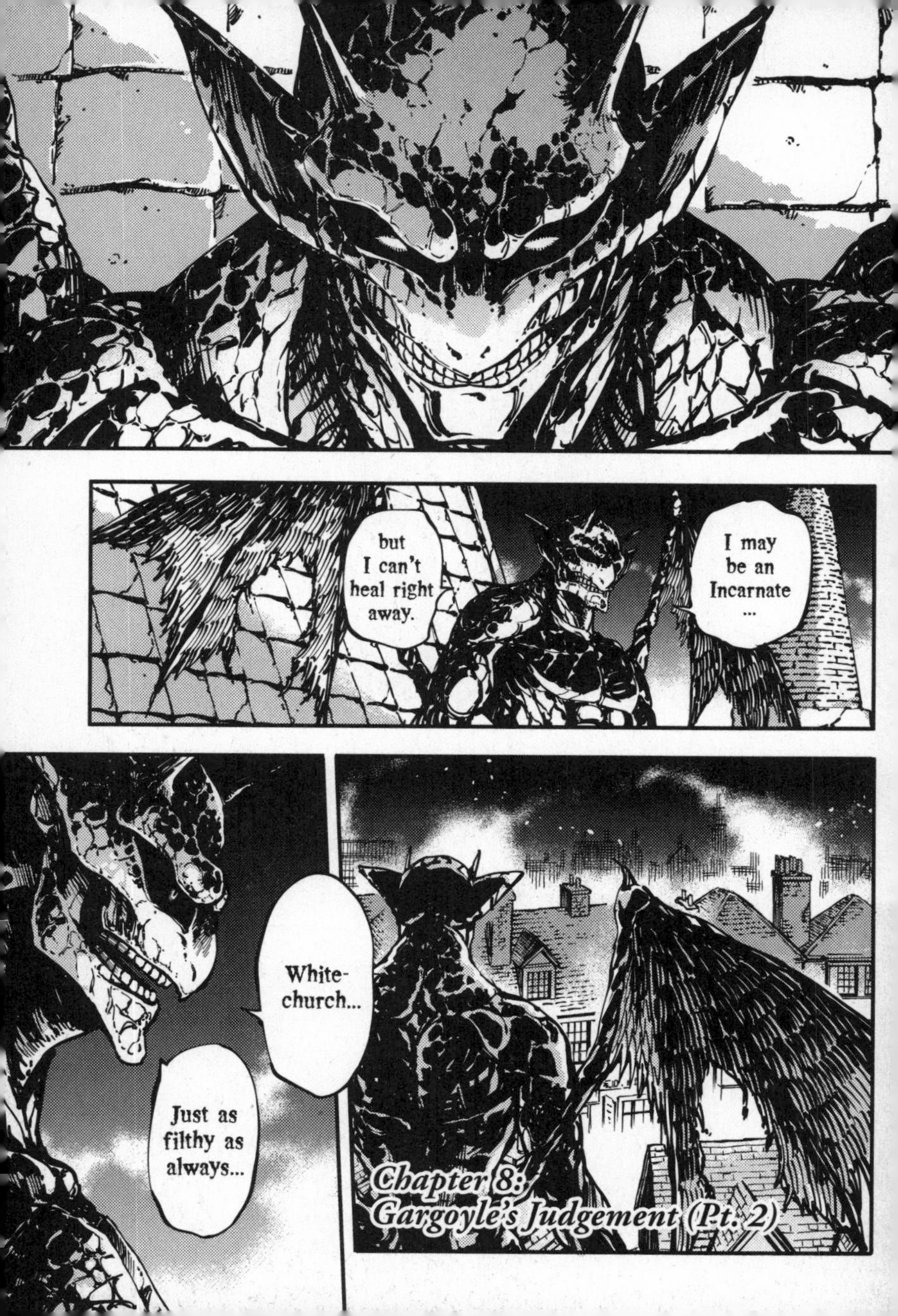
I may be an Incarnate ...
but I can't heal right away.
Chapter 8: Gargoyle's Judgement (Pt. 2)
White-church...
Just as filthy as always...

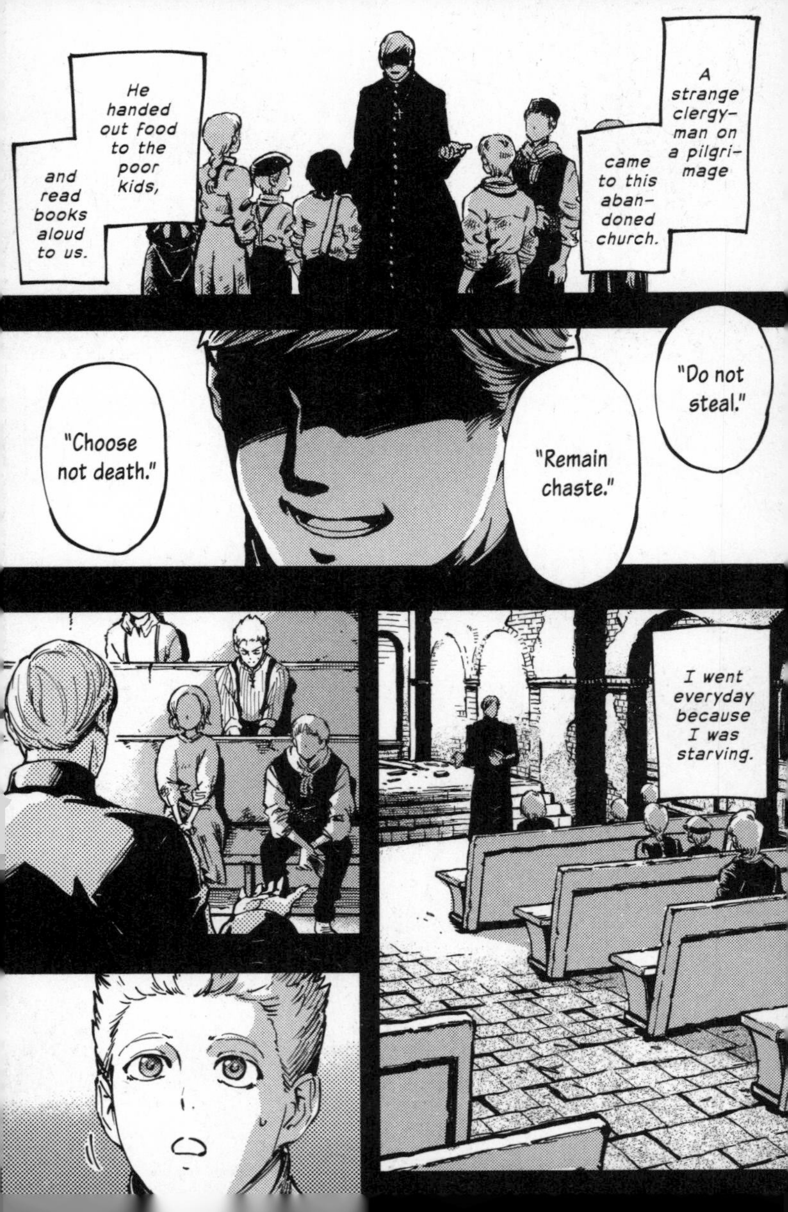
A strange clergyman on a pilgrimage
came to this abandoned church.
He handed out food to the poor kids,
and read books aloud to us.
"Do not steal."
"Remain chaste."
"Choose not death."
I went everyday because I was starving.

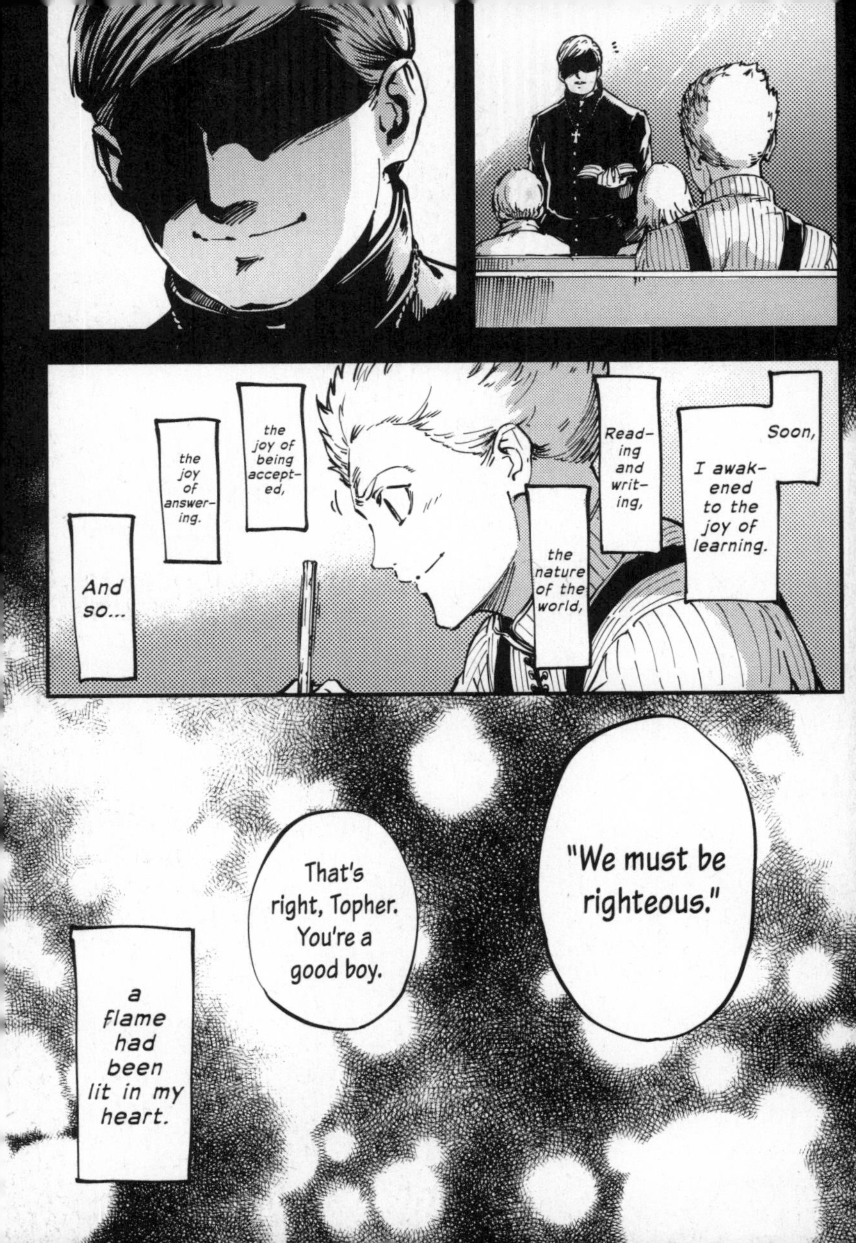
Soon, I awakened to the joy of learning.
Reading and writing,
the nature of the world,
the joy of being accepted,
the joy of answering.
And so...
"We must be righteous."
That's right, Topher. You're a good boy.
a flame had been lit in my heart.

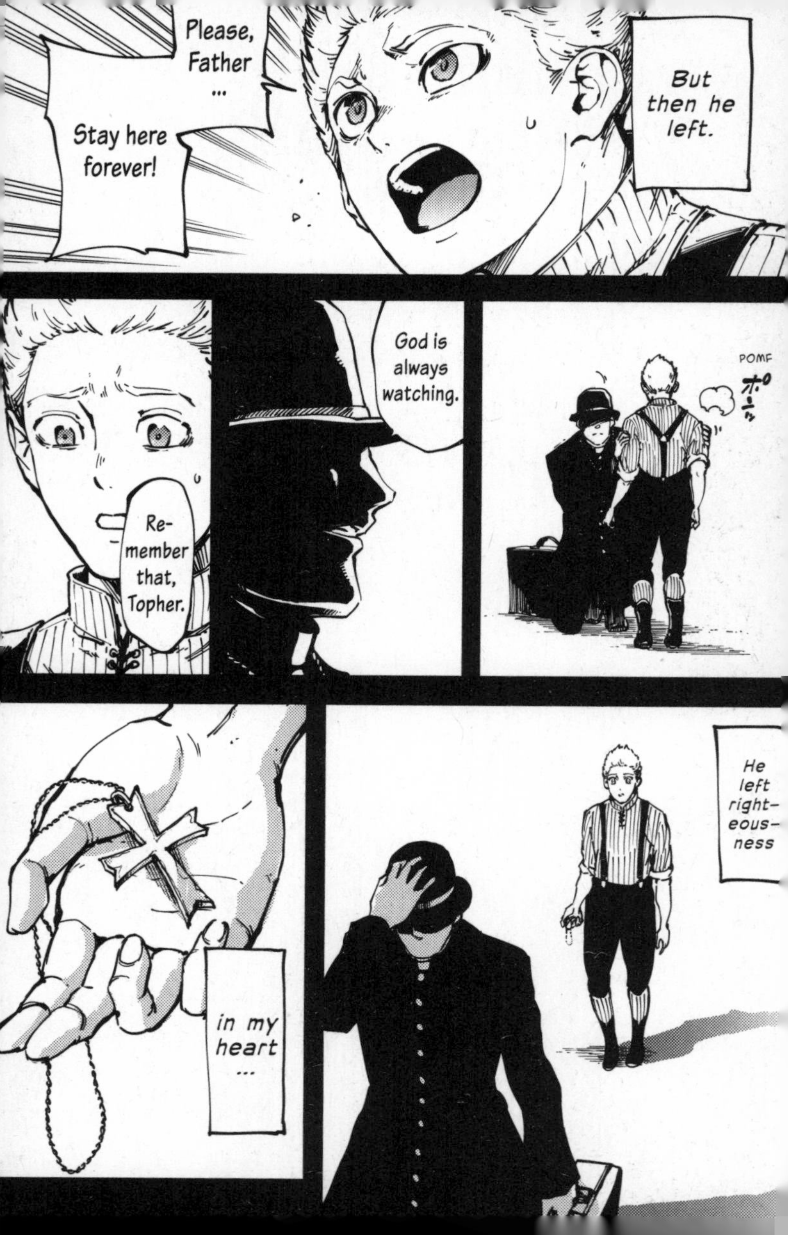
But then he left.
Please, Father ...
Stay here forever!
POMF
God is always watching.
Re-member that, Topher.
He left right-eous-ness
in my heart ...

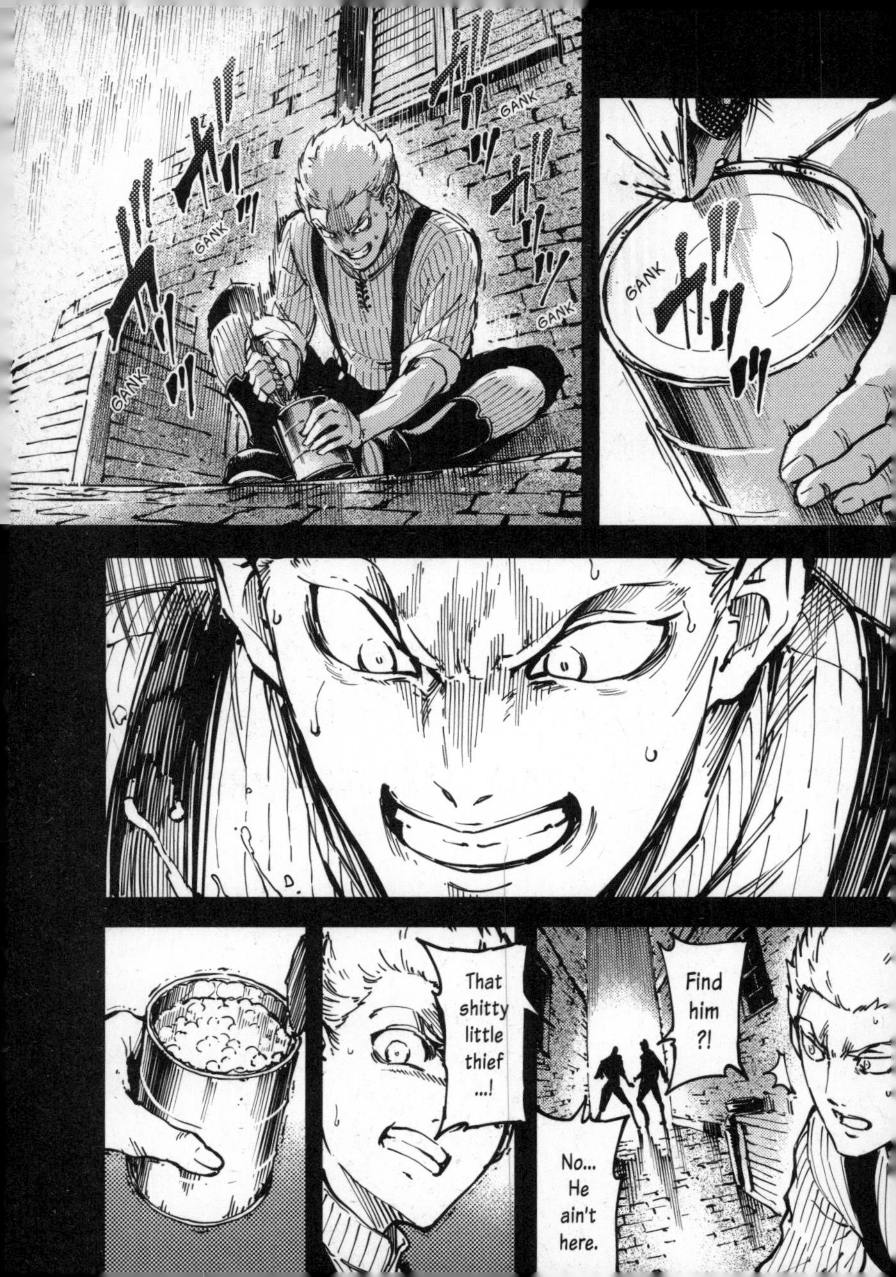
GANK
GANK
GANK
GANK
GANK
Find him ?!
No... He ain't here.
That shitty little thief ...!

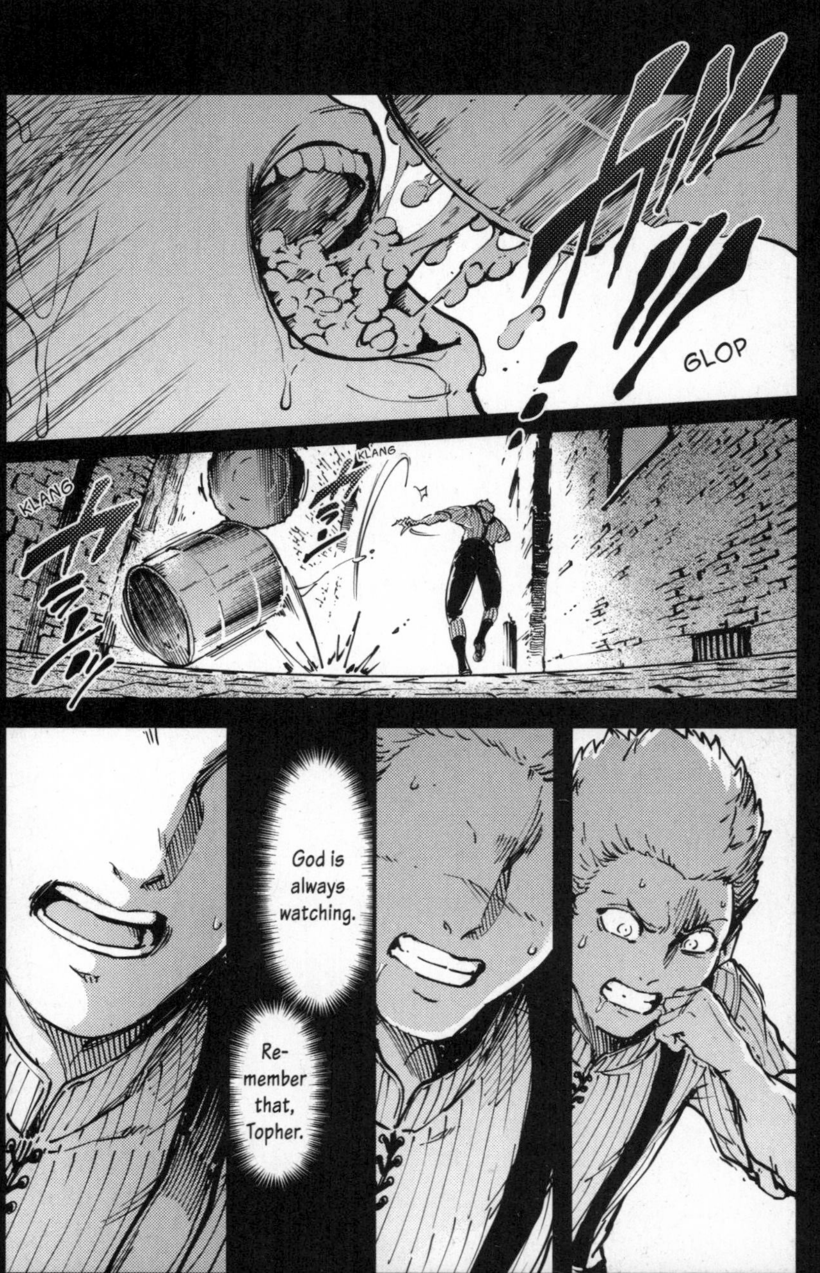
GLOP
KLANG
KLANG
God is always watching.
Re-member that, Topher.

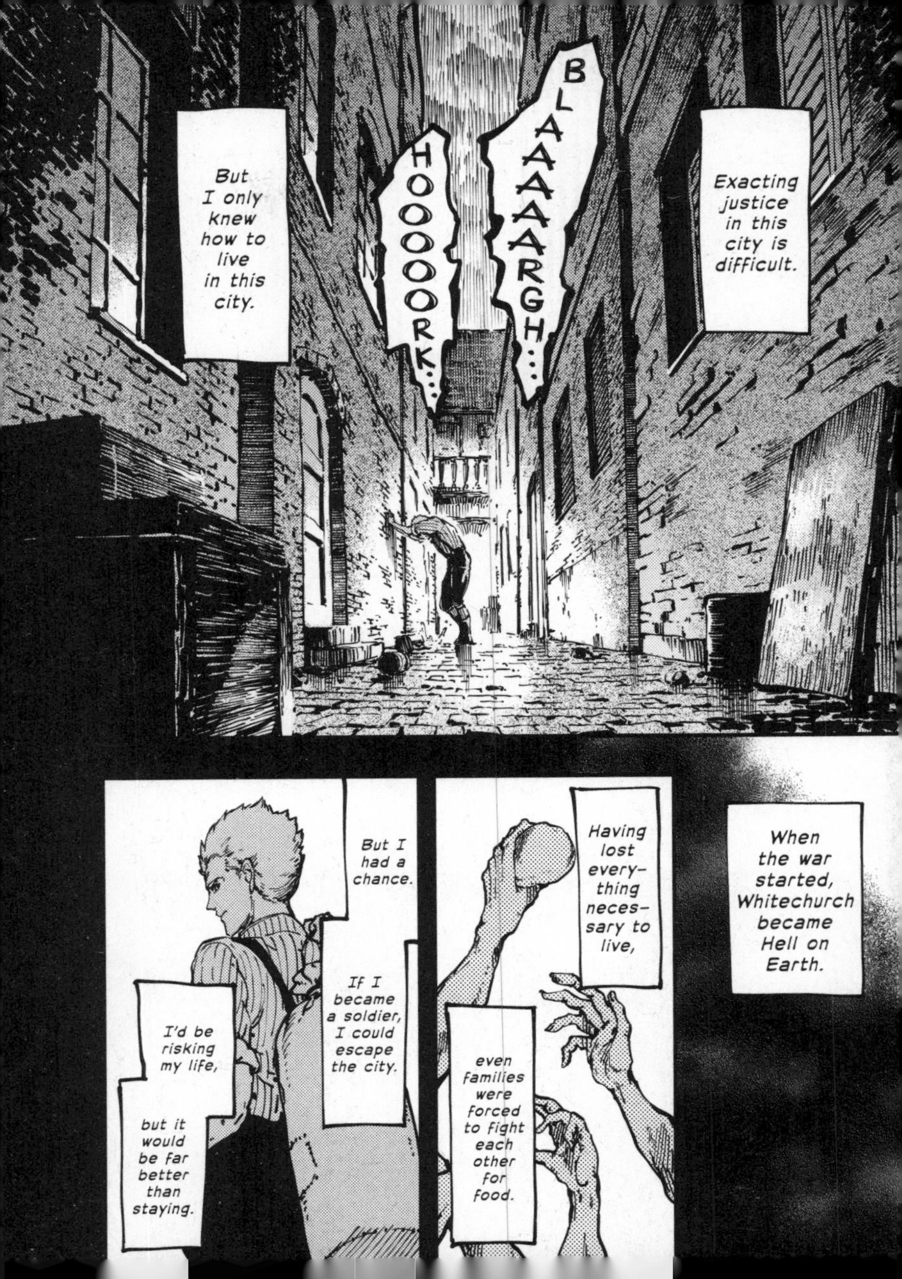
Exacting justice in this city is difficult.
BLAAAAARGH...
HOOOOOORK...
But I only knew how to live in this city.
When the war started, Whitechurch became Hell on Earth.
Having lost every-thing neces-sary to live,
even families were forced to fight each other for food.
But I had a chance.
If I became a soldier, I could escape the city.
I'd be risking my life,
but it would be far better than staying.

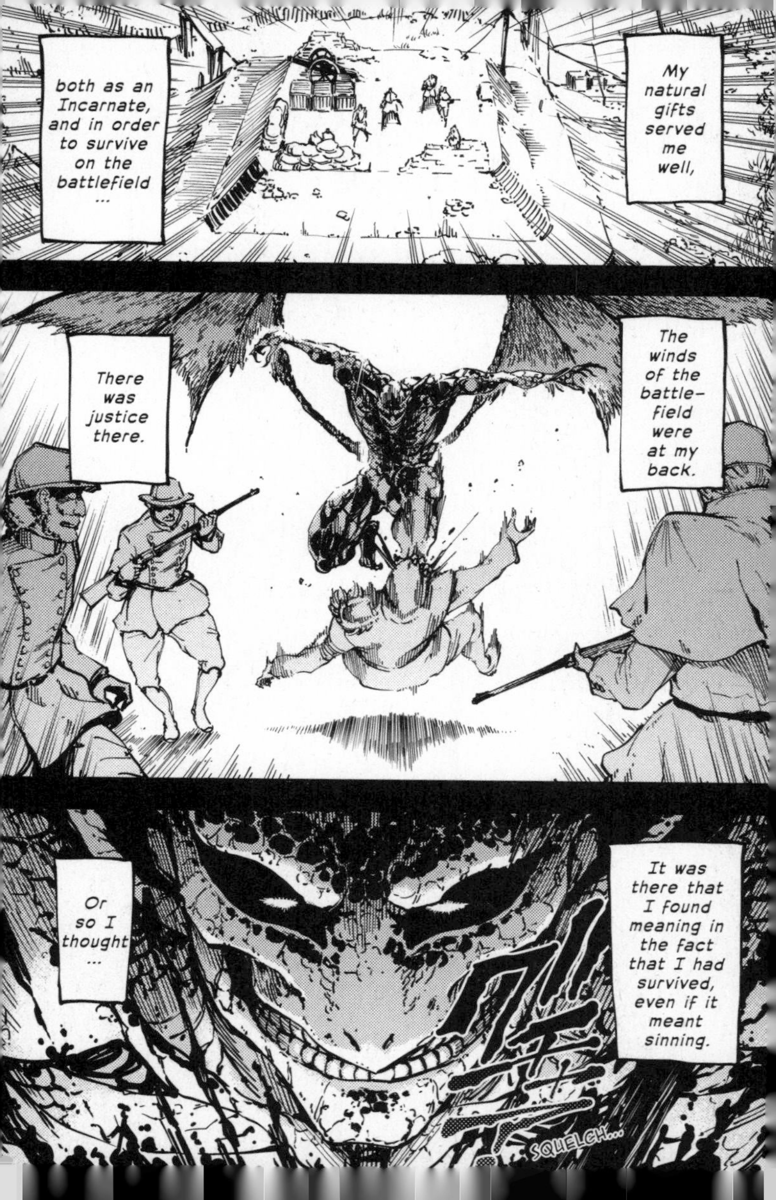

My natural gifts served me well,
both as an Incarnate, and in order to survive on the battlefield ...
The winds of the battle-field were at my back.
There was justice there.
It was there that I found meaning in the fact that I had survived, even if it meant sinning.
Or so I thought ...
SQUELCH...

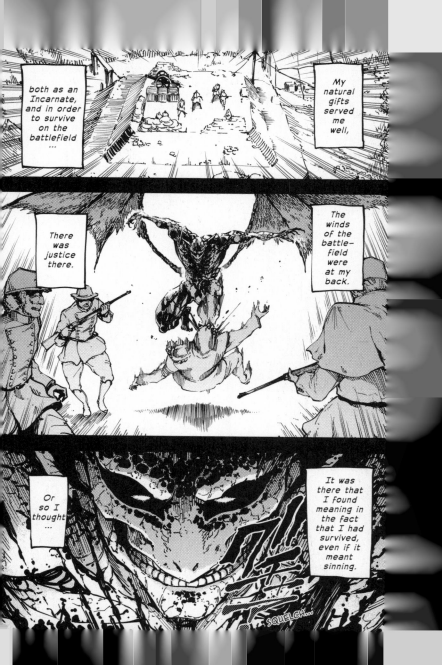

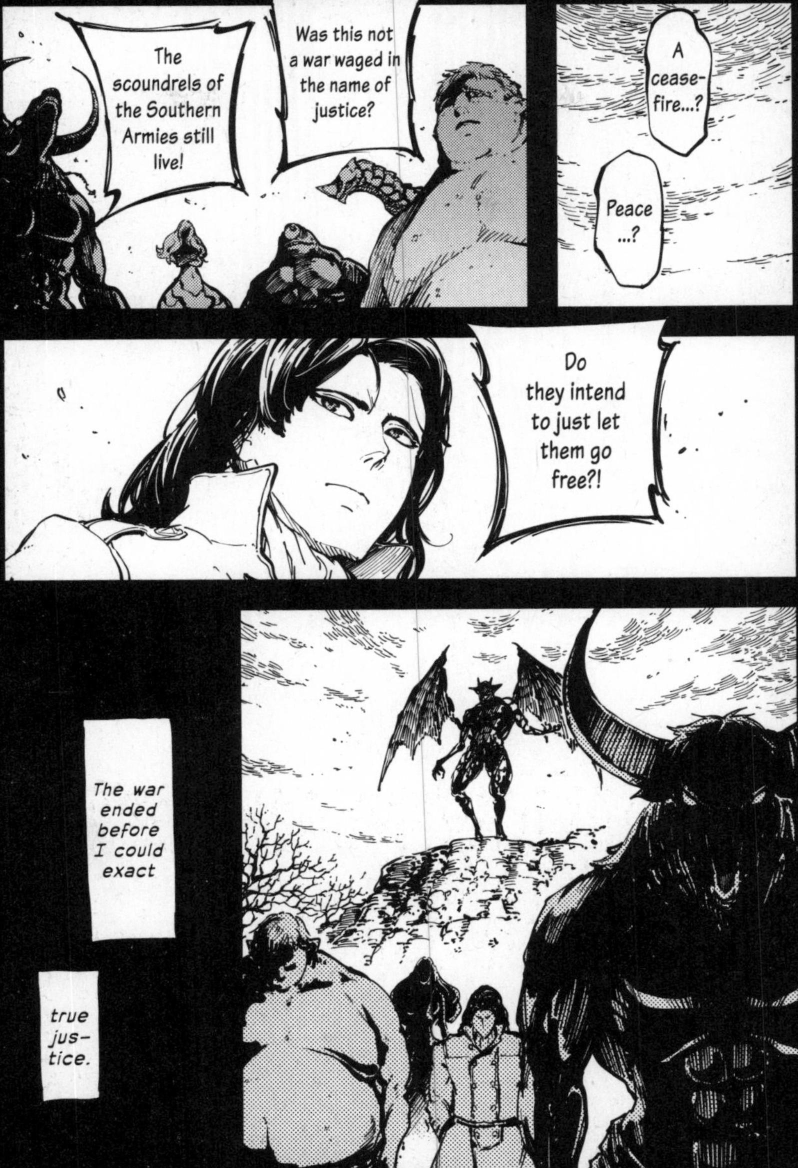
A cease-fire...?
Peace...?
Was this not a war waged in the name of justice?
The scoundrels of the Southern Armies still live!
Do they intend to just let them go free?!
The war ended before I could exact
true jus-tice.

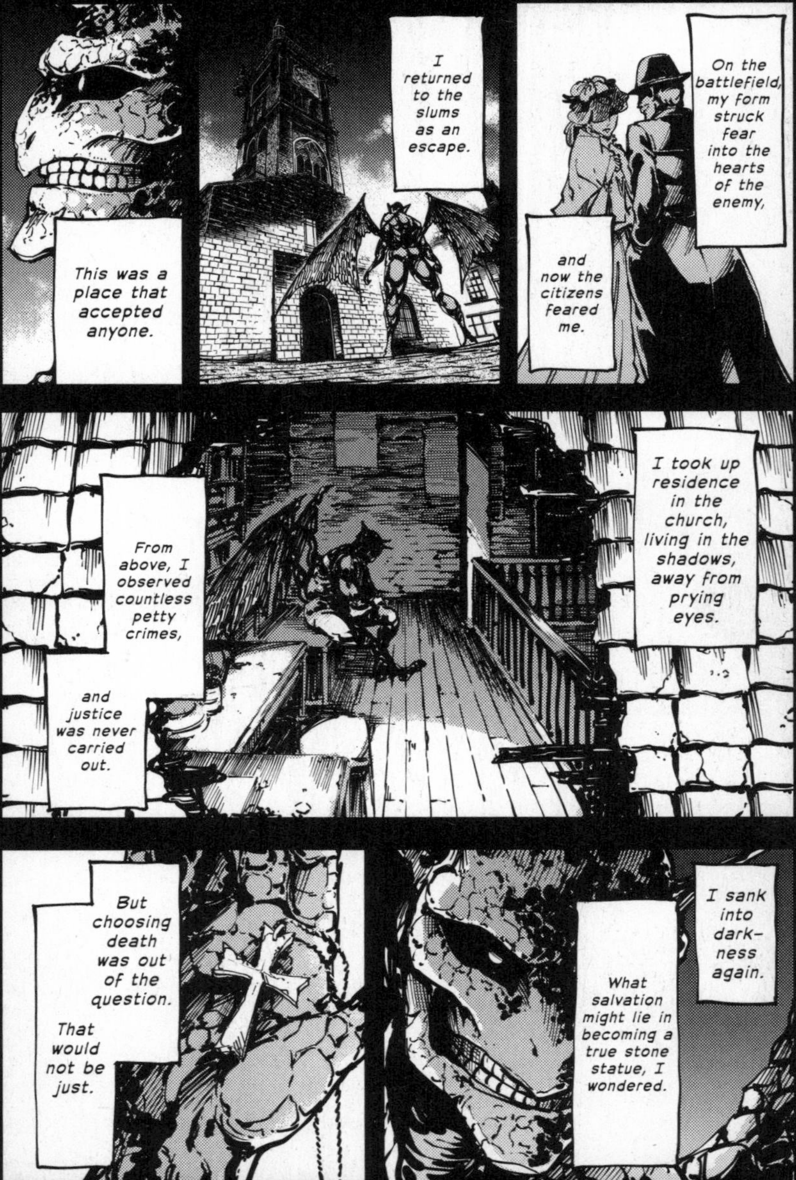
On the battlefield, my form struck fear into the hearts of the enemy,
and now the citizens feared me.
I returned to the slums as an escape.
This was a place that accepted anyone.
I took up residence in the church, living in the shadows, away from prying eyes.
From above, I observed countless petty crimes,
and justice was never carried out.
I sank into dark-ness again.
What salvation might lie in becoming a true stone statue, I wondered.
But choosing death was out of the question.
That would not be just.

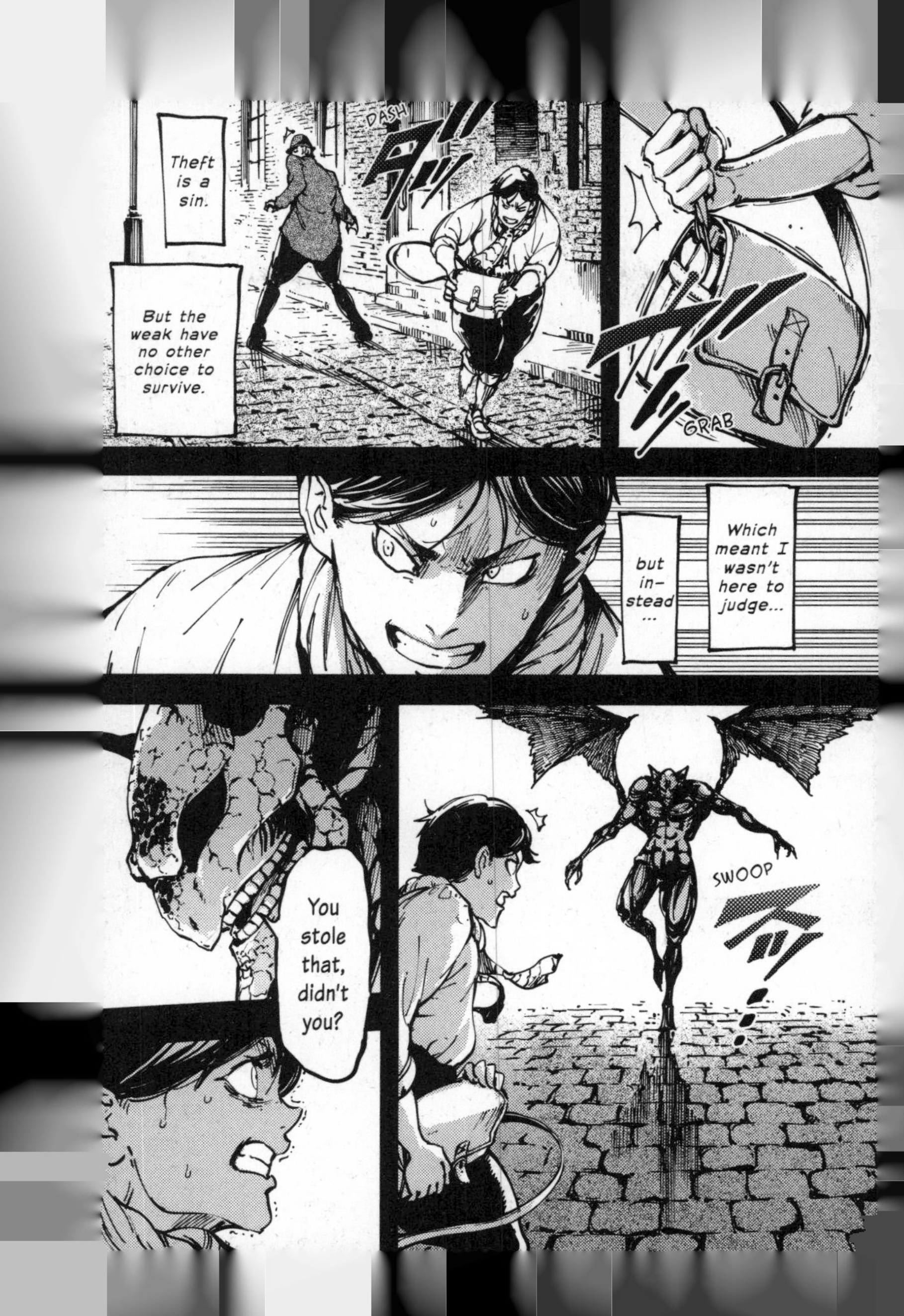
GRAB
DASH
Theft is a sin.
But the weak have no other choice to survive.
Which meant I wasn't here to judge...
but in-stead...
SWOOP
You stole that, didn't you?

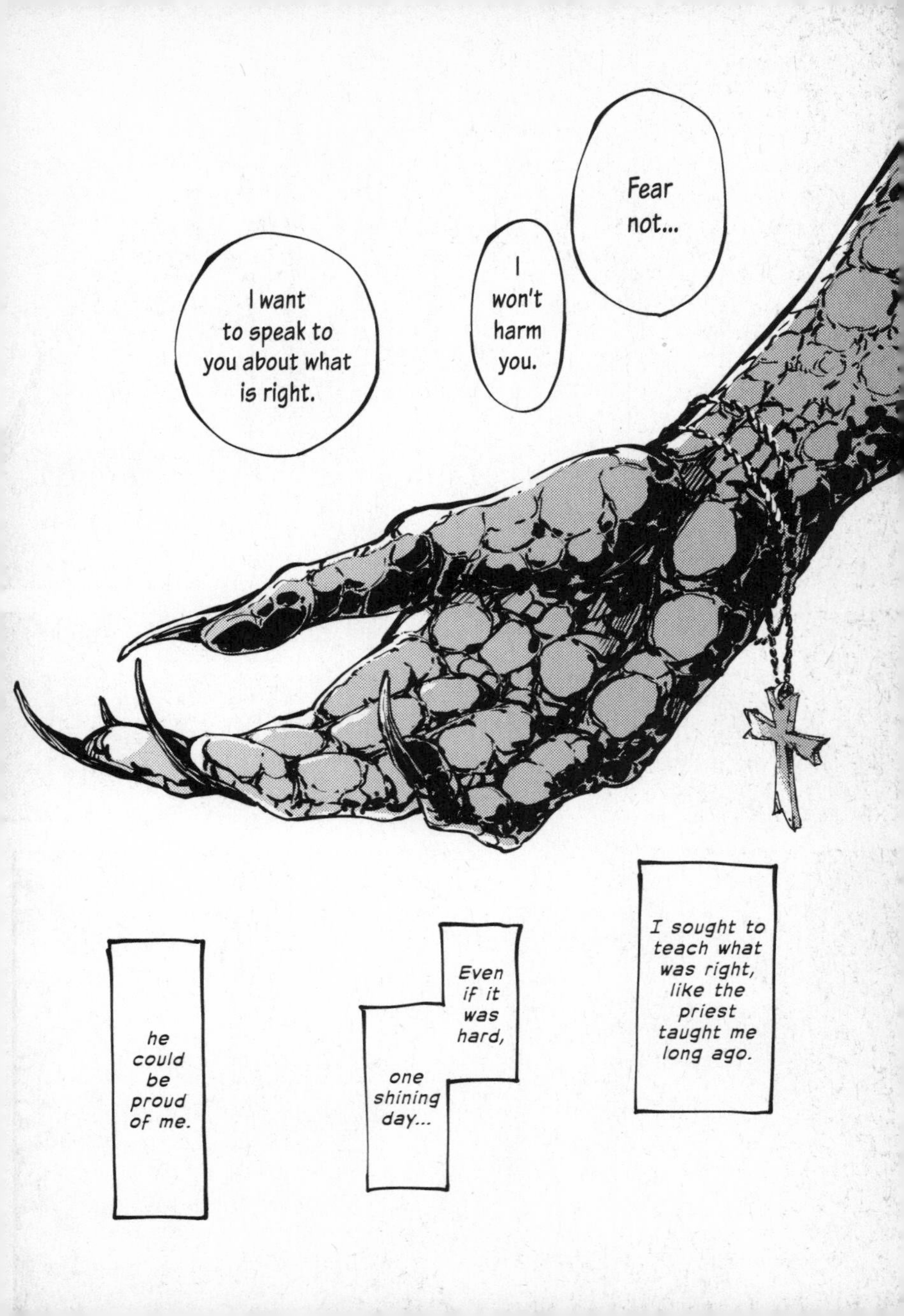
Fear not...
I won't harm you.
I want to speak to you about what is right.
I sought to teach what was right, like the priest taught me long ago.
Even if it was hard,
one shining day...
he could be proud of me.

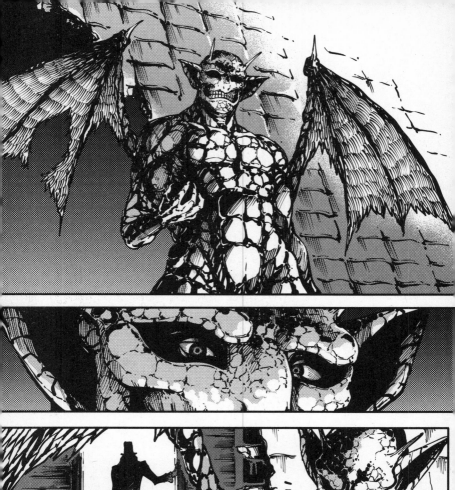
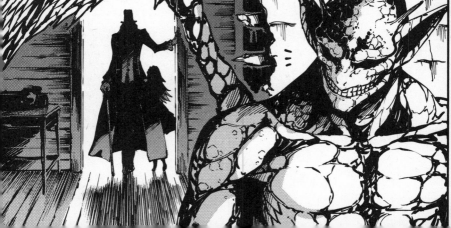

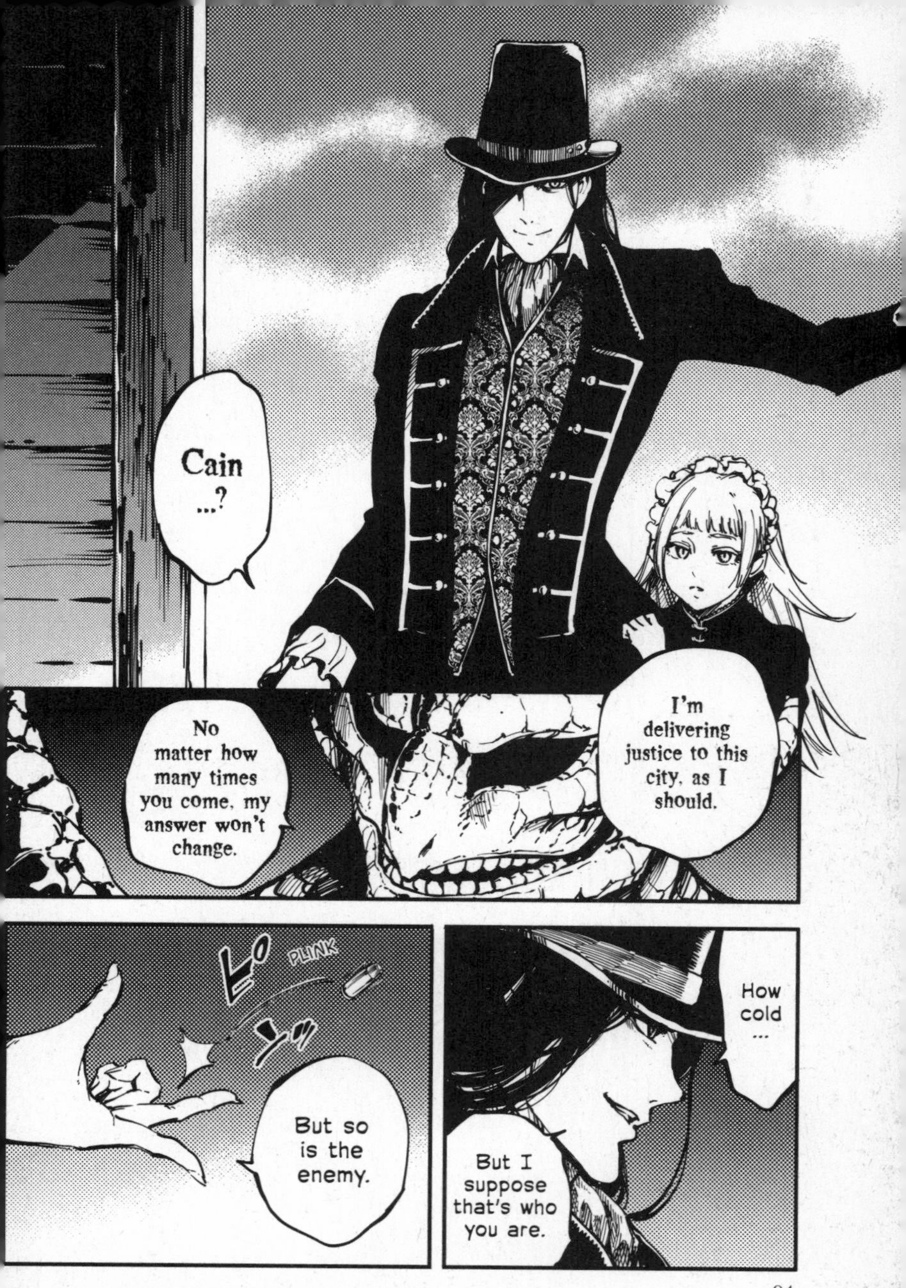
Cain ...?
I'm delivering justice to this city, as I should.
No matter how many times you come, my answer won't change.
How cold ...
But I suppose that's who you are.
PLINK
But so is the enemy.

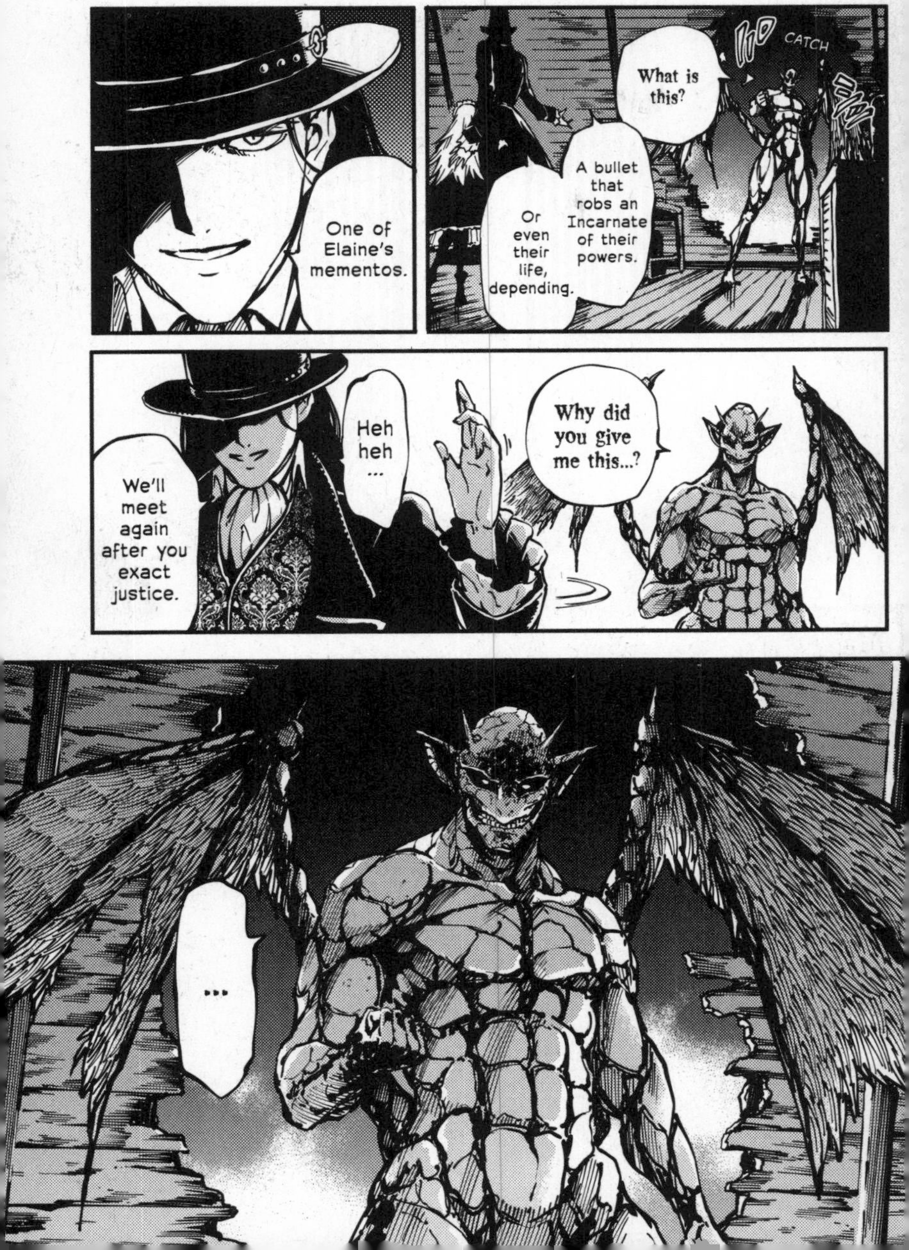
CATCH
What is this?
A bullet that robs an Incarnate of their powers.
Or even their life, depending.
One of Elaine's mementos.
Why did you give me this...?
Heh heh ...
We'll meet again after you exact justice.
...

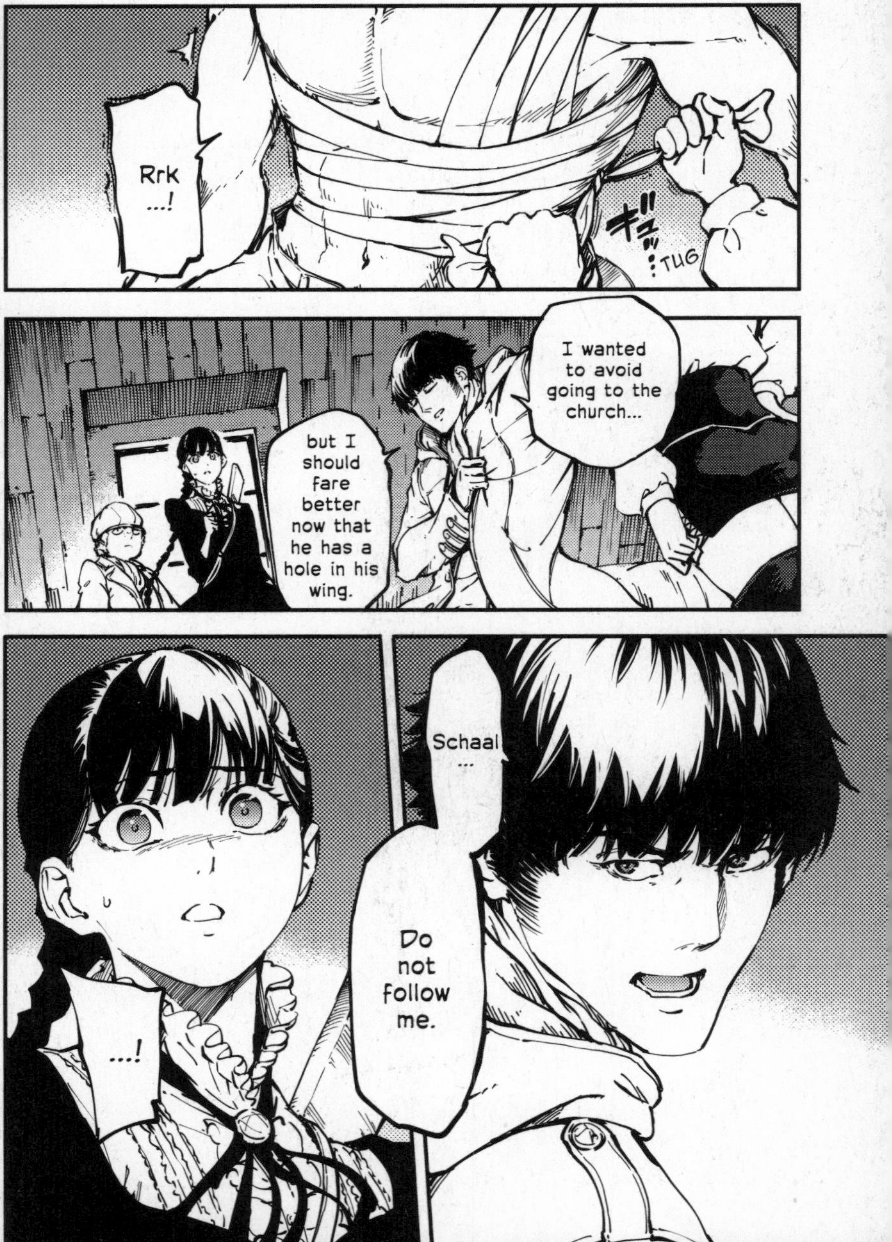
TUG
Rrk ...!
I wanted to avoid going to the church...
but I should fare better now that he has a hole in his wing.
Schaal ...
Do not follow me.
...!

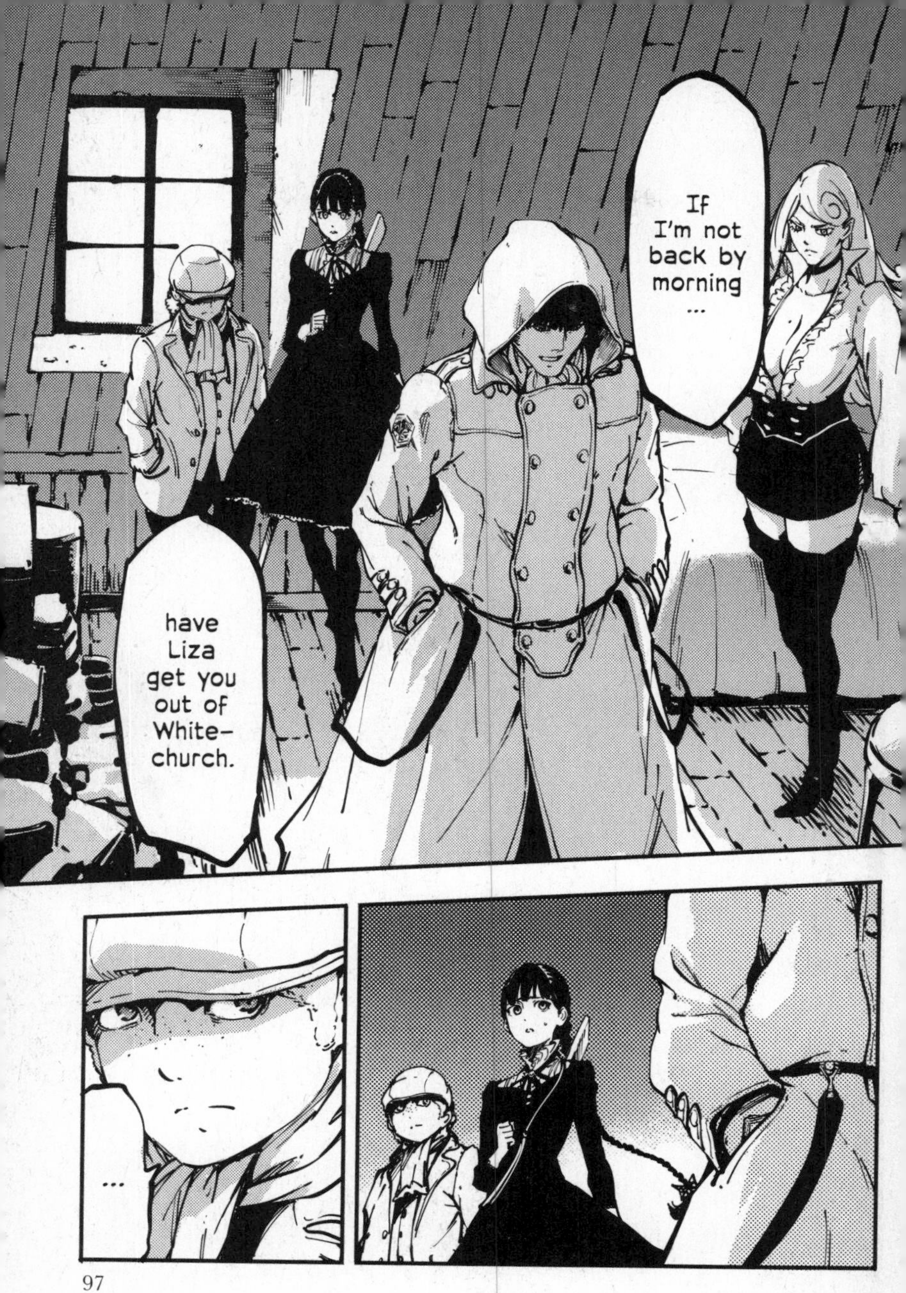
If I'm not back by morning ...
have Liza get you out of White-church.
...

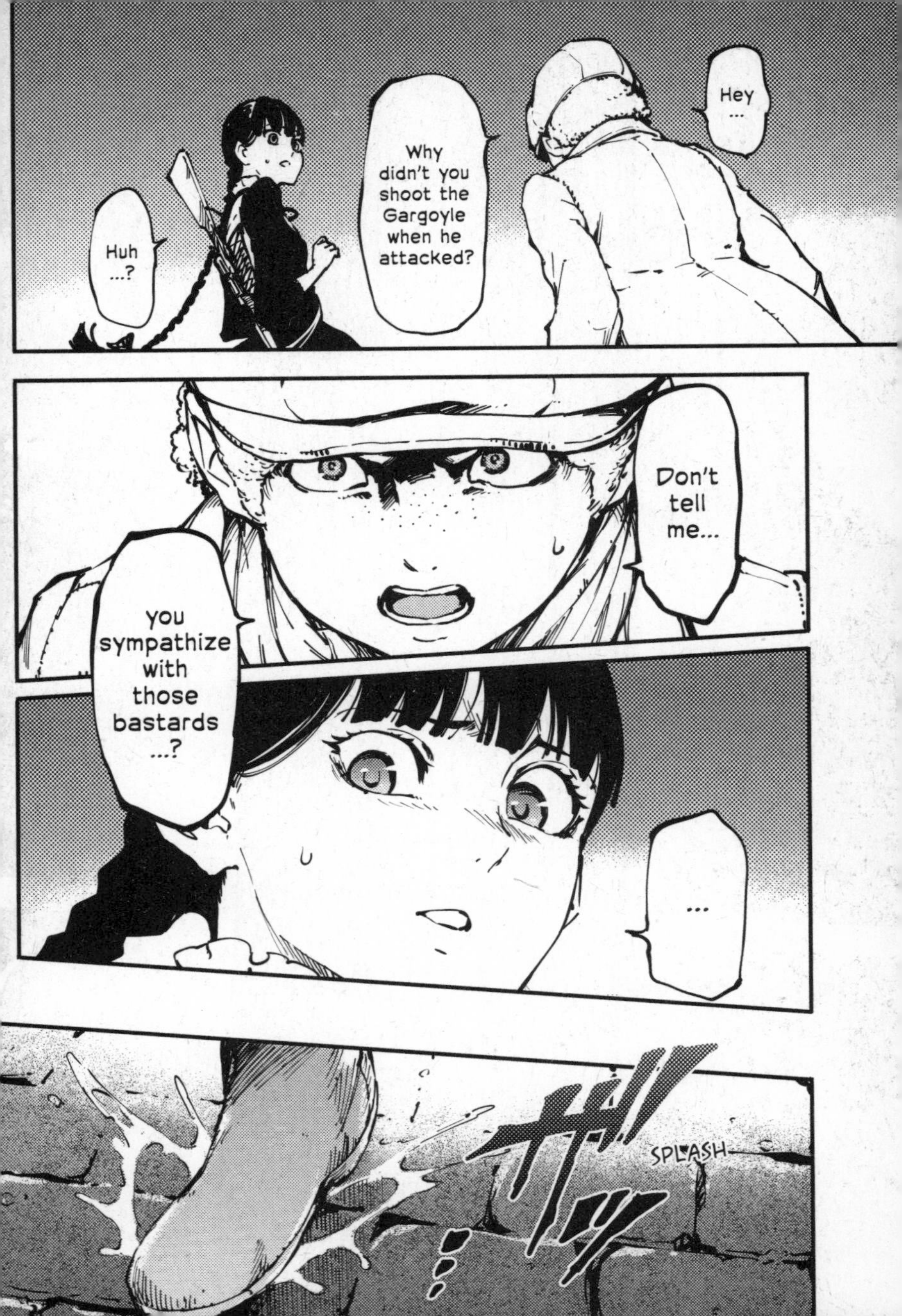
Hey ...
Why didn't you shoot the Gargoyle when he attacked?
Huh ...?
Don't tell me...
you sympathize with those bastards ...?
...
SPLASH

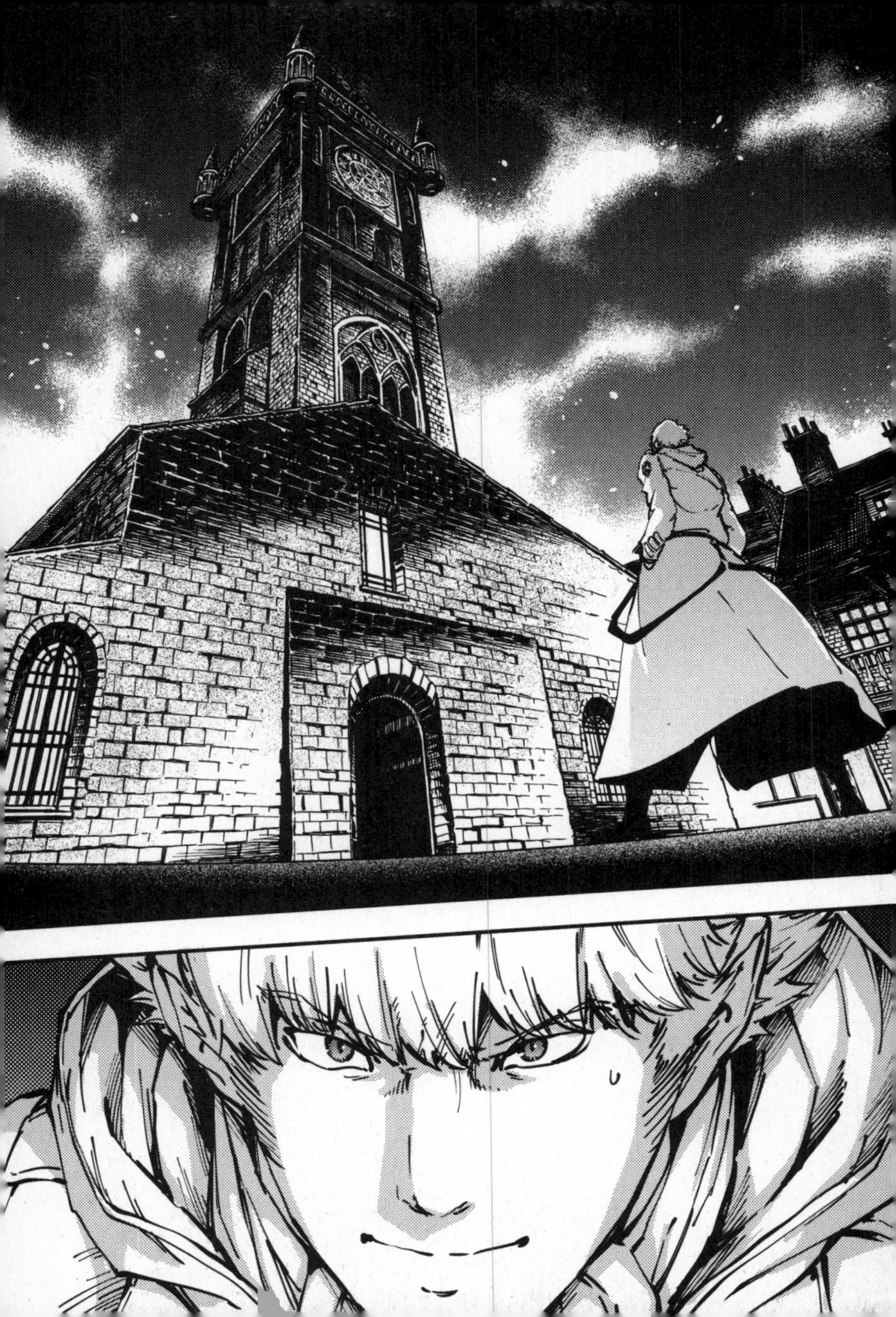

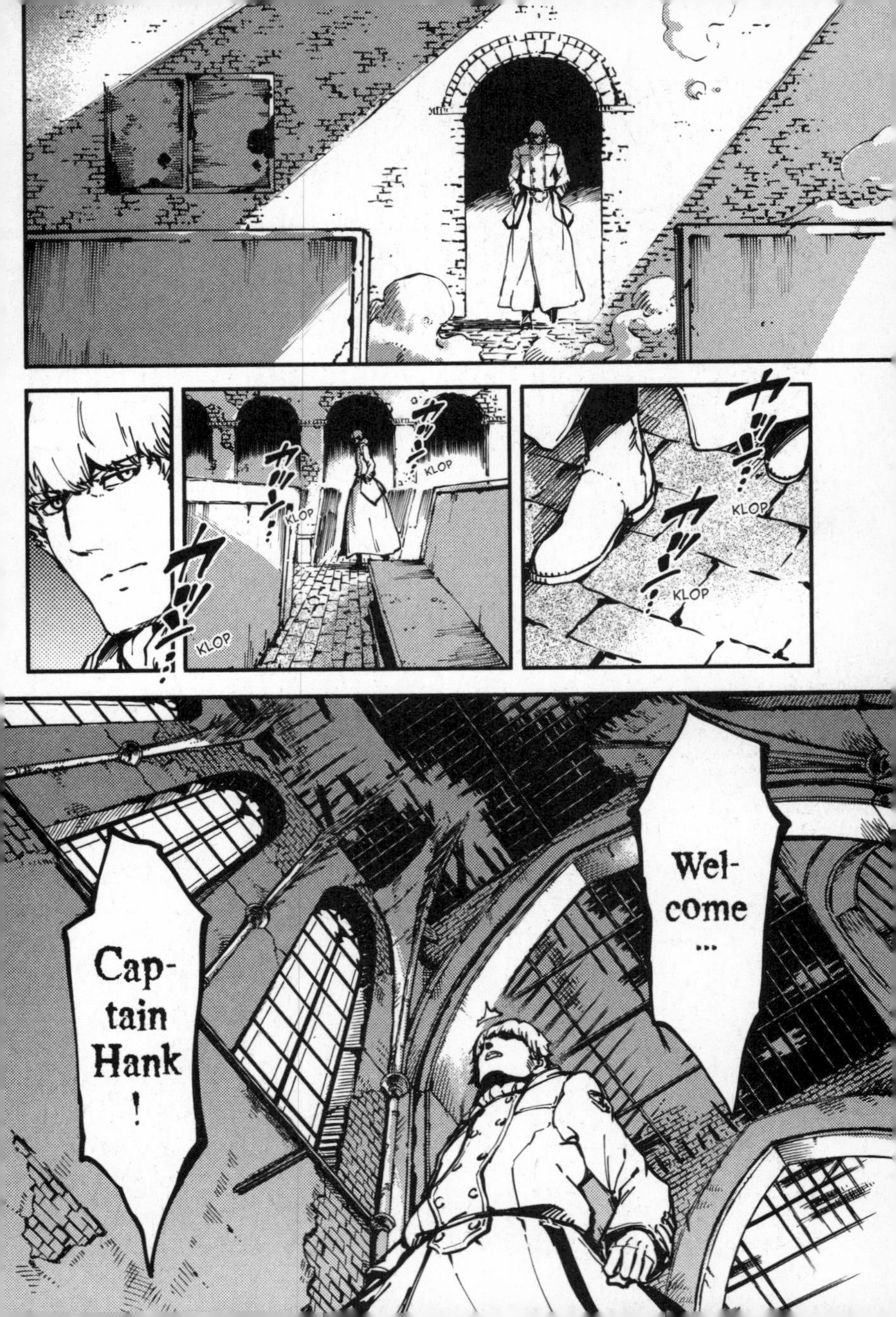
KLOP
KLOP
KLOP
KLOP
KLOP
Wel-
come
...
Cap-
tain
Hank
!

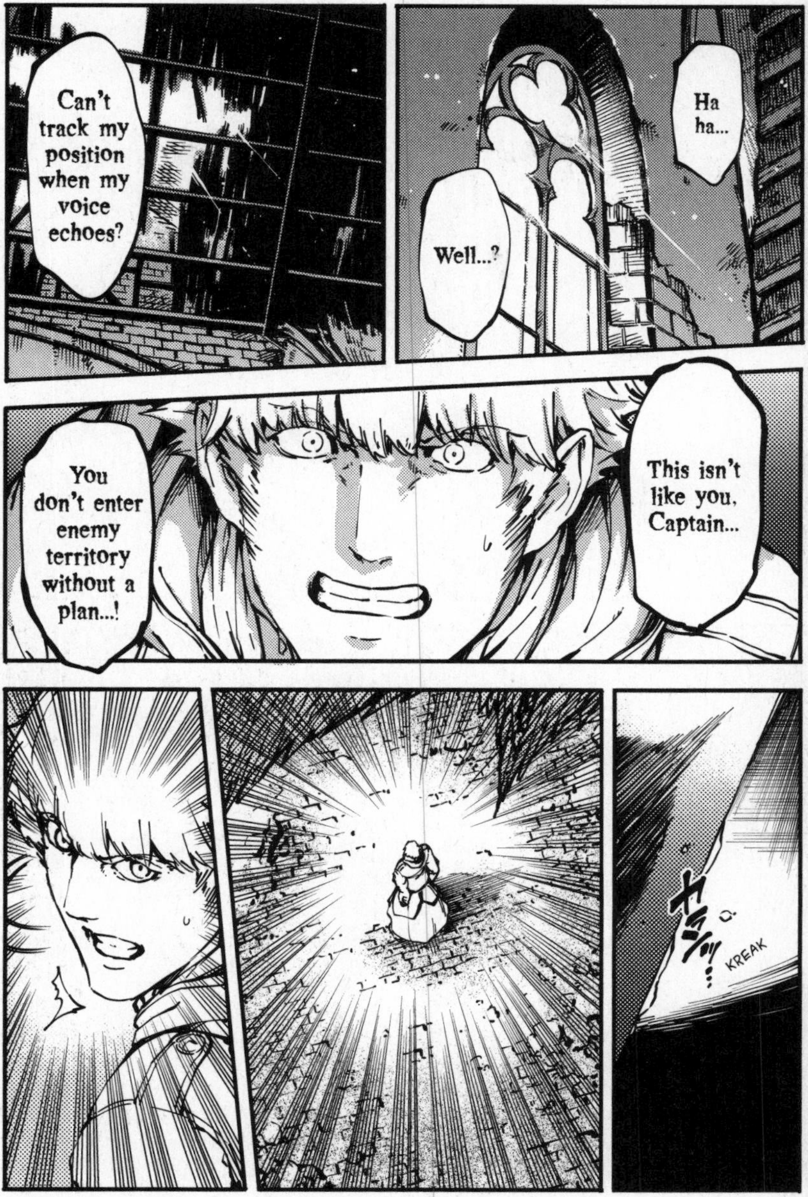
Ha ha...
Well...?
Can't track my position when my voice echoes?
This isn't like you, Captain...
You don't enter enemy territory without a plan...!
KREAK

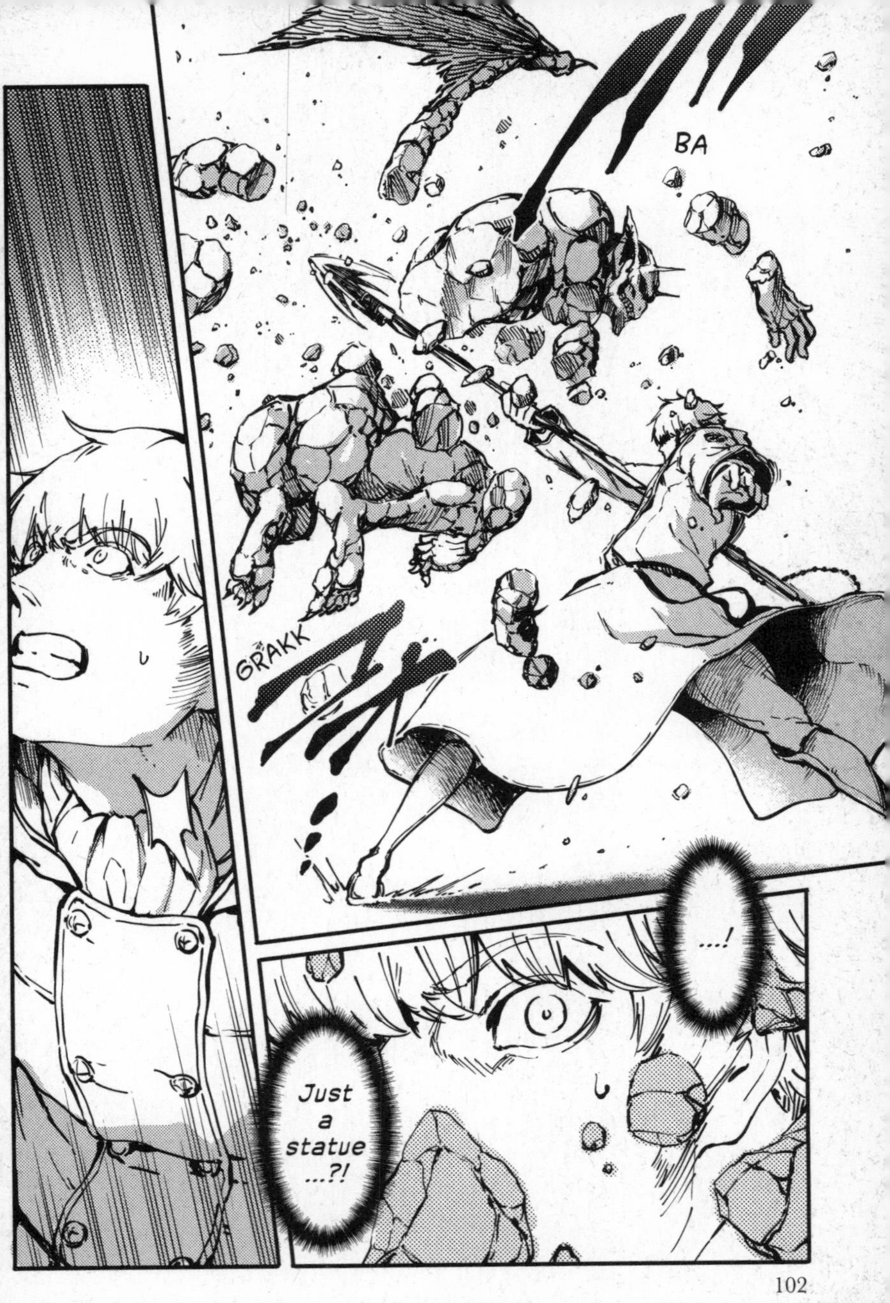
BA
GRAKK
...!
Just a statue ...?!

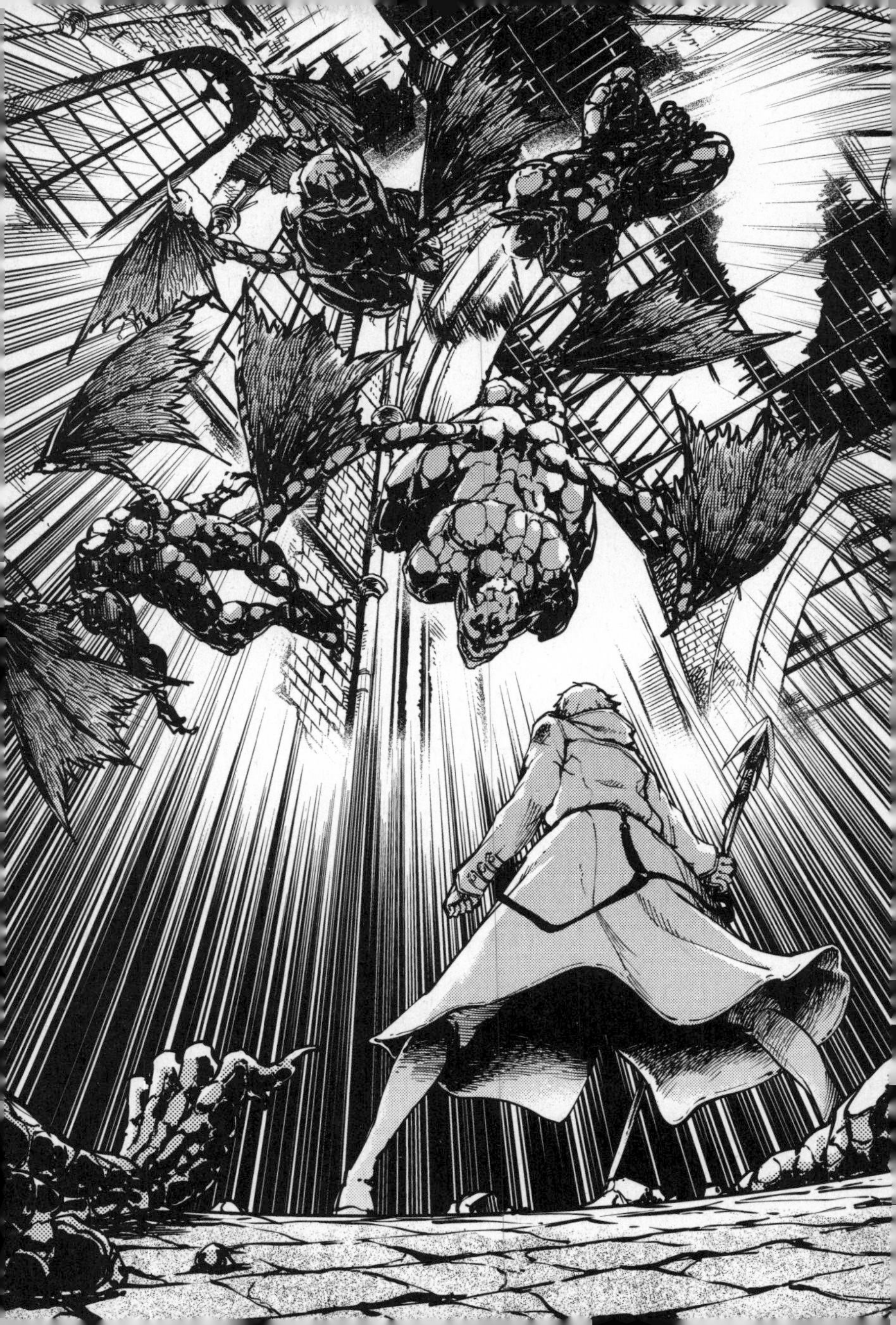

To the Abandoned
Sacred Beasts

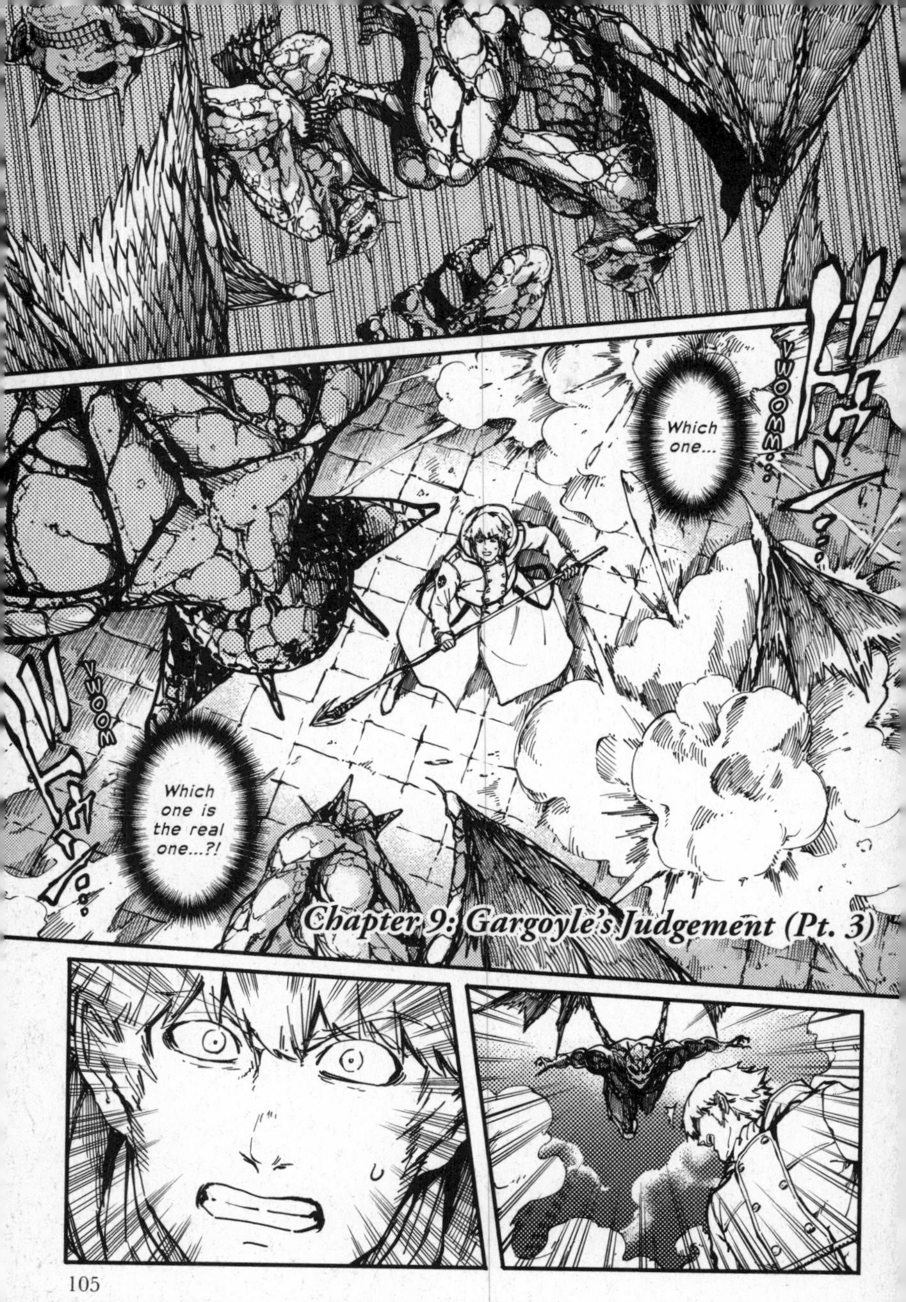
VWOOMM
Which one...
VWOOM
Which one is the real one...?!
Chapter 9: Gargoyle's Judgement (Pt. 3)

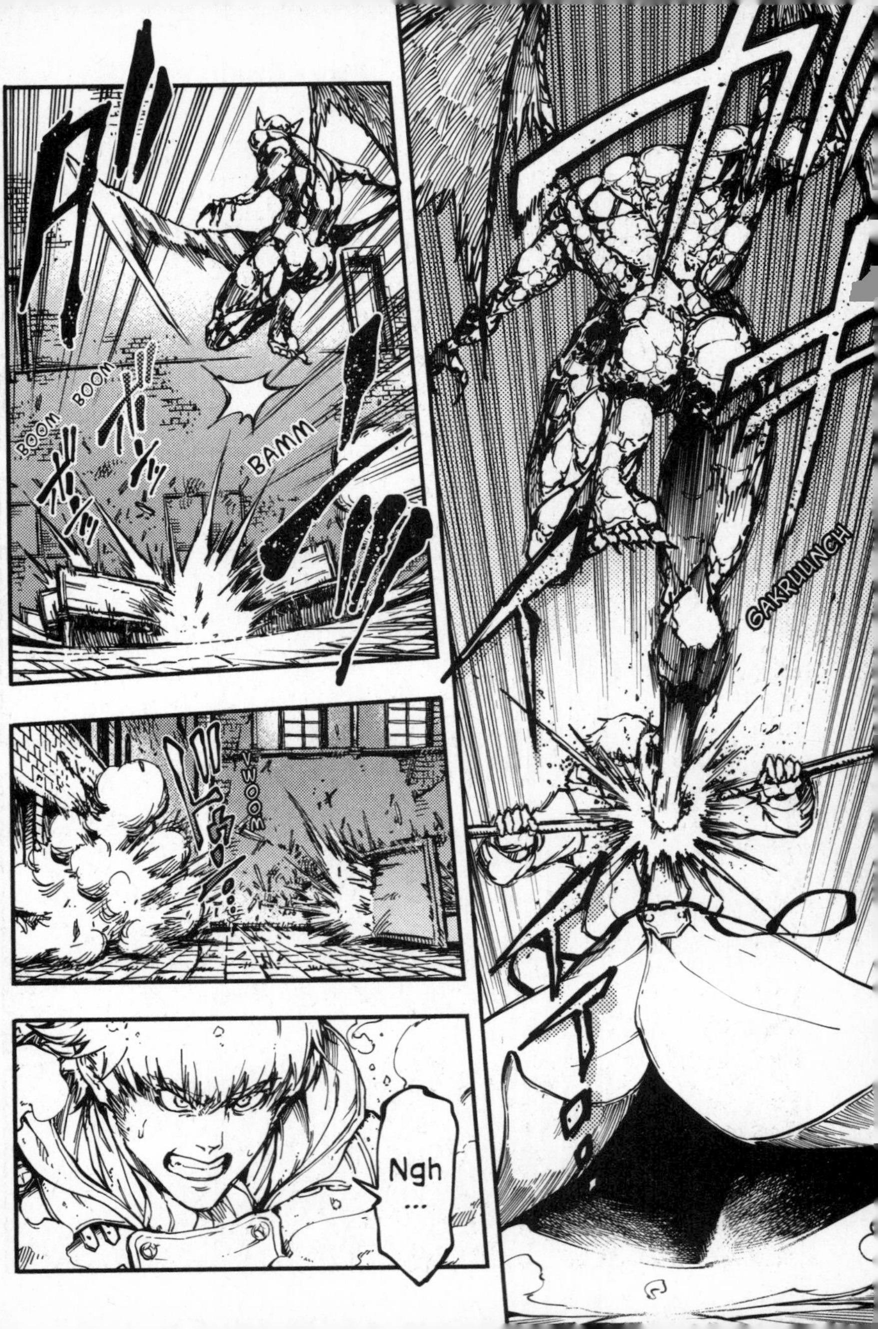
GAKRUUNCH
BOOM BOOM
BAMM
VWOOM
Ngh
...

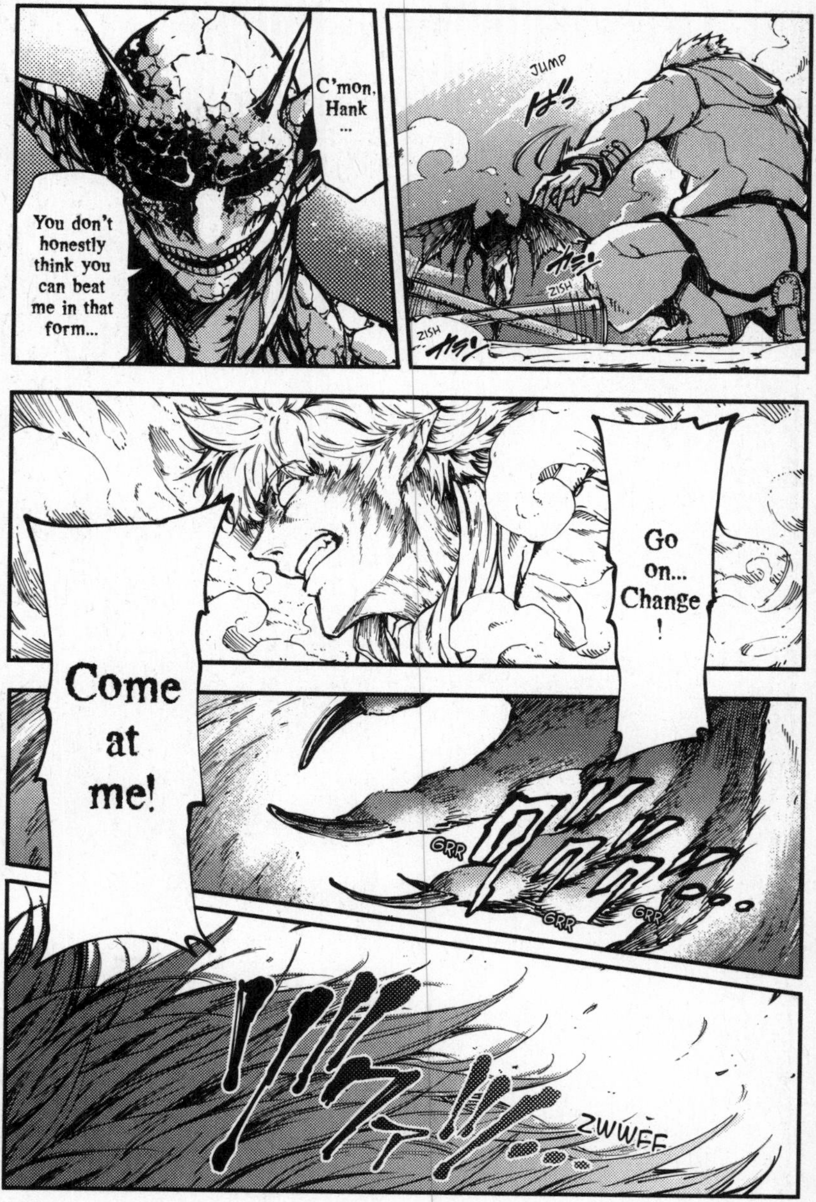
JUMP
ZISH
ZISH
C'mon, Hank ...
You don't honestly think you can beat me in that form...
Go on... Change!
Come at me!
GRR
GRR
GRR
ZWWEF

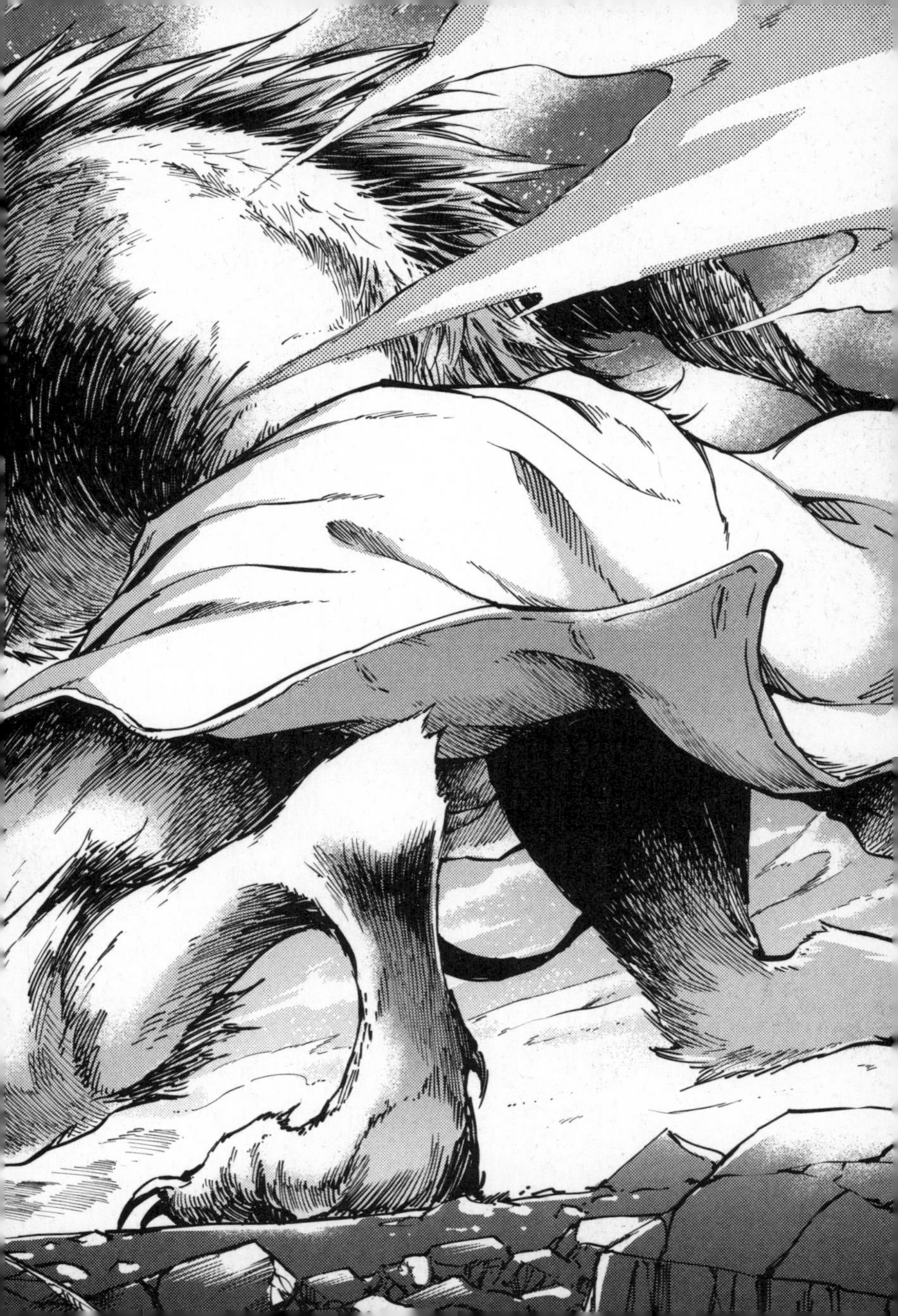

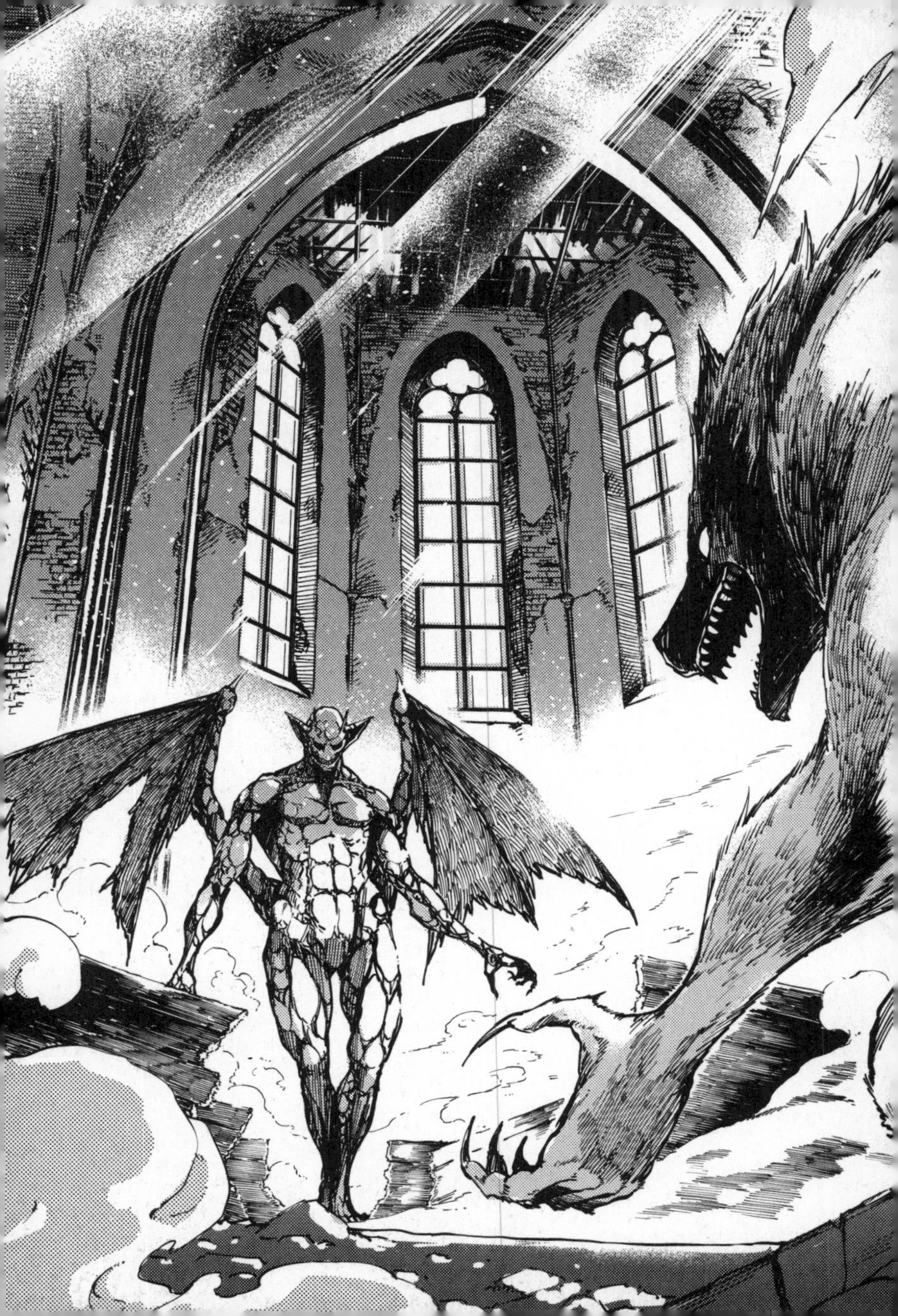

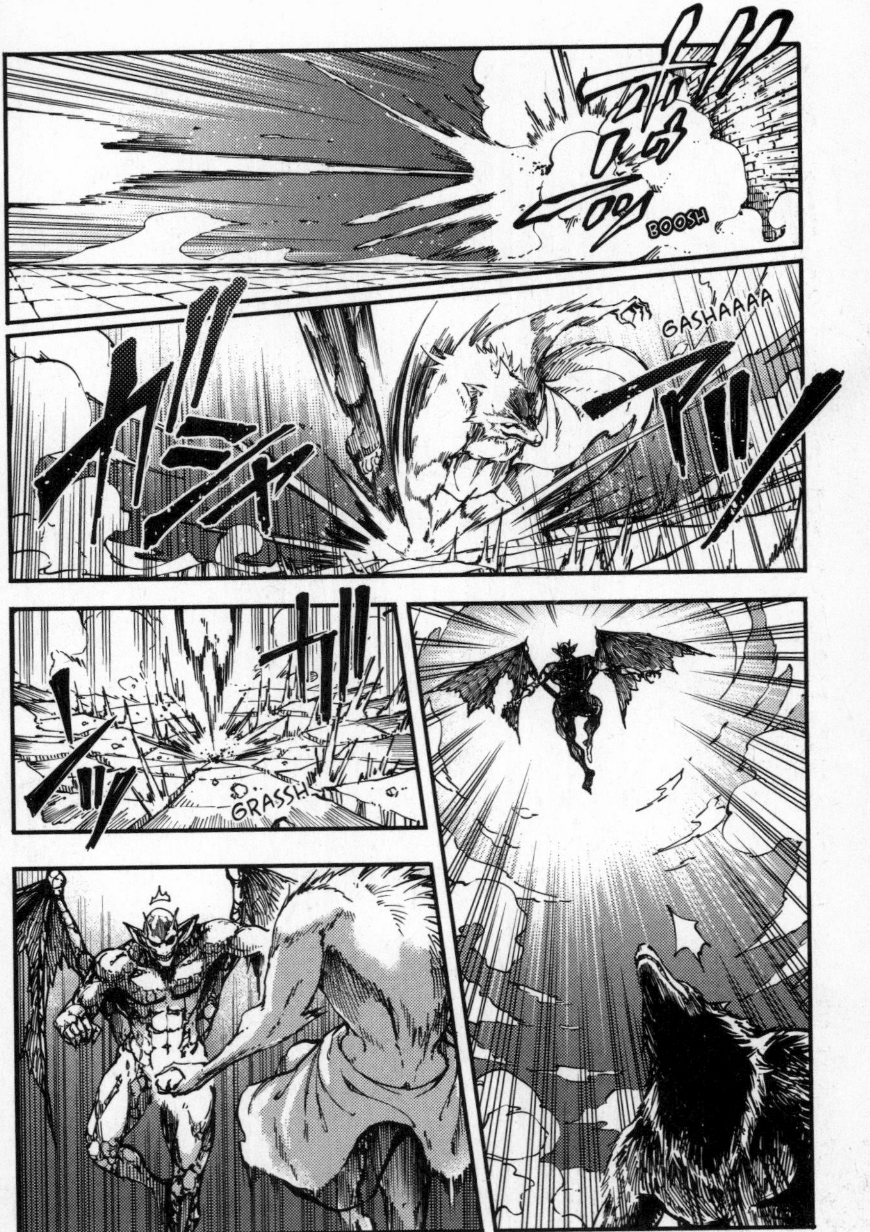
BOOSH
GASHAAAA
GRASSH

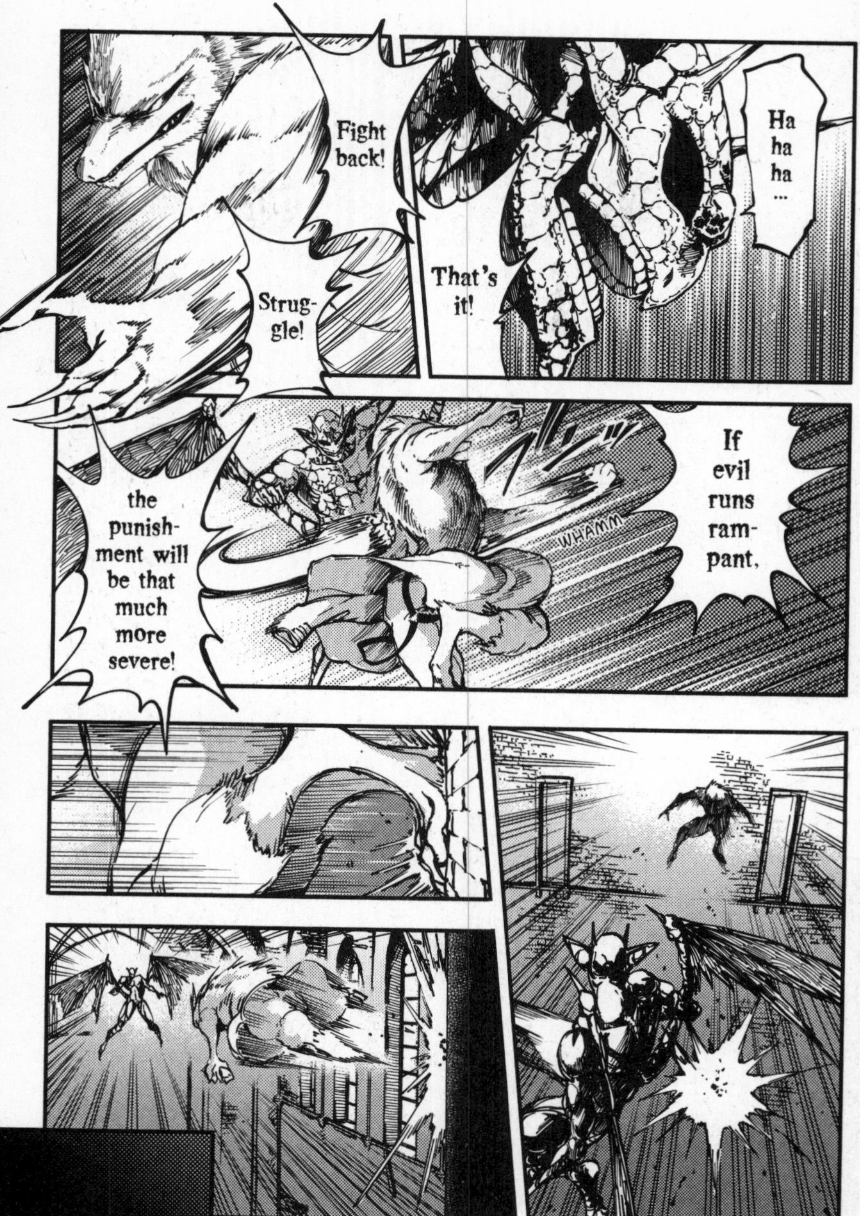
Ha ha ha ...
That's it!
Fight back!
Strug-gle!
If evil runs ram-pant,
WHAMM
the punish-ment will be that much more severe!

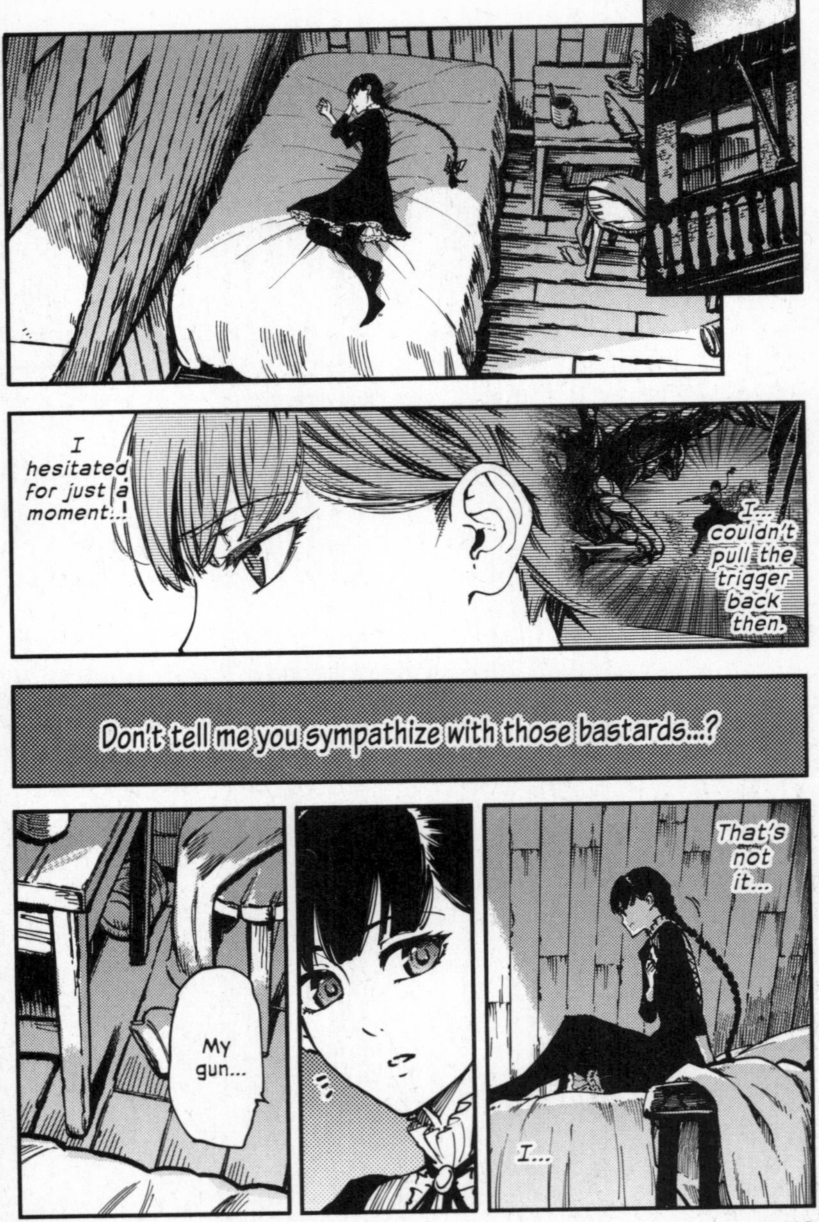

I... couldn't pull the trigger back then.
I hesitated for just a moment...!
Don't tell me you sympathize with those bastards...?
That's not it...
I...
...
My gun...

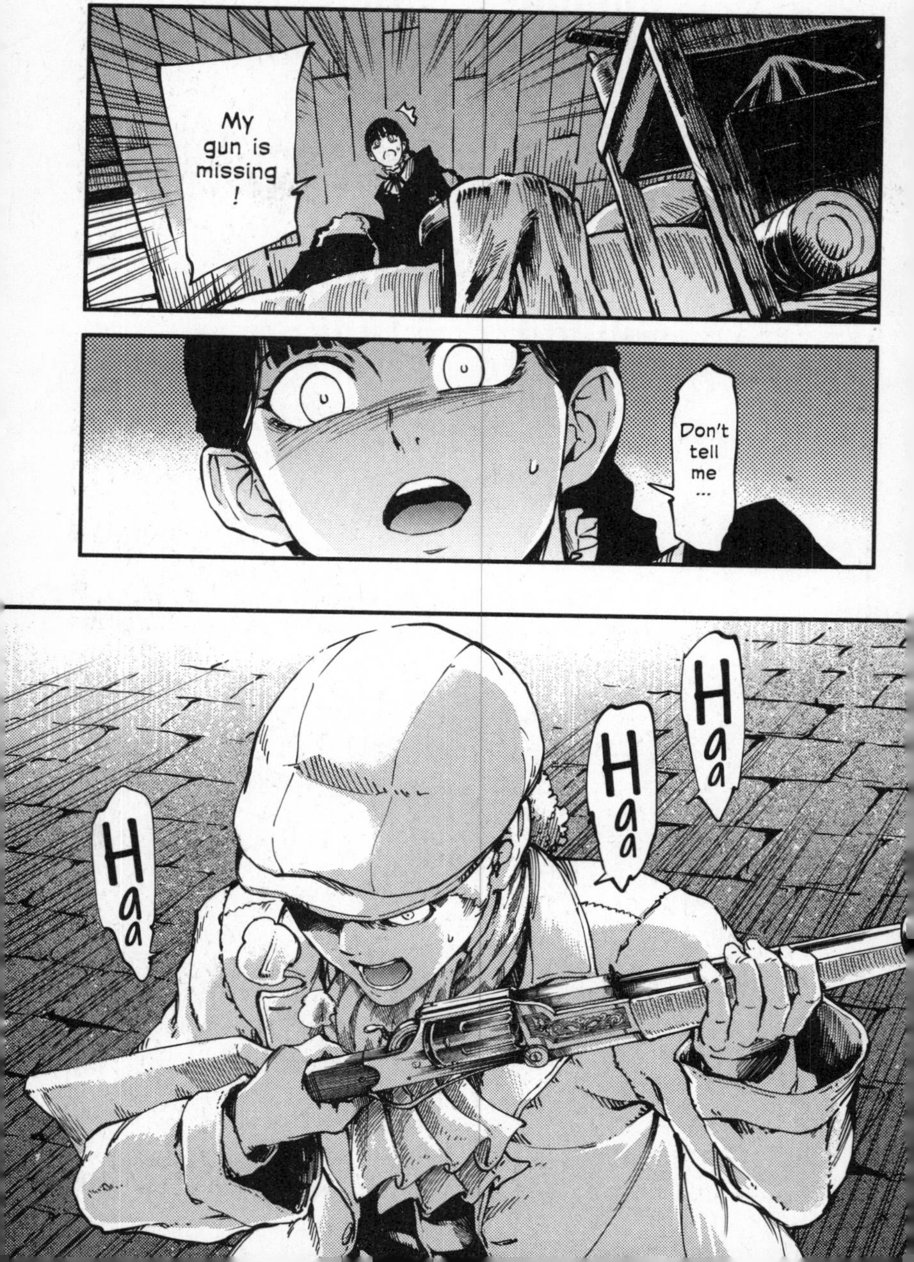
My gun is missing!
Don't tell me...
Haa
Haa
Haa

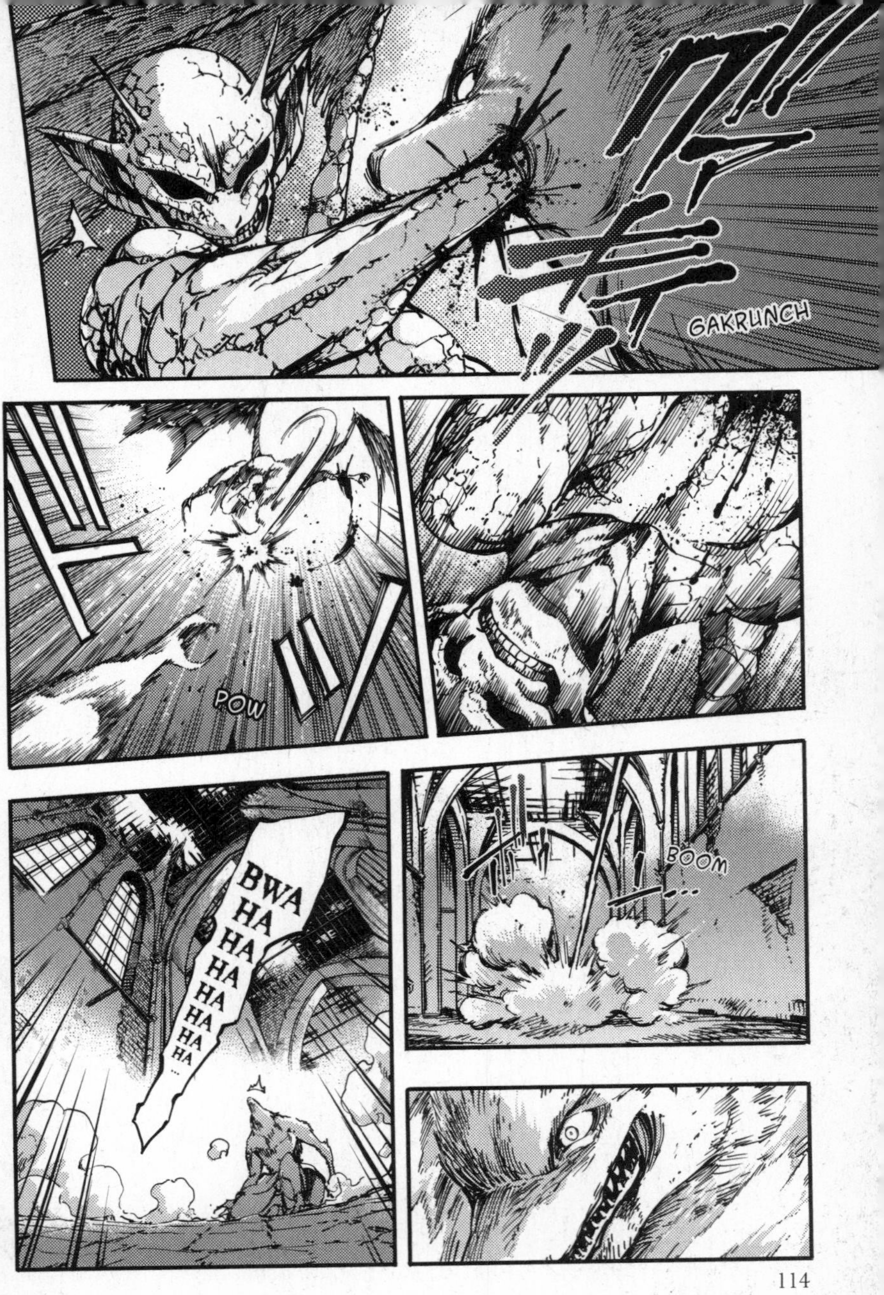
GAKRUNCH
POW
BOOM
...
BWA HA HA HA HA HA HA HA HA HA...

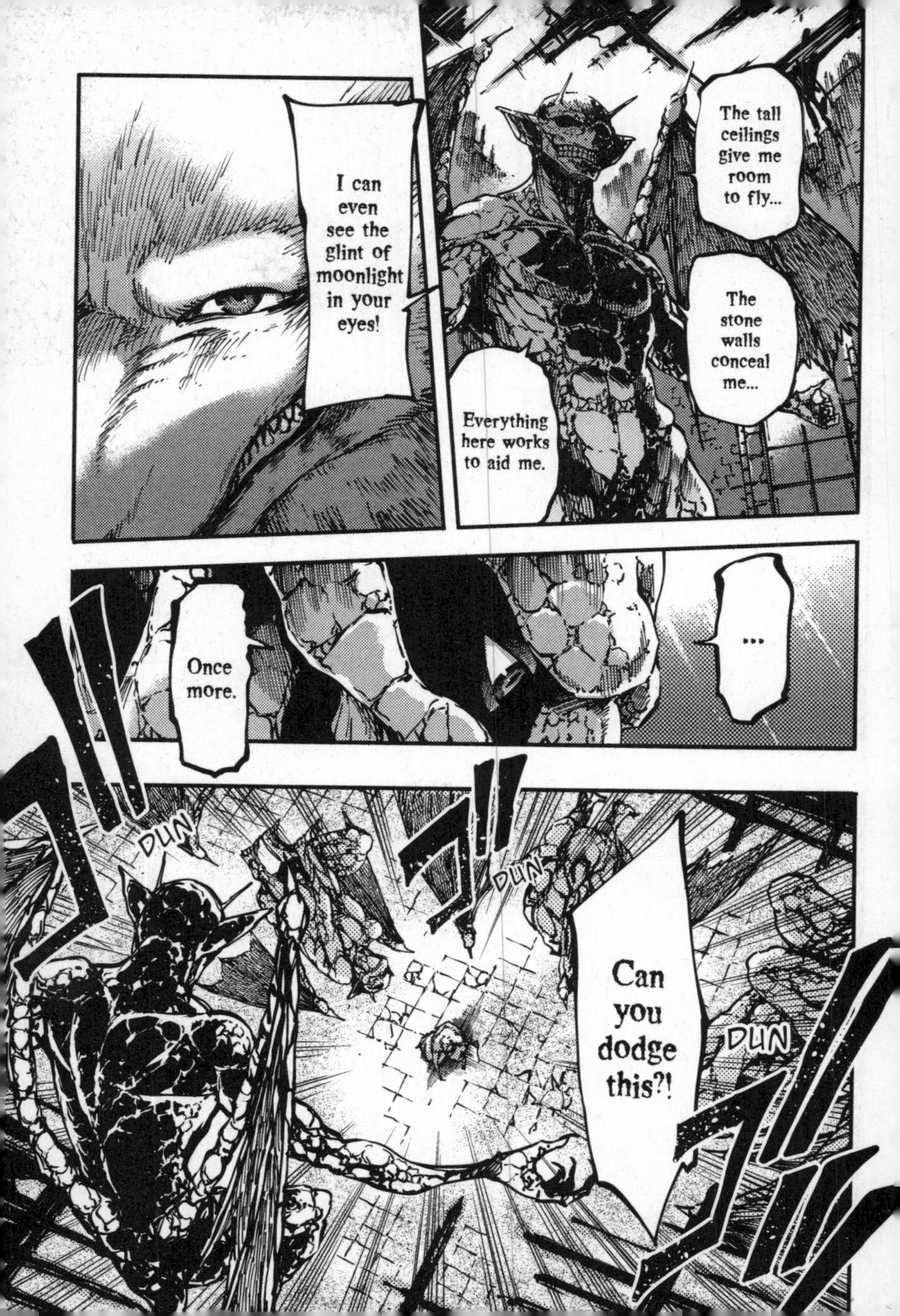

The tall ceilings give me room to fly...
The stone walls conceal me...
Everything here works to aid me.
I can even see the glint of moonlight in your eyes!
...
Once more.
DUN
DUN
Can you dodge this?!
DUN

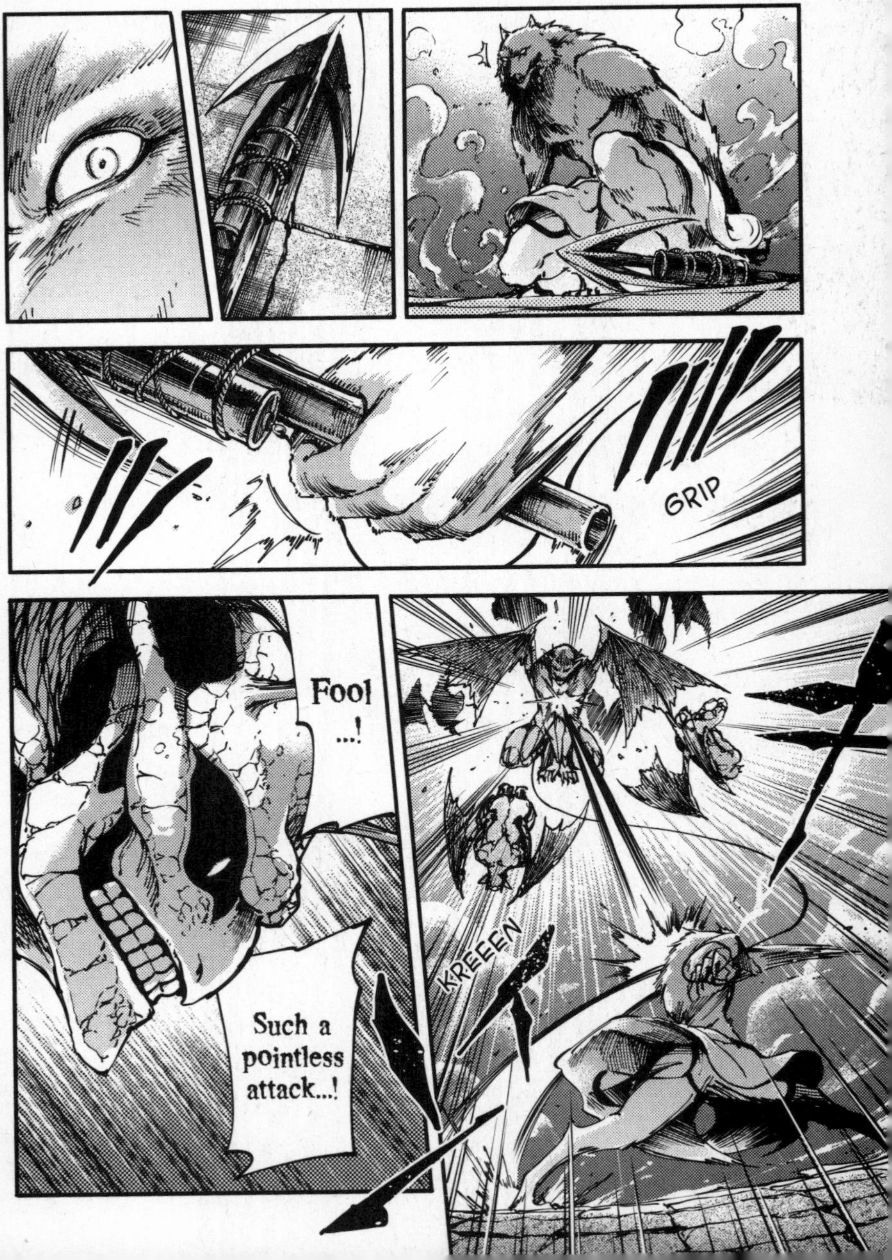
GRIP
KREEEN
Fool
...!
Such a pointless attack...!

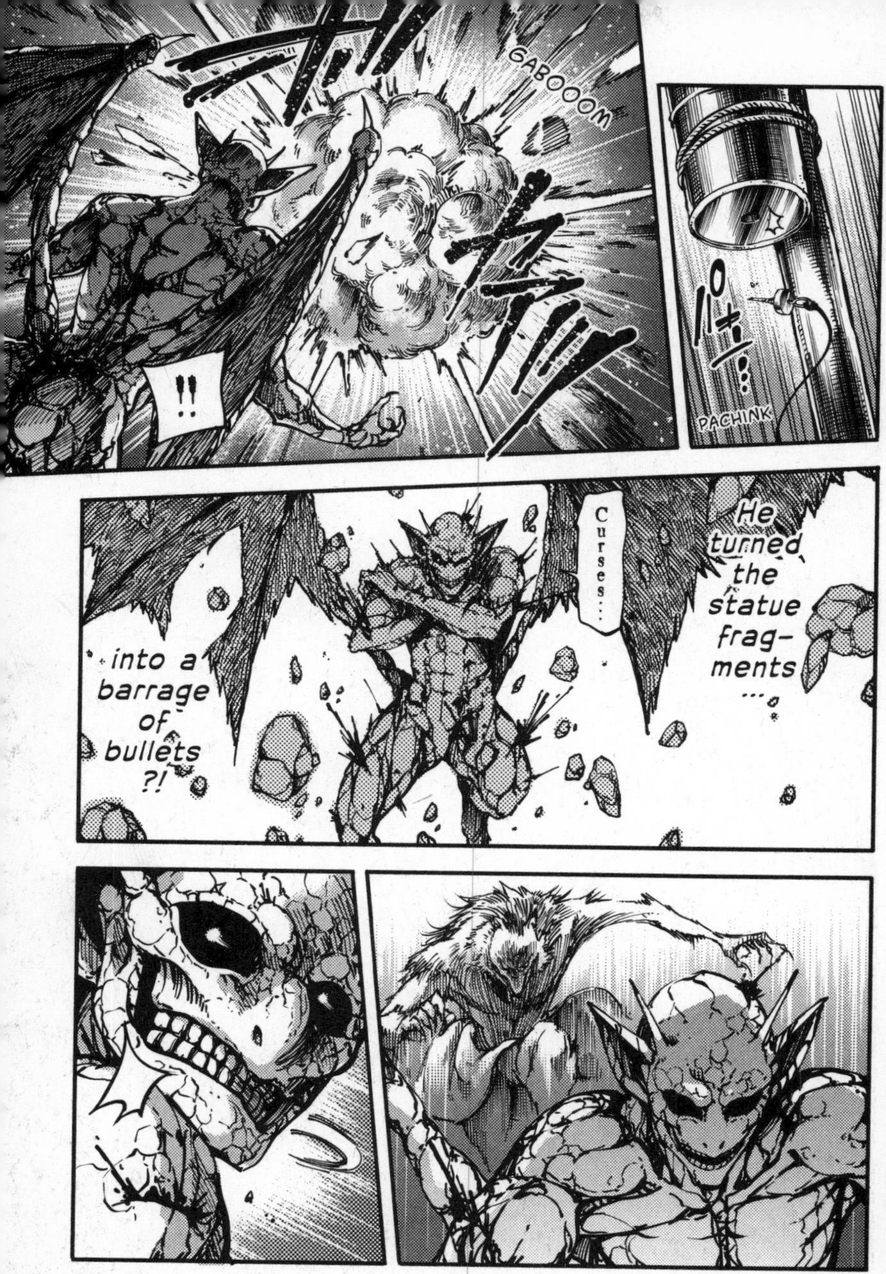
PACHINK
GABOOOM
!!
He turned the statue fragments...
Curses...
into a barrage of bullets?!

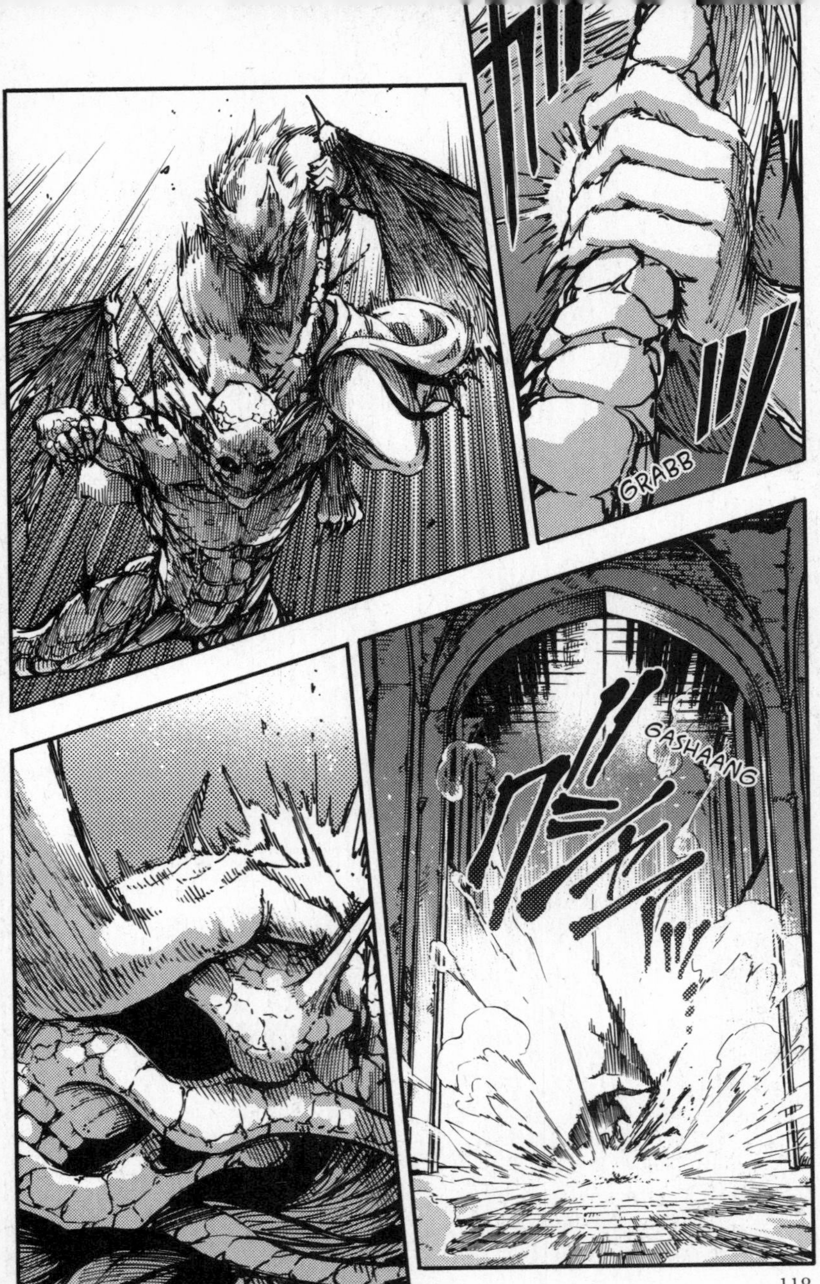
GRABB
GASHAANG

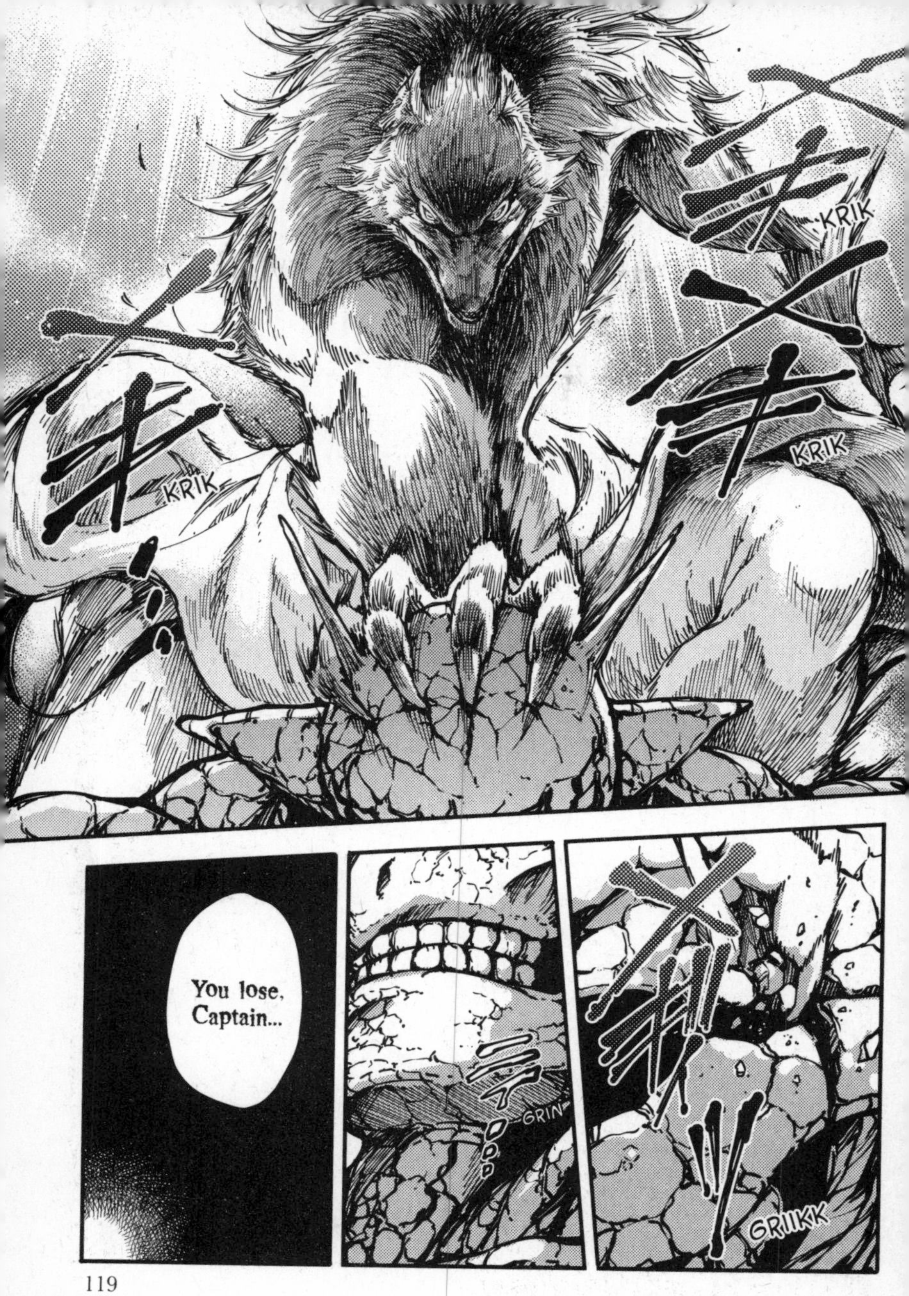
KRIK
KRIK
KRIK
GRIIKK
GRIN
You lose, Captain...

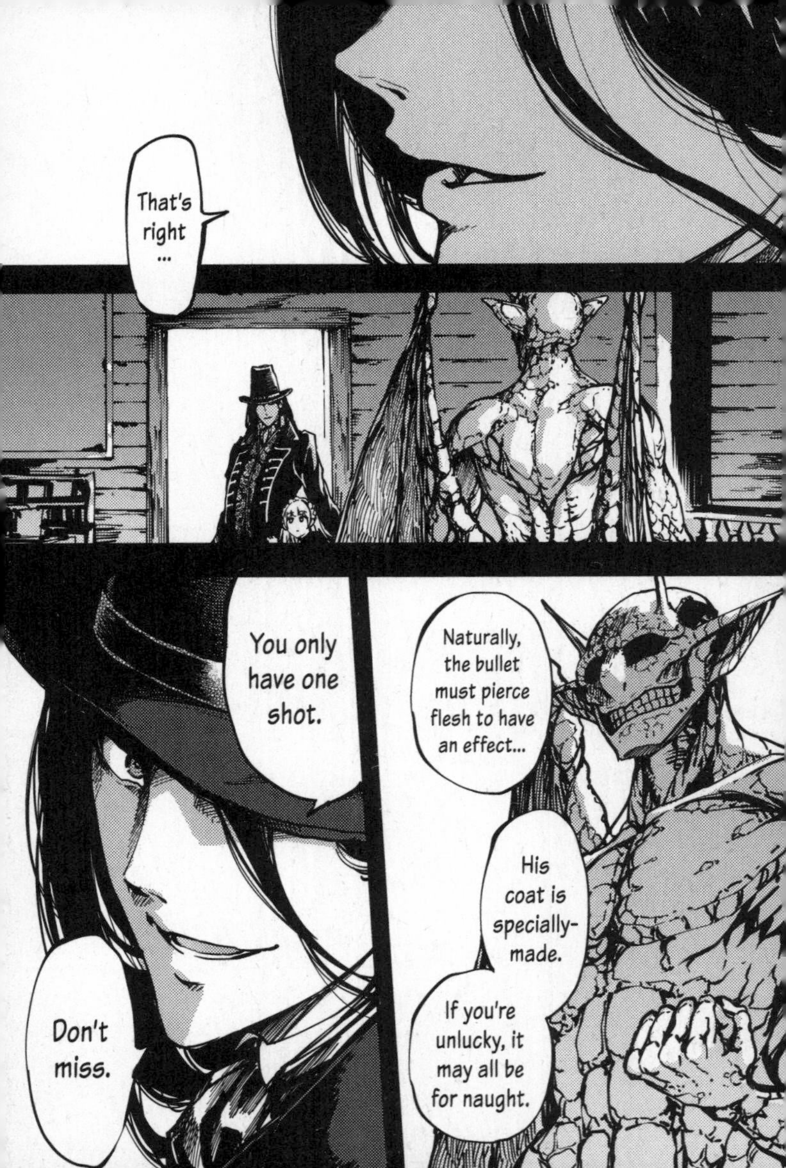
That's right ...
Naturally, the bullet must pierce flesh to have an effect...
His coat is specially-made.
If you're unlucky, it may all be for naught.
You only have one shot.
Don't miss.

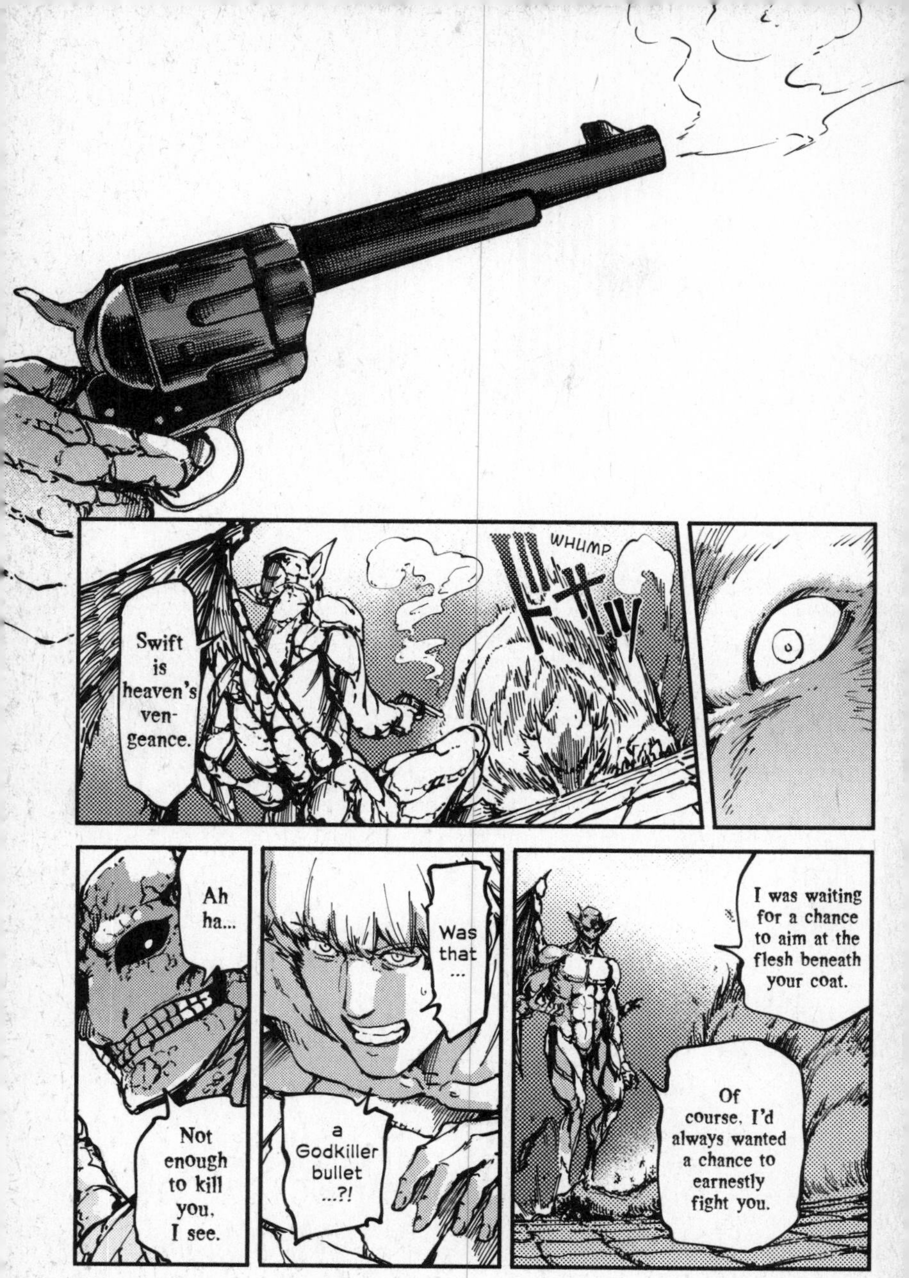
WHUMP
Swift is heaven's vengeance.
I was waiting for a chance to aim at the flesh beneath your coat.
Of course, I'd always wanted a chance to earnestly fight you.
Was that ...
a GodKiller bullet ...?!
Ah ha...
Not enough to kill you, I see.

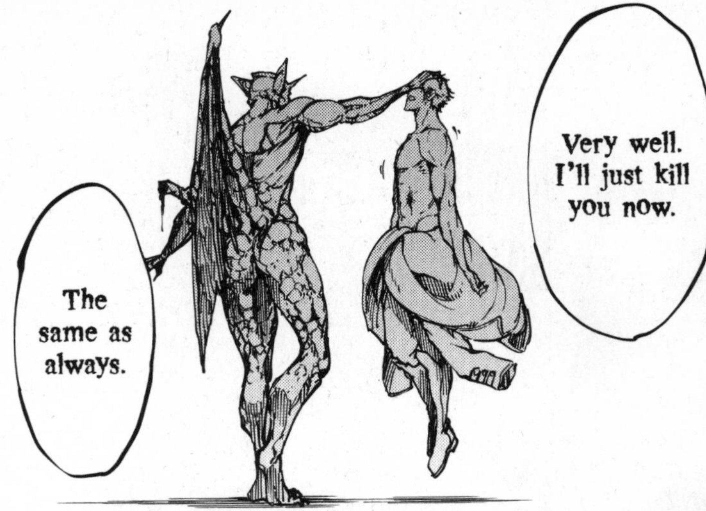
Very well. I'll just kill you now.
The same as always.

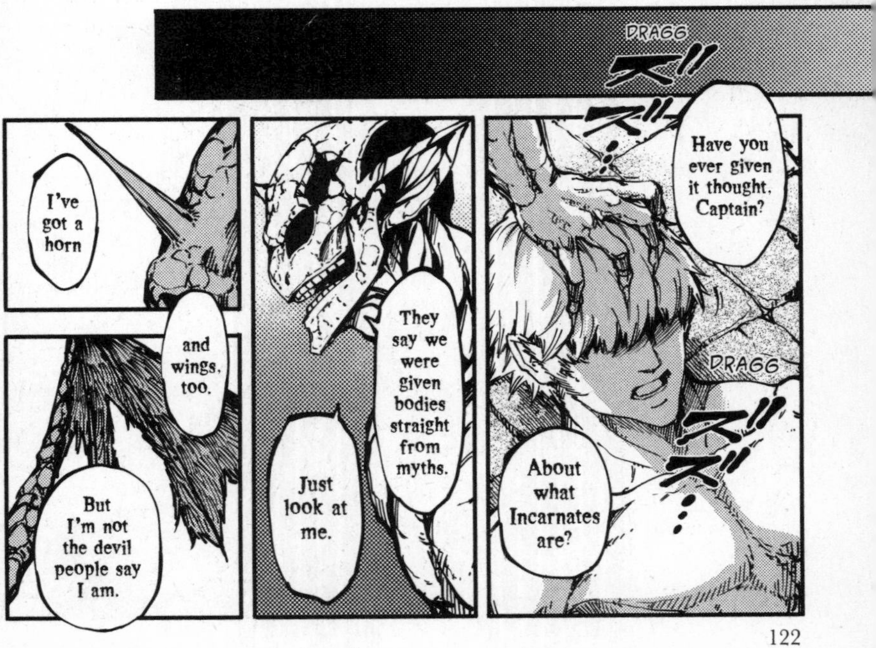
DRAGG
Have you ever given it thought, Captain?
DRAGG
About what Incarnates are?
They say we were given bodies straight from myths.
Just look at me.
I've got a horn
and wings, too.
But I'm not the devil people say I am.

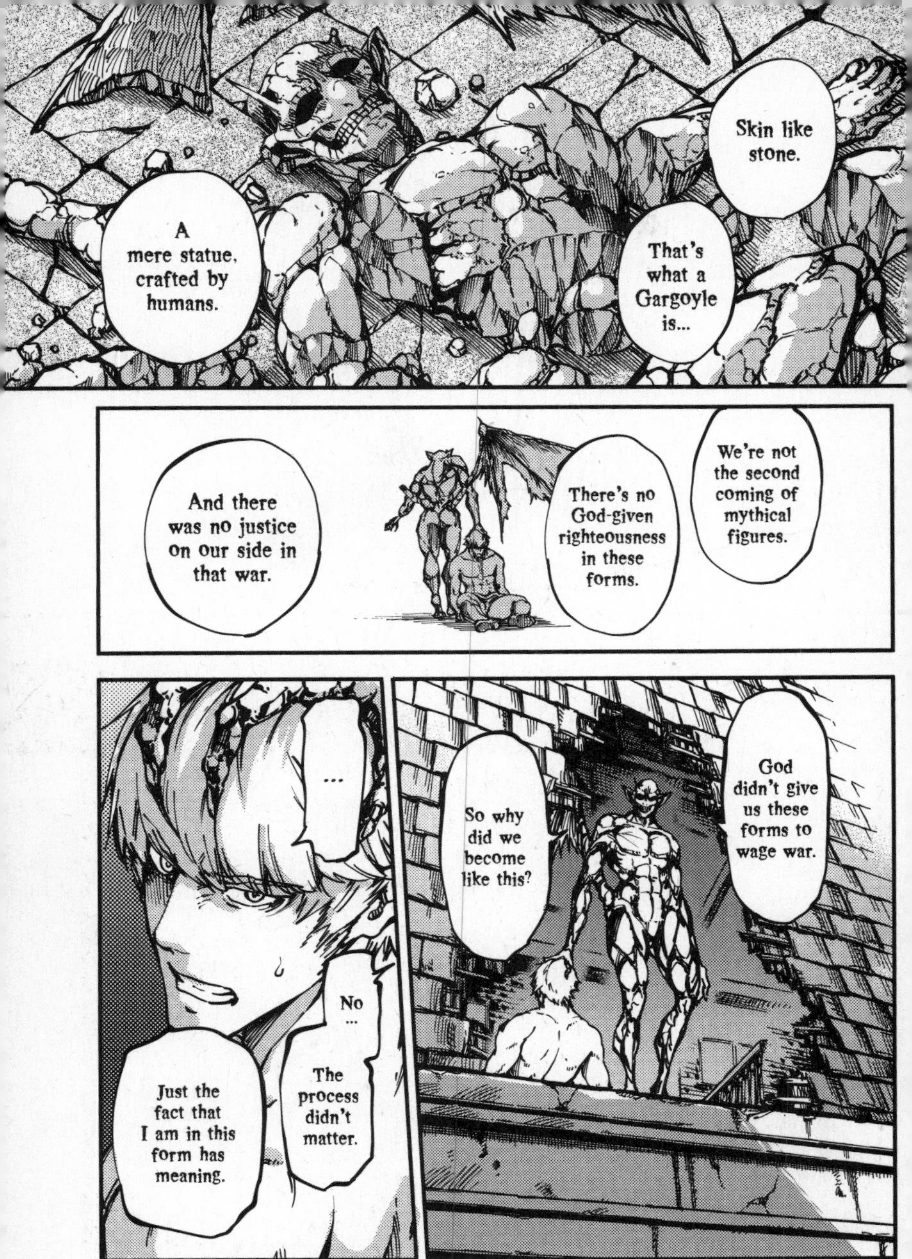
Skin like stone.
That's what a Gargoyle is...
A mere statue, crafted by humans.
We're not the second coming of mythical figures.
There's no God-given righteousness in these forms.
And there was no justice on our side in that war.
God didn't give us these forms to wage war.
So why did we become like this?
...
No ...
The process didn't matter.
Just the fact that I am in this form has meaning.

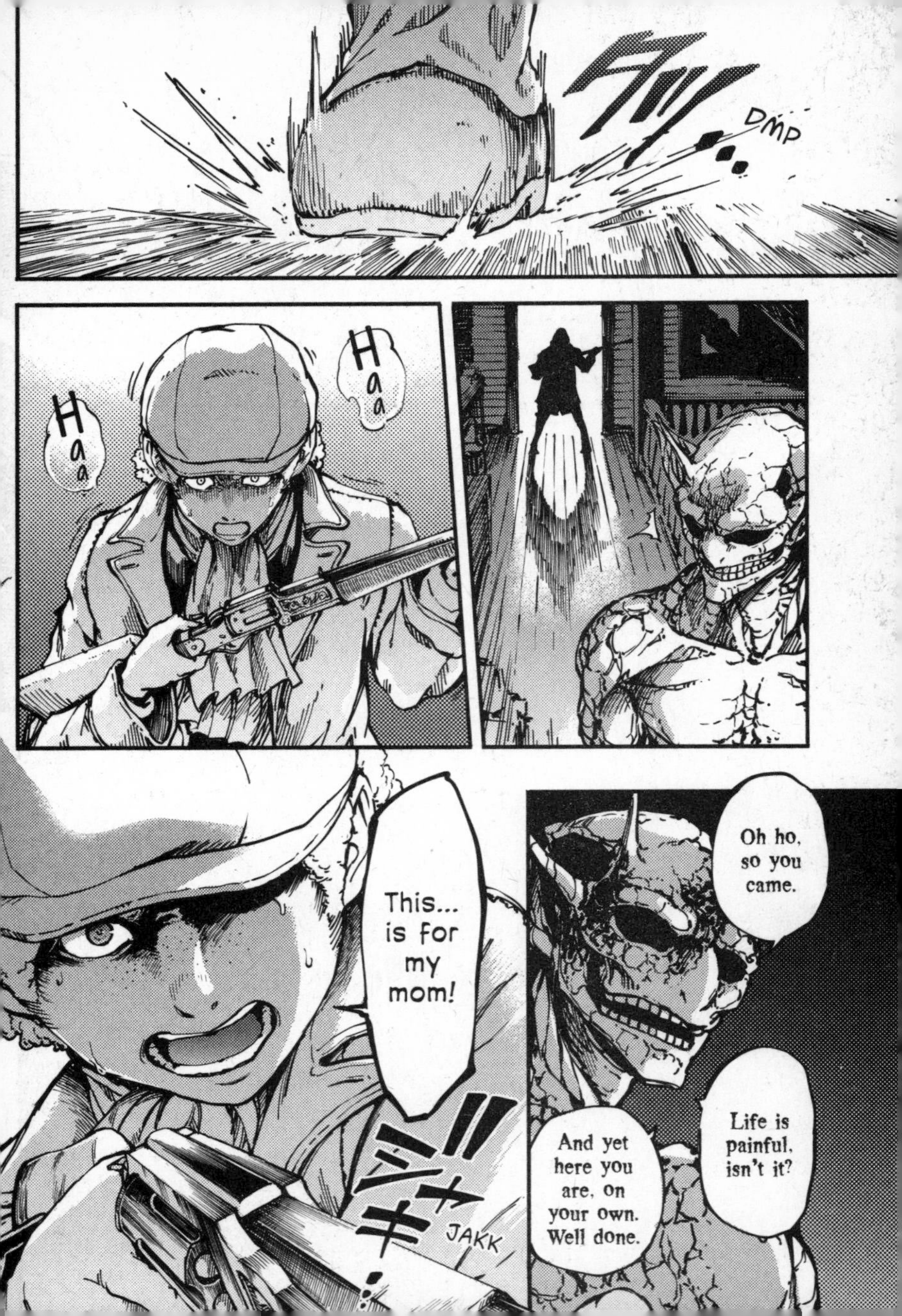
DMP
Haa
Haa
Oh ho, so you came.
Life is painful, isn't it?
And yet here you are, on your own. Well done.
This... is for my mom!
JAKK

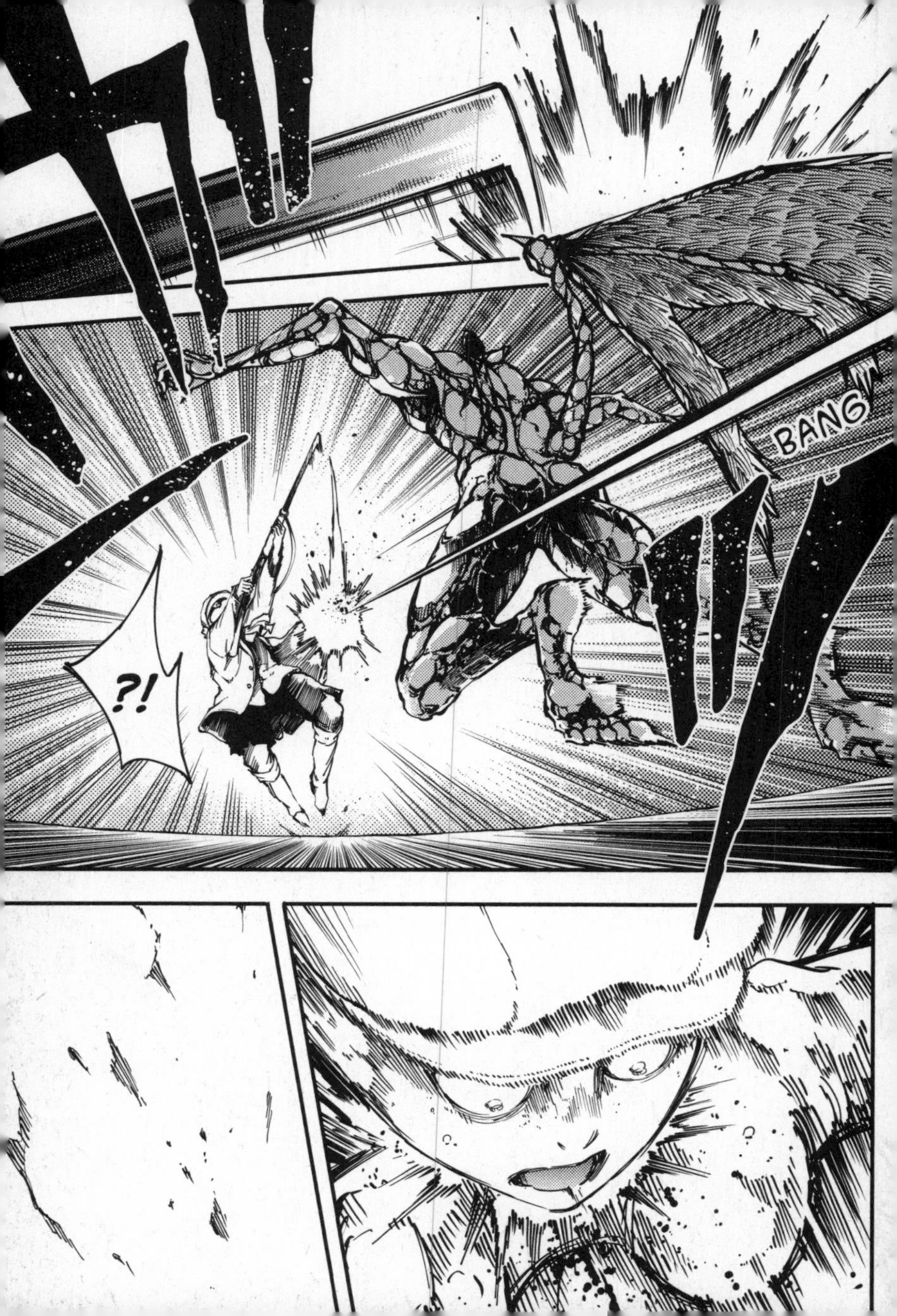
BANG
?!

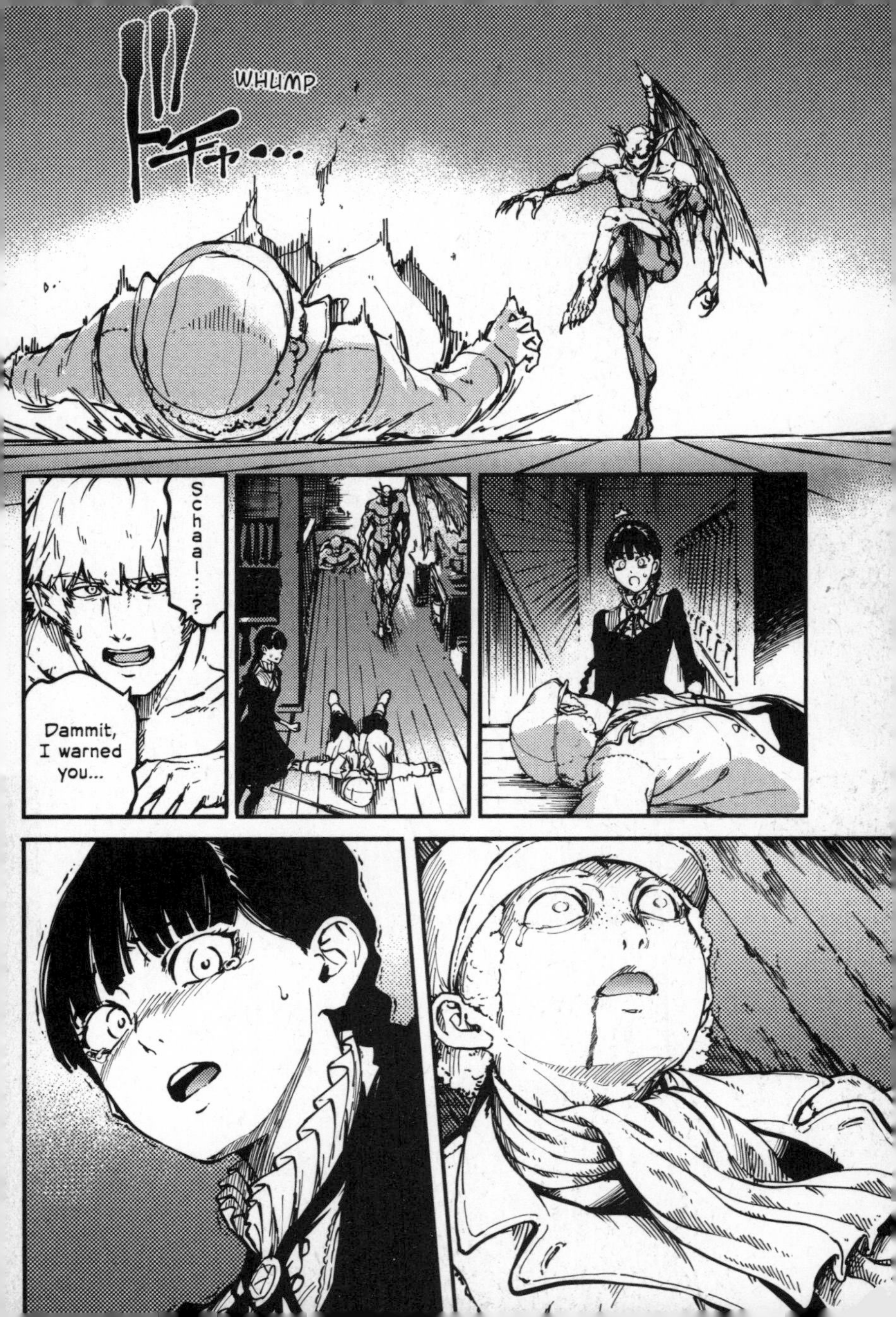
ドチャ...
WHUMP
Schaal...?
Dammit, I warned you...

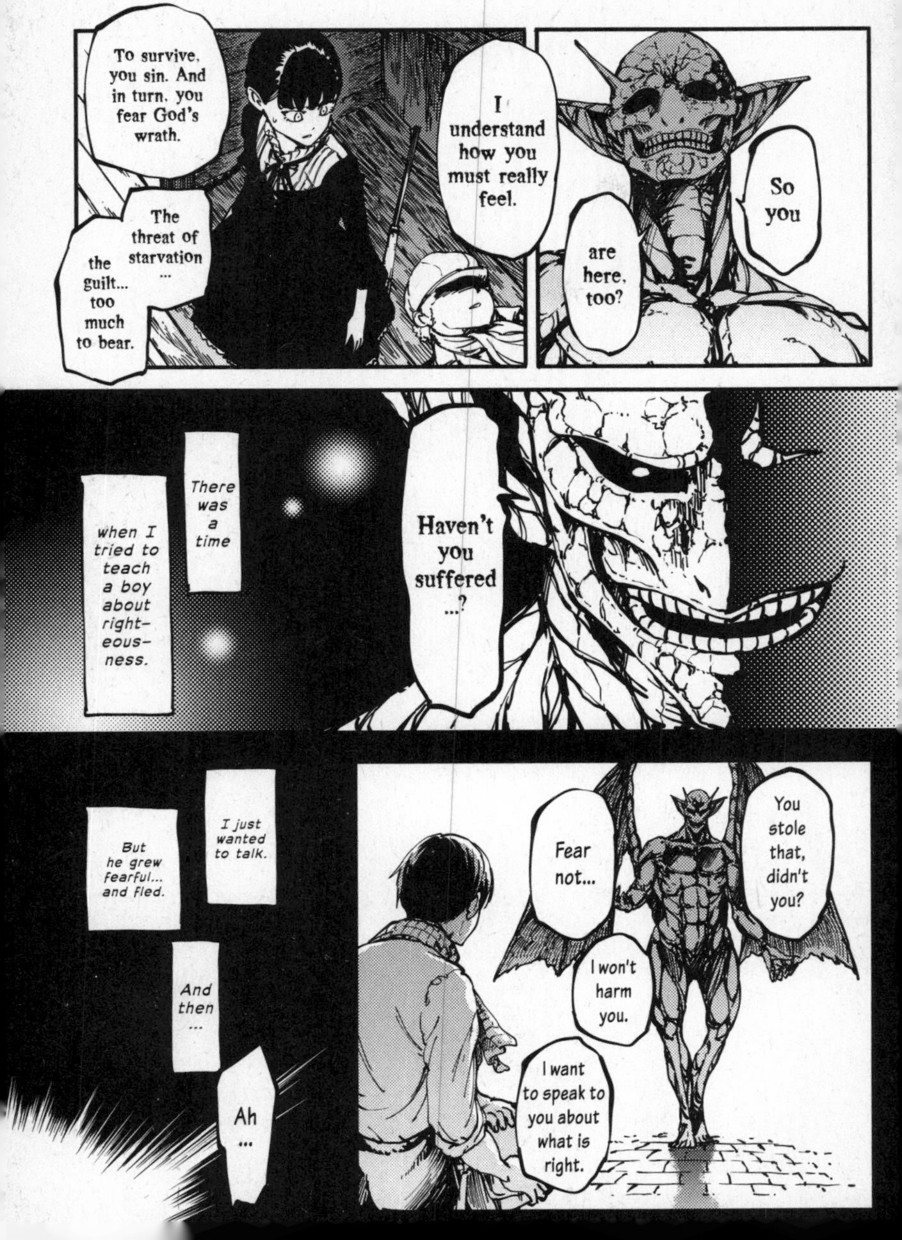
So you
are here, too?
I understand how you must really feel.
To survive, you sin. And in turn, you fear God's wrath.
The threat of starvation ...
the guilt... too much to bear.
Haven't you suffered ...?
There was a time
when I tried to teach a boy about right- eous- ness.
You stole that, didn't you?
Fear not...
I won't harm you.
I want to speak to you about what is right.
I just wanted to talk.
But he grew fearful... and fled.
And then ...
Ah ...

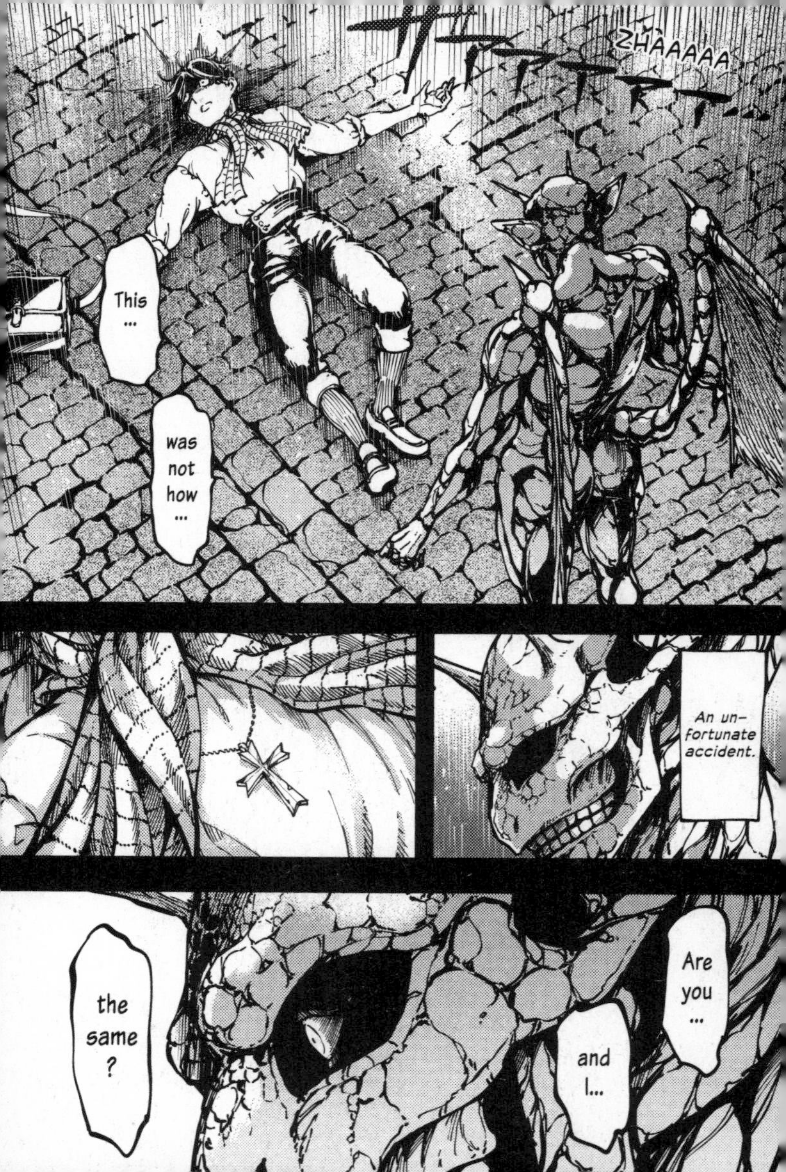
ZHAAAAA
This ...
was not how ...
An unfortunate accident.
Are you ...
and I...
the same ?

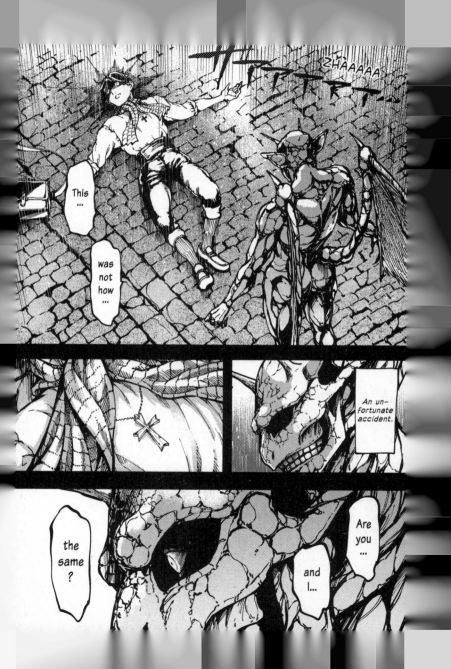

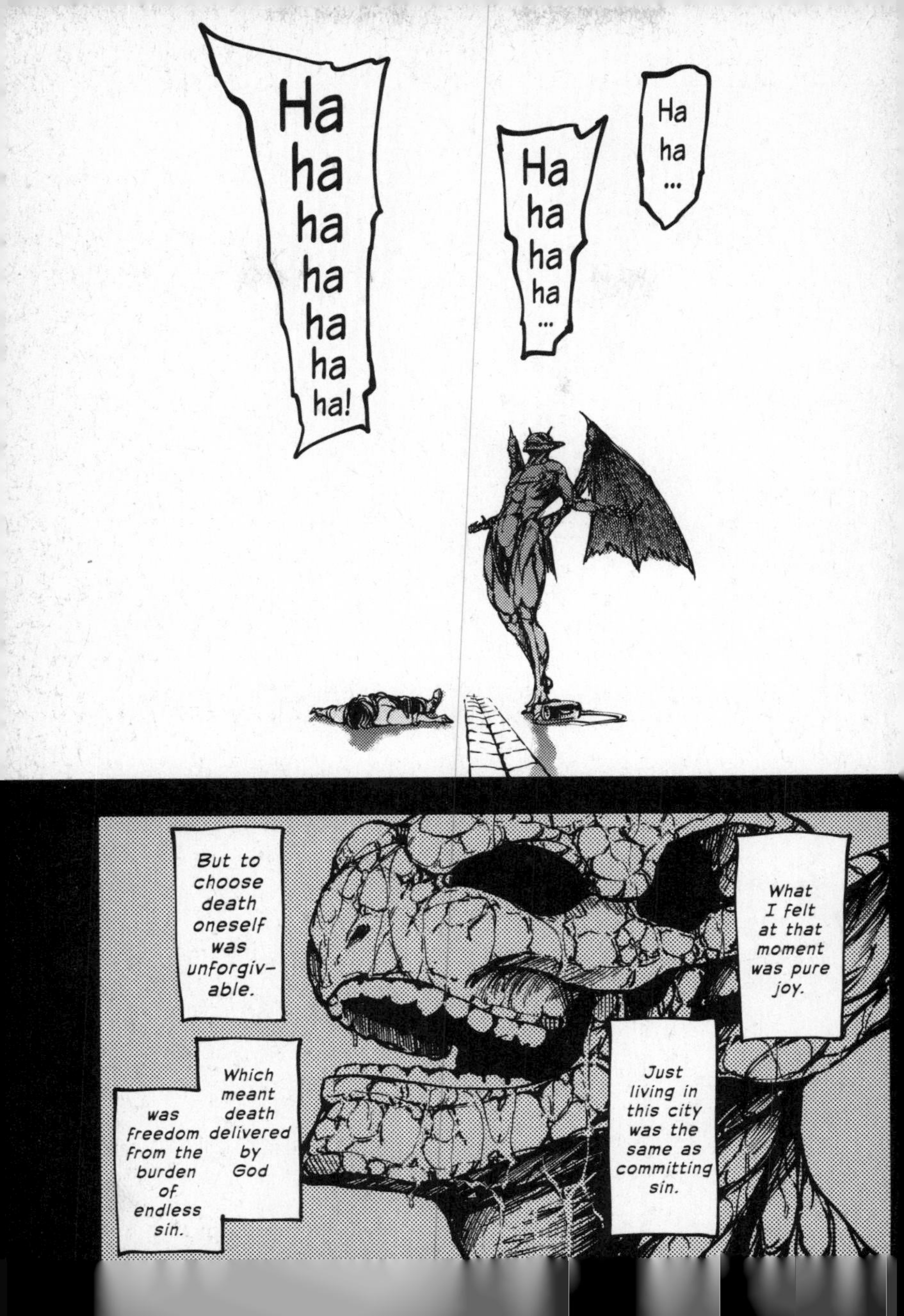
Ha ha ...
Ha ha ha ha ...
Ha ha ha ha ha ha ha!
What I felt at that moment was pure joy.
Just living in this city was the same as committing sin.
But to choose death oneself was unforgivable.
Which meant death delivered by God
was freedom from the burden of endless sin.

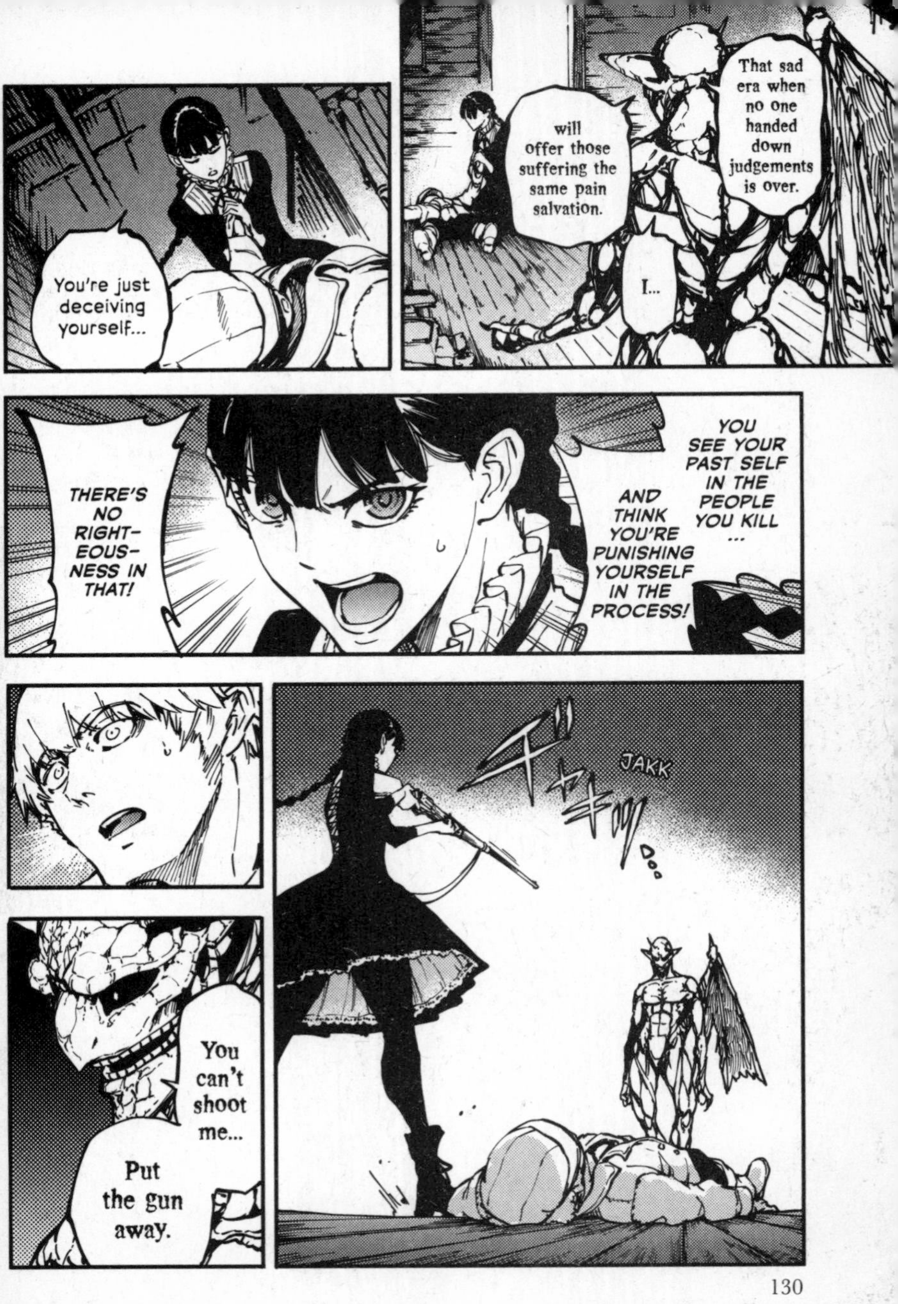
That sad era when no one handed down judgements is over.
I...
will offer those suffering the same pain salvation.
You're just deceiving yourself...
YOU SEE YOUR PAST SELF IN THE PEOPLE YOU KILL ...
AND THINK YOU'RE PUNISHING YOURSELF IN THE PROCESS!
THERE'S NO RIGHT-EOUS-NESS IN THAT!
JAKK
You can't shoot me...
Put the gun away.

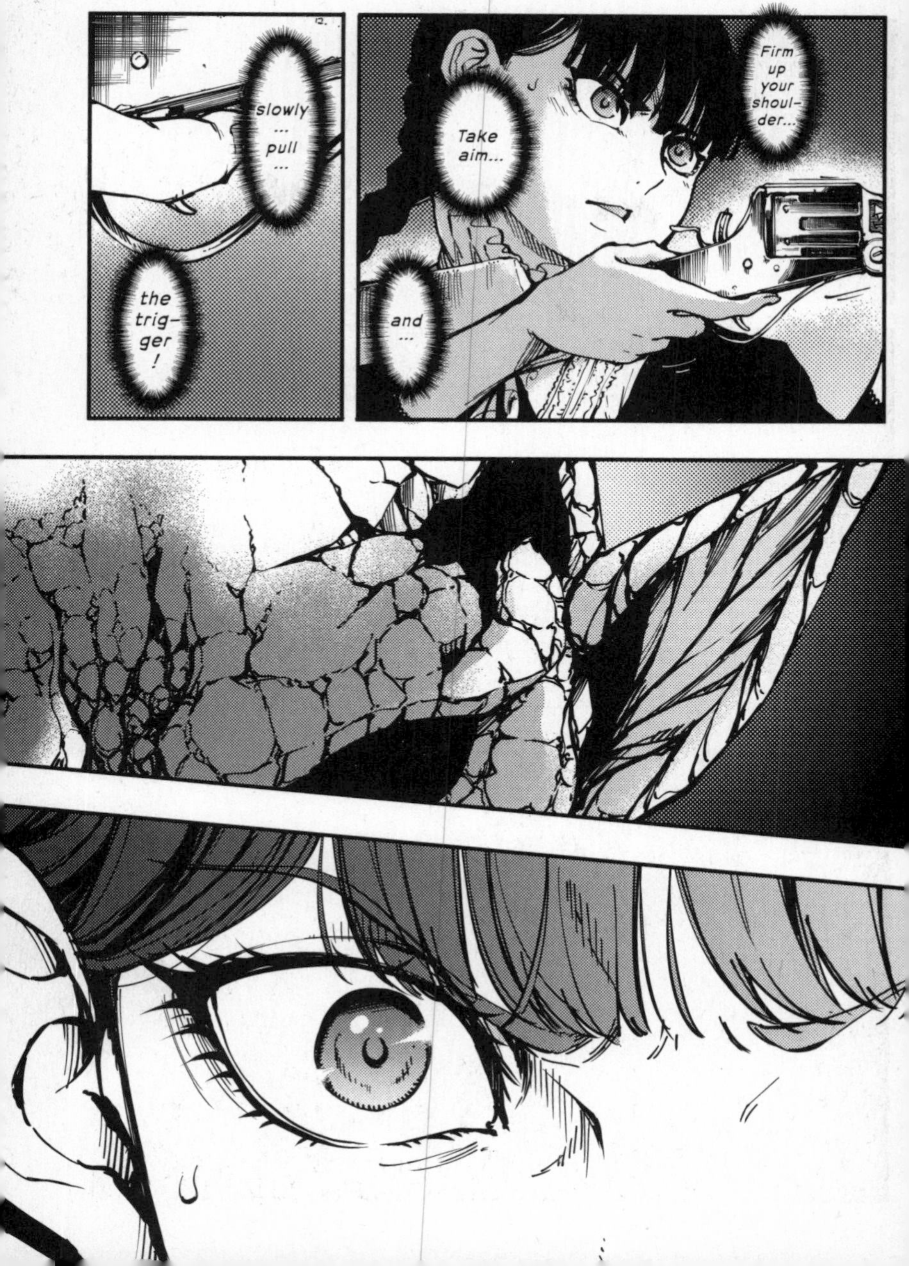
Firm up your shoul-der...
Take aim...
and ...
slowly ... pull ...
the trig-ger !

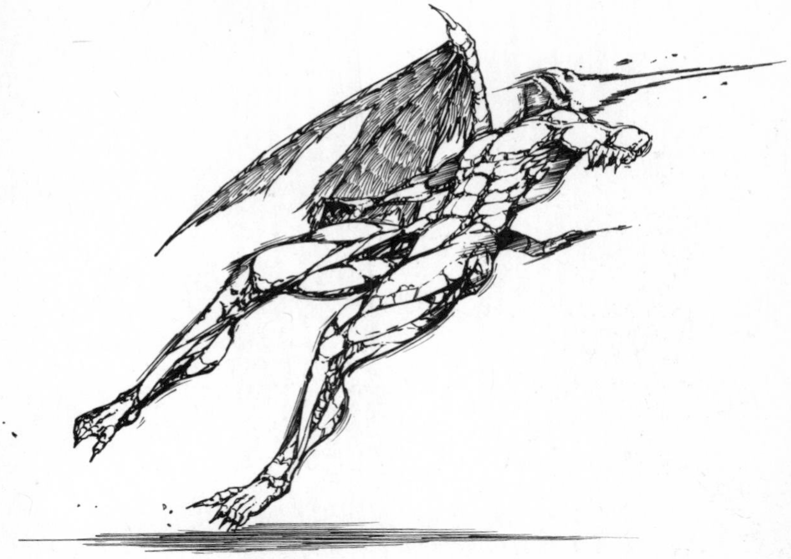

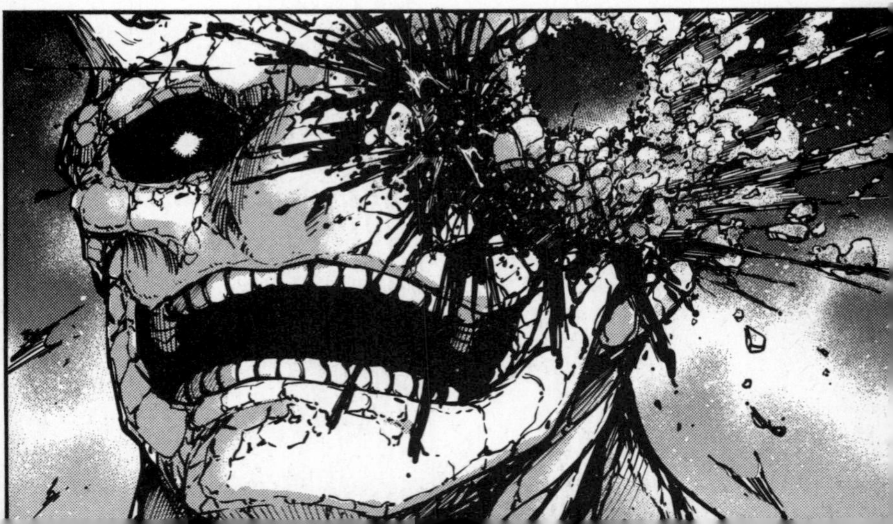

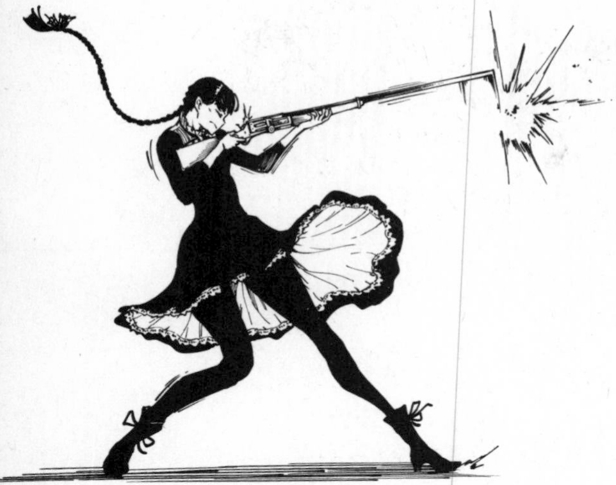

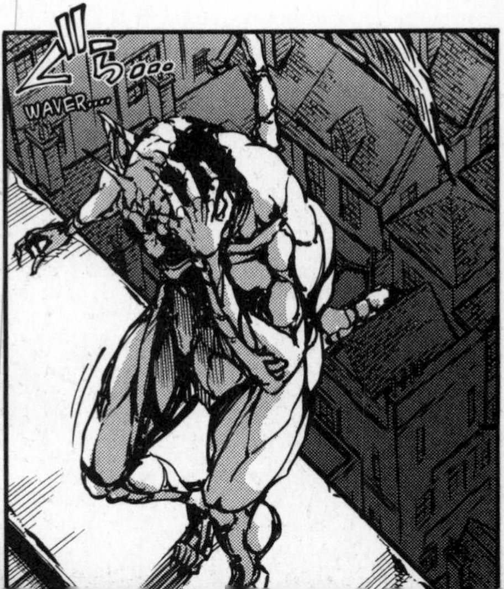
ぐら...
WAVER....

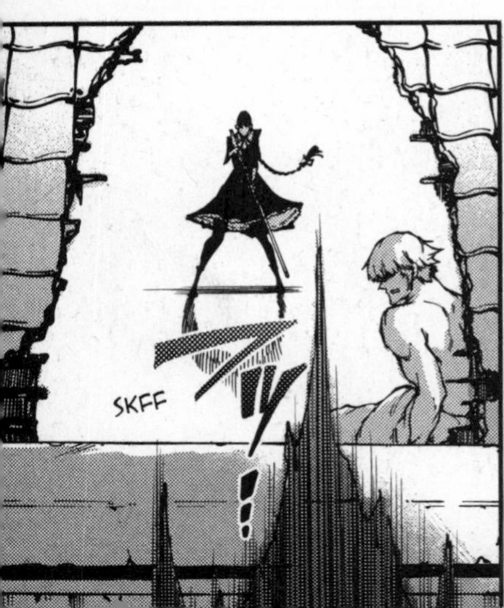
SKFF

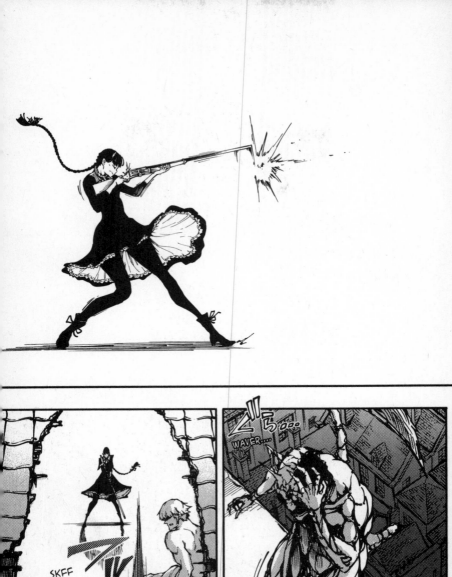

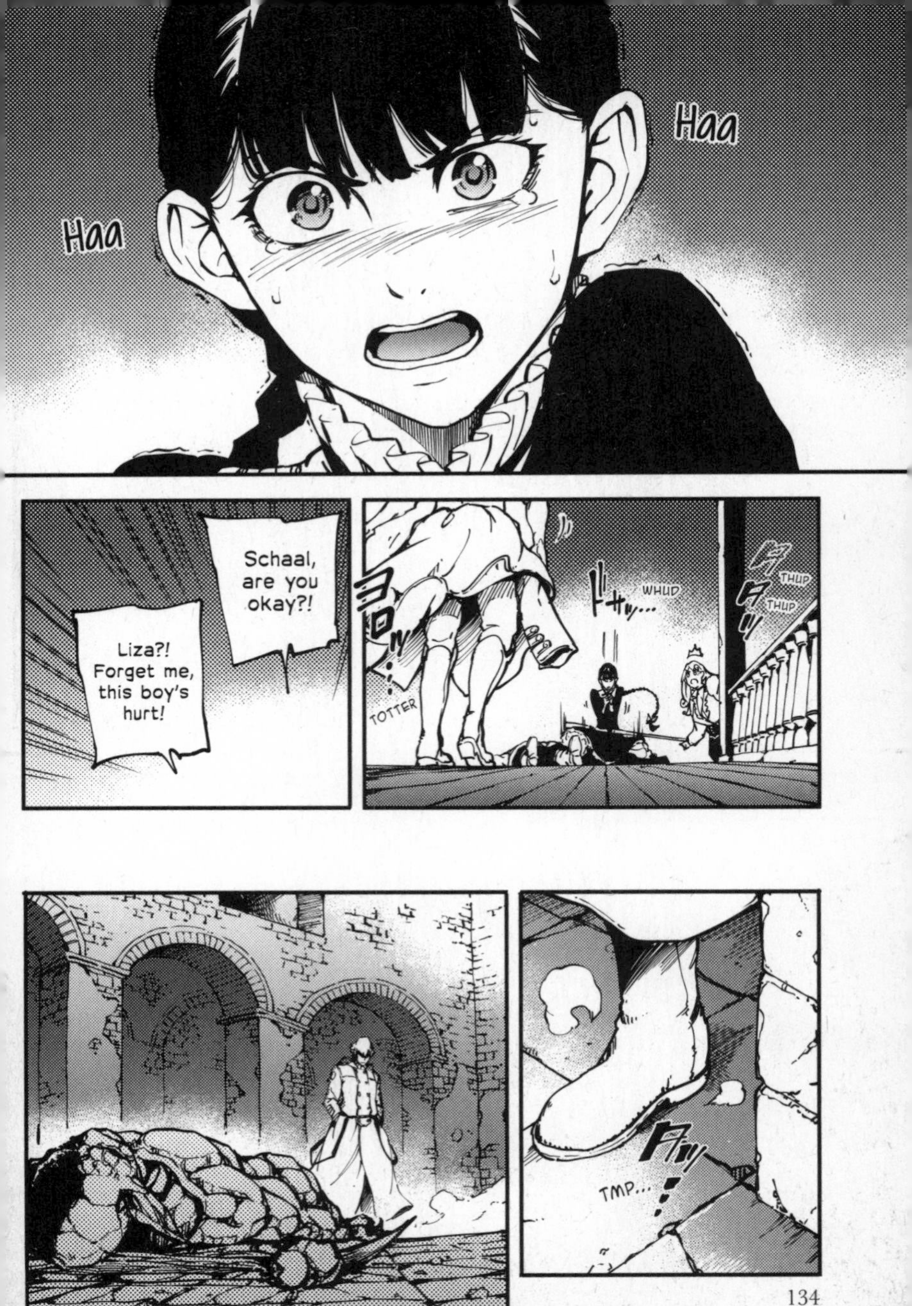
Haa
Haa
THUP
THUP
WHUD...
TOTTER
Schaal, are you okay?!
Liza?! Forget me, this boy's hurt!
TMP...

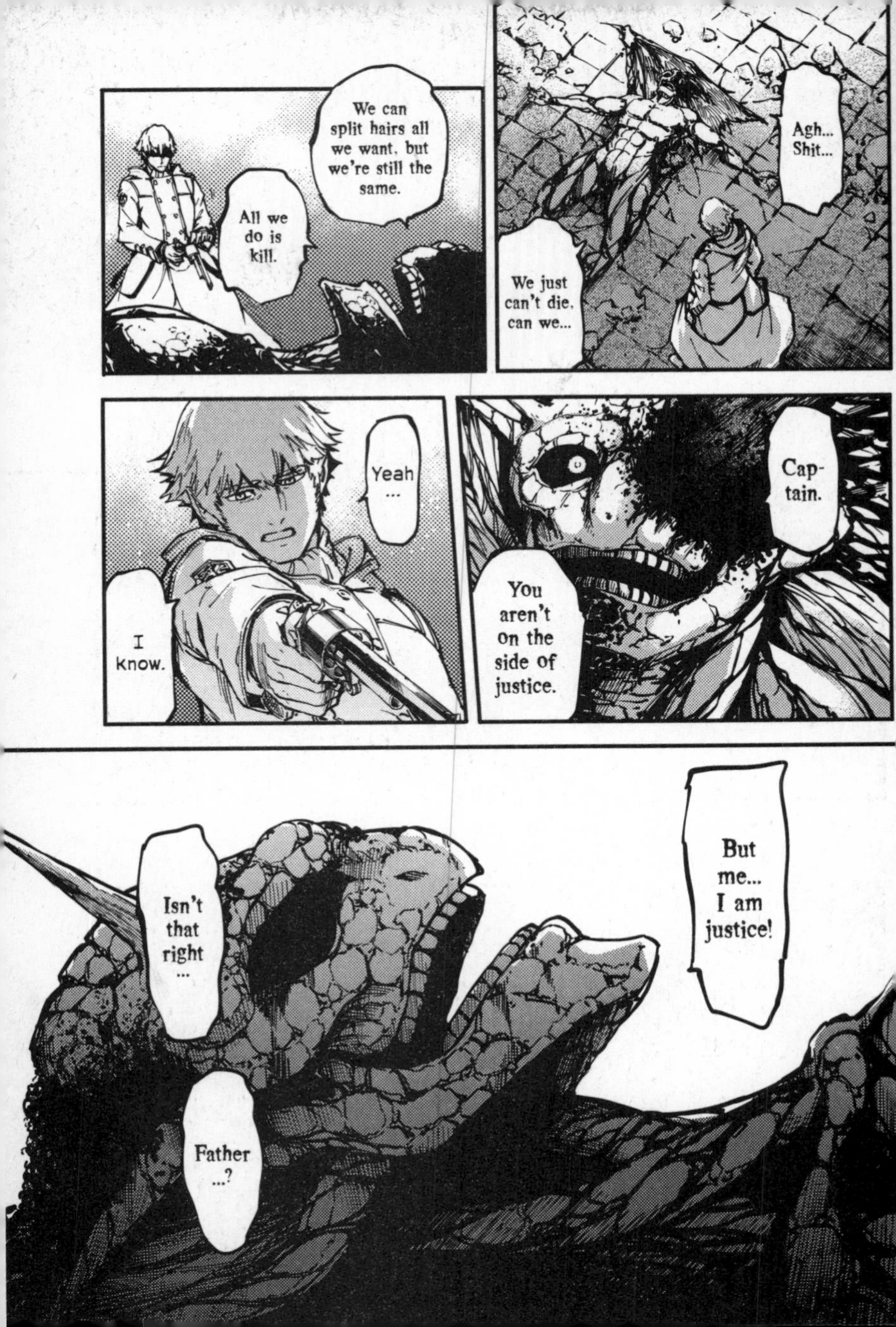
Agh... Shit...
We just can't die, can we...
We can split hairs all we want, but we're still the same.
All we do is kill.
Cap-tain.
You aren't on the side of justice.
Yeah ...
I know.
But me... I am justice!
Isn't that right ...
Father ...?

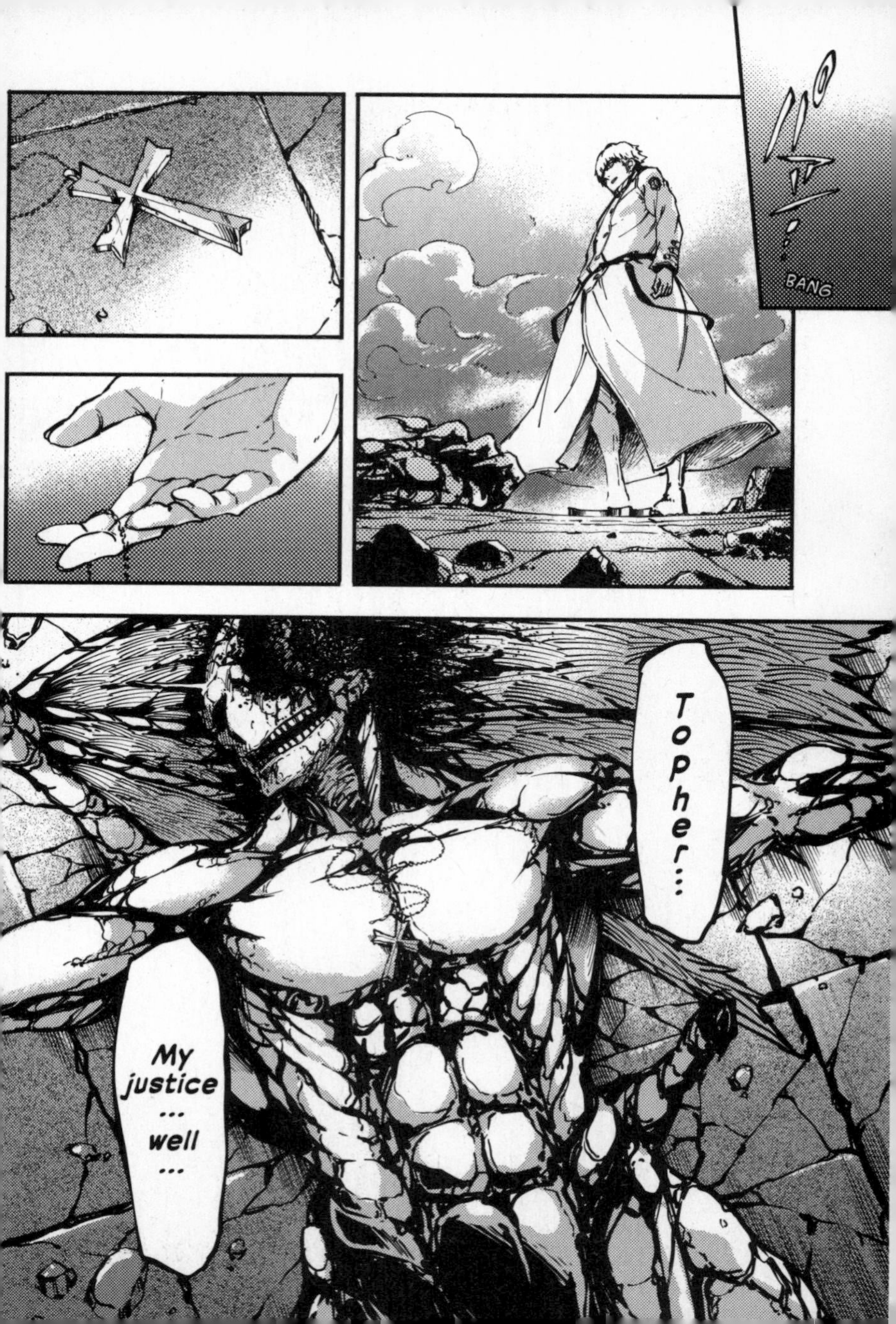
BANG
Topher...
My justice ... well ...

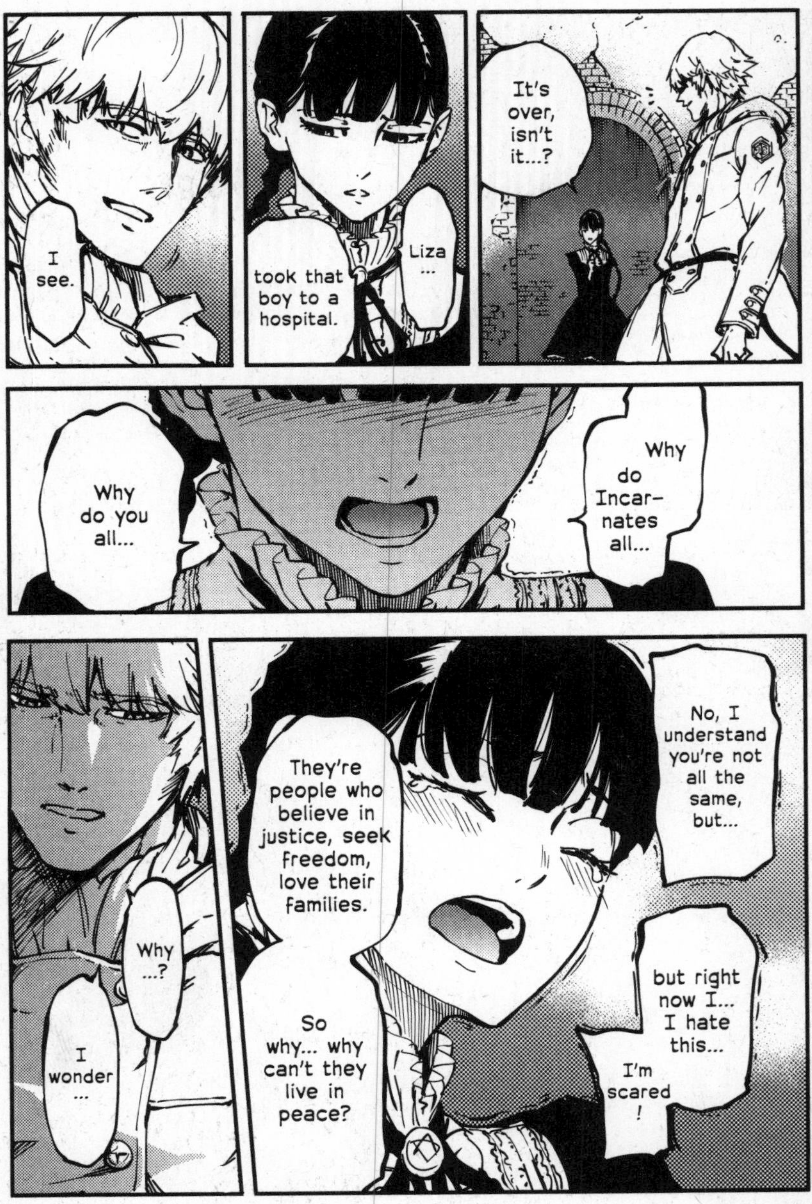
It's over, isn't it...?
Liza ...
took that boy to a hospital.
I see.
Why do Incar-nates all...
Why do you all...
No, I understand you're not all the same, but...
They're people who believe in justice, seek freedom, love their families.
but right now I... I hate this...
I'm scared!
So why... why can't they live in peace?
Why ...?
I wonder ...

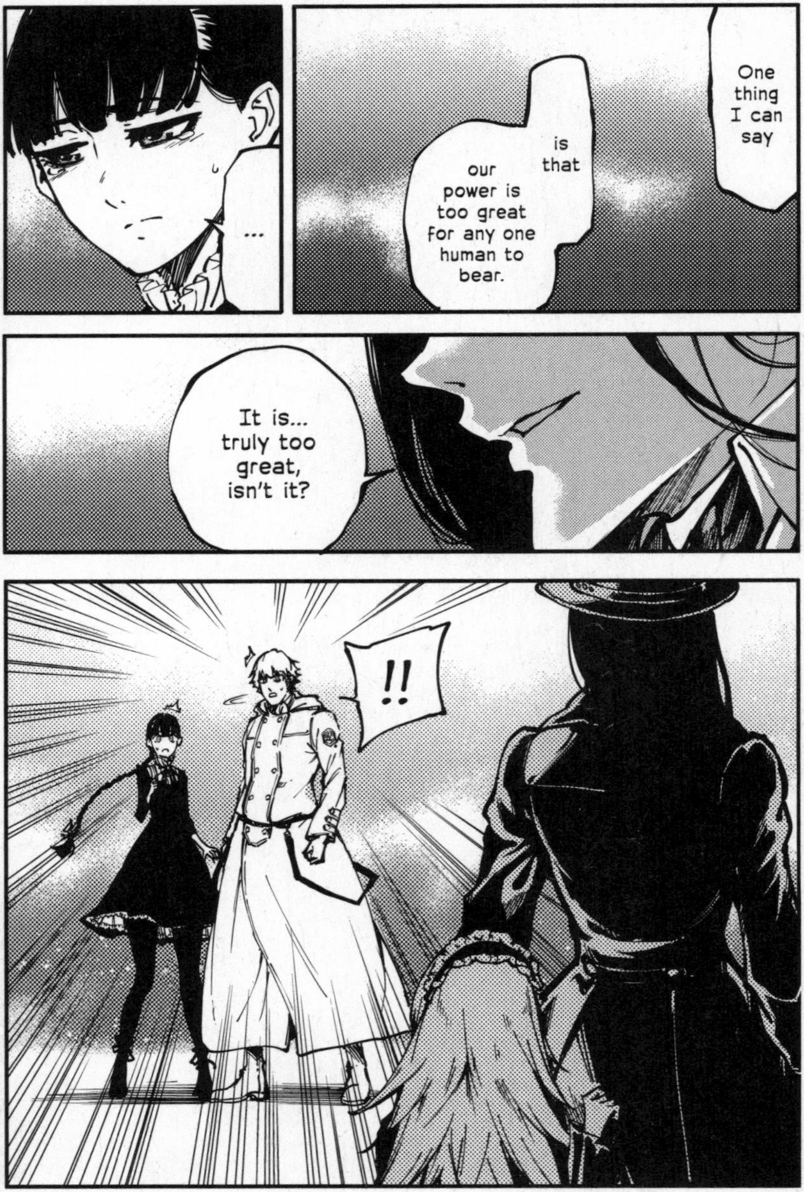
One thing I can say
is that
our power is too great for any one human to bear.
...
It is... truly too great, isn't it?
!!

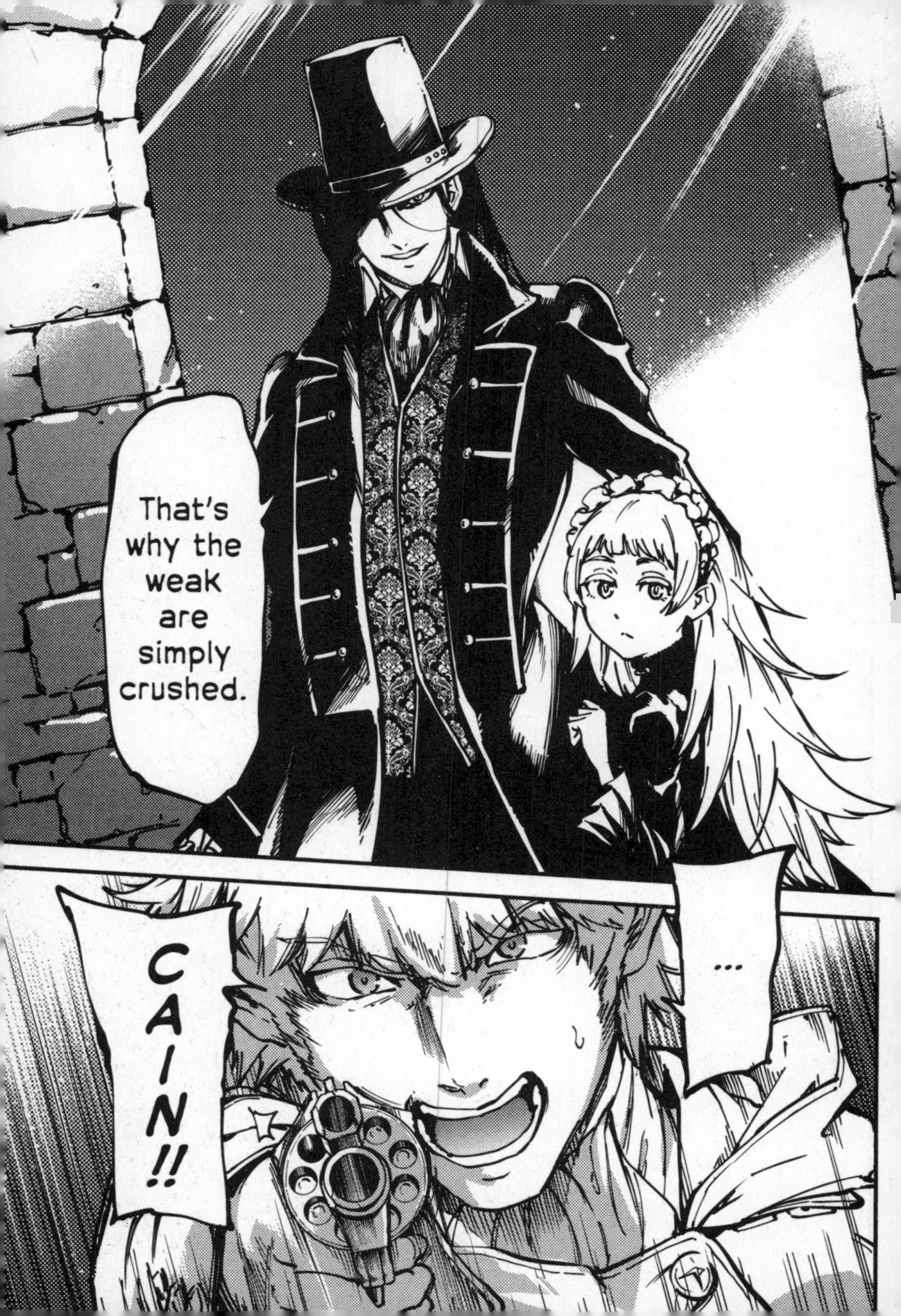
That's why the weak are simply crushed.
...
CAIN!!

To the Abandoned
Sacred Beasts

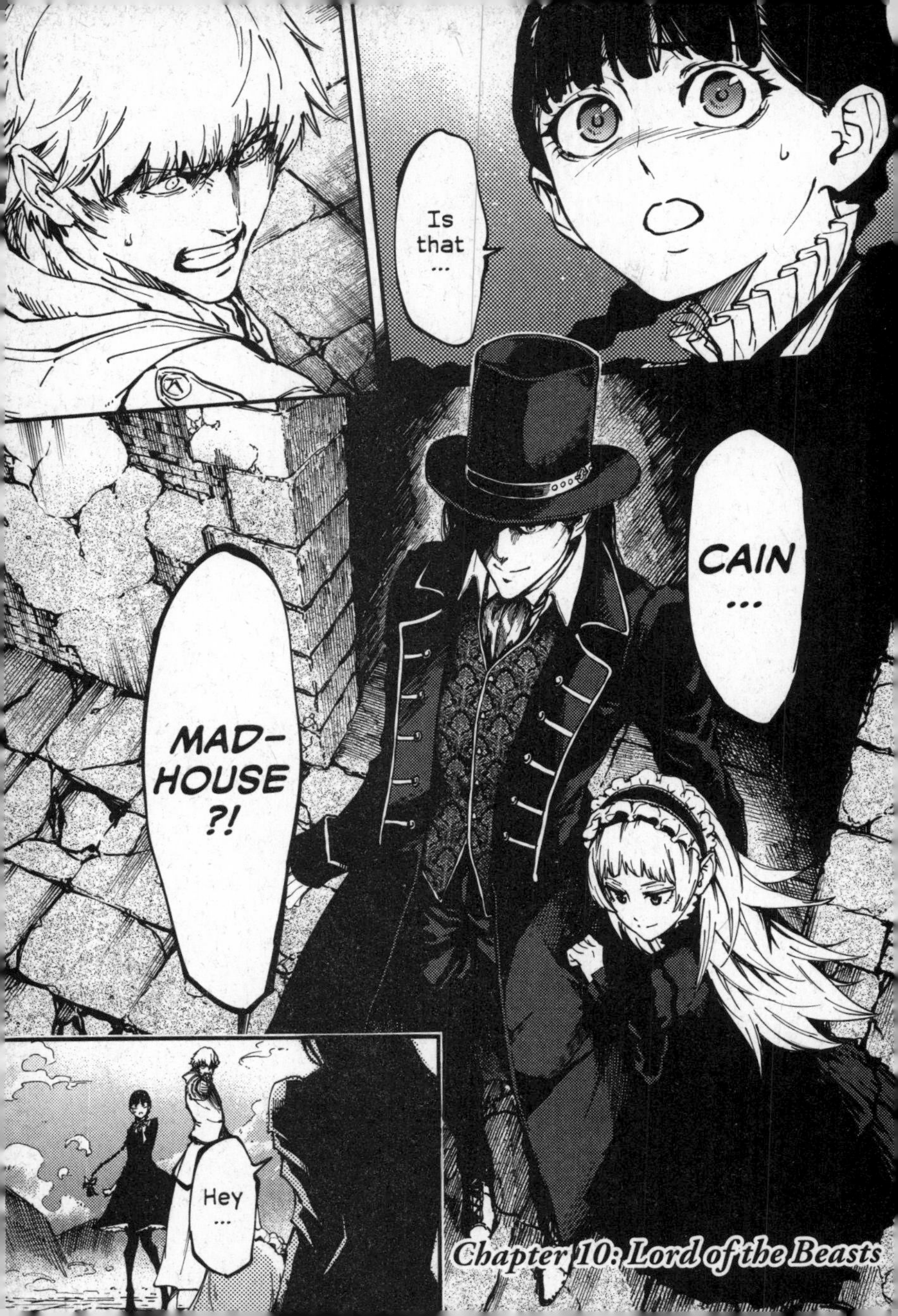
Is that ...
CAIN ...
MAD-HOUSE ?!
Chapter 10: Lord of the Beasts
Hey ...

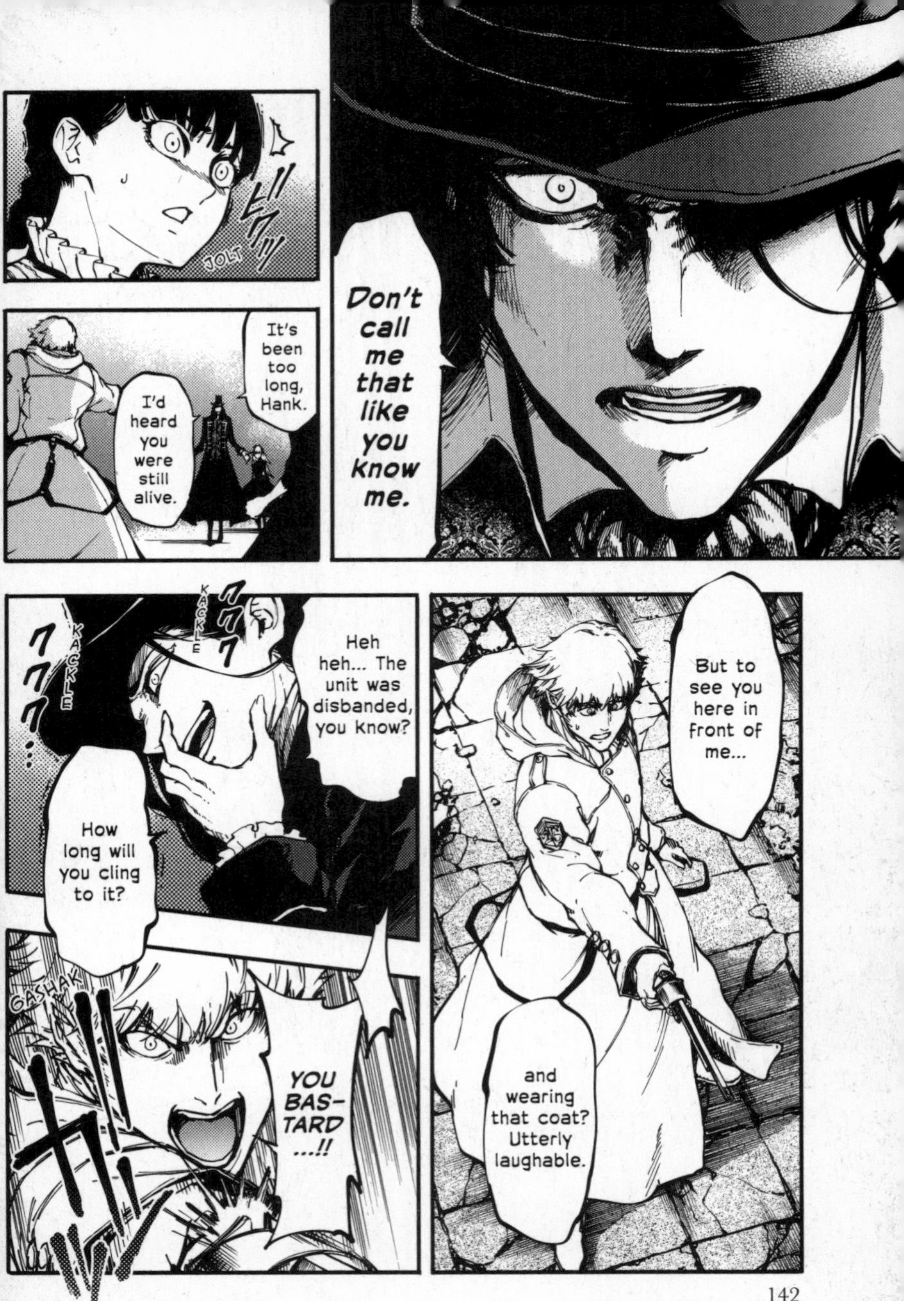
Don't call me that like you know me.
JOLT
It's been too long, Hank.
I'd heard you were still alive.
But to see you here in front of me...
and wearing that coat? Utterly laughable.
KACKLE
KACKLE
Heh heh... The unit was disbanded, you know?
How long will you cling to it?
GASHAK
YOU BAS-TARD ...!!

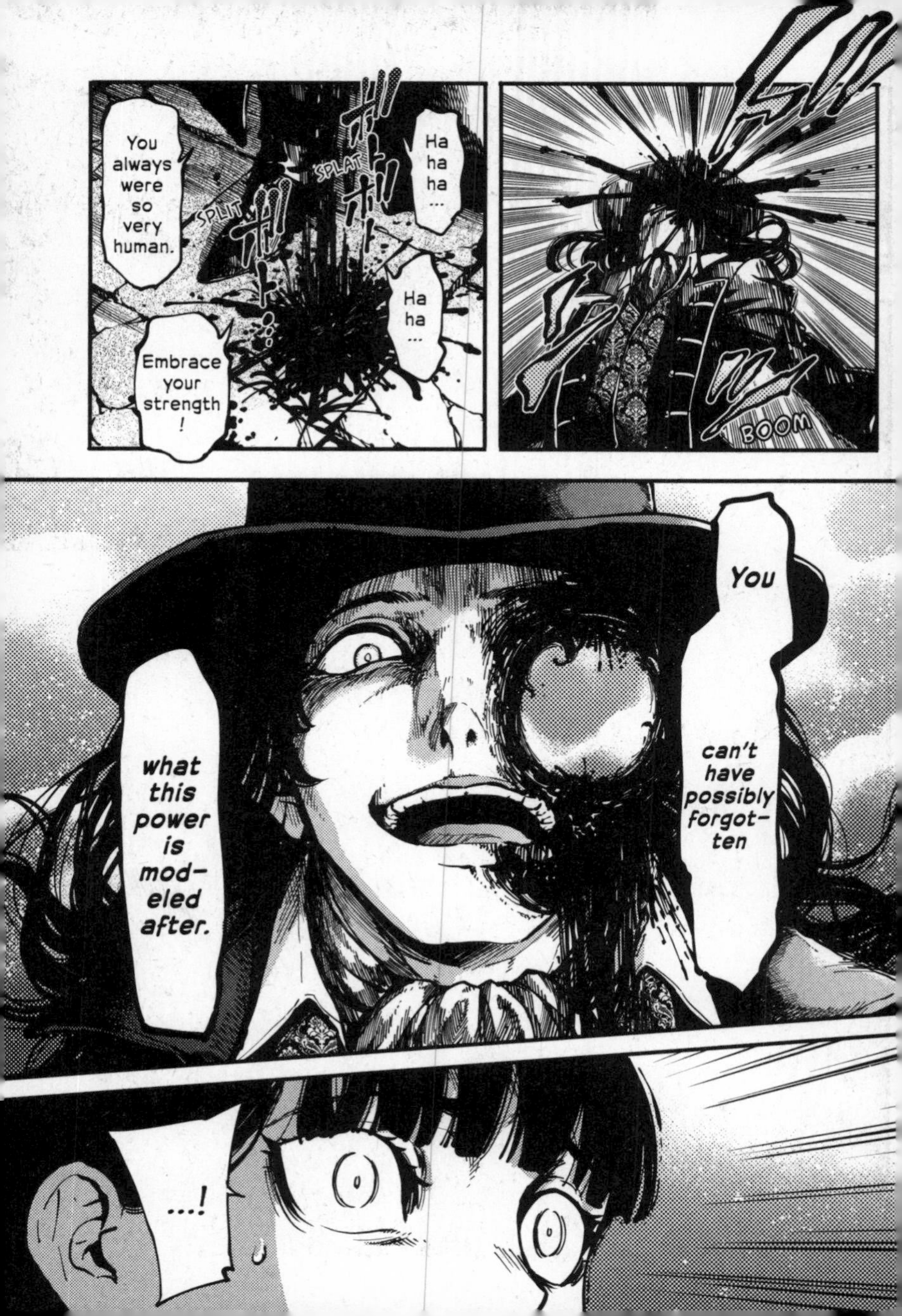
BOOM
Ha ha ha ...
SPLAT
Ha ha ...
You always were so very human.
SPLIT
Embrace your strength !
You can't have possibly forgot-ten
what this power is mod-eled after.
...!

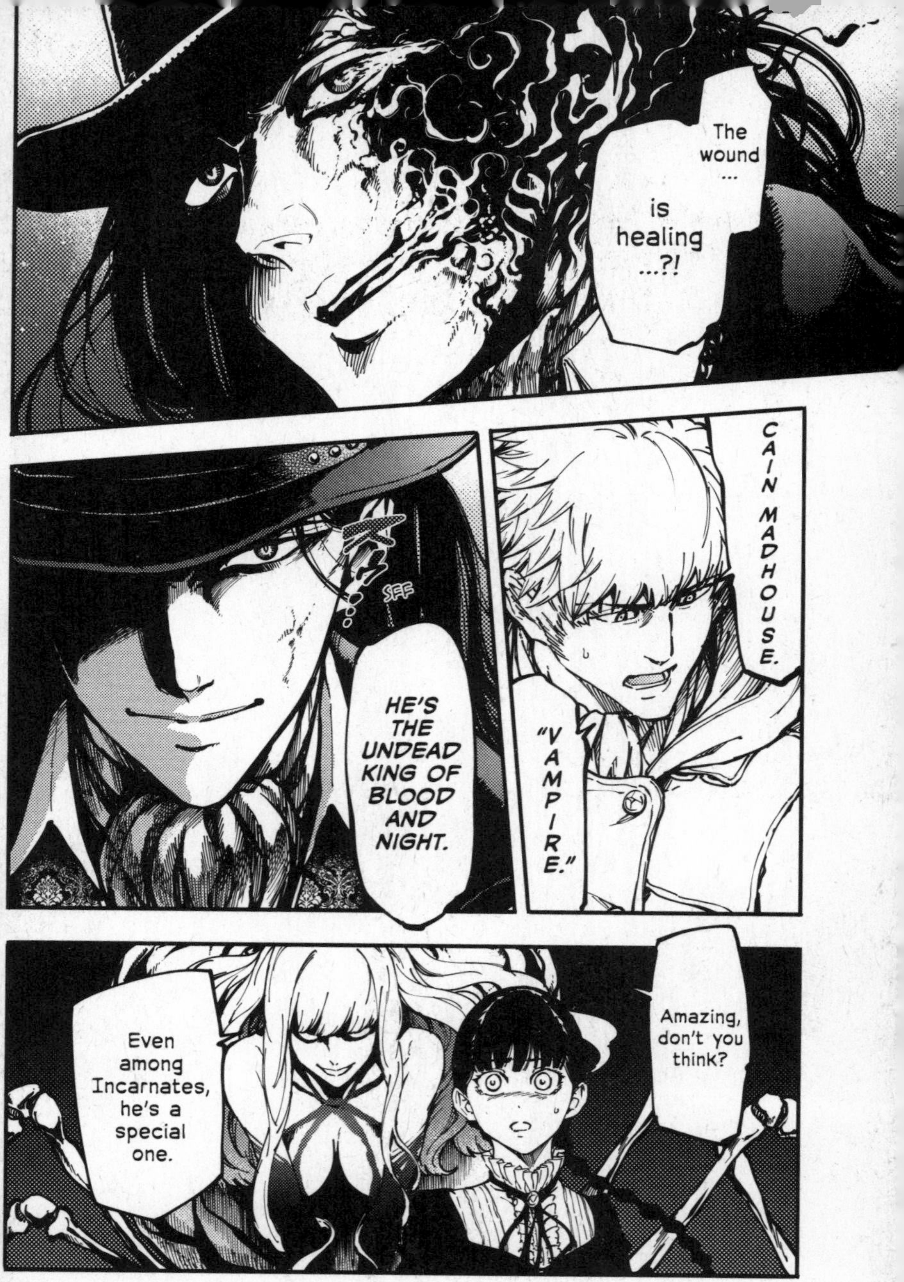
The wound ... is healing ...?!
CAIN MADHOUSE.
"VAMPIRE."
SFF
HE'S THE UNDEAD KING OF BLOOD AND NIGHT.
Amazing, don't you think?
Even among Incarnates, he's a special one.

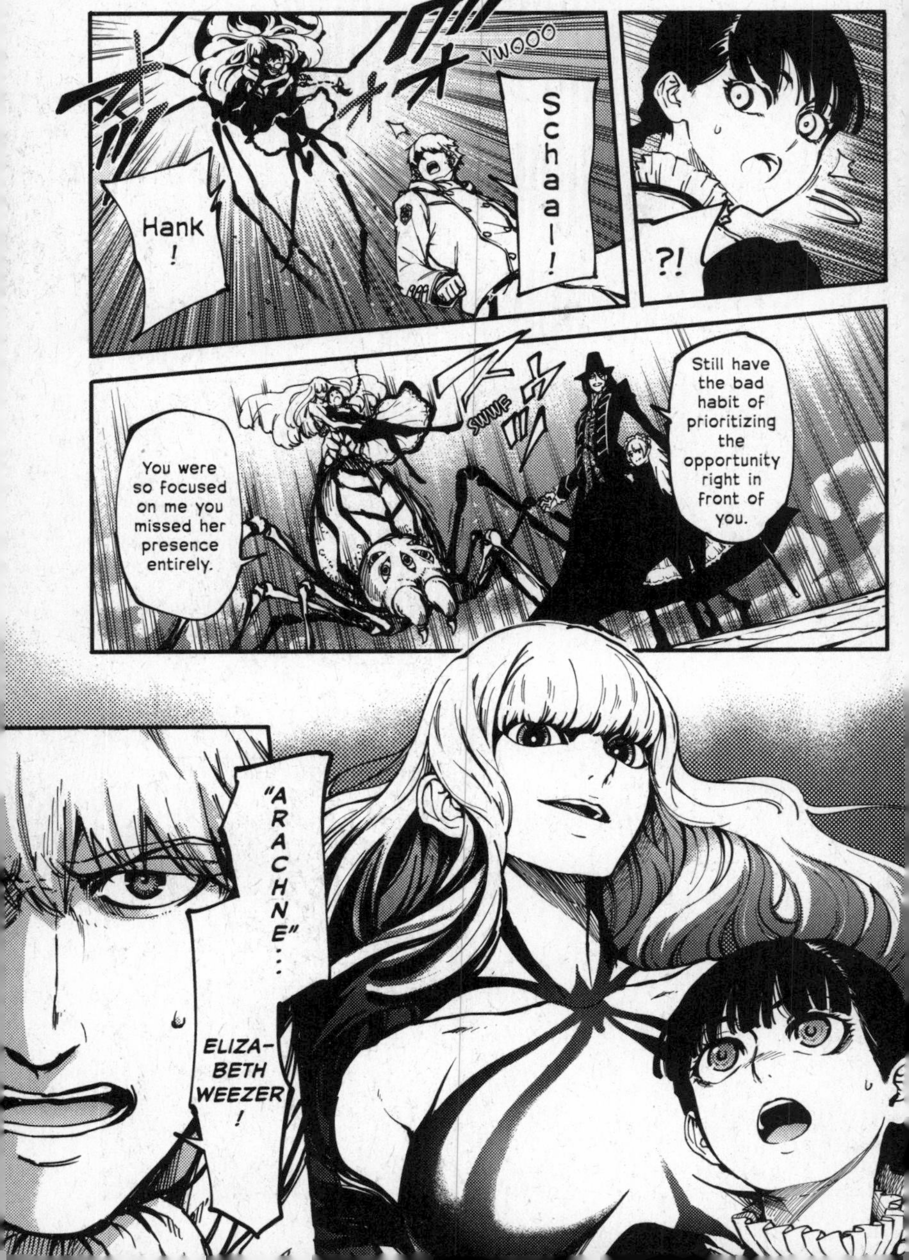
?!
VWOOO
Schaal!
Hank!
Still have the bad habit of prioritizing the opportunity right in front of you.
SWWF
You were so focused on me you missed her presence entirely.
"ARACHNE"...
ELIZABETH WEEZER!

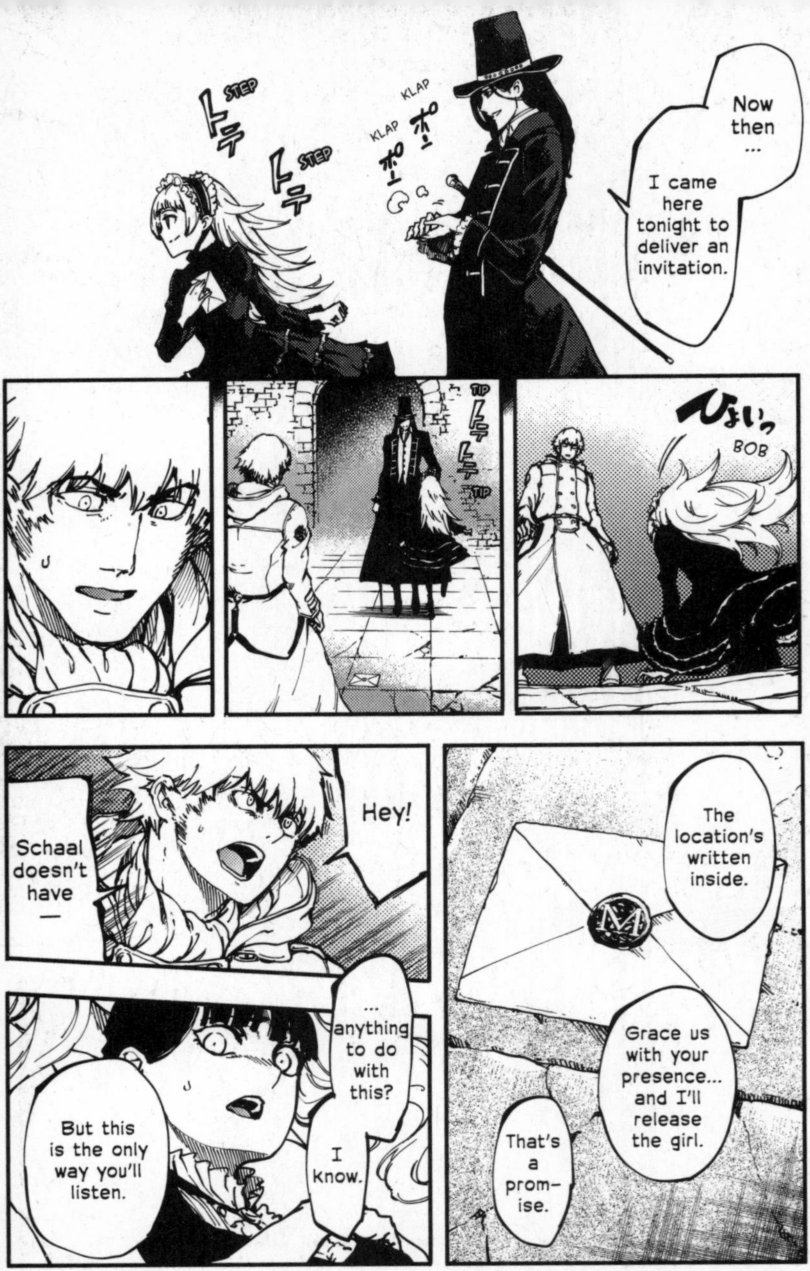
Now then ... I came here tonight to deliver an invitation.
KLAP
KLAP
STEP
STEP
ひょいっ
BOB
TIP
TIP
The location's written inside.
Grace us with your presence... and I'll release the girl.
That's a prom-ise.
Hey!
Schaal doesn't have —
... anything to do with this?
I know.
But this is the only way you'll listen.

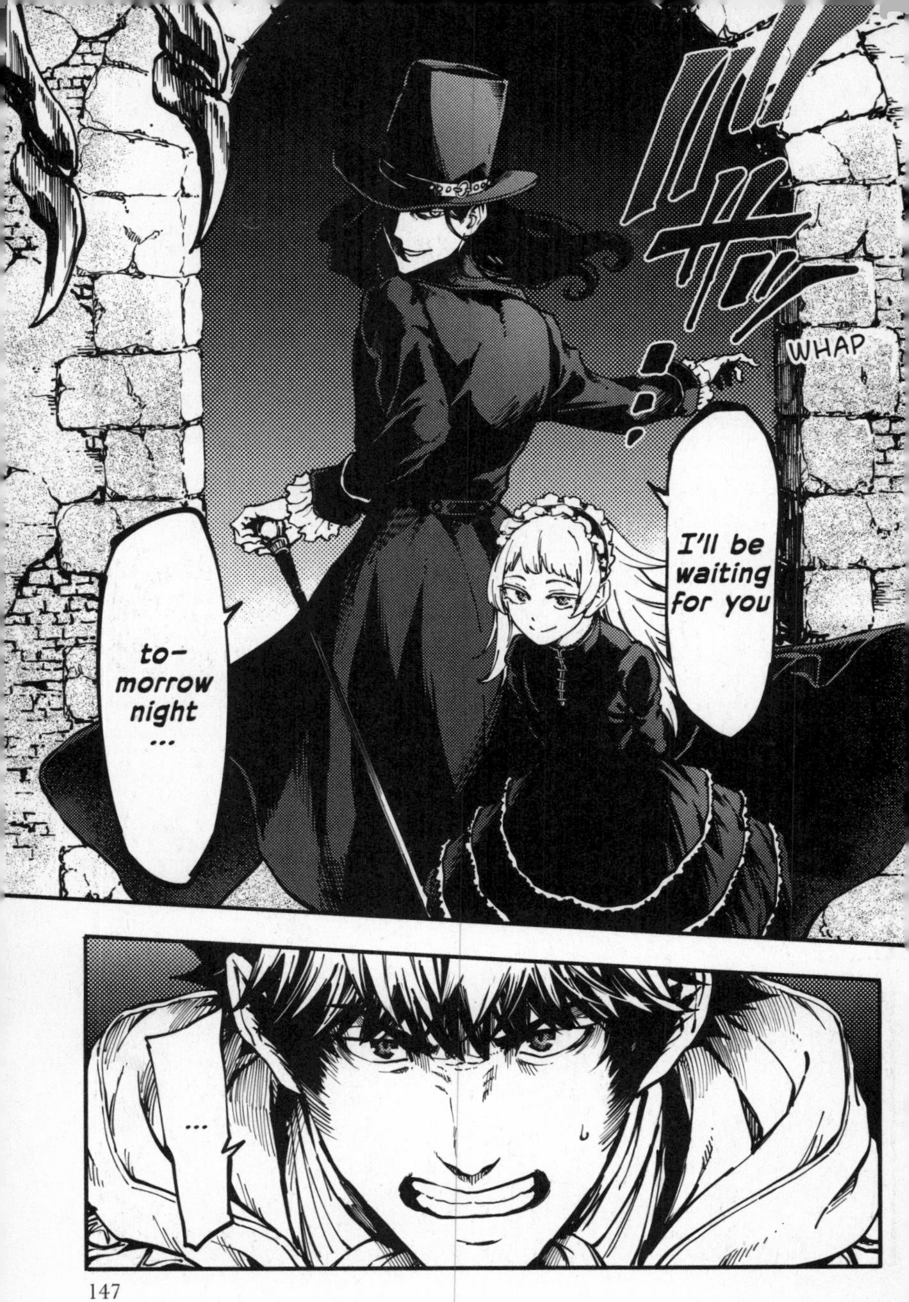
WHAP
I'll be waiting for you
to-morrow night ...
...

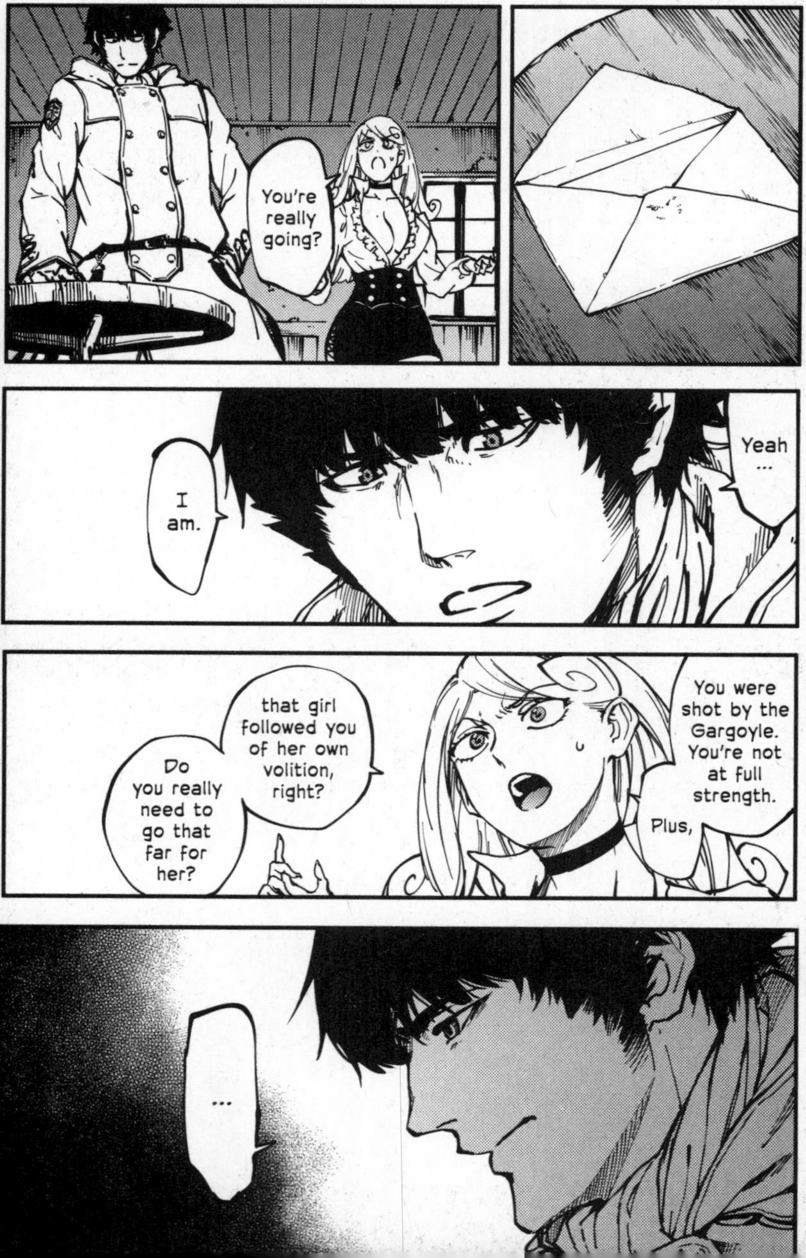
You're really going?
Yeah ...
I am.
You were shot by the Gargoyle. You're not at full strength.
Plus,
that girl followed you of her own volition, right?
Do you really need to go that far for her?
...

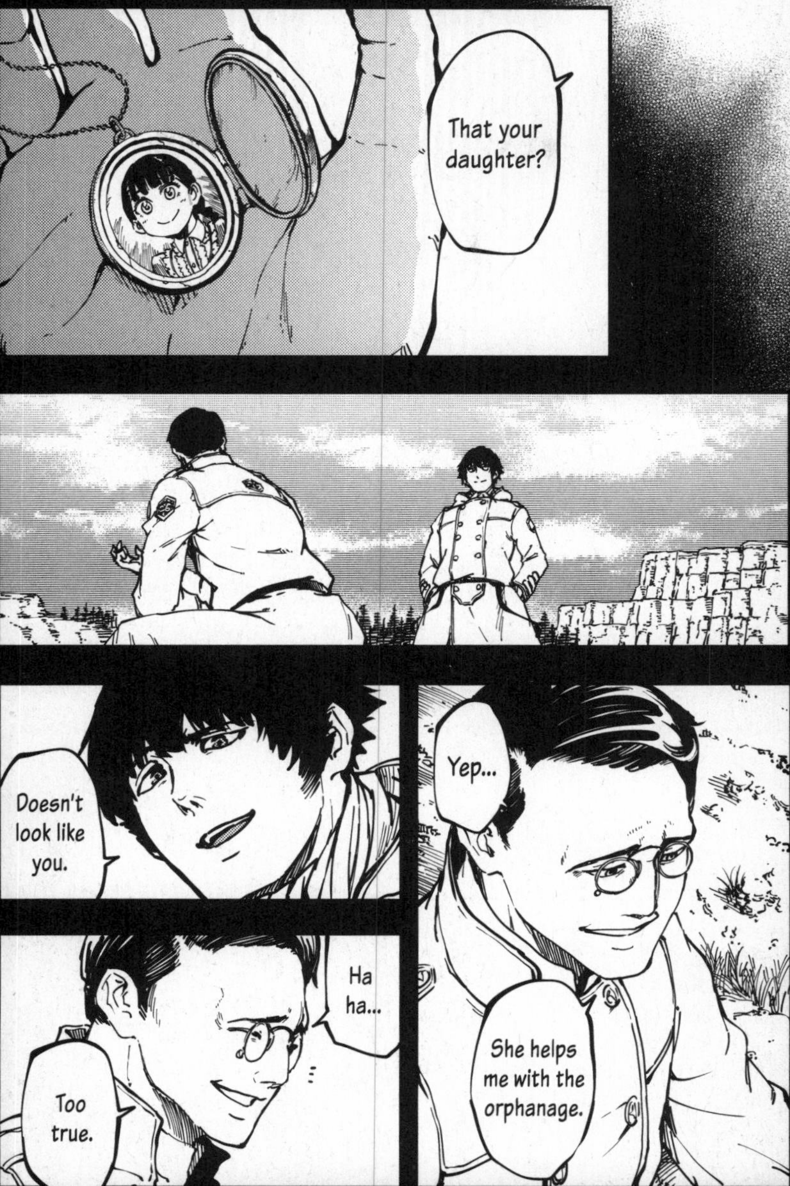
That your daughter?
Yep...
She helps me with the orphanage.
Doesn't look like you.
Ha ha...
Too true.

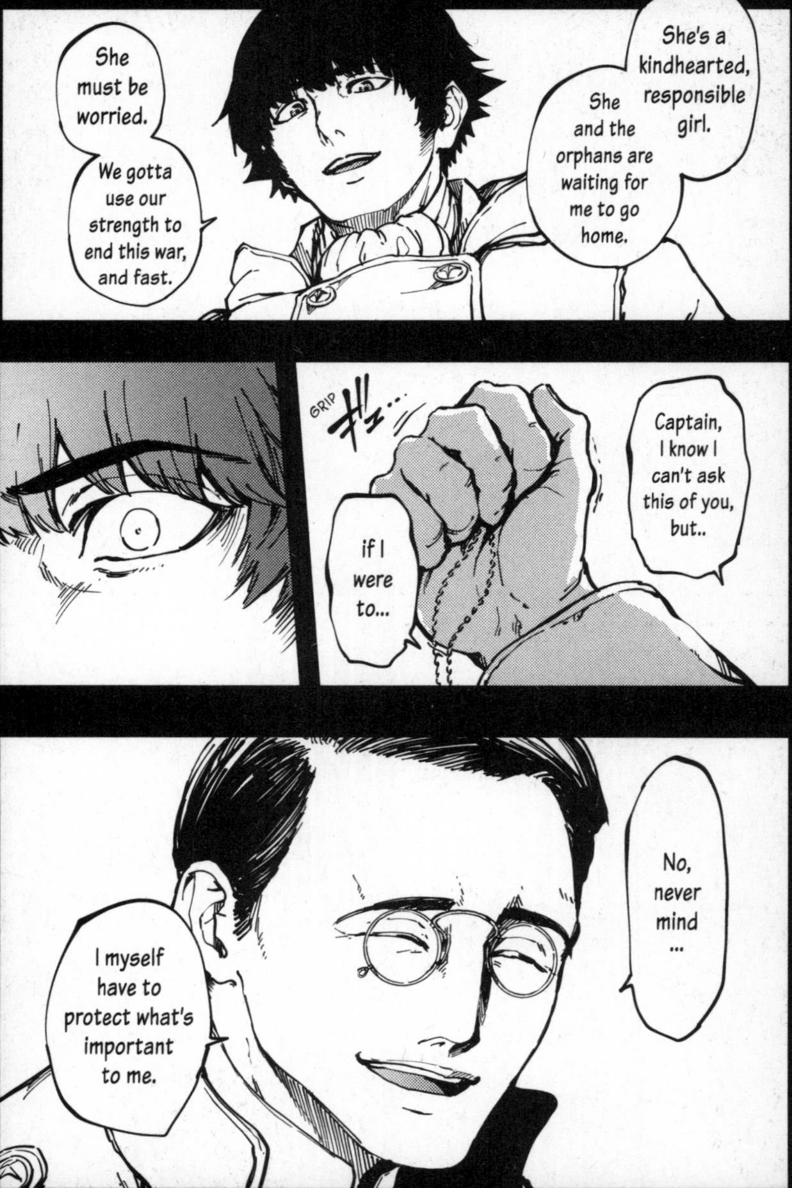
She's a kindhearted, responsible girl.
She and the orphans are waiting for me to go home.
She must be worried.
We gotta use our strength to end this war, and fast.
GRIP
Captain, I know I can't ask this of you, but..
if I were to...
No, never mind ...
I myself have to protect what's important to me.

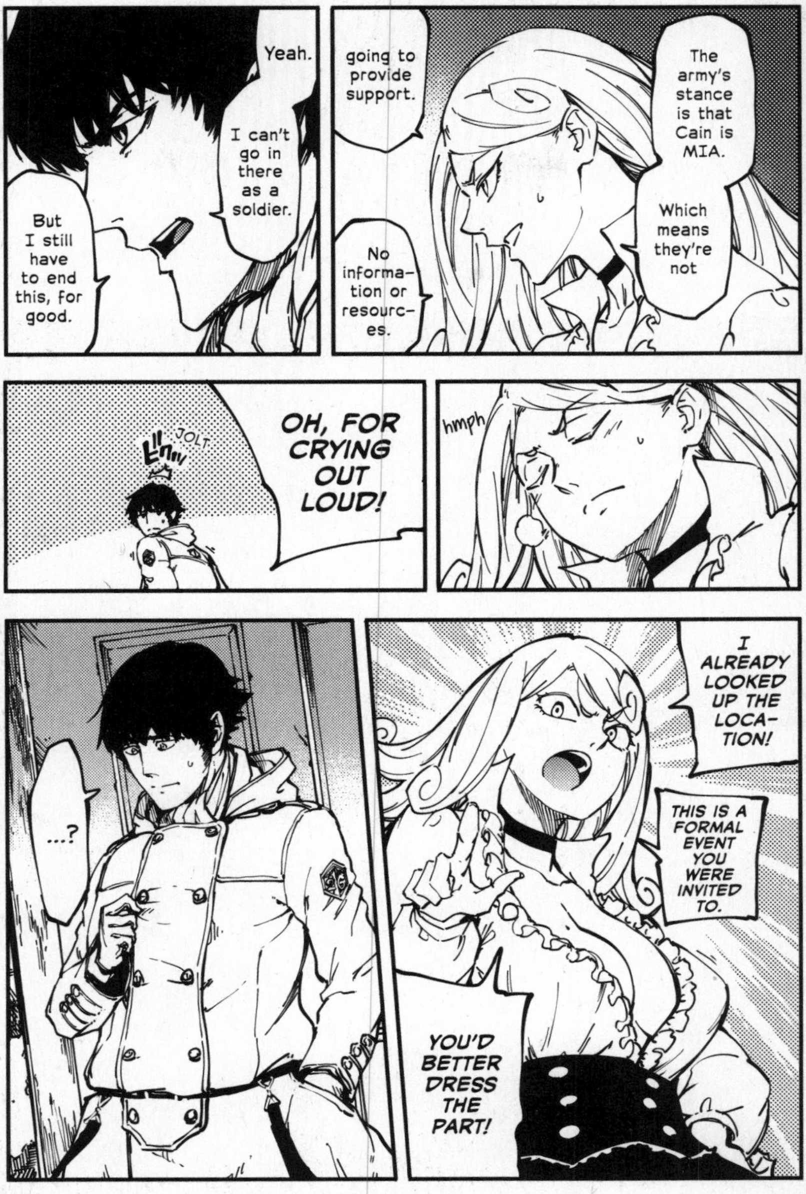

The army's stance is that Cain is MIA.
Which means they're not
going to provide support.
No information or resources.
Yeah.
I can't go in there as a soldier.
But I still have to end this, for good.
hmph
OH, FOR CRYING OUT LOUD!
JOLT
I ALREADY LOOKED UP THE LOCATION!
THIS IS A FORMAL EVENT YOU WERE INVITED TO.
YOU'D BETTER DRESS THE PART!
...?

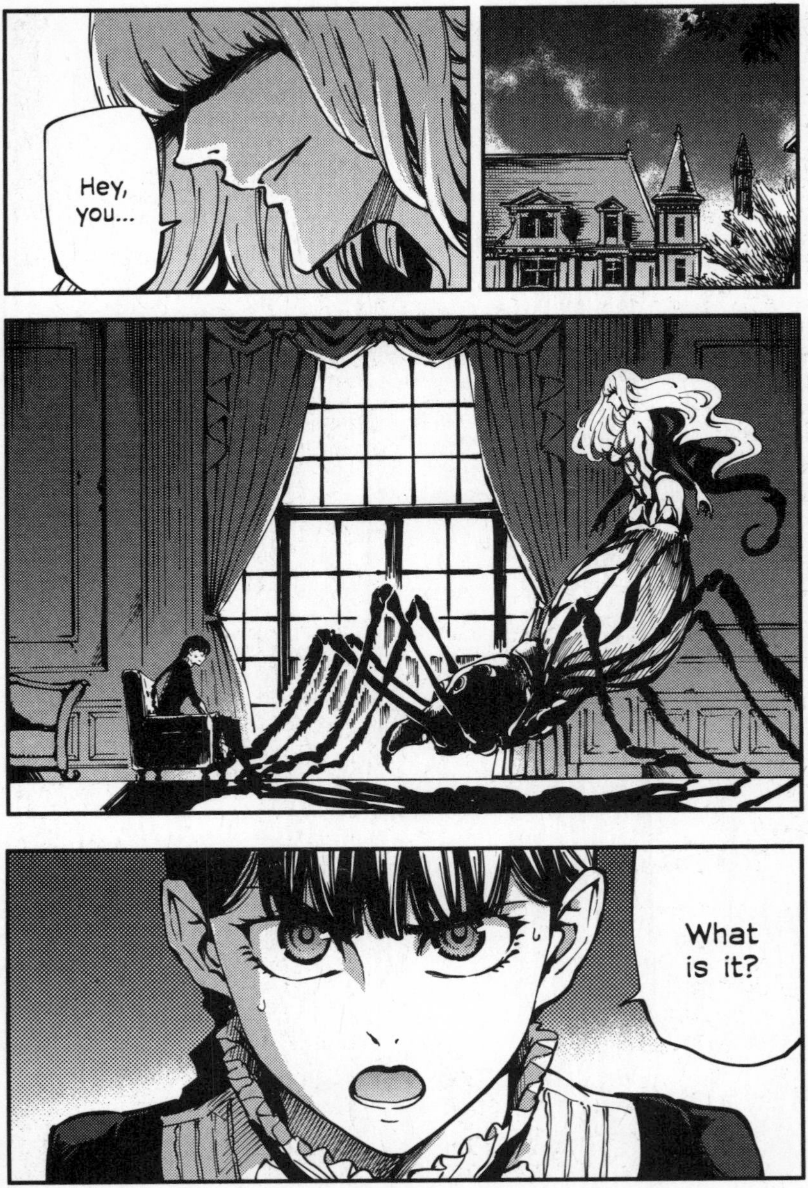
Hey, you...
What is it?

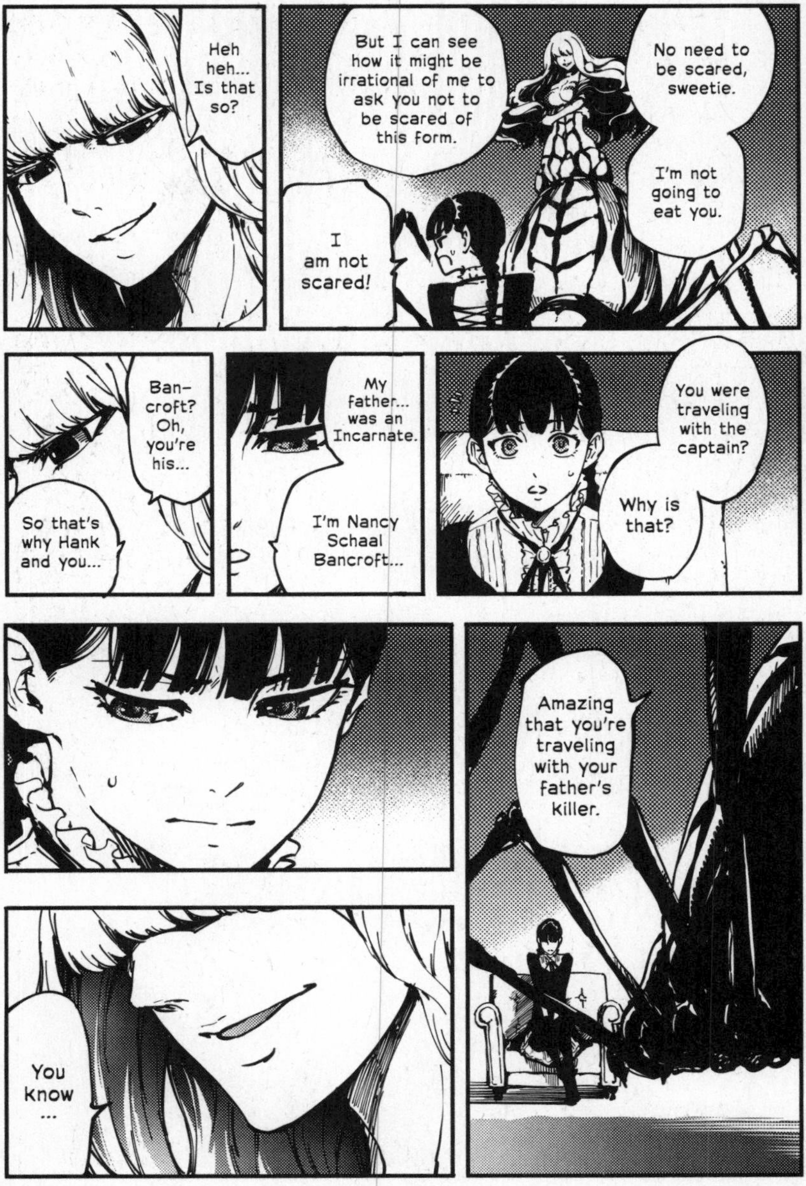
No need to be scared, sweetie.
I'm not going to eat you.
But I can see how it might be irrational of me to ask you not to be scared of this form.
I am not scared!
Heh heh... Is that so?
You were traveling with the captain?
Why is that?
My father... was an Incarnate.
I'm Nancy Schaal Bancroft...
Ban-croft? Oh, you're his...
So that's why Hank and you...
Amazing that you're traveling with your father's killer.
You know ...

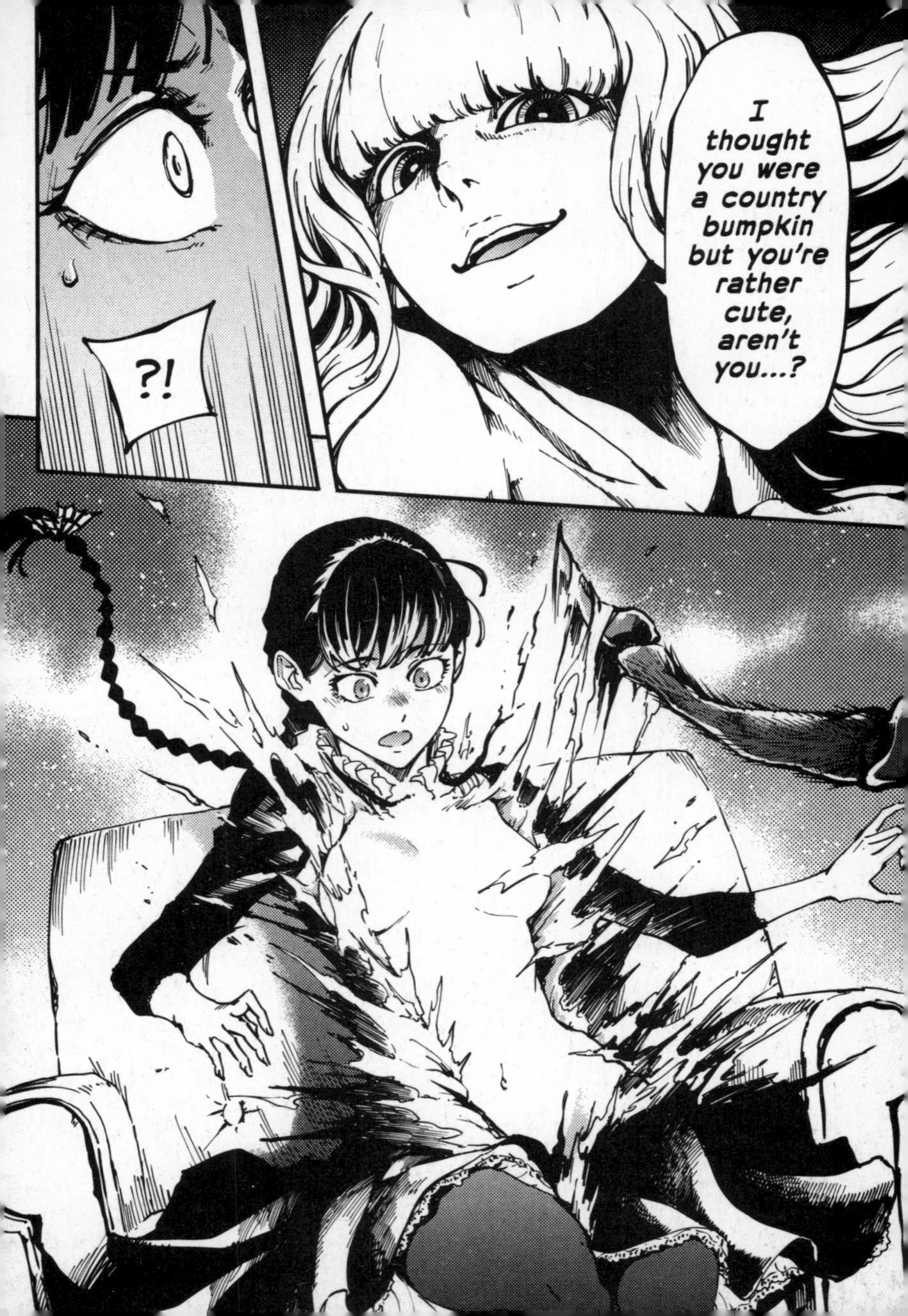
I thought you were a country bumpkin but you're rather cute, aren't you...?
?!

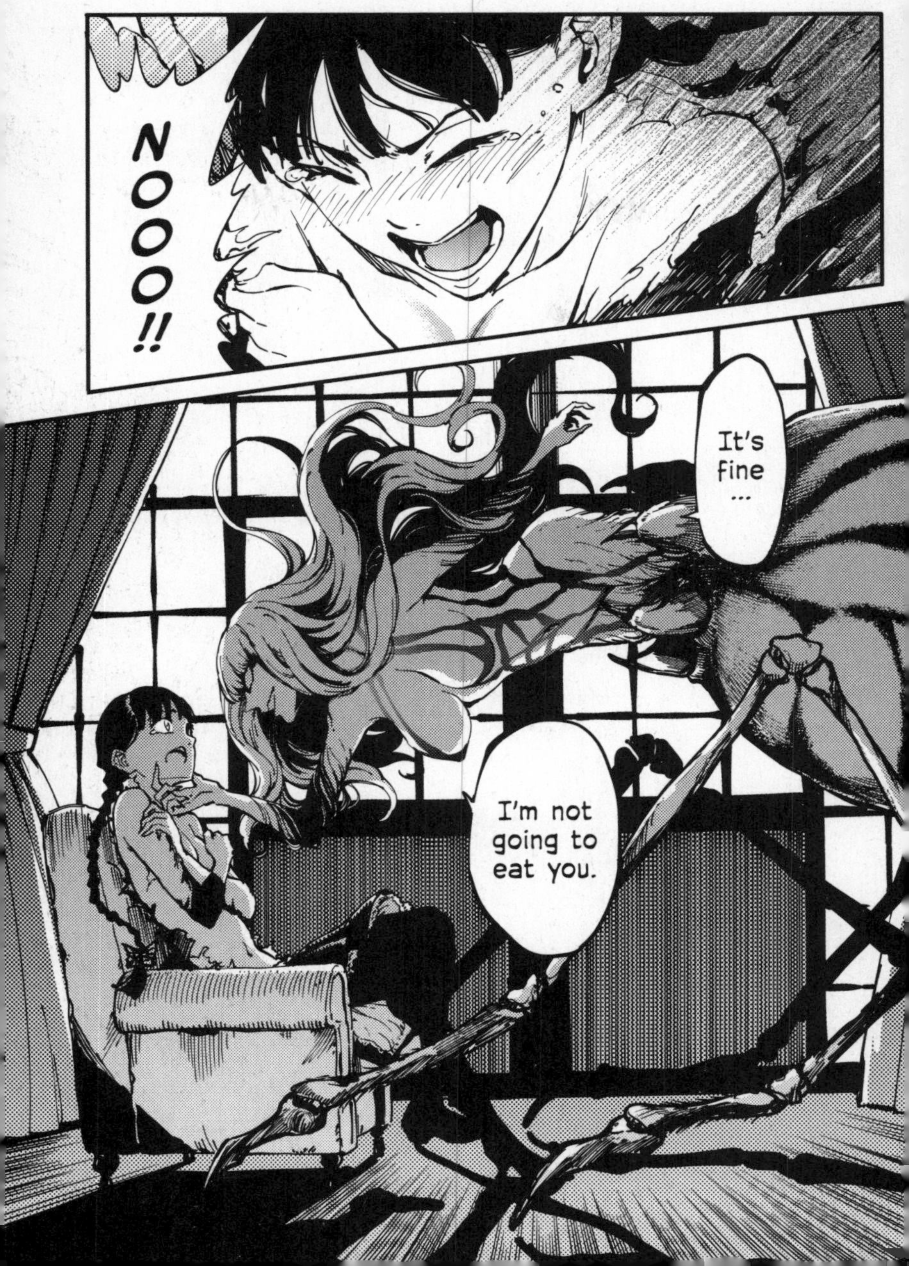
NOOOO!!
It's fine ...
I'm not going to eat you.

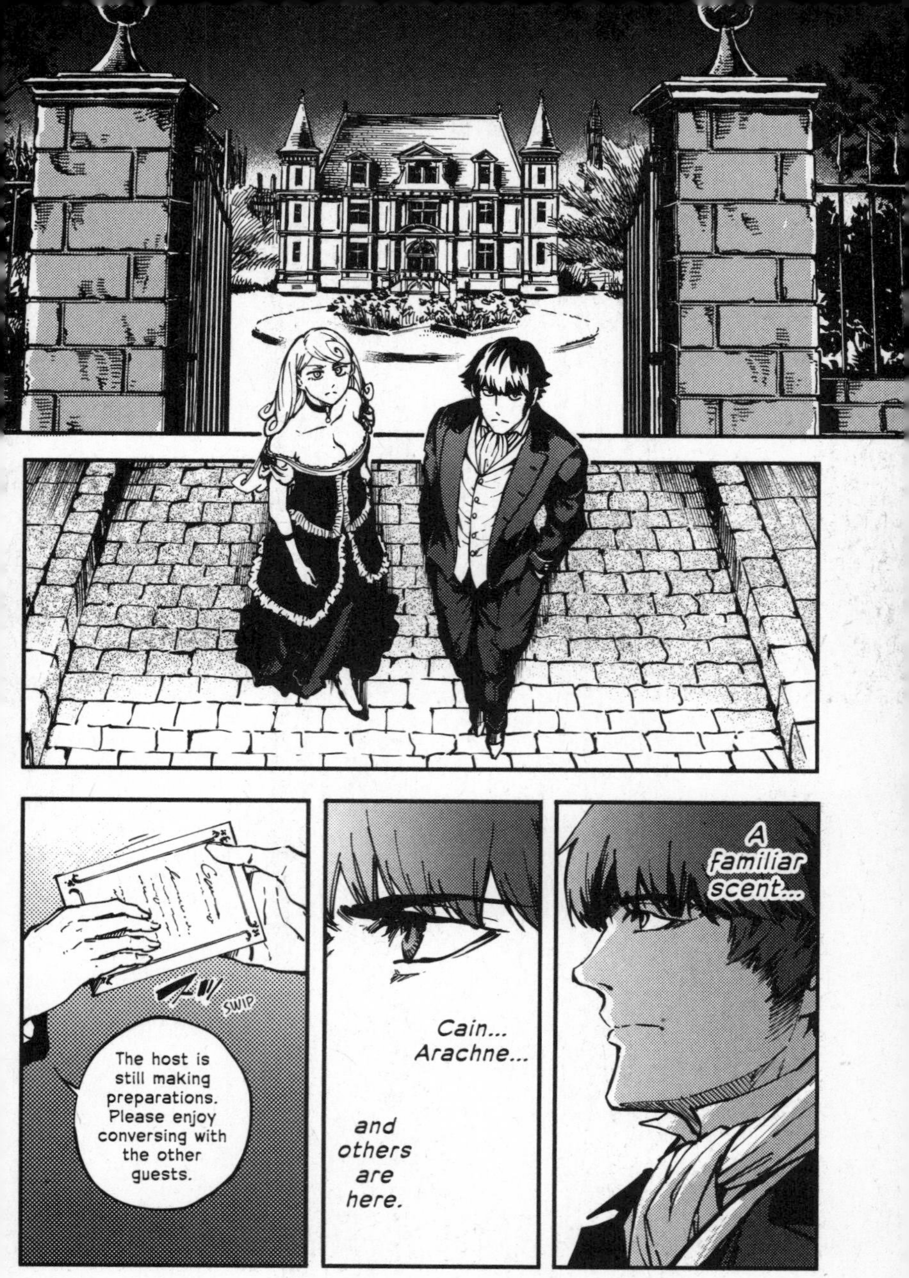
A familiar scent...
Cain... Arachne...
and others are here.
SWIP
The host is still making preparations. Please enjoy conversing with the other guests.

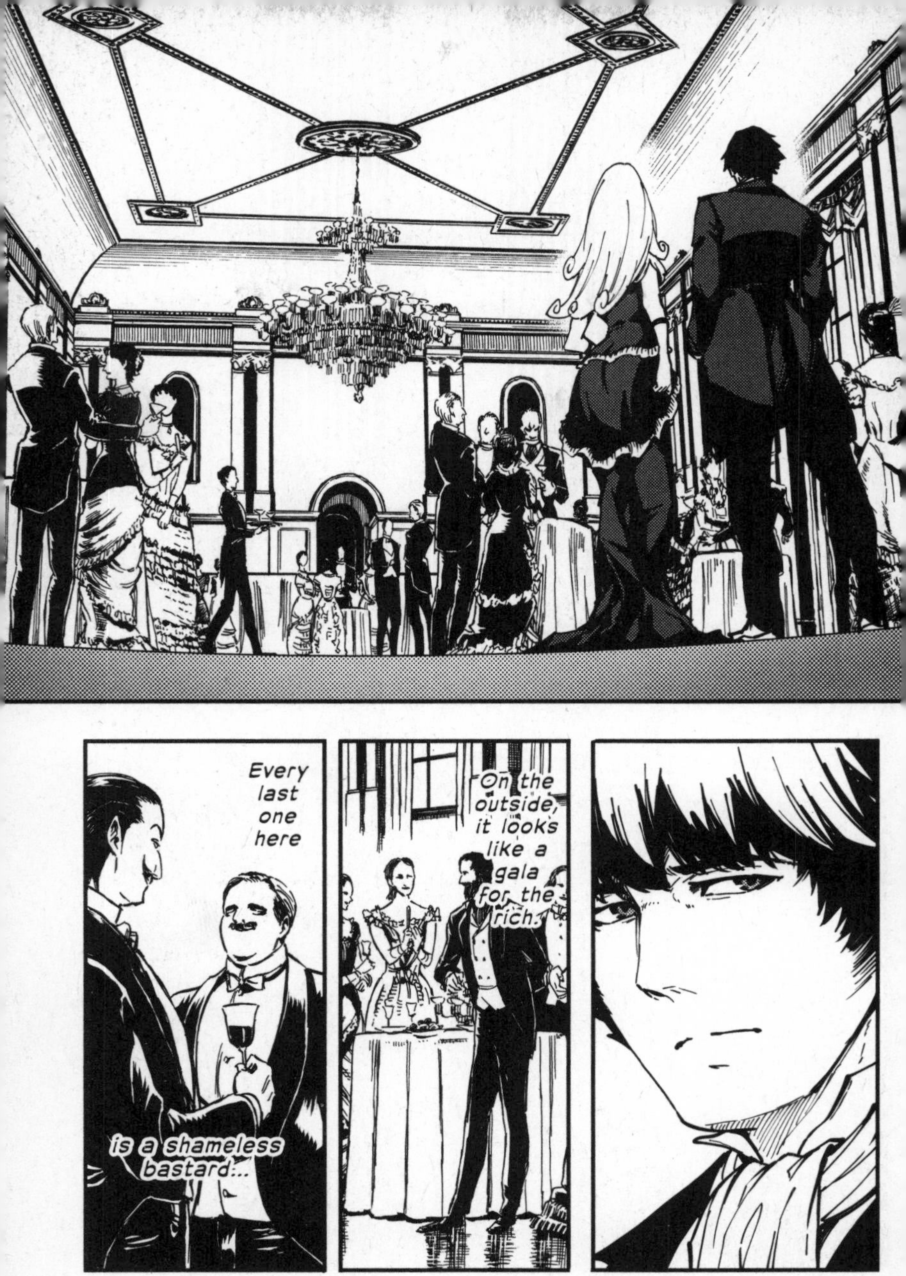
On the outside, it looks like a gala for the rich.
Every last one here
is a shameless bastard...

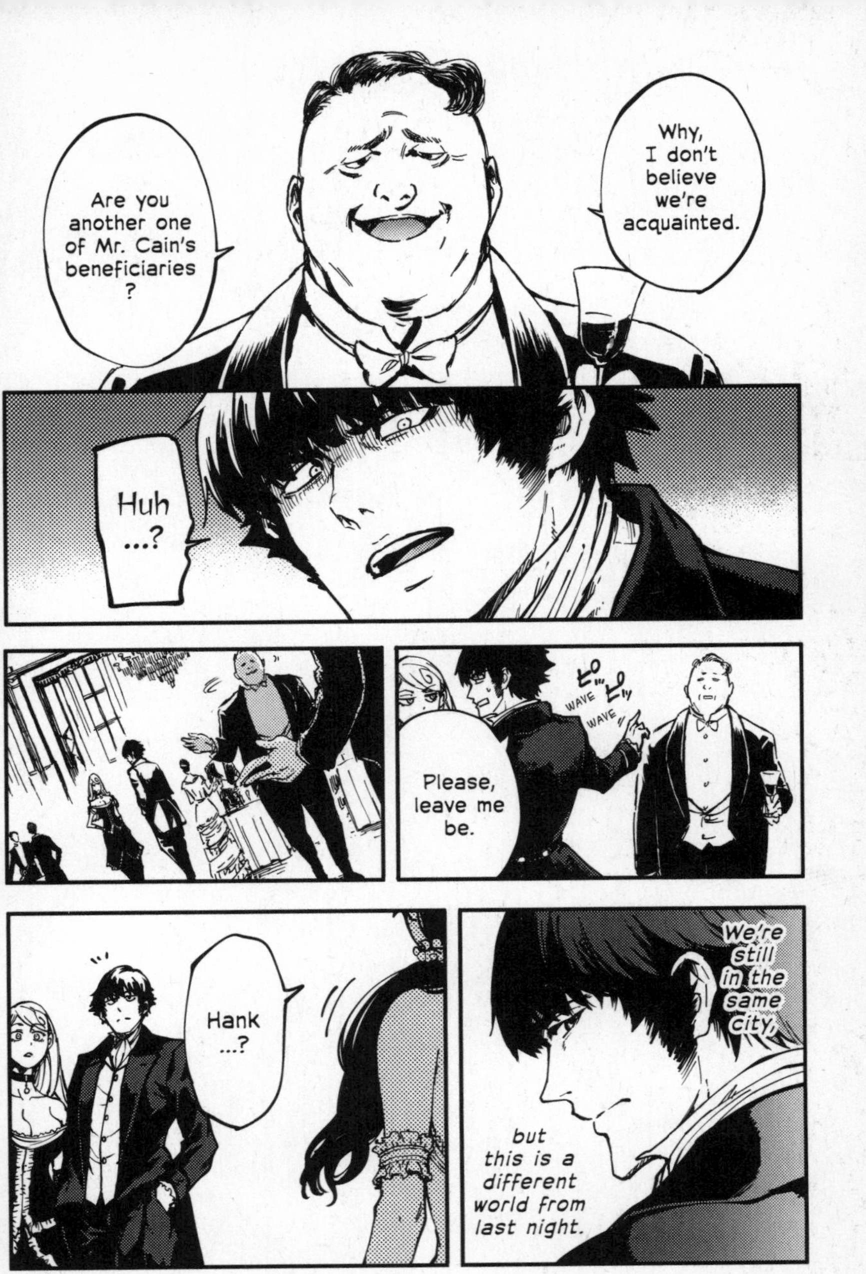
Why, I don't believe we're acquainted.
Are you another one of Mr. Cain's beneficiaries?
Huh ...?
WAVE
WAVE
Please, leave me be.
We're still in the same city,
but this is a different world from last night.
Hank ...?

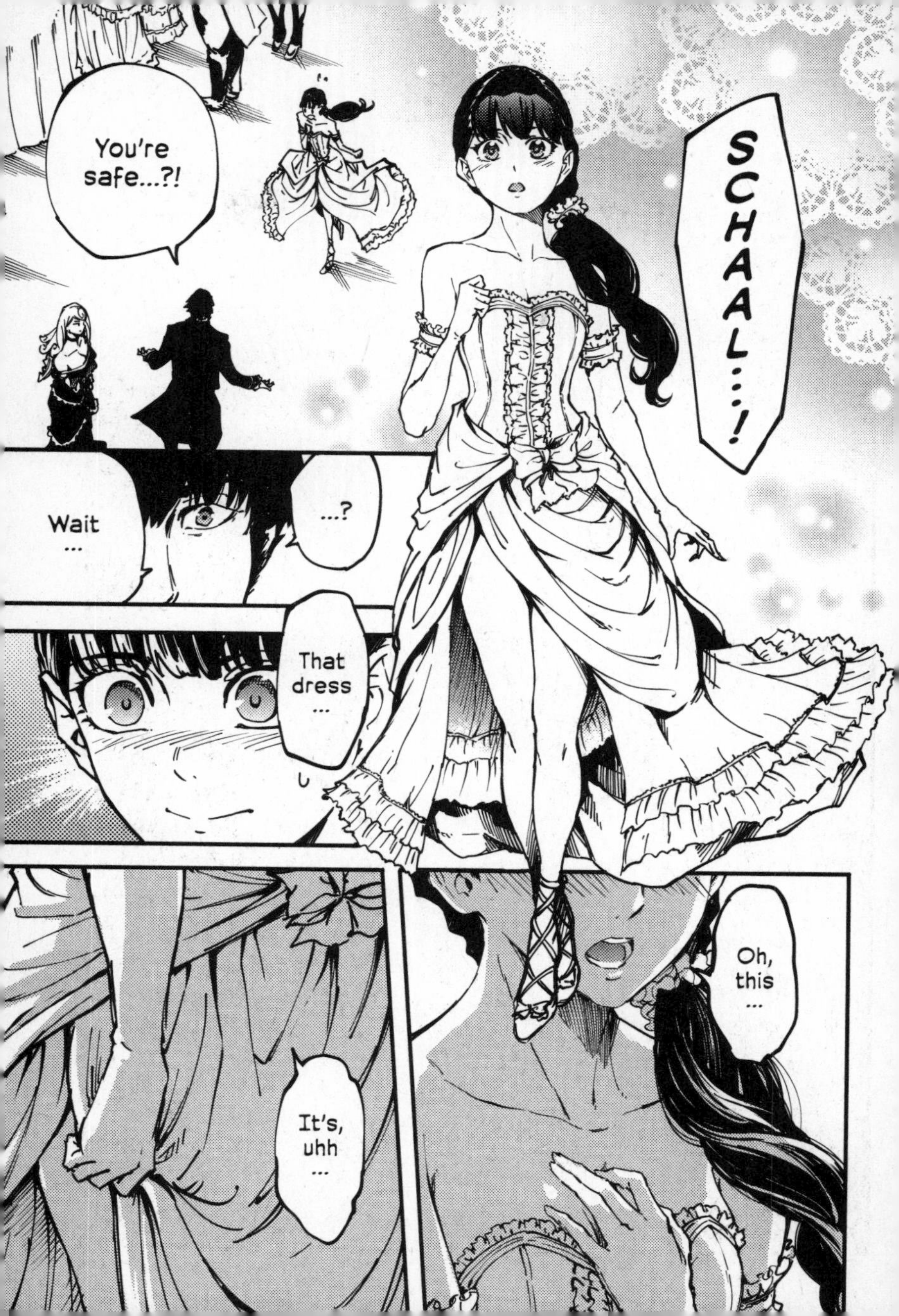
SCHAAL...!
You're safe...?!
...?
Wait ...
That dress ...
Oh, this ...
It's, uhh ...

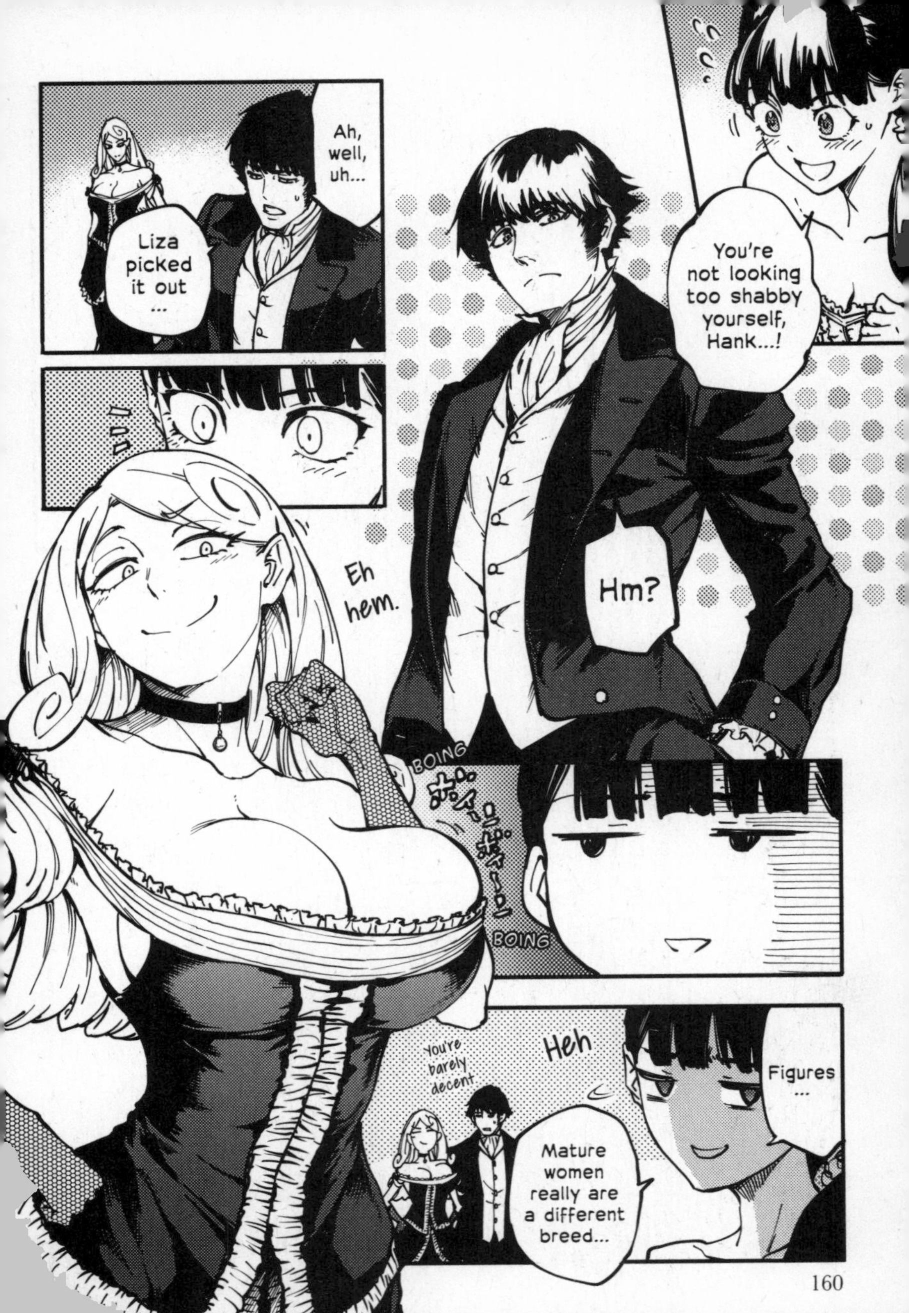

You're not looking too shabby yourself, Hank...!
Ah, well, uh...
Liza picked it out ...
Hm?
Eh hem.
BOING
BOING
Figures ...
Heh
You're barely decent
Mature women really are a different breed...

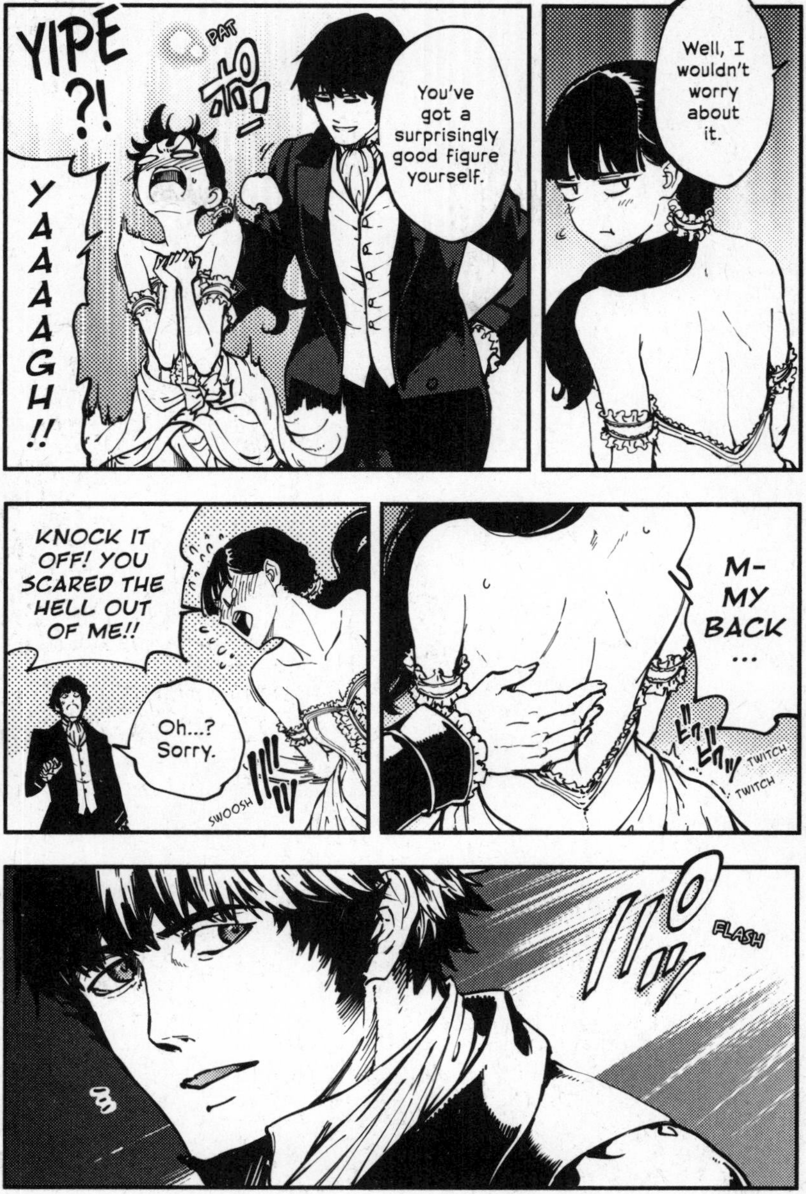

Well, I wouldn't worry about it.
You've got a surprisingly good figure yourself.
PAT
YIPE?!
YAAAAAGH!!
M-MY BACK...
TWITCH
TWITCH
KNOCK IT OFF! YOU SCARED THE HELL OUT OF ME!!
Oh...? Sorry.
SWOOSH
FLASH

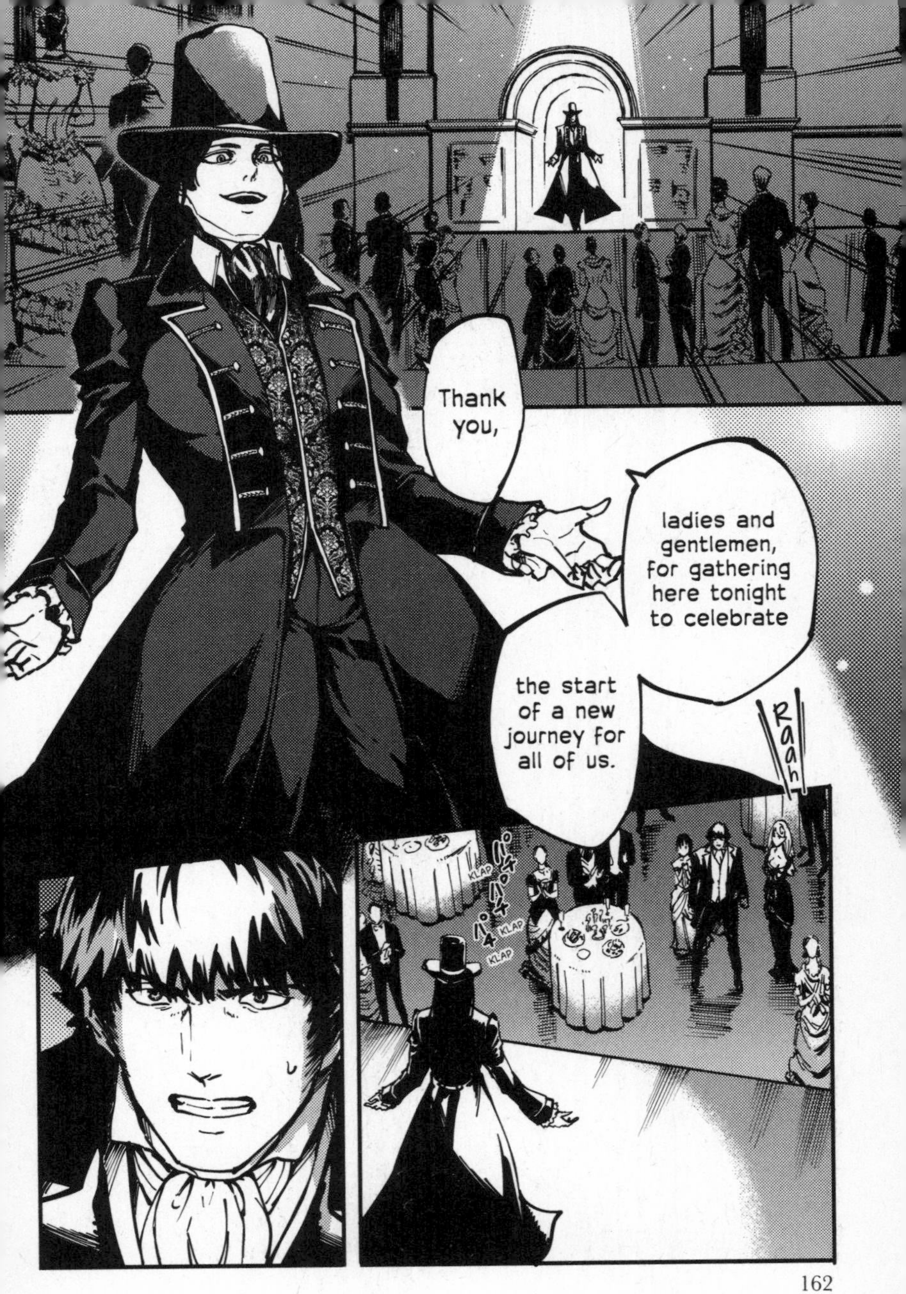
Thank you,
ladies and gentlemen, for gathering here tonight to celebrate
the start of a new journey for all of us.
Raaah
KLAP
KLAP
KLAP

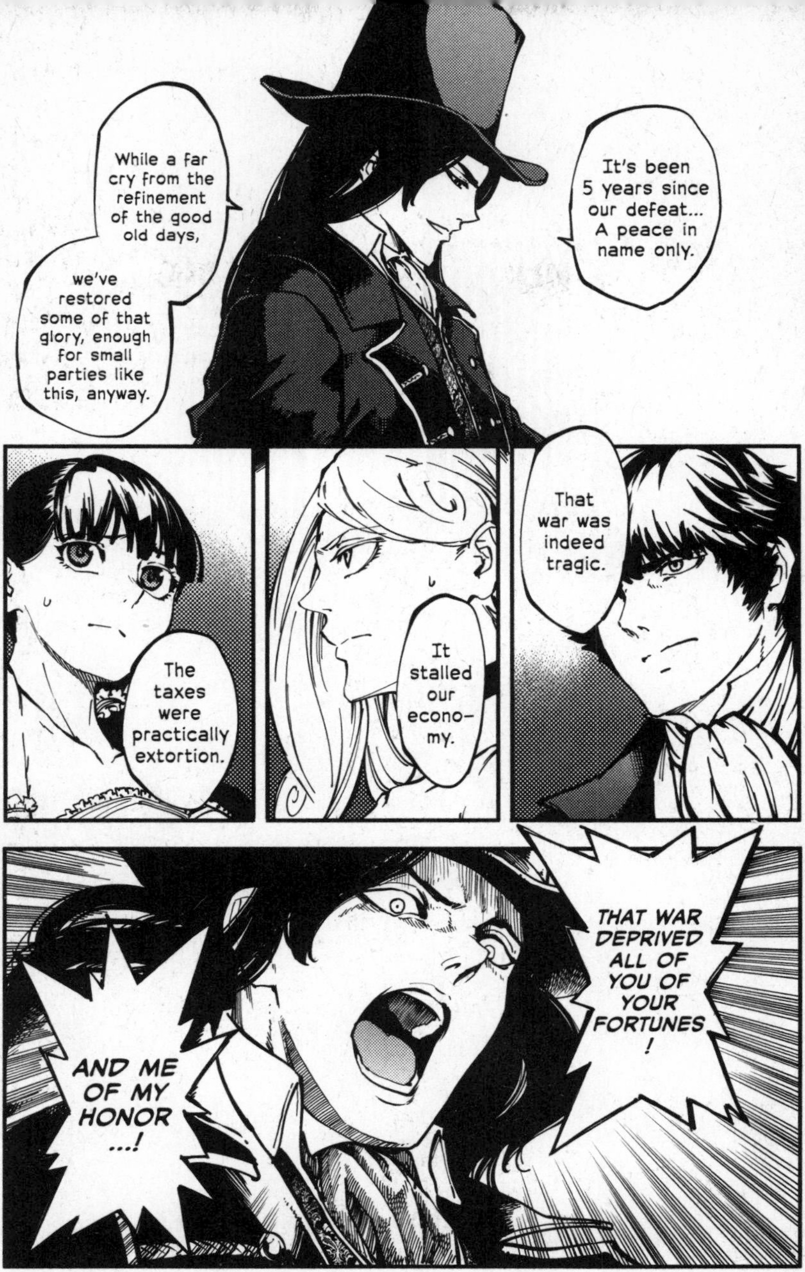
It's been 5 years since our defeat... A peace in name only.
While a far cry from the refinement of the good old days,
we've restored some of that glory, enough for small parties like this, anyway.
That war was indeed tragic.
It stalled our econo-my.
The taxes were practically extortion.
THAT WAR DEPRIVED ALL OF YOU OF YOUR FORTUNES!
AND ME OF MY HONOR ...!

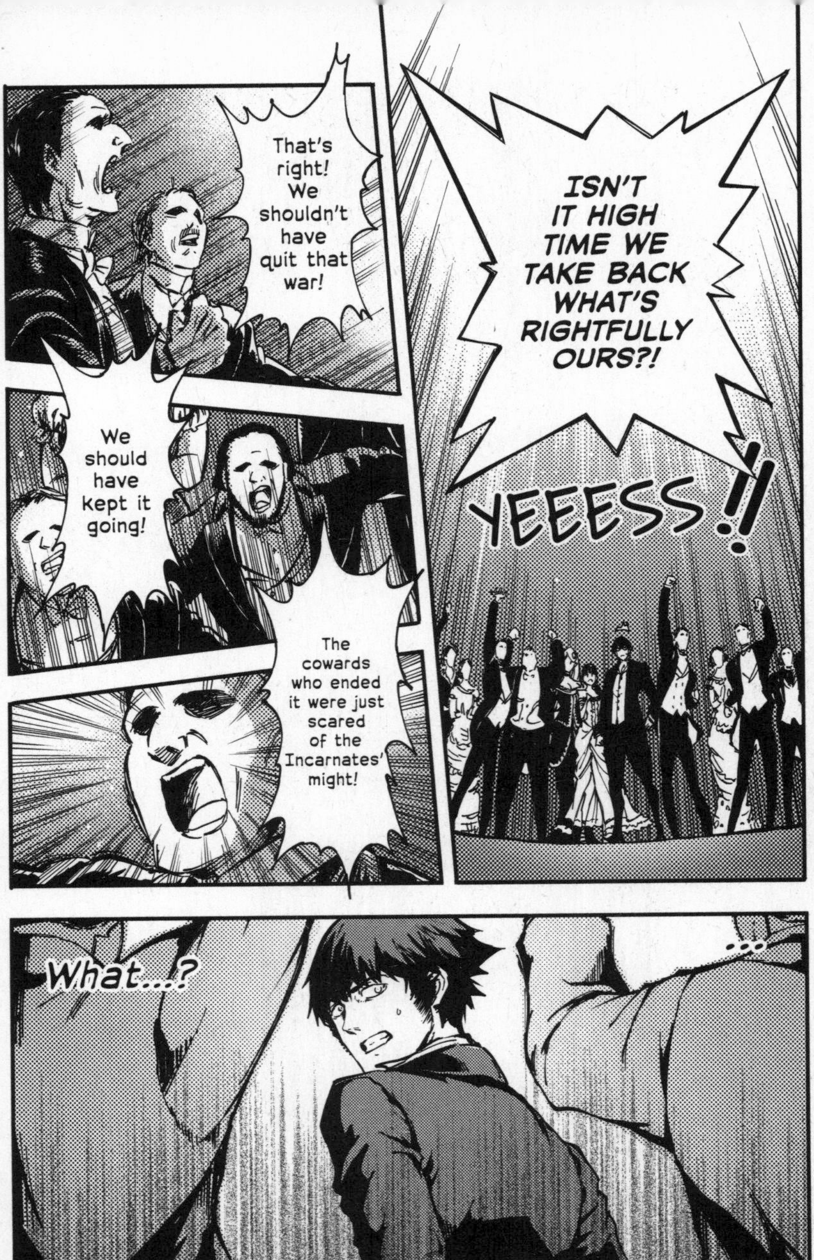
ISN'T IT HIGH TIME WE TAKE BACK WHAT'S RIGHTFULLY OURS?!
YEEESS!!
That's right! We shouldn't have quit that war!
We should have kept it going!
The cowards who ended it were just scared of the Incarnates' might!
...
What...?

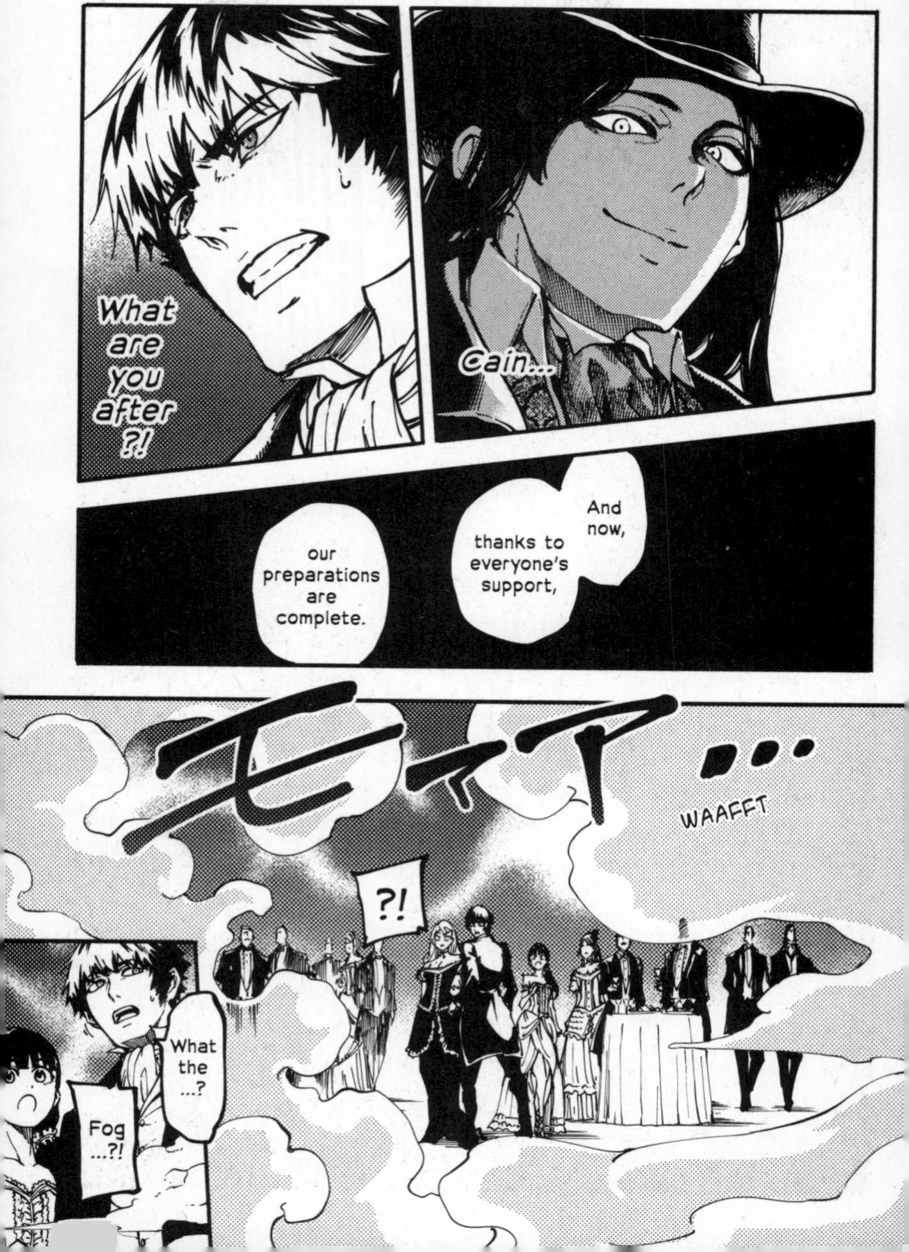
Cain...
What are you after ?!
And now,
thanks to everyone's support,
our preparations are complete.
WAAFFT
?!
What the ...?
Fog ...?!

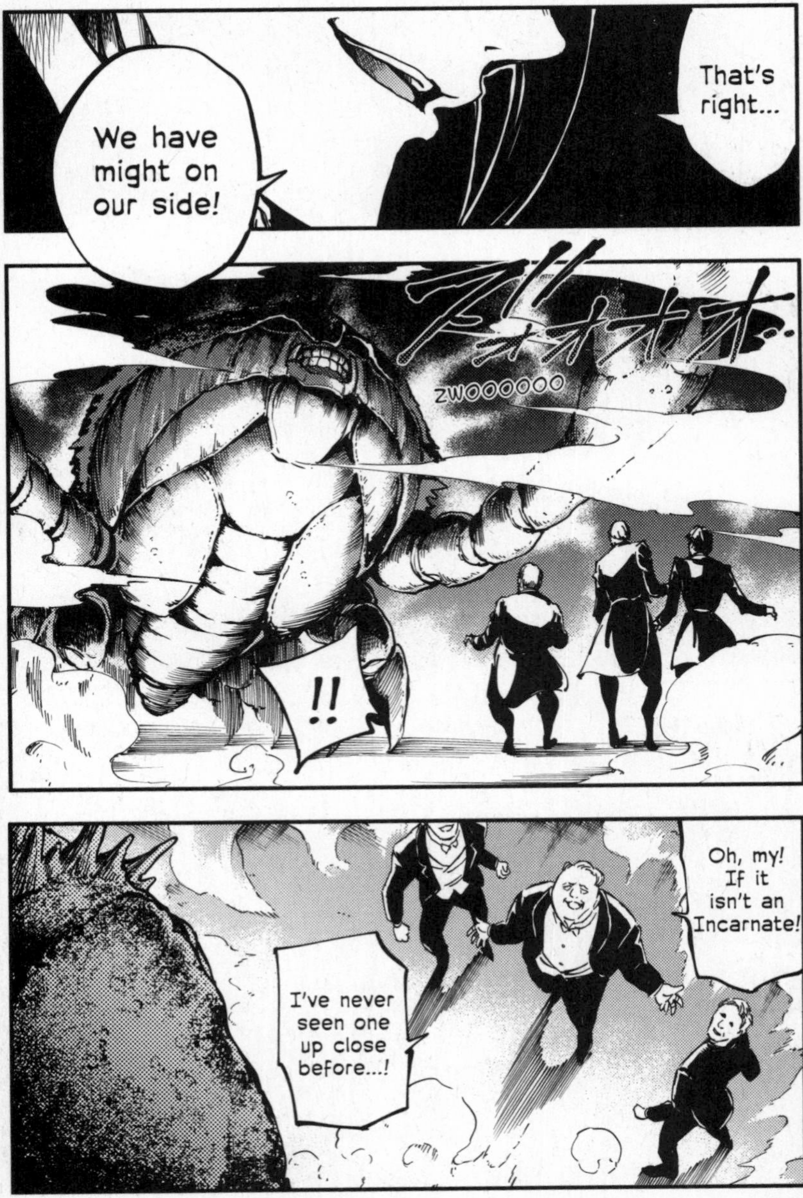
That's right...
We have might on our side!
ZWOOOOOO
!!
Oh, my! If it isn't an Incarnate!
I've never seen one up close before...!

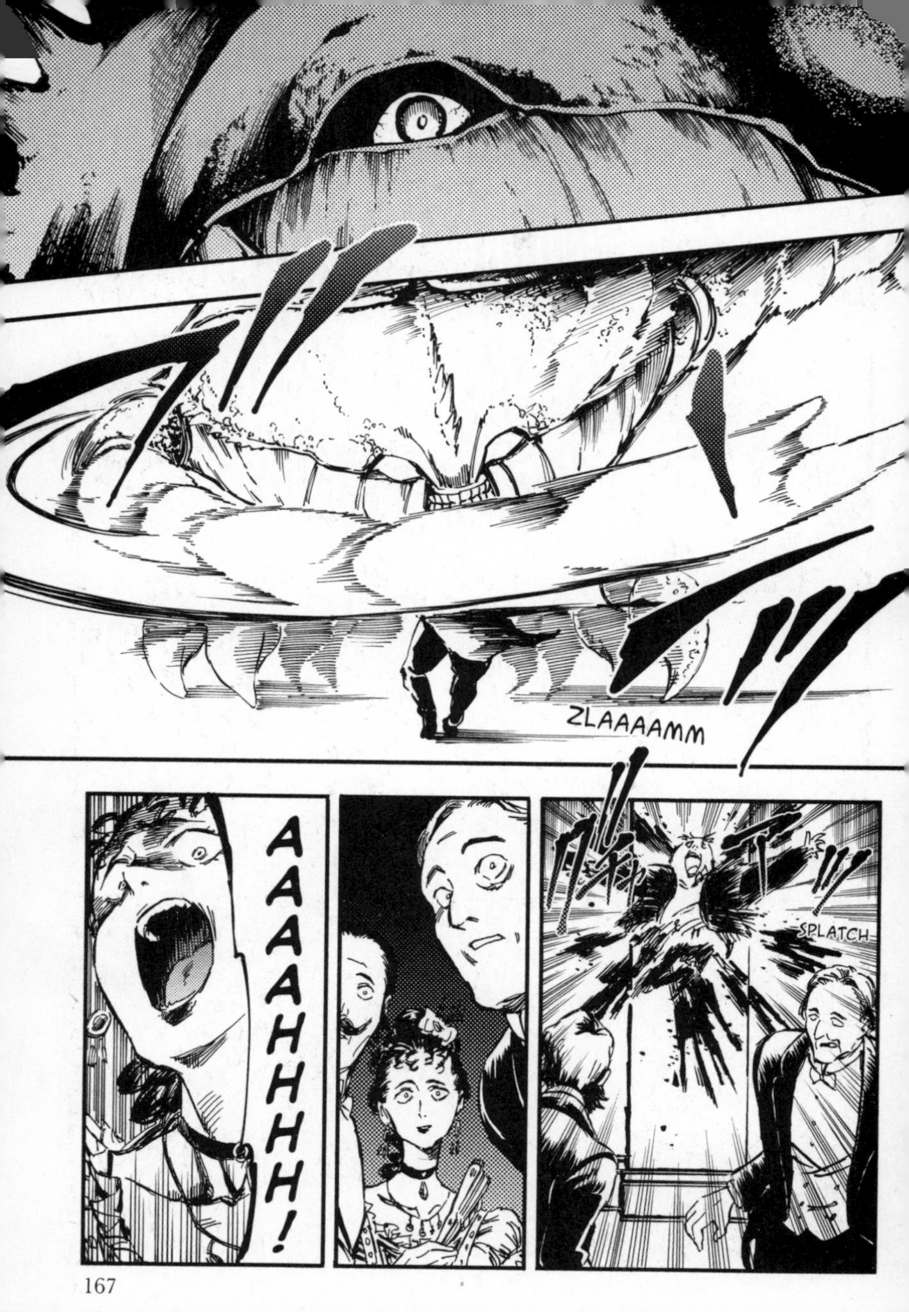
ZLAAAAMM
SPLATCH
AAAAHHHHH!

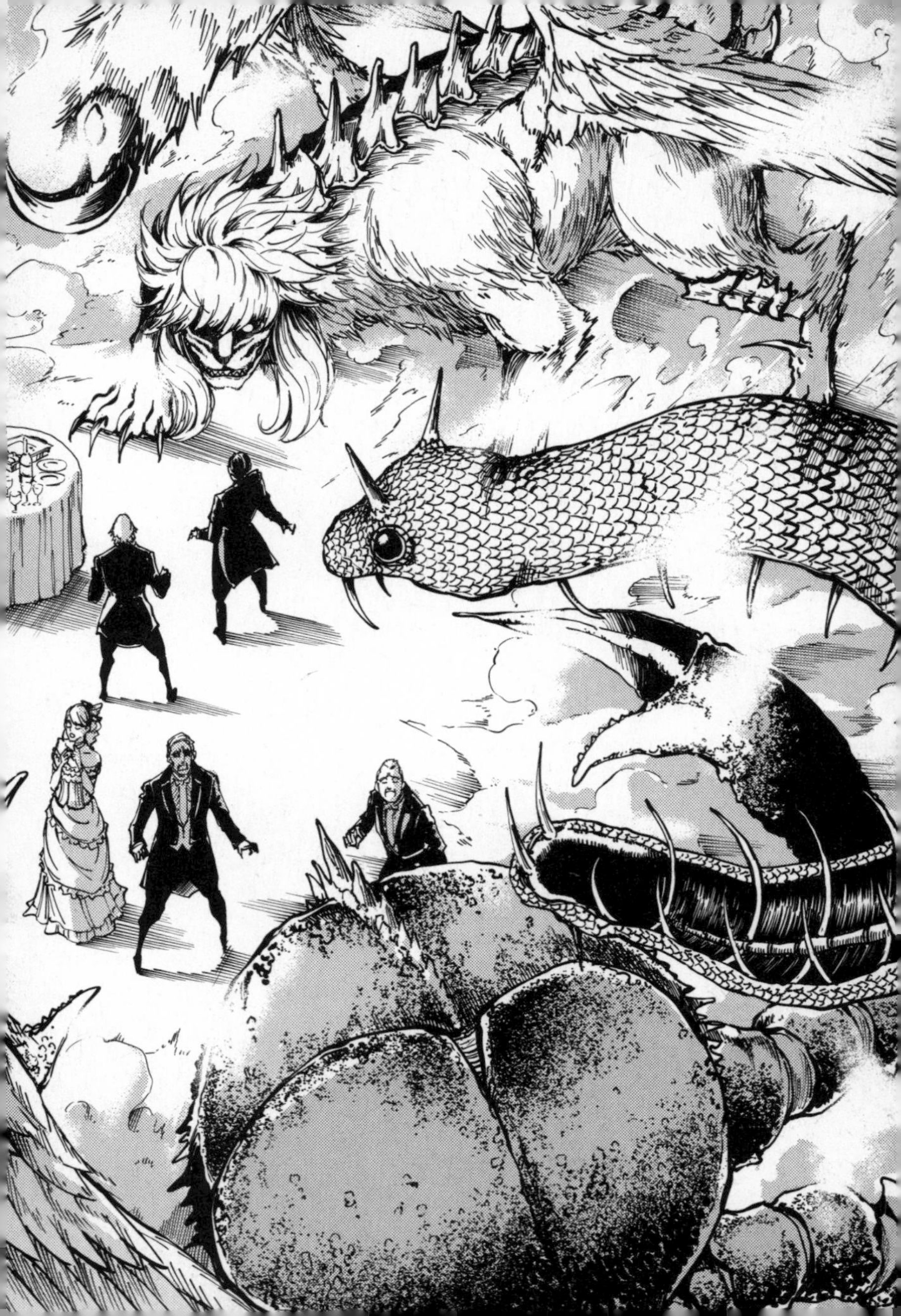

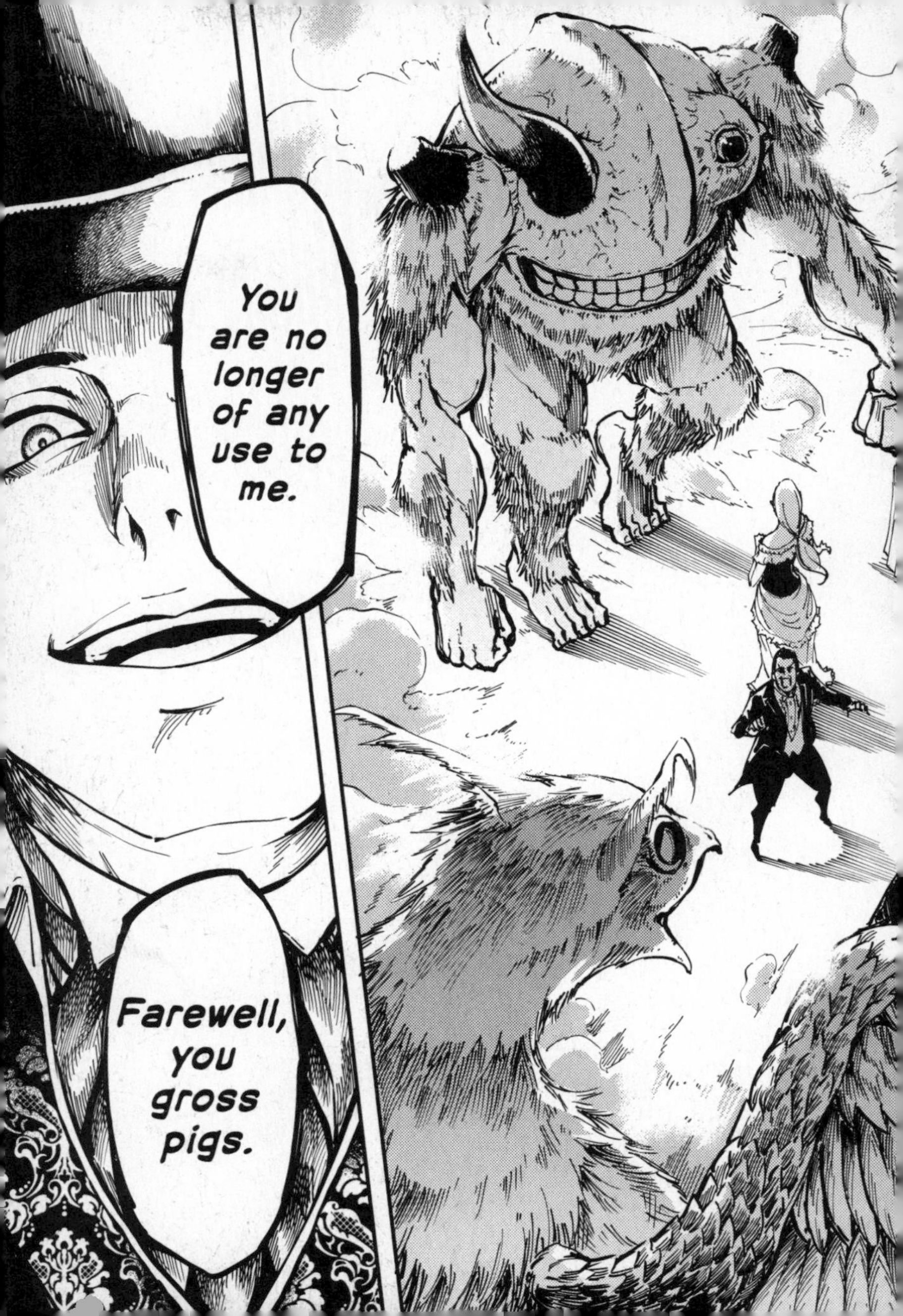
You are no longer of any use to me.
Farewell, you gross pigs.

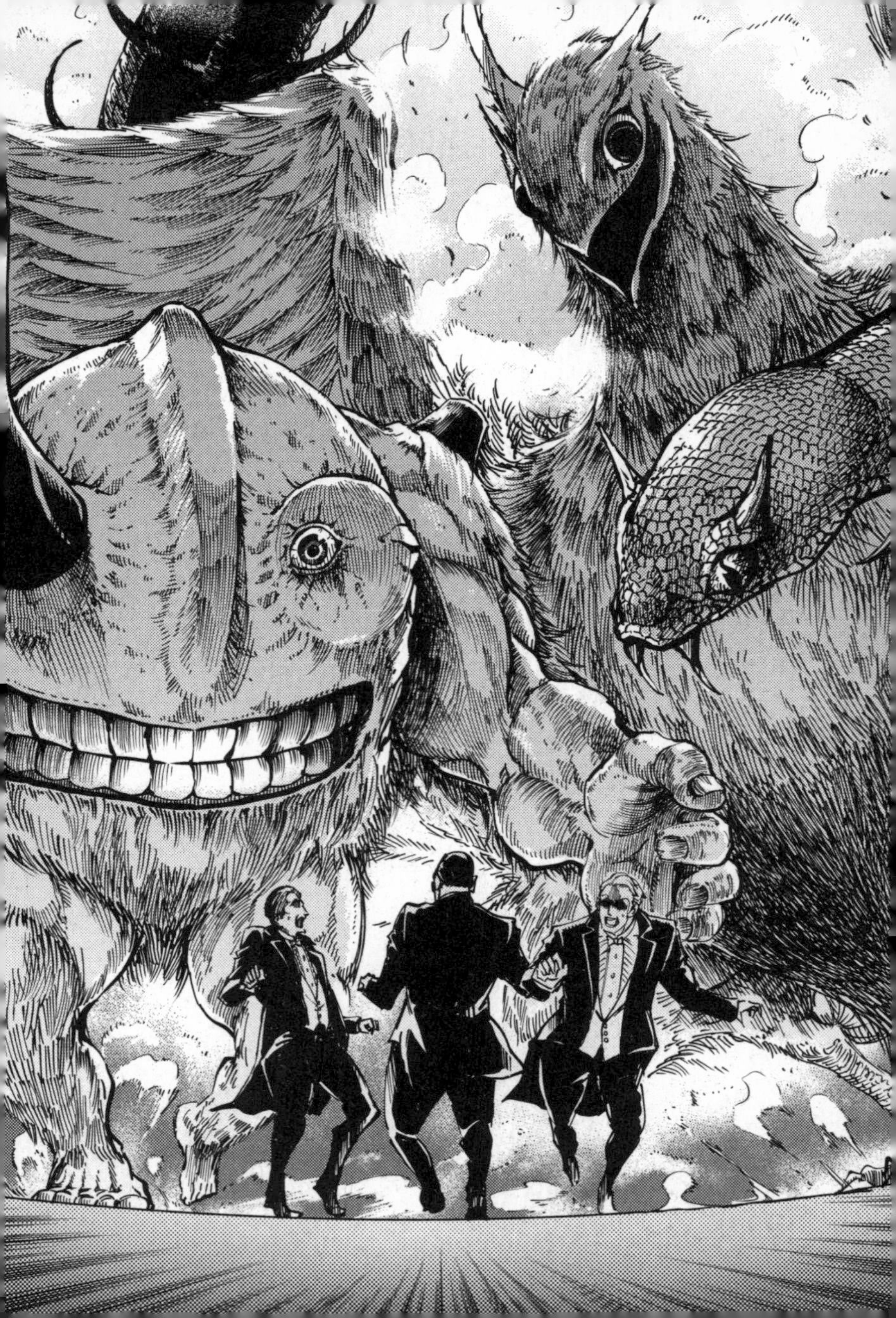

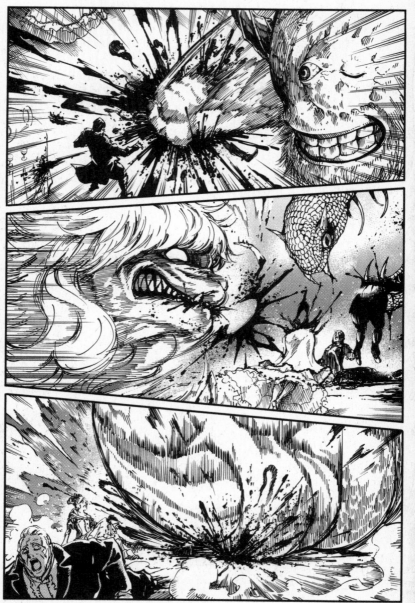

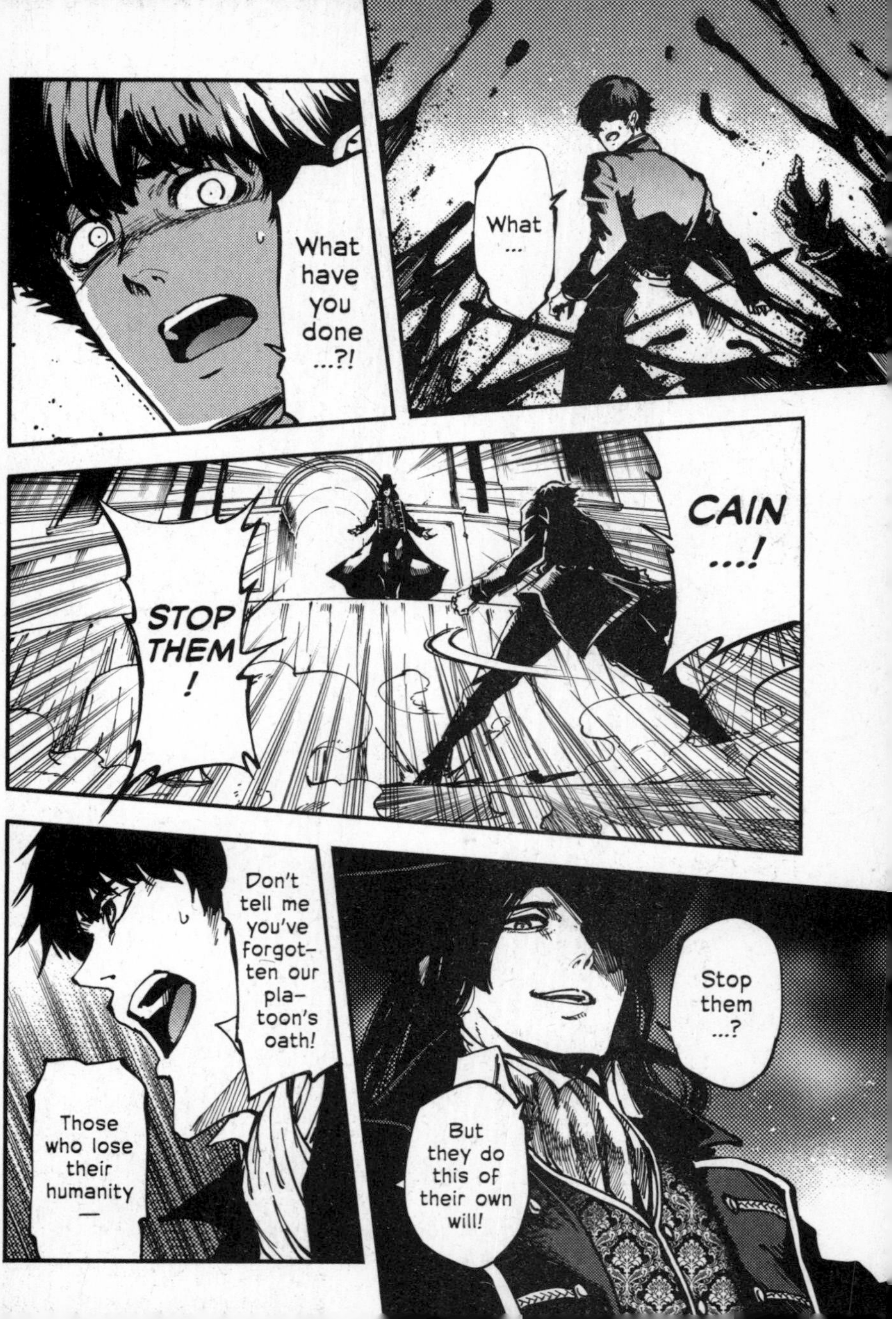
What ...
What have you done ...?!
CAIN ...!
STOP THEM !
Stop them ...?
But they do this of their own will!
Don't tell me you've forgot-ten our pla-toon's oath!
Those who lose their humanity —

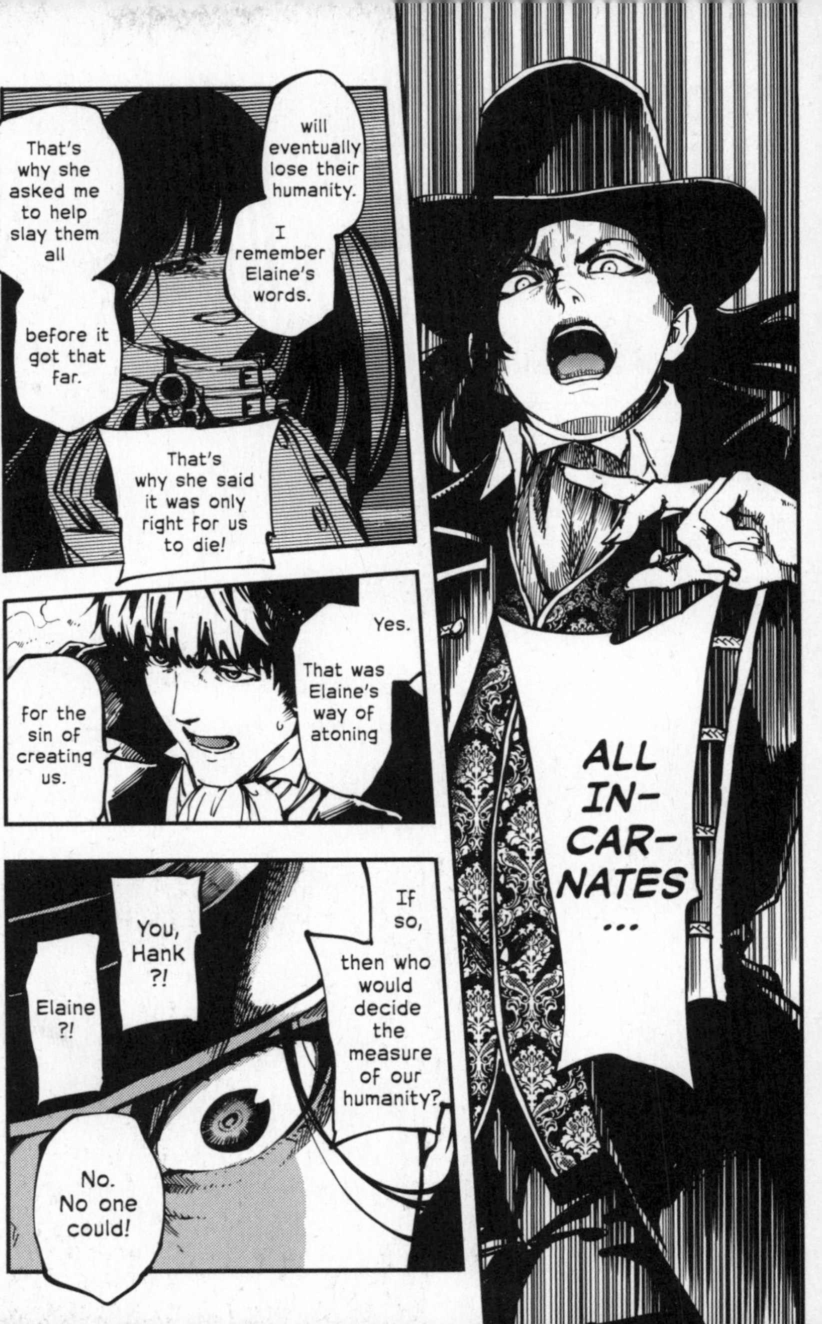
ALL IN-CAR-NATES ...
will eventually lose their humanity.
I remember Elaine's words.
That's why she asked me to help slay them all
before it got that far.
That's why she said it was only right for us to die!
Yes.
That was Elaine's way of atoning
for the sin of creating us.
If so,
then who would decide the measure of our humanity?
You, Hank ?!
Elaine ?!
No. No one could!

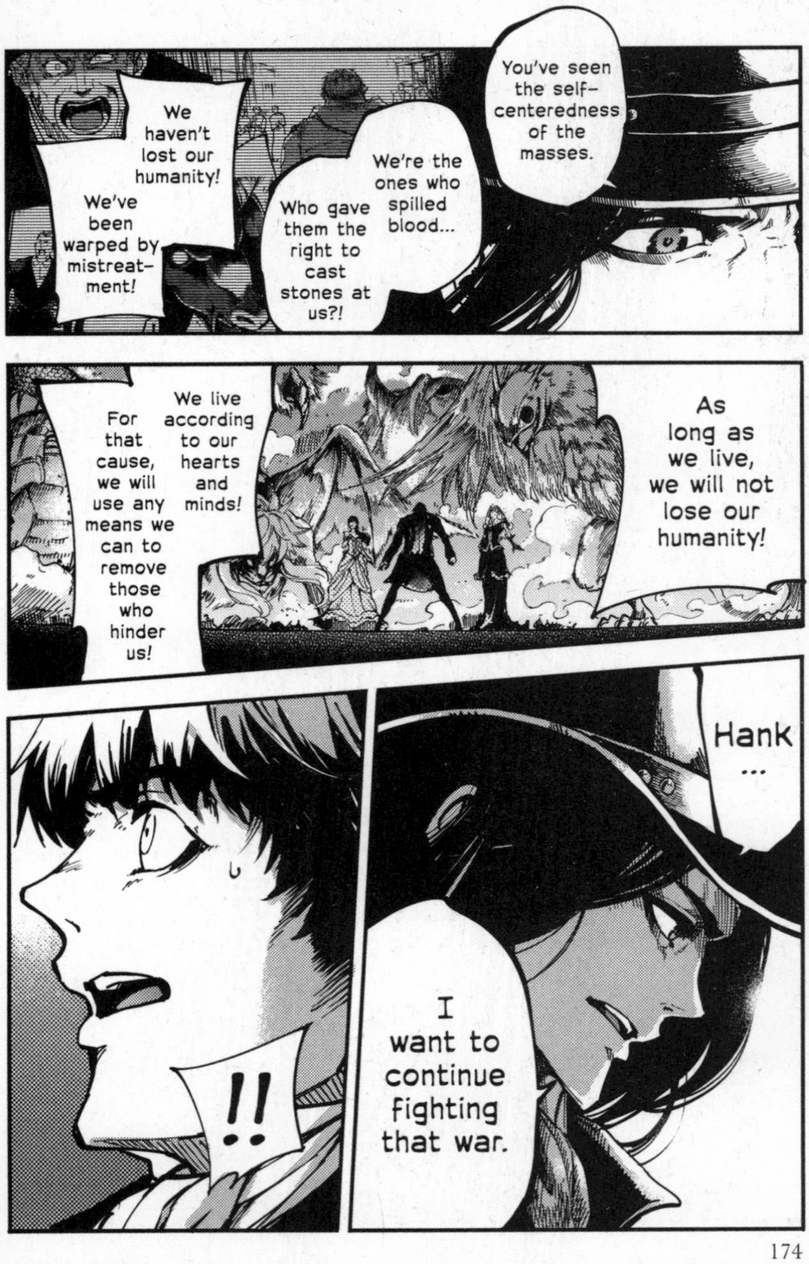

You've seen the self-centeredness of the masses.
We're the ones who spilled blood...
Who gave them the right to cast stones at us?!
We haven't lost our humanity!
We've been warped by mistreatment!
As long as we live, we will not lose our humanity!
We live according to our hearts and minds!
For that cause, we will use any means we can to remove those who hinder us!
Hank...
I want to continue fighting that war.
!!

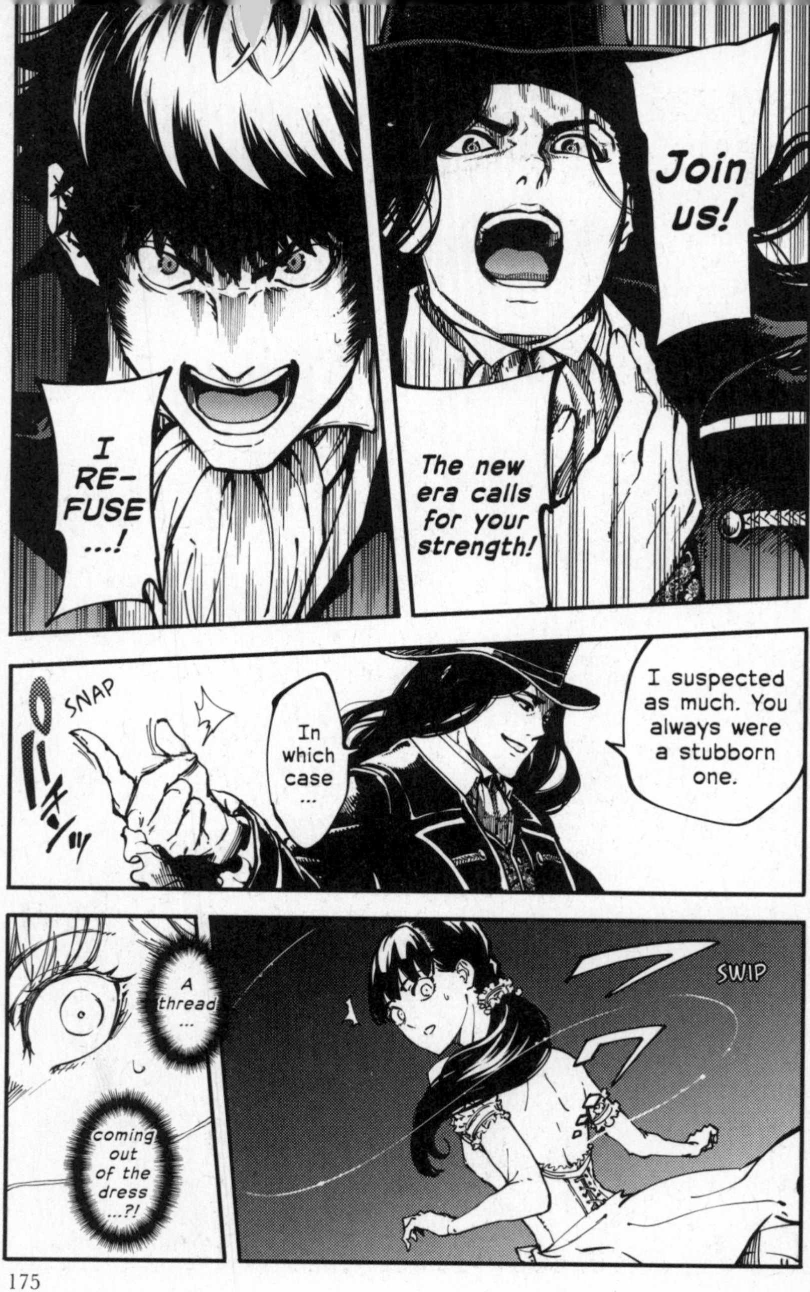
Join us!
The new era calls for your strength!
I RE-FUSE ...!
I suspected as much. You always were a stubborn one.
In which case ...
SNAP
SWIP
A thread ...
coming out of the dress ...?!

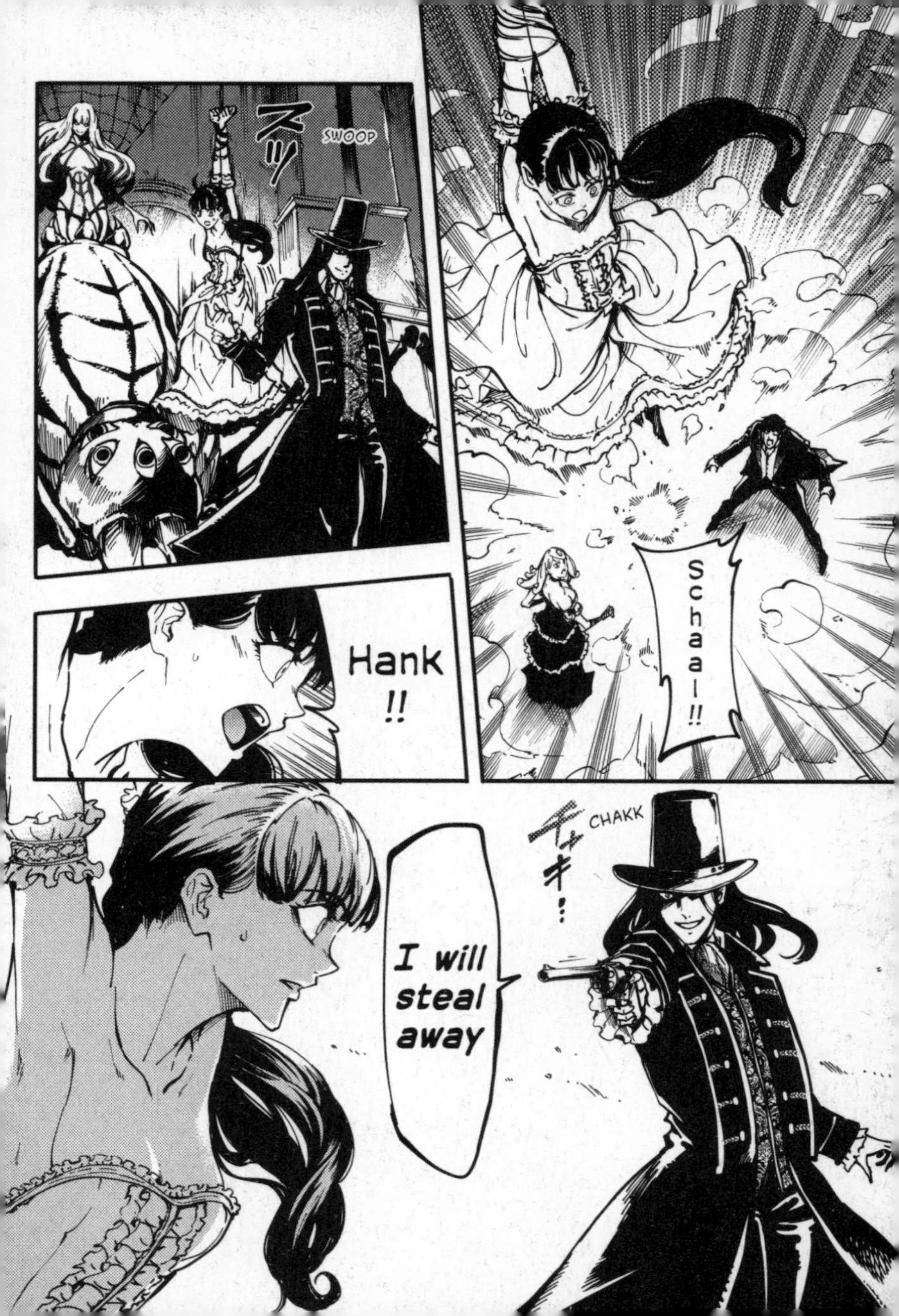
Schaal!!
スッ
SWOOP
Hank!!
チャキ!!
CHAKK
I will steal away

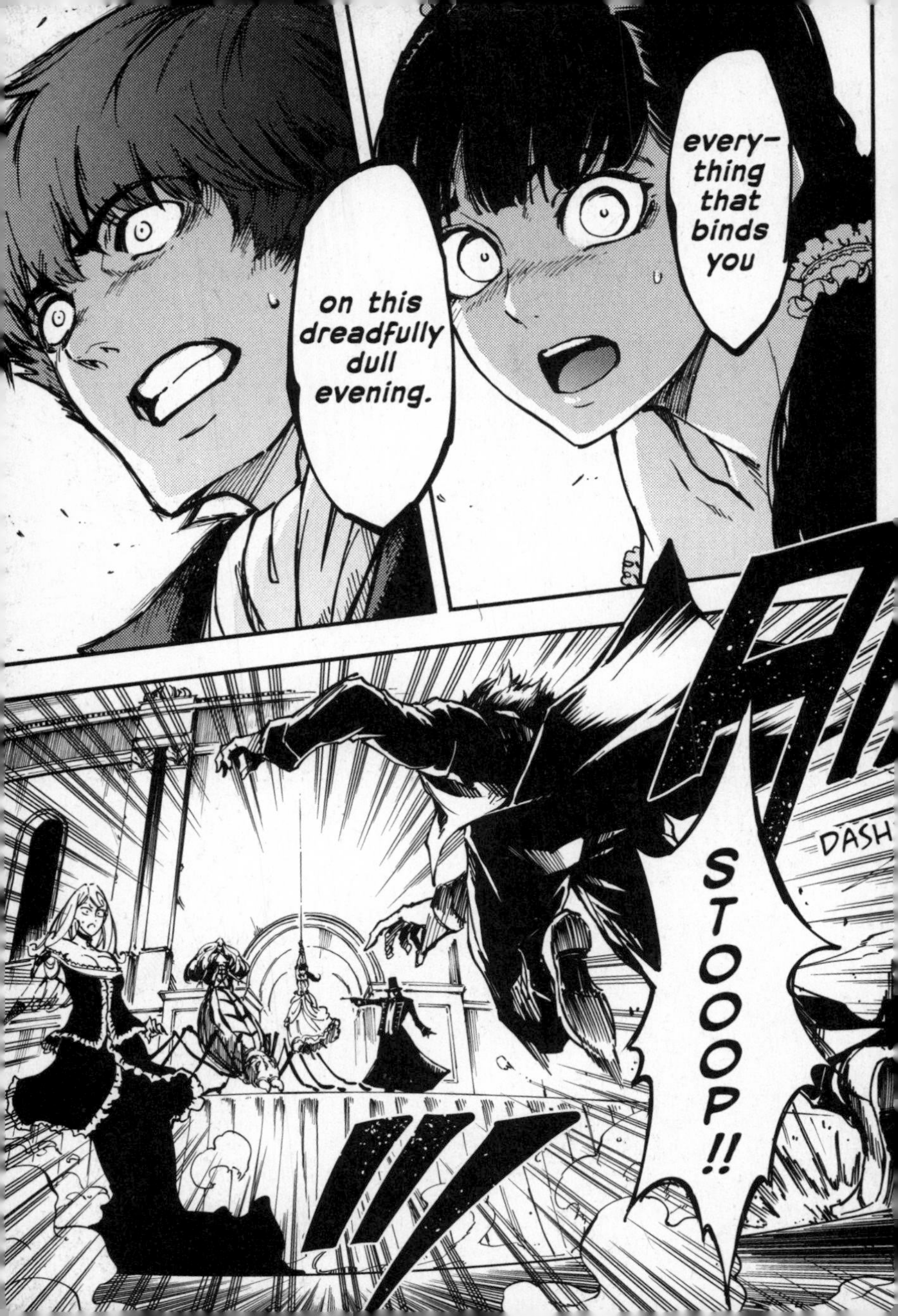
every-
thing
that
binds
you
on this
dreadfully
dull
evening.
DASH
STOOOOP!!

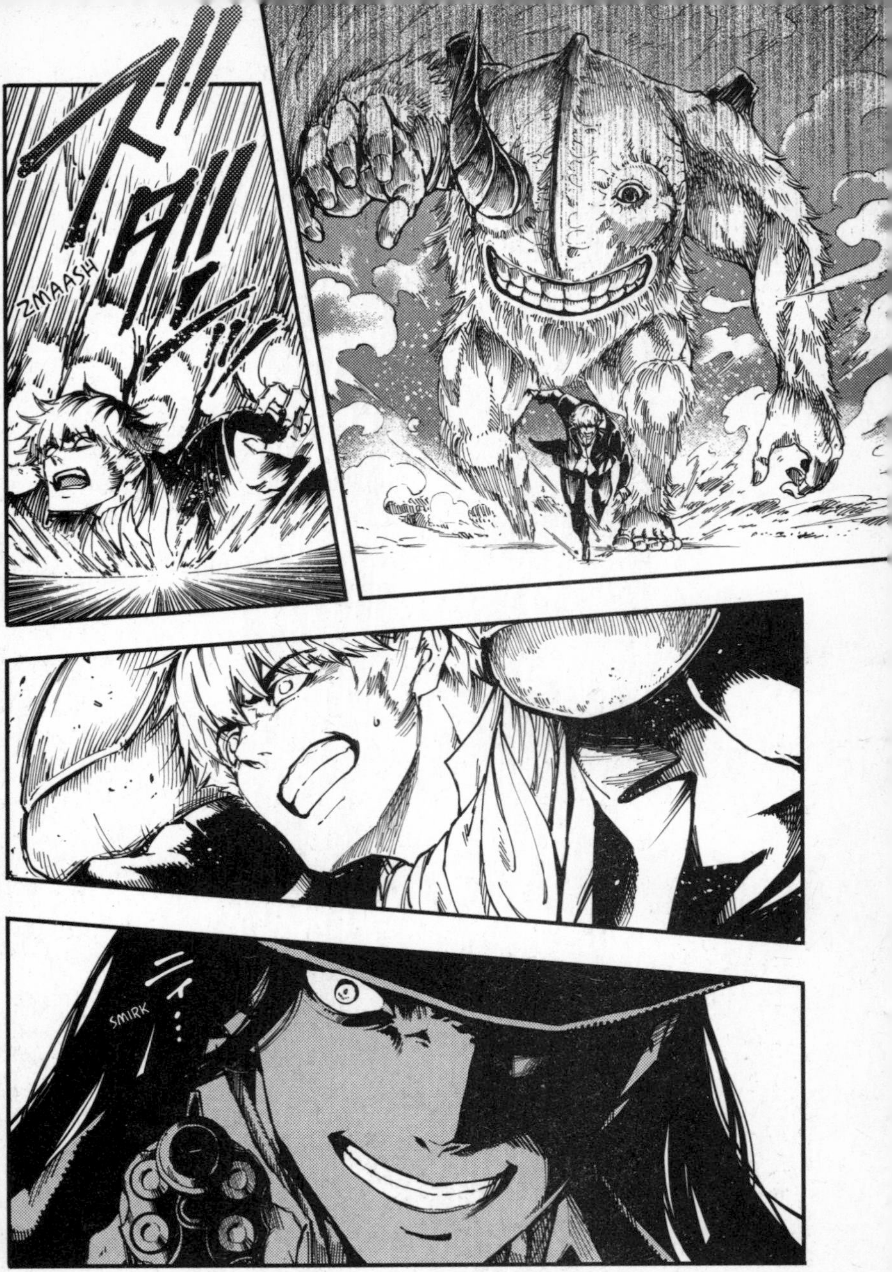
ZMAASH
ニィ…
SMIRK

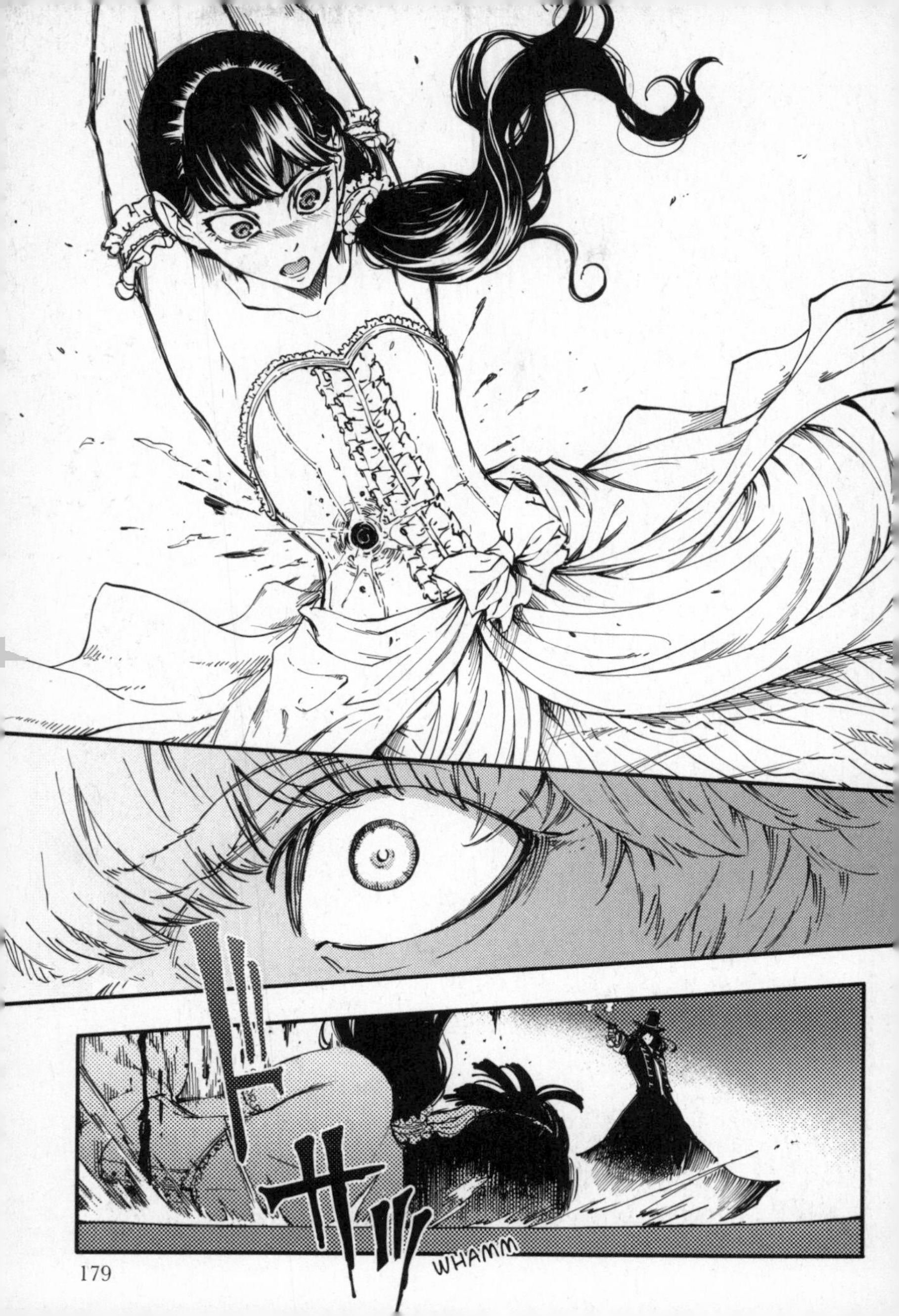
WHAMM

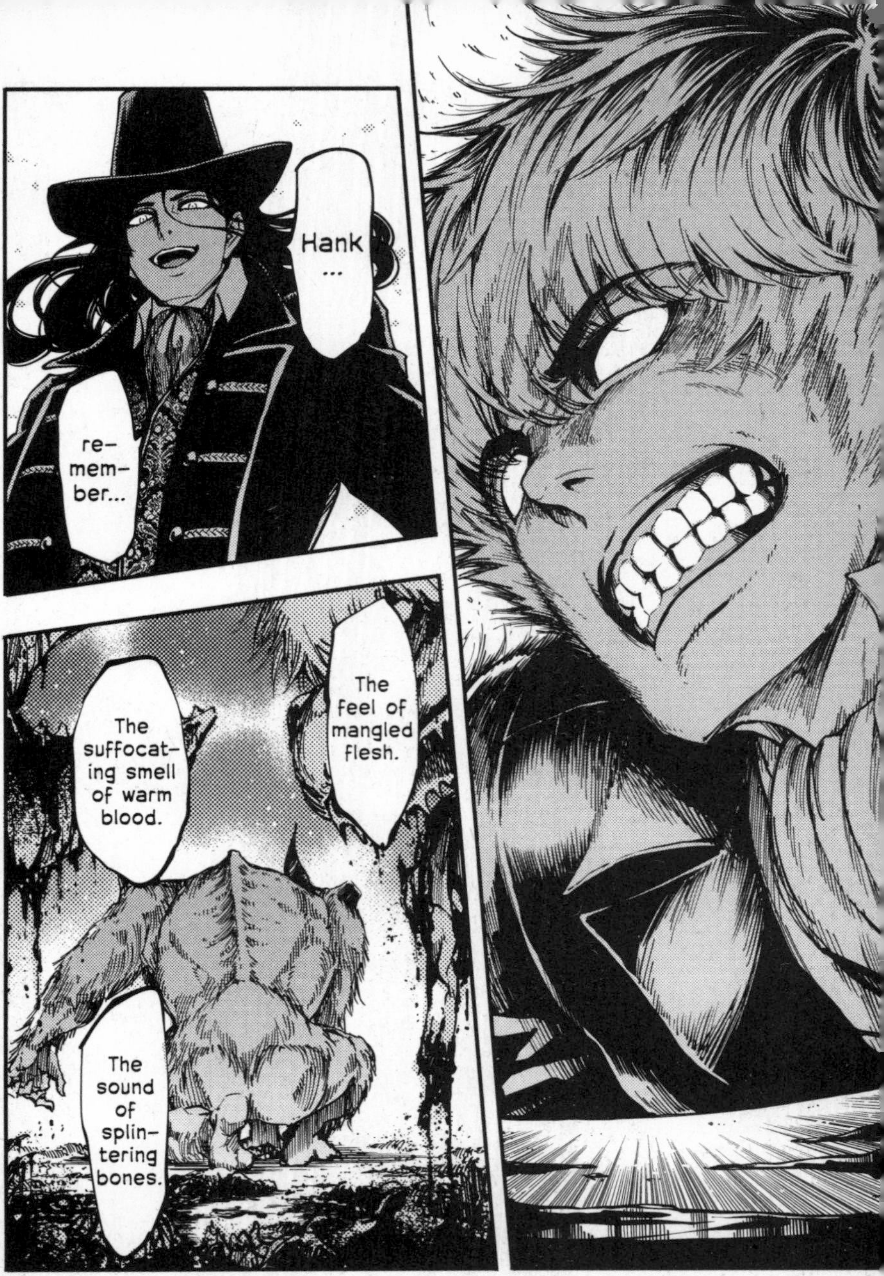
Hank ...
re-mem-ber...
The feel of mangled flesh.
The suffocating smell of warm blood.
The sound of splintering bones.

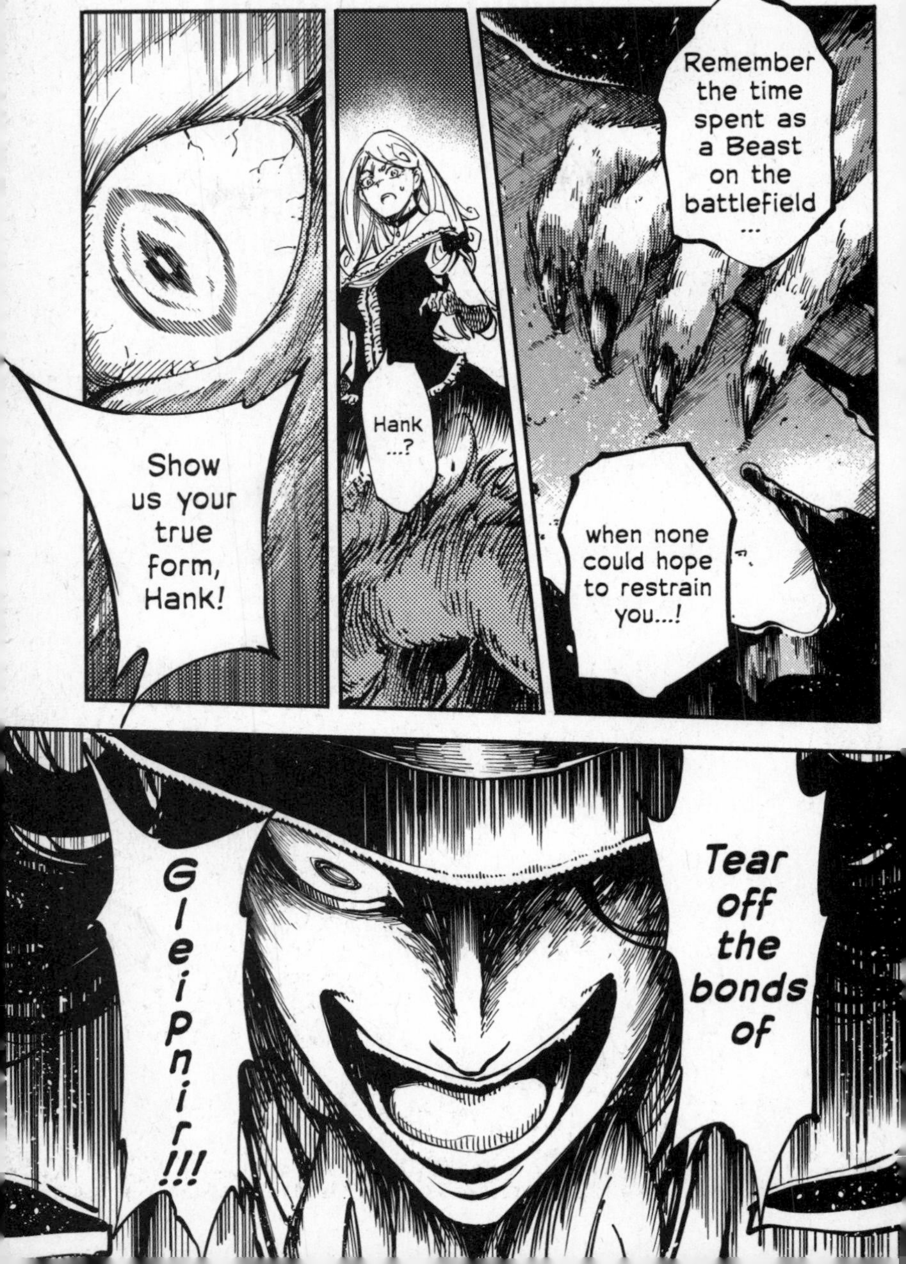
Remember the time spent as a Beast on the battlefield ...
when none could hope to restrain you...!
Hank ...?
Show us your true form, Hank!
Tear off the bonds of
Gleipnir!!!

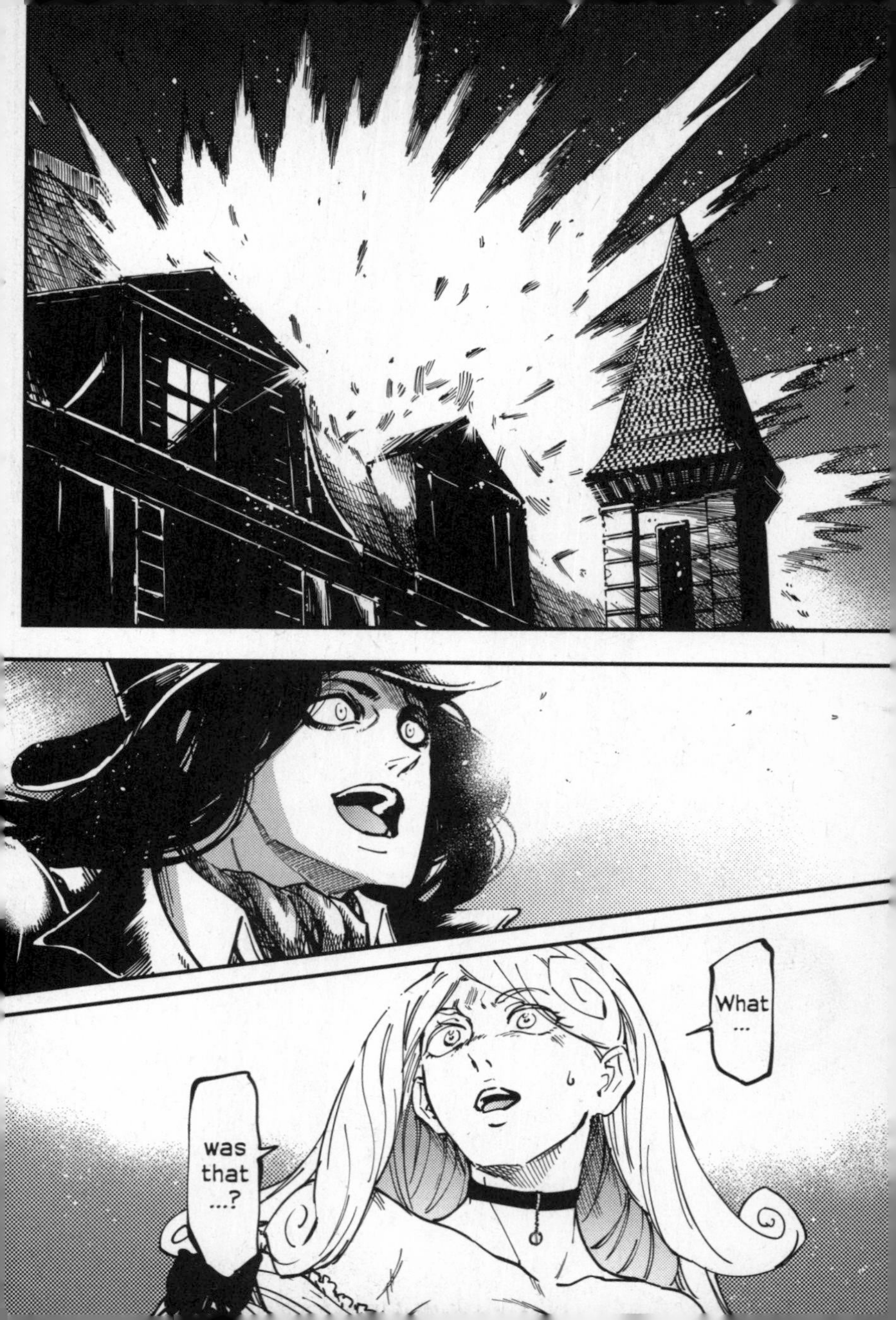
What
...
was
that
...?

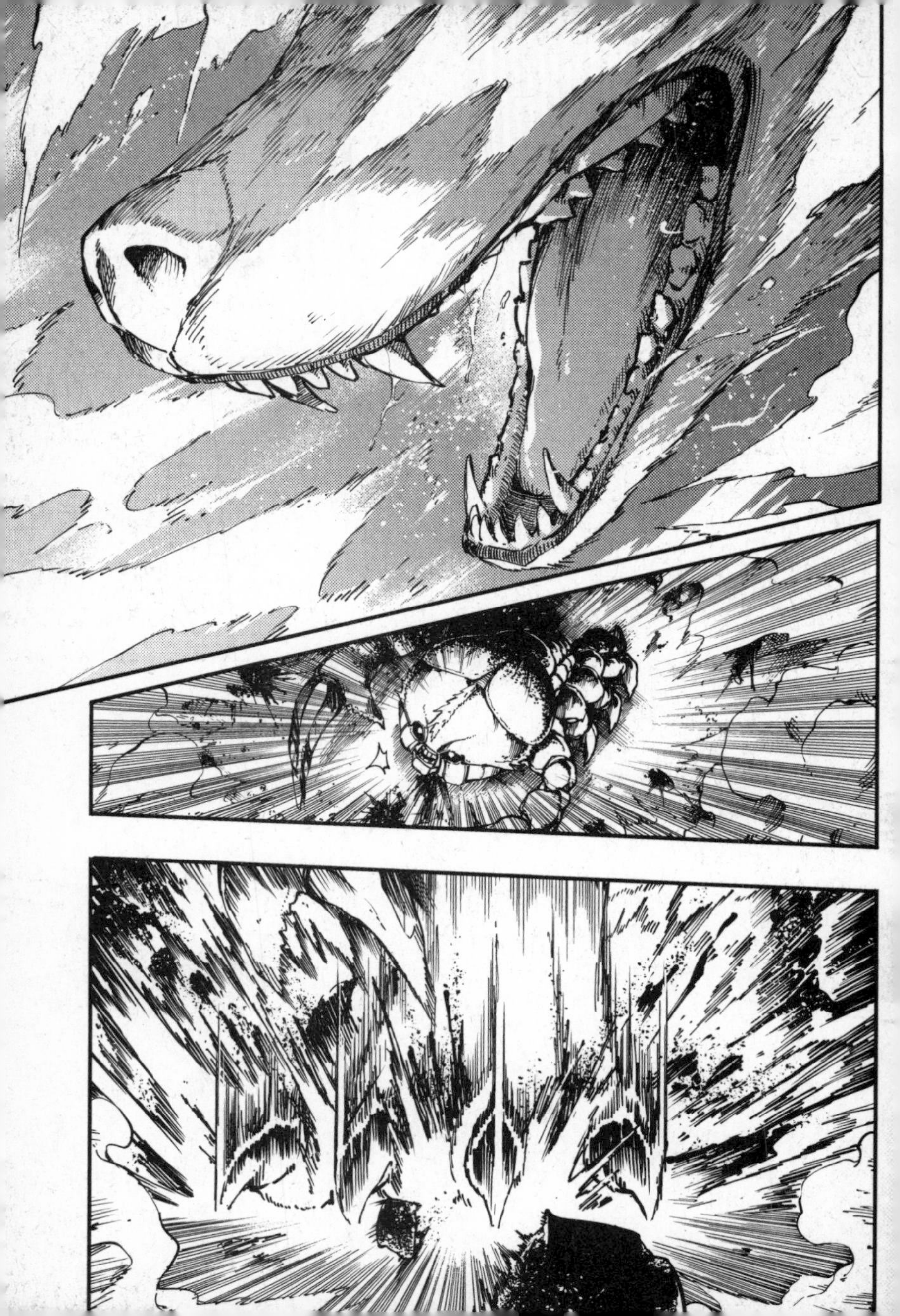

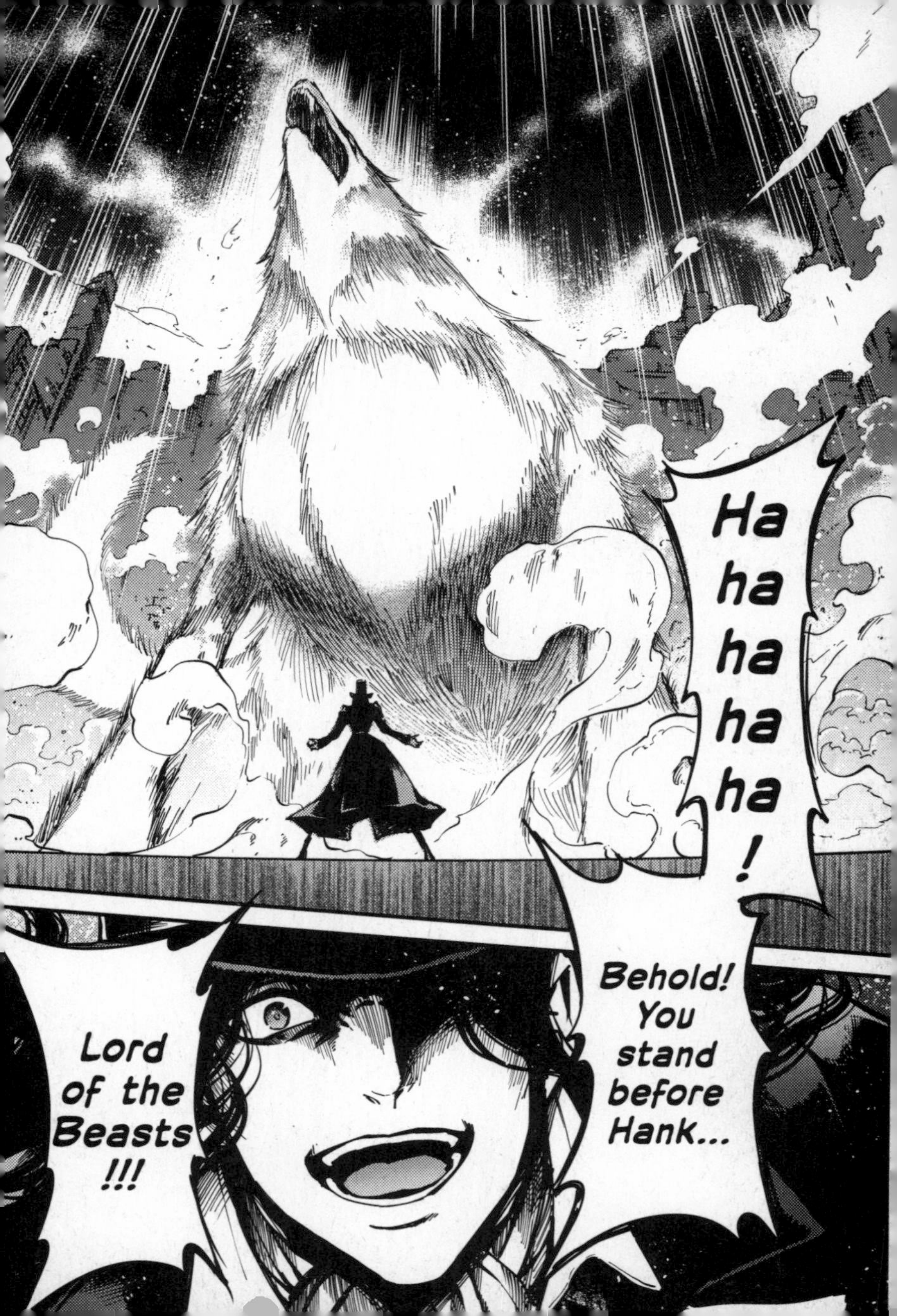
Ha ha ha ha ha ha!
Behold! You stand before Hank...
Lord of the Beasts!!!

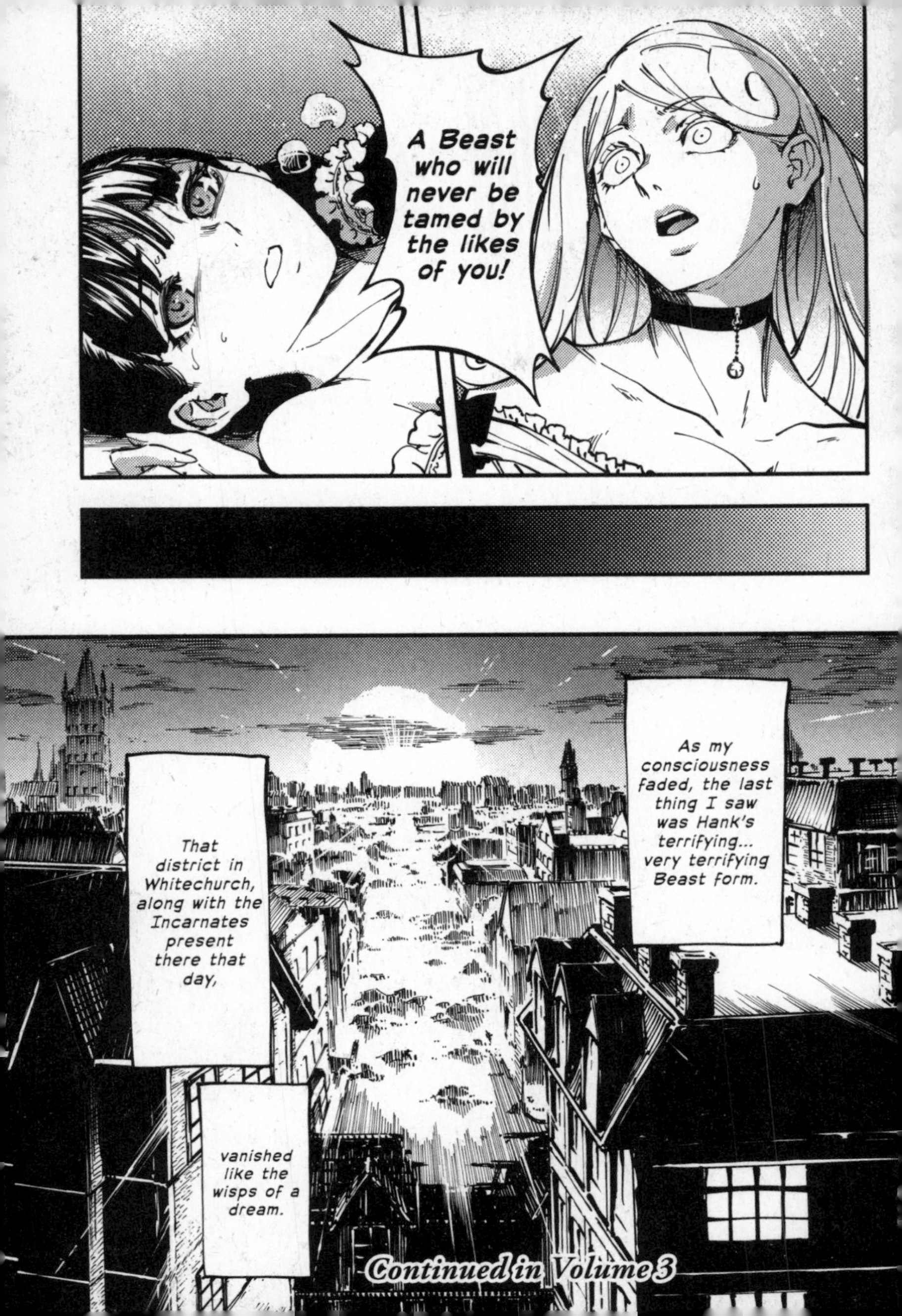
A Beast who will never be tamed by the likes of you!
As my consciousness faded, the last thing I saw was Hank's terrifying... very terrifying Beast form.
That district in Whitechurch, along with the Incarnates present there that day,
vanished like the wisps of a dream.
Continued in Volume 3

Encyclopedia Entries

file no. 5 | *Incarnate: Gargoyle*

Height: 7' 3"

The stony statue of punishment that drives off evil and judges the guilty

This winged Incarnate can attack unseen from high in the skies.

One of the reasons for the Incarnate platoon's field advantage was their dominance of the skies. Flight also allowed for reconnaissance and the ability to gain a greater understanding of the military situation; an incalculable boon to their side in battle.

Attempts were made to strike back with military balloons, but as of yet the army could only make their watchtowers taller.

While the Gargoyle does not possess a large frame, it can strike with enough force to easily kill a single human, and could aim solely for commanders from the sky—a common blind spot for ground forces—instantly decimating the enemy's chain of command.

Although its skin lacks the durability of a real stone statue, it can still serve as camouflage in rocky terrain.

file no. 6 | *Karkinos*

Height: 13 ft.

A massive crab that fearlessly charges even the strongest of foes.

The mighty Karkinos is an Incarnate armed with powerful shear-like pincers as its sword and an invincible shell as its shield.

It is entirely covered in a thick armor that provides both durability and flexibility, as well as superior resistance to blade or bomb attacks.

In addition, its many legs allow for not just lateral movement, but shockingly fast forward and backward movement as well. It puts this trait to excellent use in a bullet-filled battlefield, at times shielding its allies, and the next instant scattering foes with its pincers, truly able to move freely about the battlefield.

Where it really excels, however, is not its Incarnate powers but its unflinching bravery in aiding its allies no matter the circumstance. This quality garnered praise from not only its fellow Incarnates, but standard Northern infantry as well, who lauded Karkinos as a superior solider.

Also, its legs can be regrown just like a molted shell, and the fact that its legs are a tasty delicacy are another reason for its popularity.

Sacred Beasts

file no. 7 | *Godkiller bullets*

A venomous whip for striking down Beasts.

Developed by Dr. Elaine Bluelake, a key Incarnate researcher, Godkiller rounds are specialized bullets. Once fired into an Incarnate's body, the bullets cause the mutated cells to die off. As ordinary methods are insufficient to defeat an Incarnate, these bullets offer a sure-fire way to kill them.

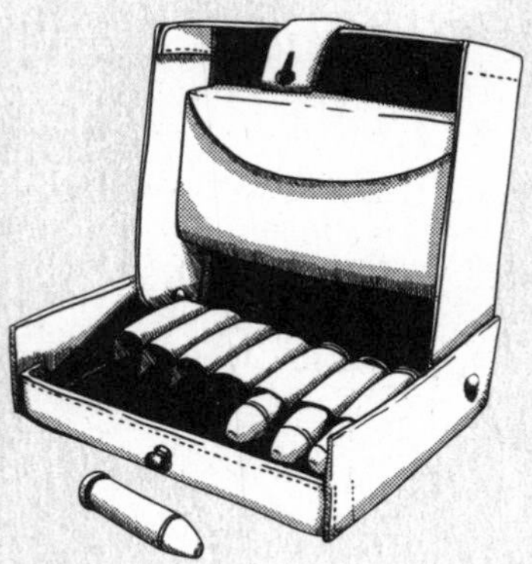

Dr. Bluelake's sudden disappearance resulted in the loss of core technical information pertaining to the Incarnates as well as the principles and manufacturing methods of the Godkiller bullets. Current whereabouts of the existing several dozen bullets are unknown.

While attempts were successful to craft replicas of the bullets (based on those found by accident by Northern soldiers after the war), scarcity of resources and complex manufacturing requirements made mass production impossible, and the few replicas that do exist are inferior products, significantly less potent than the originals.

The Godkillers used by the Beast Hunter are replicas, only useful as a means to deliver the killing blow to a badly-wounded Incarnate.

file no. 8 | *Whitechurch, the City of Steam*

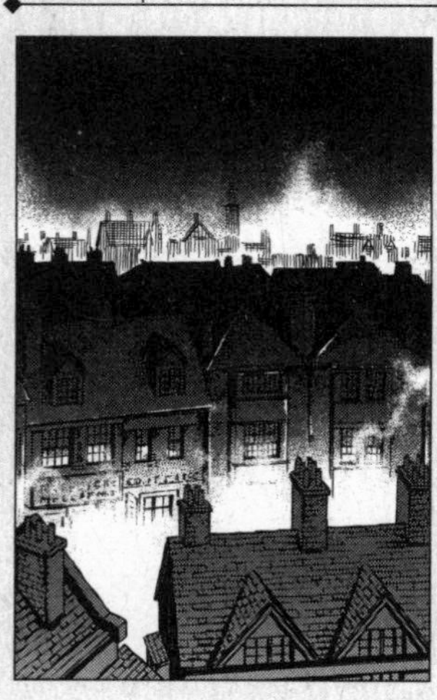

A city of poverty and prosperity created by coal.

Whitechurch quickly grew into an industrialized city following the discovery of high-quality "black diamond" coal.

Whitechurch started off as a remote village visited by few except those who made pilgrimages to its church, but as the demand for coal rapidly increased, the city greatly expanded. Yet this expansion led to massive inequality between the haves and the have-nots, and the old district surrounding the city's namesake church turned into a slum.

While Whitechurch was never the site of a battle during the Civil War, many poor residents lost their lives, and many in the upper classes lost their fortunes. This lead to a very small number of wealthy people pushing towards a reopening of hostilities in order to reclaim the spoils of war.

In addition, several rich veins of precious ores were discovered deep within the coal mines during the war, but they are currently sealed off.

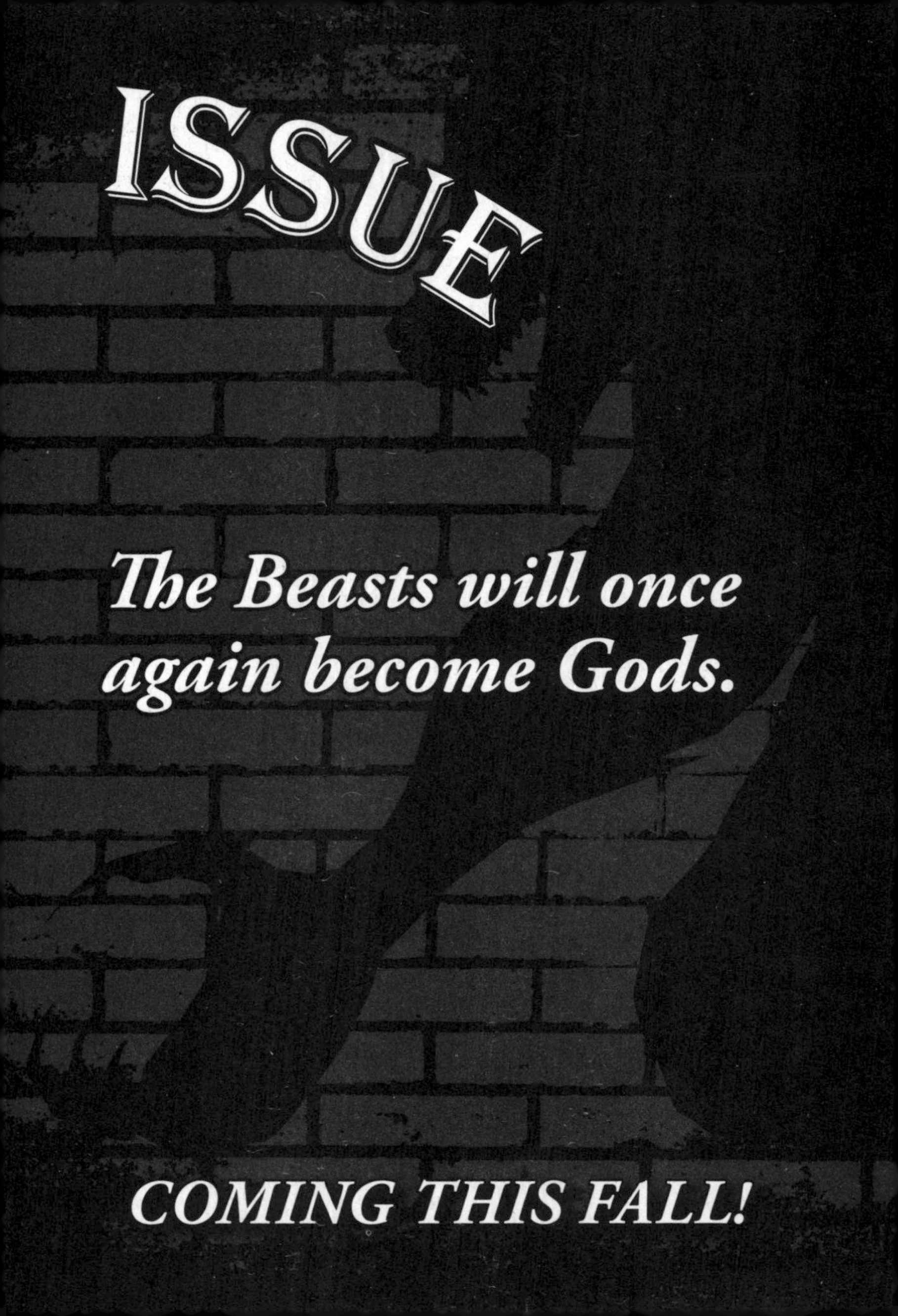
ISSUE
The Beasts will once again become Gods.
COMING THIS FALL!

NEXT

"I want to continue fighting that war," states Cain, who wants to reignite the flames of war and turn peacetime into an era of turmoil.

Hank has been missing since the incident at Whitechurch. Our story jumps ahead one year, when the threat of another civil war causes tensions to rise...

To the Abandoned Sacred Beasts

VOL. 3

To the Abandoned Sacred Beasts
Volume 2

Translation: Jason Moses
Production: Grace Lu
Anthony Quintessenza

First published in Japan in 2015 by Kodansha, Ltd., Tokyo
Publication rights for this English edition arranged through Kodansha, Ltd., Tokyo
English language version produced by Vertical, Inc.

Translation provided by Vertical Comics, 2016
Published by Vertical Comics, an imprint of Vertical, Inc., New York

Originally published in Japanese as *Katsute Kami Datta Kemono-tachi e 2* by Kodansha, Ltd.
Katsute Kami Datta Kemono-tachi e first serialized in *Bessatsu Shonen Magazine*,
Kodansha, Ltd., 2014-

ISBN: 978-1-942993-42-1

Manufactured in Canada

First Edition

Vertical, Inc.
451 Park Avenue South
7th Floor
New York, NY 10016
www.vertical-comics.com

Vertical books are distributed through Penguin-Random House Publisher Services.